VAMPIRE BYTES

Linda Grant

IVY BOOKS • NEW YORK

An Ivy Book
Published by The Ballantine Publishing Group
Copyright © 1998 by Linda V. Williams

www.randomhouse.com/BB/

Library of Congress Catalog Card Number: 99-90032

ISBN 0-8041-1862-0

This edition published by arrangement with Scribner, an imprint of Simon and Schuster.

Manufactured in the United States of America

First Ivy Books Edition: May 1999

10 9 8 7 6 5 4 3 2 1

Please turn to the back of the book
for an interview with Linda Grant

"ENGAGING . . .

You can always count on Linda Grant for believable characters and strong writing. *Vampire Bytes,* with its background in computer gaming and the LARPing angle, is fresh, fun, and a rapid read."
—*Minneapolis Star Tribune*

"Grant's stylish detective thrillers linger in the mind long after they are returned to the shelf. . . . Grant's careful plotting and excellent pacing make her version of 'vampire murder' genuinely compelling. She also has a sure sense of character. Her detective, Catherine Sayler, is brainy, gutsy, and prone to impulsive mistakes. The 'gamers' are ambiguous, some merely rebellious, others edgily dangerous. . . . Best of all is the sixteen-year-old runaway, Chloe, the key to the puzzles and crimes, who is drawn with great sensitivity. Few crime writers are currently Grant's equal."
—Baton Rouge *Magazine*

"[Grant] introduces readers to a teenage world of street and computer games that is psychologically intriguing and surprisingly attractive."
—*Portsmouth Herald*

"Solid writing and the unusual background of computer gaming and LARPing make this one a winner."
—*Hitchcock Magazine*

By Linda Grant:

RANDOM ACCESS MURDER
BLIND TRUST*
LOVE NOR MONEY*
A WOMAN'S PLACE*
LETHAL GENES*
VAMPIRE BYTES*

*Published by Ivy Books

To Megan

Acknowledgments

This book began one night when my daughter, Megan, announced, "I'm going to Cal to play the vampire game. I might be late." "Major props" and "moocoo thanks" to her for being my muse and cultural informant. I am also deeply indebted to Noah Nelson, game master extraordinaire, for sharing his knowledge of role-playing games and for his many imaginative suggestions. And to the members of Berkeley by Night for welcoming me into their game.

I am indebted to White Wolf Publishing, Inc., for permitting me to use *Vampire: The Masquerade* and *The Laws of the Night* as a background for my story. For those interested in learning more about these games, White Wolf's addresses, real and virtual, are 735 Park North Blvd., Suite 128, Clarkston, GA 30021 and *http://www.white-wolf.com*

I would like to express my appreciation to Louis Gottfried and David Williams for help with technology questions; Annie Fox, Eric Quakenbush, Rosaura Sandoval, James Guilford, and Kevin Norman for background on the computer games industry; Officer Abbie Cohen of the Berkeley Police Department; Michael Prodan of the California Department of Justice; Sergeant N. Tom Siebe of the Sonoma County Sheriff's Office; and Elizabeth Lynn, Sensei, Eastshore Aikikai.

My thanks also to Andrew Williams, Barbara Dean,

Susan Dunlap, and Janet LaPierre for their thoughtful and perceptive comments on the manuscript.

As always, I am deeply grateful to my editor, Susanne Kirk, and my agent, Jennifer Rudolph Walsh for their support and guidance. I'd also like to express my appreciation to Elizabeth Barden, for her insightful suggestions and cheerful help. And, finally, I'd like to thank an outstanding copy editor, Meredith Phillips. Any errors that remain after all this advice and help are strictly my own.

1

THE FIRST THING I noticed that Saturday night was the group of teenagers dressed in black leaning against the wall of the bank, four guys in jeans and leather jackets watching the street too attentively. Four guys waiting for something to happen.

I am suspicious by profession. Trust is excess baggage for a private investigator.

My partner, Jesse Price, noticed the group about the same time I did. He touched my arm lightly and nodded in their direction. We were headed for Peet's to pick up lattes. Instead, we found an outside bench where we could watch the watchers.

It was a warm night, a sign of the arrival of fall in San Francisco. For most of August, sunny afternoons had turned to chilly evenings as the fog blew in from the ocean. You could drive ten miles north or south and watch the sun set in clear skies, but on our side of the Golden Gate, it had been as gray as February.

"Lots of kids in black on the street tonight," Jesse said softly.

There were two sets of people in dark clothes on the crowded sidewalks, but they weren't hard to tell apart. The Fillmore regulars, hotshot young lawyers and MBAs, wore their salaries on their backs while the second group looked like they'd yet to earn a salary. I counted four other groups of the unsalaried. Two looked to be just hanging out; the third had the same watchful quality as the group by the bank, and the fourth was right behind us.

I only had a glimpse of the three of them before they disappeared into a store, but they seemed to be in their late teens or early twenties. Jesse and I waited, making small talk.

The threesome emerged from the store and leaned against a wall next to our bench. The one nearest me was tall and slender with long blond hair and strikingly sharp features. He was dressed in black slacks, a black silk shirt, and a charcoal vest. One of his companions wore a deep red poet's shirt with flowing sleeves; the other, a black turtle-neck and jeans.

The tall one glanced over at us, appearing casual but checking us out all the same. What he saw was a young black guy dressed in chinos and a sport shirt and a slightly older blond woman wearing jeans and a cream-colored sweater, not a particularly threatening pair.

"It's almost time," red-shirt said in a voice just above a whisper.

"Slinger's waiting for your signal. Take off," the tall one said. "And remember, I don't want any fighting. We move in fast with enough force so they can't resist and we're gone before they know what hit them."

The kid in the red shirt rose from the bench and headed up the street toward the bank. Jesse and I exchanged glances.

"You think they know we're after them?" the third kid asked, his voice so soft I had to strain to hear him.

"Won't matter, if Slinger does what I told him."

I searched the street for a cop, but of course, there wasn't a uniform in sight. I wasn't about to do anything stupid like taking on a gang of thugs, but my fifteen-year-old niece,

Molly, was up the street at a bakery just beyond the bank. I didn't want her walking into a crime in progress.

I nudged Jesse and we stood up and followed the kid in the red shirt. As we approached the bakery, I saw a group of three boys and a girl dressed in dark clothes coming from the opposite direction.

They spotted the gang by the bank just as they reached the bakery. And just as Molly stepped out the door.

She stopped in front of them, and before she could move on, one of the boys grabbed her arm and spun her around, swinging her between himself and the other group.

We rushed him. Jesse moved to the left and I to the right. He grabbed the kid from behind; I slammed into him from the side, throwing my shoulder between him and Molly. He let her go, and she staggered forward as Jesse yanked the kid's arms behind his back.

I turned to face an attack from the other members of the group, but they were frozen in surprise.

"Hey," Molly cried out, "it's okay. I know these guys. They're just joking around. Jesse, let him go."

We were starting to draw a crowd. The tall guy who'd been at the coffee store broke through the onlookers. "I'm sorry to scare you," he said to us. "We didn't mean any harm. Sometimes Darien forgets that you can't use people as props."

Jesse let the kid go. "This is Darien and Josh," Molly said, gesturing toward the kid who'd grabbed her and one of his buddies. "They go to Headlands." Headlands was Molly's high school. She'd be a sophomore when school started in a week.

"And I'm KZ Metzger," the tall man in black said. "I graduated from Headlands a couple of years ago."

The crowd began to move on. KZ turned toward the group at the bank who were standing nearby and made a time-out sign with his hands.

"You guys are LARPing, right?" Molly asked.

Darien and Josh nodded. "Sorry if we freaked you out."

"Not me," Molly said. "But you got the old folks going."

"LARPing?" I asked.

"Live Action Role-Playing," Darien informed me. "It's a game. Sort of like D & D . . ."

"That's Dungeons & Dragons," Molly explained for "the old folks'" benefit.

Darien ignored her interruption. "Except that you don't just sit around a board and throw dice, you act it out. Like today, we're playing Vampire. I'm a Toreador and I have to deliver the Devil's Eye, this stone of incredible power, to my clan's leader."

Josh thrust his hand over Darien's mouth. "Shut up," he ordered, "KZ's with the Brujah."

The man in black smiled broadly. "Nice of you to tell us who has the stone," he said to the abashed Darien. Turning to me, he apologized again, then to Darien's group he said, "Okay, this attempt failed so you guys move on to the next direction. We'll meet up with you later. And, Molly, you should join us for real next time. You'd make an awesome vampire."

He gave Molly the kind of smile that makes an aunt nervous and headed for the group by the bank.

"I guess we spend too much time with the criminal element," Jesse said. "Sorry about that, Mol. Hope we didn't embarrass you."

"It's okay," she said. "Actually, it's kind of cool when the game gets tangled up with real life."

My heart was finally starting to slow down, but I could still feel the effects of too much adrenaline. "What exactly is this game?" I asked. I've been responsible for Molly since her youthful rebellion turned into full-scale war and she ran away from home and moved in with me. Trapping your average felon is a piece of cake compared to raising a teenager.

"Role-playing, like Darien said," she explained. "You make up these characters and you give them special traits and skills and then you play your character. Vampires don't die, well, not usually, but they have battles and the winner gets more power, which means more traits and skills for the next game. It's . . ."

"There's Peter," Jesse said, interrupting her.

I looked up the street and saw a familiar long-legged figure approaching. Peter had promised to meet us, but he was working on a case in Berkeley, and I didn't really expect him to make it. He was wearing jeans and a blue shirt, and I entertained lecherous thoughts as I watched him approach and considered that he'd be home tonight.

He slipped his arm around me and gave me a hug as he greeted Molly and Jesse. He'd shaved his beard for an undercover job a week ago, and it still seemed a bit strange to see him without it. Strange, but nice. The beard had hidden a very sexy smile.

Peter hadn't had dinner and was in the mood for satay, so we headed down the street to the Thai place. On the way we caught him up on our meeting with the vampires. We passed two different groups of kids who were playing the game, and a boy and girl I didn't spot until I heard her say, "You do not remember anything you've seen. You will never remember it."

"Whoa, she's using Piercing Gaze," Molly said. "She must be a kick-ass character."

"How do you know so much about this game?" I asked.

"I played a couple of times in Palo Alto, before I left home."

"These guys get around," Jesse said.

"Not with these guys," Molly said. "This is the San Francisco game; there's another one in Palo Alto. There are

LARPs all over the country, even in places like France and England."

"You mean that tonight, all over the U.S., there are kids in black pretending to be vampires," I said.

"The kindred walk among you," Molly said in a mock-creepy voice.

We reached the Thai place and found a table. Knowing how Molly loves satay, Peter ordered extra. Jesse and I made our selections from the beer menu.

"So what's the point of this game?" Peter asked. "Are you out to take over the world, defeat the humans?"

"Humans are just food," Molly said dismissively. "The goal depends on the game, but mostly, it's different clans battling for power. The fun part is creating a character and messing with other players' minds. And it's a neat feeling that you know something other people don't. To everyone on the street, we're just geeky kids, but we know we're in the game and you guys are just our backdrop."

"Sort of like going undercover," Jesse said.

"Yeah," Molly said enthusiastically. "And you can be whoever you want to be."

Not quite, I thought. I played the dumb blonde too often, and Jesse spent more time pushing a broom than he liked. But she was right about the excitement of playing a role.

"Sounds like a great way for trying on different personalities," Peter said.

Molly looked blank, but I understood. I'd watched her try out different styles and poses, searching for a solid identity in the chaos of adolescence. I remembered going through the same process, and it hadn't ended when I hit twenty. I'd spent my first years as a private investigator feeling as if I were making myself up as I went along. Sometimes I still felt that way.

"Of course, some of the guys are just into the confrontations," Molly continued. "They're out to slash and burn."

"Young males are into violence," Peter said. "Better role-playing than real guns."

"I guess I've entered fogeydom," I said. "Violence has definitely lost its allure."

"Meeting the real thing will do that for you," Jesse said. His voice was serious. We'd had too many cases that turned violent.

Peter had fallen silent and I could see that Jesse's words had struck a chord. I put my hand on his and gave a gentle squeeze, but he didn't respond. He wasn't there. He was back in Guatemala, where he'd gone with a forensic anthropologist and ended up in a military jail. He wouldn't talk about what had happened there, but it had scarred him, and he was still a long way from recovering. Sometimes I felt I was living with a stranger.

"Hey," I said. "Enough grimness. Let's go back out and vampire-watch."

Peter smiled, but it took an effort, and I knew that now it was he who was playing a role. "Yeah," he said, "here's to a world where the violence is only play-acting."

I didn't look at my watch, so I don't know what time it was. But it must not have been too long before the game in Palo Alto turned deadly, and role-playing became the only way to survive for a girl not much older than Molly.

2

BEN MINOR TURNS left, pauses, then tries to go back, but it's too late. A ball of fire speeds toward him until it fills the computer screen and a maniacal laugh echoes mockingly from the speakers. The screen goes black, then lightens to show a grave with his character's name on it.

"Awright," he says, particularly pleased with the leering skeleton on the tombstone. He took it from a book of photos of old graveyards in New England. "Bones with attitude," he calls it.

He checks his watch. Bummer, it's almost midnight. Not much chance Matt Demming will come now. He was really looking forward to showing Matt his game. Hot damn! It'd be so cool to have one of the greatest game designers in the business check out your work. But not tonight.

He should have known it was too good to be true when Matt said he'd drop by. A guy like Matt, with a game just about to hit the market, has places to go, people to see. But he did seem interested in Ben's game. He could come another time. It could still happen.

After all, he and Matt had really kicked it before the vampire LARP last week. He is pretty much a neophyte to the LARP, and he'd felt weird talking to his idol, but he couldn't miss the chance. He'd told Matt how much he loves *Cult of Blood*, how it was the game that had made him decide to develop one of his own.

He'd tried not to gush, not to be too horribly geeky, but it's hard when your goal in life is to be this guy's clone. Every gamer dreams of designing a game that goes from underground classic to hot commercial property. And Matt had done it, but he was so fabulously cool about it, not stuck up at all. He'd even been willing to tell Ben all about the new version of *Cult*. The coolest game ever.

The script hadn't changed. You still played the vampire Sebastian whose sire had been killed by a more powerful vampire, and you spent the first part of the game figuring out the identity of the killer and building up your power to kick his ass. Then you had to track him and finally defeat him. But now you had choices about how to play Sebastian. The original character had bulked up on physical traits, but now you could choose to make him stronger in social or mental traits, and the game changed depending on which you chose.

Some annoying kid had interrupted them before Matt could tell him more about the new features. Damn, if he'd just been able to go to the LARP last night he could have found out more and reminded Matt to come by tonight. Next week he won't miss the LARP, that's for sure.

It's midnight, but there's still time to check out the chat room and message board on his buddy Dan's Web page. Dan's dad is CEO of his own company, and there isn't a techie toy Dan doesn't have. His Web page makes lots of commercial sites look shabby. And part of its coolness is Ben's graphics.

Ben logs on to his server and it takes him to the Internet. In a few seconds, the black crushed-velvet background of Dan's page fills his screen, and bright red letters proclaim, YOU HAVE ENTERED THE OUTER SANCTUM. There's Dan's welcome-to-my-page statement, which is pretty lame in Ben's opinion, then a very cool gravestone that Ben copied from the cemetery book. The gravestone lists the areas you can visit on the site.

Ben clicks on INNER SANCTUM. The background changes to a rotting wooden door in a stone wall. I need to do a new graphic for that, he thinks, as he types in his ID and password to move into the private area.

The menu screen for the message boards and chat rooms has four choices. Ben clicks on *The Meat Rack*—Chat, and another of his graphics appears. It's a drawing of a meat rack; along with sides of beef, the hooks hold ghouls, vampires, and a werewolf.

There are three people in the chat room tonight, and while they all use handles, the computer equivalent of pseudonyms, Ben's pretty sure he knows who two of them are. Most of the regulars go to Paly High School. *The Extra Rib* is Sherri Klatz, and *Cosmic Slime* is a kid named Kent something. He doesn't know *Frodo's Toe*.

The discussion is about Chloe Dorn, who's also a member of the *Rack*, as they call it. He scans the most recent entries.

The Extra Rib: "If she ran away, how come she didn't take any of her stuff?"

Cosmic Slime: "Probably didn't want to alert her parents."

The Extra Rib: "I don't buy it. She's not the type to take off."

Frodo's Toe: "So I suppose there's some psycho out there snatching pretty young things off the street. Better watch your sweet ass, Rib."

The *Toe*'s response pisses off Sherri, and her flame hits both his anatomy and his parentage.

Ben usually enjoys the flame wars, but tonight he wants to know more about Chloe Dorn. He likes Chloe, not like a girlfriend but a friend-friend. She isn't one of those girls who treat you like hot stuff one day and rat scat the next.

And she's interested in cool things. She reads Isaac Asimov and Carl Sagan, and gets it.

"What's up with Chloe?" he types in.

Seconds later his question appears on the screen.

Sherri answers him. *"No one knows, but the Goat put up a bulletin that she's missing."*

The *Goat* is Dan, whose handle is *The Three-Horned Goat.* Ben leaves the chat room and signs on the message board. At the top in screaming capitals is the bulletin: *LISTEN UP BOYS AND GIRLS: CHLOE DORN WENT MISSING SATURDAY NIGHT. SECURITY FORCES ARE ON HER TRAIL AND ANYONE WHO KNOWS HER SHOULD EXPECT A CALL FROM THE BACON.*

There are already six responses to the *Goat*'s post. All of them assume she's run away. Ben wants to believe that, but he doesn't. Chloe wouldn't take off and leave her friends to worry. He shivers as he rereads the bulletin.

I WAS LATE getting to my office on Monday morning. I'd promised to go by a client's warehouse in south San Francisco and check the alarm system. The problem wasn't a serious one, but it took almost an hour to fix, and it was ten o'clock before I got back on the Bayshore Freeway and headed home to San Francisco.

It was a beautiful day, sunny and clear with just enough wind to sweep the sky clean. As I rounded Hospital Curve, the city spread out before me. I've driven this route hundreds of times, and that first view of the city still knocks me out. Today, it was especially grand with the tall buildings glittering in the sun. Even the Marriott Hotel, whose chrome-and-glass art deco facade resembles a giant jukebox, looked good beneath the cloudless blue sky.

It took another twenty minutes to get to my part of Divisadero Street, a few blocks up the hill from Mount Zion Hospital. As usual, there were no parking places on the street. It's a neighborhood of small shops and restaurants and a few Victorian houses converted to offices. I pay the mortgage on one of those Victorians, and sometime in the next century it will belong to me instead of the bank.

The advantage to this location, besides its proximity to several cheap ethnic restaurants, is the fact that it's only three blocks from my apartment. As I often do, I parked at home and walked to work.

My secretary, Amy, thrust several message slips at me as I walked in the door. "Call the one on top first. He's phoned three times this morning, and he's beginning to sound a bit hysterical."

"Good morning to you, too," I said. "Did he tell you what it was about?"

"Sorry." She smiled apologetically. Amy has the pale-pink skin of the British Isles. I'm not sure what color her hair is because it changes from month to month. Recently, it's been a sort of auburn, and today she'd pulled it back on one side with a barrette and braided a skinny lock at the temple on the other side. It gave her face a strange, uneven appearance. I hoped she wouldn't ask my opinion of this latest "do."

"The company's named Astra, and he wanted to talk with Jesse," Amy said. "But Jesse's in Seattle. So he asked for you. Said we'd been recommended by Ian Smith at ZephyrGraphics."

"Ah, the bang-you're-dead crowd," I said, recognizing the name as a computer game company where Jesse had recently done an undercover job. I got a cup of coffee and headed for my office.

The name on the message sheet was Ari Kazacos. I dialed the number. A man with a deep baritone voice answered.

"Hello, this is Catherine Sayler. I'm . . ."

"Thank God," he said, interrupting me. "I've got a hell of a problem down here and not a lot of time to solve it. If I hired you, how soon could you start?"

Most problems in security demand an immediate response. At least, most of the people with the problems think they do. "I'll need to know more about your problem before I can answer that," I said.

"I want you to find a guy. My lead programmer. He's stolen something, and I need it back, fast."

"Have you contacted the police?"

"No, I don't really want to involve them in this." His voice changed tone, just slightly. Just enough to tell me there was more to the story than the version he'd offered.

"What exactly was stolen, and how?" I asked, hoping I wouldn't have to play Twenty Questions.

"Source code," he said in a lowered voice. "You know what that is?"

"In general, yes. What kind of source code are we talking about?"

"Game code. We're a game company, computer games. I don't know how much you know about the games business, but everything you see on the screen is driven by code. The quality of the code literally determines the quality of the game. To change anything in the game, fix anything, you need to work with the source code.

"But the source code isn't made for speed. It slows the game down. So we have to compile the code, put it in a form that's more efficient. Then the game runs faster. But once it's compiled, the code can't be changed anymore. So if there are problems, you've got to go back and fix them in the source code. With me so far?"

"Yes."

"So the source code's been stolen, and I need it back now. We got bugs to fix, and this game's gotta ship for Christmas sales. We miss that deadline, we're history."

"How do you know the thief is your lead programmer?"

"Because the bastard left a message on my e-mail. Look, can we talk about this in person? Can you send someone down here today?"

The phone number I'd dialed had a 650 area code, so "down here" was someplace on the Peninsula. Jesse was the logical one to take the case, but there was no telling how long he'd be in Seattle. Since my assistant Chris was taking a well-deserved vacation, I'd kept my calendar fairly clear. I'd planned to spend the morning catching up on paperwork. That could always wait.

The address Ari Kazacos had given me for Astra was in Redwood City, one of the less affluent corners of Silicon Valley, about twenty-five miles south of San Francisco. I picked up a sandwich to eat in the car and got there a little before noon.

It took another ten minutes to locate Kazacos's office because it was in a part of town where few owners had seen the need to post street numbers. I found it in an industrial park that had little industry and no park, just a couple of large buildings that appeared empty and a number of smaller ones with inexpensive signs on their doors. Astra Software was the third door in a low stucco building that might once have been white.

I rang the bell and waited. The door was opened by a tall guy in jeans and a *Star Wars* T-shirt so faded that C3PO looked like he was beginning to rust. He greeted me with a tentative smile that widened when I introduced myself.

"The private eye," he said. "Come on in." His voice was soft with a slight midwestern accent. "I'm Bill Griffen, call me Grif." If his sandy brown hair hadn't been receding from an already high forehead, he'd have looked about fifteen years old. He was all long bones and big extremities, his hands and feet a size too large, the way they often are in adolescent boys.

"Ari's in the back," he said, stepping aside and motioning me in. We were standing in a small lobby with a receptionist's desk, a mauve couch, two chairs, and a couple of unhealthy-looking ficuses. Pretty standard low-budget outer office, except for the three poster-sized drawings that adorned the walls. They were strikingly beautiful and disturbing at the same time. All three were set at night, done with dark colors that created a sinister, moody feel. The backgrounds were richly drawn with a nice sense of depth.

The first showed two men in formal evening attire squaring off as if to fight, but their hands held no weapons. Instead the sense of combat and menace was conveyed through body language. One faced outward, his gaze intense and threatening. Between snarling lips gleamed the sharp eyeteeth of a vampire.

The other two posters featured a beautiful, raven-haired woman with deathly pale skin and full red lips. In one the background was nineteenth-century London, and a young man in a topcoat followed her. In the other, the setting was contemporary New York with the Brooklyn Bridge in the distance, and she held the slumped body of a teenage boy in her arms. In both she wore a knowing smile, and sharp vampire teeth glistened between her lips.

Grif watched me as I studied them. "They're art from the game," he said. "You like them?"

"They're very powerful."

"Powerful," he repeated, "yeah, that's good. They're mine, I mean, I drew them. Ari thinks Sabrina, that's the woman, should be a blonde. What d'you think?"

Before I could answer, a male voice from the back called, "Grif?"

"Coming," Grif said and motioned me toward a half-open door behind the receptionist's desk.

Beyond the door, the standard office illusion collapsed. There was a single large room that looked like a high-tech crash pad. A jumble of electronic equipment covered desks and tables, none of which looked like they had come from the same place. Five-foot-high gray partitions created two smaller spaces against the right wall, and taller beige panels marked off four spaces on the left.

Toward the back of the room, two ratty armchairs faced two color monitors. Arms and feet protruded from the chairs indicating they were occupied, and the screens flickered as the images changed but there was no sound.

Behind the chairs was a makeshift kitchen, and near the left wall sat an old rust-colored couch and three bean bag chairs in psychedelic prints from the sixties. Two bikes leaned against the wall and a pile of sleeping bags and clothes was stuffed in the corner.

Grif led me to the first of the partitioned areas, where a man I assumed to be Ari Kazacos met us in the doorway. He was about average height with a stocky build. Thick dark hair reached just below his collar, and his nose canted slightly to one side as if it had been broken when he was younger. His lips were full and sensual; thick lashes framed his dark eyes.

He was dressed casually, in chinos, a dark plaid sports shirt, and loafers without socks. He was probably in his early thirties. From our phone conversation I'd pictured him as slightly older, and Astra as a more established company. Sounding older and more established was clearly an advantage for a start-up.

"Thank you for coming so quickly," Kazacos said. "Time is really crucial." He motioned me into his cubicle office. It was high-tech meets high camp. Two computers, two printers, a copy/fax machine, and every space creature and craft available in miniature form. An army of brightly colored, often scaly aliens marched across the bookshelf, the entire cast of *Star Wars* perched on one computer terminal, and the *Enterprise*, several X-wing fighters, and an assortment of other spaceships awaited launch on top of the file cabinet.

Kazacos offered me a folding director's chair that was crammed into the corner next to the bookshelf. The tiny aliens were exactly at eye level. They seemed to stare straight at me, a dusty Lilliputian army taking my measure.

"You said that your lead programmer had disappeared."

Kazacos nodded. He'd taken the chair by his desk. Grif leaned against the file cabinet. "Yeah, Matt Demming. The bastard's stolen the source code for our new game, and we've got to get it back to debug the program," Kazacos said. "This game, *Cult of Blood*, is our first product, our *only* product. Time is crucial."

"You're sure Demming stole it?"

"Oh yeah. He left me a note."

"Can I see it?"

"It's right here on the e-mail," Kazacos said, turning to his computer. With a few clicks of the mouse, he brought up the electronic mail.

"Ari, you son of a bitch," it read, *"I've got the source code and the archives. When you've got the papers give me a call. And don't worry about trying to pull up the current backups. They're history."*

"What's the reference to papers?" I asked.

"Business agreements. A contract. We didn't have one. I

haven't had time to get it drawn up yet," Kazacos said impatiently. "But I gave the bastard my word. That should have been good enough."

Obviously it hadn't. "What are the archives?"

"The backups. All the former versions of the program. Every so many days we archive the backups just in case we lose data. Son of a bitch took those, too."

"Did you try to call him?"

"Of course," he said. "I called him the minute I got the message. No answer. And there's been no answer yesterday or today, either. The bastard's messing with my mind."

I read the message again. "Strange that he'd tell you to call him, then not be there," I said. "When was the e-mail sent?"

"Saturday at four-thirty P.M."

"And you called him how many times?"

"Twenty, maybe thirty. At least once an hour. I sent him e-mail, too, so there's no question that he knows I want to talk to him."

"May I see your e-mail message to him?" I asked, wanting to know if Kazacos had agreed to Demming's terms.

He had. The message was short and simple. *"You'll have the papers Monday morning. Now stop fucking around."*

"Do you have any idea why he hasn't replied or where he might be?" I asked.

"Why is because he wants to make me sweat. Maybe he's planning on hitting me up for more money. Where is what I'm hiring you to find out."

I produced a contract of my own and watched while Kazacos read and signed it. "Tell me a little about Demming," I said. "What kind of guy is he? Is he unstable?"

"He's a programmer," Kazacos said, as if that were a character description. "He's brilliant, probably one of the best minds in the field, totally obsessed with *Cult*. Never seemed unstable before."

"And the source code and backups, how big are they? What do they look like?"

"They're disks, CDs. One for the source code; a stack for the backups." He spread his hands to indicate the size of the stack. "Demming's laptop has a copy of the source code on the hard drive, but he always keeps it with him."

"I'll need a recent photo," I said. "And I'd like to search his office." Please, let him have an office, I thought, remembering the chaos of the room behind me.

"Sure, Grif can show you. He can also take you to Matt's apartment. He lives in Menlo Park, about fifteen minutes from here. Grif's got a key."

I'm not up on the legal fine points of entering a house without the owner's permission. Since we had a key, I figured it wasn't breaking and entering. Criminal trespass, maybe.

"I checked it out this morning," Grif said. "His laptop's gone, and there was no sign of the source code or the archives."

"I could kill the bastard," Kazacos said. "I'd like to wring his damn neck."

I didn't pay much attention at the time. Later I'd wonder if maybe I should have.

DETECTIVE LOU MARTIN stares down at the body and sucks in the corner of his lower lip. Across from him, the evidence tech reads his scowl and keeps his mouth shut.

The body lies on a wooden walkway above the marshy waters near the southern end of the San Francisco Bay. The sky stretches overhead like a giant bowl, deep blue at the center, fading to turquoise at the horizon. A lonely place, Martin thinks, desolate and exposed. The stiff breeze that always blows on the bay cuts through his sports coat, making him shiver involuntarily.

This isn't the first time he's been called to the Baylands to investigate a homicide. The remote area is a good place to dump a body and it offers the choice of dry land or the bay. They've had two floaters in the last year, though Martin suspects that one of them was gently nudged across the county line by a colleague from the neighboring jurisdiction.

This body wasn't dumped. It's been carefully laid out on the wooden planks of the boardwalk leading to a sailing ramp. It lies on its back with its head pointing north, the hands crossed over the chest, the way an undertaker would do it.

A white male, probably midtwenties, medium height, medium build. He's dressed all in black—black jeans, long-sleeved black shirt, black running shoes. His dark brown hair is long and held back in a ponytail. No visible scars, tattoos, or other distinctive marks. Except for the scraped spot on his forehead and the two small wounds on his neck.

It's the neck wounds that grab Martin's attention. They're no more than an eighth of an inch in diameter, close together, on the right side of the neck. A small, dark bruise rings one wound; the other is clean. Martin studies the distance between them and tries to block out the sharp point of pain in his gut. It feels like the hot ash of a cigarette burning its way through his intestine. In a move that has become almost automatic, he pulls the roll of Maalox antacids from his pocket and pops a couple of tablets into his mouth.

The staccato click of high heels on the boardwalk announces the approach of Joyce Lim, Santa Clara County

Medical Examiner. He's gotten over being surprised to see the petite, fashionably dressed woman at grisly crime scenes, though he still thinks it strange that a woman would choose to spend her life examining dead bodies.

When he arrived, she was already there, busy talking with two guys from the crime scene team. She's impeccably dressed in a deep purple suit. Eggplant, he corrects himself, remembering his daughter's admonition that when a woman wears that color, you do not call it purple.

As he looks up from the body, he can't help appreciating Lim's legs, shown to perfection by her short skirt. Martin is a leg man, and Joyce Lim has great legs.

"The way I see it, you're looking for a vampire or a lawyer," she says, her voice crisp.

He is used to her jokes. They are better than the last M.E.'s. Outsiders would consider them in poor taste, but that is the hallmark of cop humor.

Lim nods. "I'm afraid they're just what they look like. Puncture wounds. I won't know until I dissect them out, but they look to be about over the carotid artery. After they finished with the photos, I lifted his shirt and checked his back. There's no lividity."

Martin lets out a low whistle. Lividity refers to the bruiselike discoloration created when blood pools in a dead body. "No lividity means no blood," he says. "That's why he's so gray, I bet."

"You got it. If those wounds are the cause of death, this guy didn't just bleed to death. He was bled."

The pain in Martin's gut grows sharper.

"Of course, we don't know that they're the cause," she cautions. "They could be symbolic or meant to throw us off. I found a gash on the back of his head when I turned him to check for lividity. That could also be the cause of death."

"He was smacked on the head and fell forward. That's where he got the scrape on his forehead," Martin suggests.

"Could be," Lim says. She's already told him a lot more than most M.E.'s would. It's hard as hell to get an M.E. to commit to anything before a full autopsy. It's not just that they hate to be wrong, they're afraid that incorrect information will throw an investigation off. He takes Lim's willingness to speculate as a sign of trust.

They are interrupted by the sound of heavy boots on the boardwalk and a high nasal voice. "I'll bet it was a gay thing," Carl Rainey says.

Martin looks like he's just smelled something foul. Rainey is one of his least favorite people in the department. The patrolman thinks anything out of the ordinary is a "gay thing." He's young, only twenty-four, but youth doesn't excuse everything, and Martin doubts that he'll be any less stupid or narrow-minded when he gets older.

"Why would you think that, Officer?" Lim asks sweetly.

"Because it's so weird. The way the guy's laid out, the wounds. I'll bet it's some kind of S and M thing gone bad."

"I didn't know you were an expert on deviant sexual practices," Lim says. Her tone drips sarcasm, but Martin doubts that Rainey hears it. Anything short of a board in the face is too subtle for him.

Martin can see George Prizer, Rainey's partner, coming toward them. Prizer is tall and trim with a runner's build. There's a precision to his movement and his dress. You could cut yourself on the crease in his pants. Though he is at least ten years older than Rainey, he's clearly in better shape.

Martin doesn't know Prizer well, but he's worked several cases with him. He knows that Prizer has applied to move into the investigation division. For reasons he can't explain to anyone, including himself, he does not entirely trust the man.

Prizer stops just behind Rainey and gives a low whistle as he studies the corpse. His already thin lips compress into a flat line and his bushy eyebrows creep toward each other as his forehead draws itself into a frown.

Martin is uneasy. There are too damn many people tramping around the crime scene. He does a quick inventory of who is there and realizes it isn't such a crowd. Just the crime scene guys, Lim's people, and Prizer and Rainey, the patrolmen who caught the original call.

It isn't the numbers, he realizes, but his instinct to keep this thing quiet. At the thought of what the press would do with this bizarre killing, the pain in his gut burns sharper. He can see the headline, VAMPIRE KILLER STRIKES IN PALO ALTO. That'd be the lead story on the evening news, and not just the local news either. The reporters would be on this one like vultures on a carcass.

Prizer's voice interrupts his thoughts. "Strange wounds. Were they the cause of death?"

"We won't know cause of death until the autopsy," Lim says.

Martin doesn't like the way Prizer is studying the corpse. He doesn't want the patrolman spreading word of what they've found.

"You attended the seminar on cult crime, didn't you, Lou?" Prizer says.

Martin nods, suppressing a groan. It was almost a year ago that the department sent four "volunteers" to a daylong seminar on cult crime. At the time, Martin thought it was a bunch of crap, and he hasn't found any reason to revise that judgment. His dislike of Prizer can probably be traced to the drive home, during which the patrolman gushed with enthusiasm for the cult cops' presentation.

"This sure fits the profile," Prizer says.

"What profile?" Martin says scornfully.

"Well, there're the wounds to start with. And the head is pointing north."

"The walkway runs north-south," Martin objects. "There's a fifty-fifty chance the head would point north."

"That's probably why this walkway was chosen," Prizer says. "It's in an isolated area, another possible indicator."

He's memorized the damn checklist, Martin thinks, remembering the pack of materials they were given at the seminar. He takes another Maalox from his pocket and pops it into his mouth.

"I'd like to help on this, Lou, if you're agreeable. I've done a good bit of studying about cults since the seminar. I think I could be useful to you," Prizer says. Then he adds, "There's been some action by vampire cults on the East Coast. At least one murder. This could be connected."

Martin can't think of much that he'd find less agreeable than working with Prizer. He suspects that Prizer is the type of guy who just loves the limelight.

"Thank you very much," he says. "I appreciate that. I do need your help. I need to make sure that word of this doesn't leak to the press."

Prizer looks surprised and isn't completely successful in masking his disappointment.

"As you said, George, there's enough that's strange about this case to attract the attention of the media," Martin continues. "That'd just make our job harder. I've instructed everyone to keep this off the radio, so with luck it'll be a while before the newshounds get wind of it."

"But you can't . . ." Rainey objects.

"We can't suppress the fact that we found a body," Martin says, trying to sound more patient than he feels. "But we don't have to tell them the exact nature of the wounds, or George's concern that this might be cult-connected. We'll release the information that we've found an unidentified body dumped in the Baylands. More than that, we don't tell anyone who isn't *directly* connected with the investigation."

"Don't we have the responsibility to warn the public?" Prizer tries to make it sound like a question. "I mean, if this is the work of Satanists, others could be at risk."

"I think we'll do a little more investigating before we assume that," Martin says. He'd like to tell Prizer he's acting like a bloody fool, but he wants the man's cooperation. "I need you gentlemen to make sure that no one here runs their mouth to the press, or anyone else for that matter. A weird crime always makes a good story, so they'll be tempted to talk about it. We've got to impress on them to keep quiet about this one. Can you do that for me?"

Martin learned years ago to pick the guy most likely to break a rule and make him responsible for enforcing it. He figures that approach will work with Rainey; Prizer is more problematic.

As he expects, the younger patrolman nods enthusiastically. Prizer merely dips his chin in what Martin hopes is a sign of grudging assent. "Whatever you say, Lou," Prizer says, then turns and walks back down the boardwalk toward the crime scene guys. Rainey follows him.

"It could be cult-connected," Lim says, when the patrolmen are out of earshot.

"Could be," Martin admits. "Could even be Satanists involved." He looks up at Lim with a grim expression.

She meets his gaze. "God, I hope not."

5

I FOLLOWED GRIF to Matt Demming's "office" in the cubicle next to Ari Kazacos's. No extraterrestrials here. Instead, one wall was covered with pages from comics and
graphic novels. The images made Kazacos's office look like
a day care center. Demming's companions were sharp-
featured, ominous figures, grotesque monsters, and vicious
half beasts. The opposite wall held sheets of butcher paper
with an elaborate chart of notes in a dense, spidery hand.

I studied the chart and realized it was a time line of sorts.
At the beginning in large letters was written LUCIFER. At
various points, there were dates and names followed by
notes that started small and rapidly became too tiny to read.

"That's the chronicle," Grif said from behind me. "That's
what makes the game so cool."

"The chronicle?"

"Like the story line, except it's a lot more. It spans cen-
turies and it's got all these different clans and characters.
What's so cool about vampires is, they're immortal, so the
same character can be in Egypt when they're building
the pyramids and in Troy during the war and in Paris in the
Middle Ages. And in San Francisco right now.

"That's one of the things I love about it. I get to do these incredible backgrounds for different historic periods, so it's
like, you don't just shoot it out in front of some clunky castle,
but you move through this world we've created.

"It's not some brainless shoot-'em-up. It's got a real story line, and the characters have different motivations. They're not all evil. A vampire is only part-beast, so the good ones are struggling against the beast in themselves as well as the evil outside them."

He seemed anxious that I see the game as something more than a slick product for adolescents. "Sort of like a quest," I said, thinking of *The Odyssey* and King Arthur.

"Exactly." He smiled broadly. "Like *Star Wars*. A hero's quest."

I looked around Demming's decidedly unheroic office and thought of my own quest. Grif seemed to read my mind. "So what do you want here? Maybe I can help you find it."

"I'd like names and phone numbers for his friends and family for starters. Is that likely to be on his computer or does he keep an address book?"

"Probably on disk," Grif said. "Matt always prefers electronic solutions." He reached over and flipped the power switch on the computer. He clicked on a couple of icons, and in a matter of seconds, Matt Demming's address/phone list was on the screen.

"He's got another one, but it's password-protected, so I can't get us in there."

The most valuable information is usually the hardest to get. I wondered who Demming had in the file he'd protected.

"You know any way around the password?"

"Not me. I'm a fair programmer, but Matt's really good. Anything he wants protected is beyond me."

I asked Grif to print out the unprotected list and we went over it together. "First, tell me who's missing," I said. "Often people don't enter the numbers they call most frequently."

"No, I think it's pretty complete. I mean, Nate Sessler's

there, and if Matt knows anyone's number by heart, it's his."

"Are they close friends?"

"I guess. They've known each other forever. Nate worked with Matt on the vampire shareware. That's, like, 'I'll share this with you for free and if you like it, send me money.' Matt did the programming; Nate did the art. It was back when they were in college, before Matt decided to go for the big bucks and teamed up with Ari."

I put a double check by Sessler's name. We went down the list and Grif identified as many people as he could. Most were other programmers or people in the computer games industry. Three were men Grif described as friends whom Matt had hired to work as game testers.

"Those two guys at the other end of the room are testers," he said. "At this stage the only way to find the bugs is to play the game endlessly. We've got two teams of three guys who play around the clock.

"Three of the guys are professional testers, the others are friends of Matt's who're really into games. They thought they'd died and gone to heaven when he offered them five bucks an hour to play. We'll see if they still feel that way at the end of the month."

"From what Mr. Kazacos said, you've already found some bugs."

"Yeah, we have. There's stuff that doesn't work right, but none of the bugs causes the game to crash. So far, anyway. Ari's keeping the test going in the hopes that we won't find anything too serious. But, like he said, we can't fix anything without the source code."

"If they work around the clock, someone must have been here when Demming took the code. Do you know who?"

"Ari figures it was the day shift, ten to six, on Saturday. That's Joe and Aaron, the guys who're here now. He's talked to them. They say Matt was here. They saw him take the backups, but he didn't speak to them."

"You keep the backups on site?"

"Yeah, I know that's dumb. We got sloppy."

That was an understatement. "Are either of the testers here now Matt's friends?" I asked.

"You mean from before? No. Two of those guys work the early morning shift, and the other's on night shift."

I searched Demming's office and didn't find anything else that might tell us where he'd gone, so I suggested it was time to try his apartment.

"Sure," Grif said, "but I rode my bike to work, so we'll need to take your car." Leading the way to the front door, he moved rather like a Great Dane, with an awkward delicacy. As if he still weren't quite used to his long legs.

As we pulled out of the parking lot, I said, "What do you think of Demming's disappearance?"

"It's a shitty thing to do, but Matt won't be losing any sleep over what it does to the rest of us." There was a harsh anger in his voice that I hadn't heard before. He took a deep breath, then added in a softer tone, "I suppose from his point of view it made sense. Programmers always get screwed. The company promises them the moon to get them started, but the contracts never get written and then the project is done and suddenly it's, 'Oh, we didn't mean a percent of gross, we meant net.' Then they do a Hollywood accounting and the damn thing's never in the black.

"Or they offer the guy a big pot of money that's really not nearly as much as the original deal, but since there's no contract, he takes what's offered just to be safe. Matt doesn't have the money to hire someone to sue Ari, and by the time we get *Cult of Blood* out, we'll all be so broke we'll be desperate for cash."

"How's this affect you? Are you on contract?"

"Ari's been paying me a salary, just enough to keep me

from starving. When the game comes out I get more, and I got a fat stock option for when we go public. I've got it in writing, not a fancy contract, but I think it'll be okay."

"But Matt didn't have that?"

"No, see, Ari and Matt are supposed to be partners. Matt had the game; Ari had the connections and the start-up money. The shareware version of *Cult* was, like, an underground classic. It had a sophistication you don't often see in shareware. People really dug it.

"Ari was a producer at one of the big game companies. His team did *Desert Wars* and *Castle Doom*, both big sellers. He used the money from them to start Astra. He needed a hot product. Matt needed the backing to take *Cult* to a new level, so they teamed up."

"If Astra's a partnership . . ." I said.

"It was *supposed* to be a partnership, but Matt doesn't know jack about business and didn't care enough to pay attention. He just left all the legal stuff to Ari. Then last week his uncle, who's a hot-shit lawyer in Chicago, came to town. It didn't take long for him to figure out that there weren't any partnership papers. He did a bit of checking and the fit hit the shan, so to speak."

"So the papers Demming refers to aren't a contract; they're a partnership."

"That's the way I understand it, though most of the time, they were yelling at each other, and it was hard to tell exactly what was going on, except that Matt was madder than hell."

So Kazacos had lied to me, more or less. No surprise there. Clients often lie, especially when the truth makes them look bad. They seem to think I won't work as hard if I know they failed the exam for sainthood.

We got on the freeway heading south. It wasn't far to the Willow Road exit. From there Grif directed me to a neighborhood of small, well-kept houses. Our destination turned out to be one of the larger houses on the street, at least thirty years older than the ones surrounding it.

"Does he live with his parents?" I asked.

"No, they're back East. He lives in the garage."

We walked down the driveway to an old wooden garage that had been converted into a cottage. Wisteria vines snaked up the side of the building and draped themselves over the roof. There was only one small window, covered with a curtain.

Grif unlocked the door and stood aside for me to enter. Anyone who hadn't lived with a teenager might have assumed the place had been tossed. But the piles didn't look much different from those in Molly's room.

The made-over garage was a single large room with a door that I assumed led to a bathroom at the far end. Next to the bathroom was a small refrigerator and a table containing a hot plate, a couple of pans, some dishes, and several boxes of cereal. At the other end of the room was a mattress with rumpled bedclothes and a desk. Its surface was the neatest place in the cottage.

I went to the refrigerator and opened it. It held milk, orange juice, a carton of leftover Chinese food, and a pound of ground beef. Either Demming wasn't planning on a long absence or he'd never had to clean a refrigerator full of food gone bad.

I checked the bathroom next. Unless he had a spare, Demming hadn't taken his toothbrush. Nor had he taken allergy medicine from the cabinet. As I was leaving I noticed a hairbrush that had fallen behind the toilet. It looked more like a woman's brush than a man's.

A search of the closet and the desk didn't turn up the source code or the backups for *Cult of Blood*. Nor did we find the laptop. We did find thick files of papers covered with the same spidery writing I'd seen at the office. There were eight labeled CHRONICLES, numbered with Roman numerals.

I searched a small table standing next to the mattress. Beneath it I found a used condom. "Does Demming have a girlfriend?" I asked.

"Not that I know of."

"Well, he had someone here. Any idea who?"

Grif looked uncomfortable. "No," he said. "He's never talked about anyone." I wondered why the sight of the condom should make him so uneasy, and for the first time, I had the feeling that the animator knew more than he was telling.

"What're you going to do now?" he asked.

I let him change the subject. I'd come back to it later. "Talk to people, see if anyone knows where he is. Is this Nate Sessler his best friend?"

"I don't know about best," Grif said, "but they go back a long way. Matt even got him a job at Astra."

"I thought you were doing the art for the new game?"

"I am. Nate's doing the supplementary documentation. Ari didn't want to spend money on it, but Matt insisted that the game had to have an introduction to the vampire cosmos, the clans and politics, a lot of stuff that's cool to know but not really required by the game. And he wanted Nate to do it."

"Nate did the art for the original game?"

"Yeah. They teamed up when they were in high school, but Nate's really not that good. The animation was the weak point of the first game. It was just sort of clunky, okay for shareware but not nearly sophisticated enough for a commercial game. That's why Ari hired me."

I switched off the light, and as I was relocking the door, I said, "You know Matt pretty well, why do you think he's hiding?"

Grif gave a short, harsh laugh. "I don't know him all that

well, but I do know Matt's real good at looking out for number one."

JOYCE LIM, SANTA Clara County Medical Examiner, stares down at the mortal remains of the John Doe found at the Baylands. "The victim," she likes to tell her assistants, "is the last witness. And it's our job to give him or her a final say. The body has a story to tell; you have to learn to read it."

She's been reading this body with fierce concentration for several hours. A faint tightness across her forehead threatens to become a tension headache, and a hollowness in her stomach reminds her that she skipped lunch. The autopsy was completed twenty minutes ago. Her observations have been recorded, tissue and blood samples taken and sent to the appropriate labs. Her assistants have gone on to other work, leaving her alone in the chilly autopsy room.

This body, this nude male body mutilated first by a killer and later by her, has a lot to tell. But it's a tangled story, and she doesn't want to miss any of the clues. There's so much here that would be easy to misread.

Like the neck wounds made to look like a vampire bite. Only one of them was inflicted before death. The second hole missed the artery altogether. By the time it was made, there was little blood left in the body. Tiny hemorrhages under the skin near the first hole suggest that the killer used a smaller needle to locate the artery. And that it took several tries.

She's studied the wounds for some sign of the instrument that made them. If it was a needle, and that's the most likely candidate, it was a big one. Bigger than the ones used to draw blood. Maybe an embalmer's needle or one used for large animals.

A tiny flame of pain flickers behind her eyes and forces itself into her awareness. She yawns and rubs her temples, then walks to the door and calls a technician to put the body back in the refrigerator.

In her office she mulls over the case as she eats the turkey sandwich she bought at the deli on her way to work. She wishes Martin hadn't been called away in the middle of the autopsy. She's anxious to talk with him.

The sandwich is only half-finished when the phone rings. It's Martin. "Sorry I missed the party," he says. "What's the word? We got a serial here?"

"Hard to tell," she says. "Whatever we've got, it's not a crime of passion. I'd say it was carefully planned."

"How'd he die?"

"You probably noticed the wound behind the right ear. That was made by a heavy blunt object. I'd say he was struck from behind and knocked unconscious. There was a fair amount of surface bleeding, cerebral contusions, subdural hemorrhage. That blow didn't kill him but it knocked him down.

"You saw the bruising and minor lacerations on the upper left side of his forehead. It's what you guessed, he got that when he fell. It didn't bleed much so the killer didn't wrap it, but he did wrap the back of the head. We found fibers of white cotton cloth in the wound and in nearby hair."

"So the killer smacked him on the back of the head and knocked him out, but why wrap his head up?"

"I'd guess it's because he or she needed to move the body

and didn't want to get blood around. The victim was definitely killed somewhere else. The body may even have been wrapped in plastic. I found little bits of the black plastic used for garbage bags caught on a couple of sharp edges on his belt buckle."

"I may have a lead on where he was attacked," Martin says. "I'm following up on a 911 call. You find anything that might tell us where he was moved from?"

"Not yet, but we may get something when we analyze the trace evidence. We do know that he didn't die immediately. There's pooling and clotting of the blood in subdural areas, some bruising under the skin. The heart had to be pumping for that to occur."

"Any way to know if he was conscious?"

"I doubt it. There's slight bruising on the wrists and ankles, which indicates that he was tied up, but if he'd struggled, they'd be more pronounced."

"And the wounds on the neck?"

"One of them goes right into the carotid artery. It's probably the cause of death. The heart was empty of blood, but there was still a little in the cranium, so his head was probably lower than the rest of him." She tells Martin the rest of it, about the second wound and the smaller needle sticks.

"It's not the easiest thing to hit the carotid artery," she tells him. "You can feel the pulse in the throat, but it's fairly deep under the skin, not nearly as easy to find as the blood vessel on the wrist or the inside of the elbow. And the wounds are just deep enough to hit the artery, but not so deep as to go straight through. That took some skill. And bleeding him out without making a mess. That took skill, too.

"When you're looking at the victim's associates, pay particular attention to anyone with experience in medicine—medics, nurses, emergency workers. Same goes for morticians or vets." She paused. "Of course, it could be, he just did his research in the library."

"You're saying 'he,' " Martin interrupts. "You think it was a guy?"

Lim pauses to consider the question. "Nothing solid," she replies, "but your victim is a good-sized guy, not easy for a woman to move from one place to another, especially if she had to be careful about getting blood around."

"Okay."

"Back to the neck wounds," Lim continues. "Likely source is a big needle, very big. You might want to check reports of thefts from veterinary clinics or mortuaries."

"Okay," Martin says. There's a pause, and she assumes he is making notes. "What's your take on this vampire stuff? Do we have a weirdo running around?"

Lim knew they'd get to that question. She wishes she had an answer. "It's very possible," she says. "I've saved the big news for last. When we took the shirt off, we found a pentagram carved on the back of the victim's right forearm, an inch and a half below the elbow. The wound was post-mortem, probably done with something like a pocketknife."

"Jesus, Mary, and Joseph," Martin exclaims. "A pentagram? That's a satanic symbol, isn't it?"

"I'm afraid so. And if we have a cult that's taken up killing, this won't be their last victim."

7

I FOUND MATT Demming's friend Nate Sessler at the software store where he worked in Mountain View, about twenty minutes south of Menlo Park. The store was almost empty, except for two boys who were about twelve years old. They stood in front of a display of computer games featuring men in uniform and weapons of mass destruction, debating the merits of *War III* versus *Kill Zone*.

The guy behind the counter looked like Norman Rockwell retouched by Nine Inch Nails. He had reddish hair, a wide grin, and a nose sprinkled with freckles. But the red hair stood straight up and was cut flat across the top, and the nose wore a silver ring through one nostril. At the base of his throat, a tattoo of the head of a bat glared at me malevolently above the neck of his T-shirt.

It was hard not to stare at the bat. It was an evil-looking creature with wicked, sharp teeth. A vampire bat, no doubt. I wondered if this guy had ever considered how his bat would look when his neck was forty years old, then realized that kids never believe they'll be forty. "I'm looking for Nate Sessler." I said.

"At your service," he said, giving me a mock salute. "What can I do for you?"

"I was hoping you could help me find Matt Demming."

"Matt?" He shook his head. "Haven't seen him for a couple days. Why?"

"He doesn't seem to be around, and his boss needs to talk to him."

"Ari?" Sessler seemed surprised, then delighted. "I'll bet that means Matt still hasn't given him the code."

I was curious to know how Sessler had learned of the theft. He acted as if it were common knowledge. "How did you find out about it?" I asked.

"Matt told me Saturday night. He was really pissed at Ari."

"Have you seen him since then?"

He shook his head. "You work for Ari?" he asked. His manner was open and curious. I was watching for signs that he was nervous or trying to hide something, but didn't see any.

"Yes," I said. "He's agreed to Mr. Demming's terms, but he can't find him. Do you have any idea where he might be?"

He leaned on the counter, resting his forearms on it, and I was struck by the tattoo of a wraithlike figure on the back of his right arm.

"You like my tattoo?"

"Like" wasn't the word I'd have chosen for the disturbing figure that stared defiantly from his arm, but I said, "It's very impressive."

"Yeah, that's the main character from the game Matt and I developed. I did the art. Designed the tattoo myself."

I could see why Ari had demanded another artist. Sessler's figure was too raw, too disturbing for a commercial game. I asked again where he thought Matt might be.

"You checked his place?" Sessler asked.

"Yes."

"Damn, I don't know where else he'd be. But to tell the truth, if Matt doesn't want anyone to find him, I'm sure as hell not going to rat him out."

Sessler'd been watching too many B movies. "This isn't a manhunt," I said. "And Mr. Kazacos is ready to give Mr.

Demming what he asked for. I'm just trying to find him to tell him that."

Sessler studied me, his brown eyes bright with curiosity. "Well, I haven't seen Mr. Demming since the game on Saturday."

"What game?"

"The LARP. The vampire game." He watched me closely for a reaction as he said it.

Playing dumb is often more useful than revealing what you know. "What's a LARP?" I asked.

"Live Action Role-Playing. It's a group game. A bunch of us get together Saturday nights to play. Let's see how I can describe it." He paused, then continued, "It's like a cross between improvisational theater and D & D. Each person makes up a character, usually a vampire, though it could be a human or a ghoul, and there's a sort of rough story line, like maybe two groups are searching for the same thing and someone in the game has it but no one knows who, so the action is everyone trying to figure out who has this thing so they can get it.

"That's the improv part. The D & D part is that characters have traits and powers, like strength, stealth, perception. When two characters clash, they have a sort of duel to see who wins."

"And you and Matt were both at the game?"

"Yeah, we go most Saturday nights. We started back in high school. He pretty much dropped out when he went off to college, but he started up again about six months ago."

"And he told you about taking the source code."

"He told everybody. He was really wired. He'd just . . ." Sessler was interrupted by the sound of a bell that announced the opening of the door. We turned to see a character out of Grif's sketches slouching toward us.

He was dressed entirely in black—high lace-up boots, leather pants, and a silk shirt with flowing sleeves. And metal. Lots of metal, much of it hanging from his ears, nose, and one eyebrow. His longish black hair was much too dark for his pale skin. I checked for long eyeteeth and was relieved not to find them.

"Hey, Damion, what's up?" Sessler said.

"I brought you back the game," the apparition said, in a soft voice that didn't match its owner's exterior. "Thanks for letting me play it." He handed Sessler a CD in a clear plastic case. I noticed that the back of his forearm was disfigured with an ugly scar that had been darkened with ink in a homemade tattoo. The shape was a crudely drawn pentagram.

"Sure," Sessler said. "You like it?"

"It was okay. Third level plays sort of slow, but the fifth's cool." Metal flashed as he talked—a silver stud in the middle of his tongue.

"Yeah, the fifth's the bomb," Sessler said.

The kid named Damion just nodded. He shifted from one foot to the other and after an awkward silence said, "So, you want to play again sometime?"

"Sure," Sessler said with forced enthusiasm. "Yeah, sure. I'll bring *Dungeon Lords*."

Damion nodded. "Okay," he said. He turned to go, but Sessler stopped him with, "Say, you were at the game Saturday night. Have you seen Matt since then?"

"No."

"This lady's looking for him. Any idea where he'd be?"

Damion turned his dark eyes on me. He would have been a good-looking kid without all that metal. He was probably seventeen or eighteen, too thin for his height. But as our eyes met, I realized that it was more than his dress that made me uneasy. There was an intensity to his gaze that was unsettling.

He shook his head slowly. "Haven't seen him," he said. Then he turned and left the store.

Sessler shook his head when Damion had gone. "That's one crazy fool," he said. "A true lost soul. I give him shareware games to play sometimes 'cause I feel sorry for him. Doesn't have many friends as far as I can tell. You shouldn't judge the game by him. He's the only Goth who plays."

"Goth?"

"That's what they call themselves. The kids who dress like that. It's short for Gothic. My mom calls them punks, but punks are different. Damion's a Goth."

I didn't care what Damion called himself. I just hoped he wasn't mixed up in my case. "How well does he know Matt Demming?" I asked.

Sessler shrugged. "Who knows? People tend to avoid him since he's so weird. Some folks are even scared of him; they think he's crazy. But with Matt, you never know. He has some strange friends."

I tried to get the names of some of those friends, but Sessler clammed up immediately. I decided to try a different approach. "You're working for Astra now, I understand."

"Yeah, I'm doing some documentation."

"I'd think you'd have an interest in seeing the game get finished on deadline," I said.

"Well, it's not like they're giving *me* a stock option. Matt has an incentive to meet the deadline. I get paid one way or the other."

"Who else was at the vampire LARP game?" I asked.

"Lots of people, mostly regulars, and a few new folks. The person to tell you about that is Tony Torres. He's the game master."

"He runs the game?"

"Yeah. He makes up the story and assigns roles, decides when to schedule games. It's his baby."

To my surprise, he gave me the game master's phone number. I tried for more. "Does Matt have a girlfriend?"

"Oh, no. Matt's my buddy. You'll have to get someone else to tell tales on him."

THE TRAFFIC ON the freeway made me think fondly of the days when rush hour was only sixty minutes long, but as I passed Redwood City it lightened up and I made good time to San Francisco. The poor souls heading in the opposite direction were not so lucky.

I was in a hurry to get back since I'd promised an aikido buddy that I'd help her with a self-defense class she was offering to girls at a neighborhood recreation center. The center was just off the freeway and I arrived with about twenty minutes to spare. Just long enough to find a place to change into my *ghi* and *hakama*, the long split skirt worn over the *ghi* by black belts.

My friend Cheryl was similarly attired in white *ghi* and navy *hakama*. "We're not doing anything you couldn't do in street clothes," she said, as we dressed, "but they'll take it more seriously if we look like martial artists."

"Think that'll work with Molly?" I asked.

"Nothing works when you're the mom," Cheryl said with a laugh. She has a sixteen-year-old.

There were eleven girls in the large, multipurpose room—several races, many sizes, all on the verge of teenhood. We did some stretching exercises to get them started. Then Cheryl asked a volunteer to come forward. "What do you do if someone grabs you like this?" she said, grasping the girl's wrist. The girl immediately pulled back but couldn't break the grip.

"You kick the guy in the balls," a diminutive, dark-haired girl said.

"Nu-uh," another countered. "That just makes 'em hella mad. Then you can really get hurt."

I remembered the same discussion from my youth. Scream, run, and kick him in the balls were the three self-defense techniques we were offered. I hadn't had much confidence in any of them. Maybe that was why I'd started aikido.

"There's a lot simpler solution," Cheryl said. She held out her hand and nodded for me to grab it. I did, and she simply twisted her wrist slightly and slipped it out at the point between my thumb and index finger. "The strongest grip is still weak at that point," she said. "Take partners and try that," she said.

Most of the girls got the hang of it quickly, though some still had a tendency to pull back.

"What do you do next?" one girl asked.

"Depends on the situation," Cheryl said. "You might want to run or shout; sometimes breaking the grip is enough to let the other person know you're not an easy target.

"How did it feel when someone grabbed you?" she asked.

"Scary," a gangly redhead answered. "It's like my mind sort of stopped working for a second."

"Dealing with fear's one of the main things we'll be working on," Cheryl said. "It can really get in the way and destroy your ability to act. It can even keep you from seeing clearly what's happening.

"Let's say you're walking down the street and you see a scruffy-looking guy watching you. Your mind immediately invents scenarios. This guy is a mugger, maybe a rapist. Your mind's going a mile a minute. Meanwhile, the real mugger is behind you, and you won't even see him because you're so busy worrying about the scruffy guy in front. That's what fear can do.

"The first rule of self-defense is to be aware of what's happening around you. That doesn't mean be scared, just be aware."

We did several more exercises, and Cheryl dismissed the class. Later, as we were changing, she said, "They always say that about kicking a guy in the balls. It's the damnedest thing."

"It's what my mother told me."

"Same here. She never mentioned breaking a nose, and that's an easier target."

"You know what a shrink would say about that," I said.

"Spare me."

I called Tony Torres, the game master, as soon as I got home.

He had a pleasant, well-modulated voice; would have made a good announcer. When I explained about Matt's disappearance, he became evasive and tension crept into his voice.

"I'm awfully busy just now," he said. "I really can't take time off. And I don't have anything to tell you."

A straight-on approach wasn't going to work with this guy, so I tried something different. Knowing he loved games, I said, "I'm surprised. Matt Demming's set up one hell of a game and you don't want to play."

"What do you mean?"

"Just what I said."

A long pause, then, "I could see you tomorrow night. It'd have to be in the city. I've got a class at State. I could see you afterward."

We arranged to meet at ten o'clock at a coffeehouse near the campus.

* * *

Dinner was hamburgers, for the third time in a week. Molly was learning to cook, and Peter and I were trying to be supportive, but it was time to nudge her into an expanded repertoire.

"Peter makes a terrific spaghetti sauce," I said. "I'll bet he'd show you how."

"And Catherine is a whiz at stir-fry," Peter countered.

"Do either of you know how to make lemon meringue pie?" Molly asked.

"I don't even know how to bake Toll House cookies," I said. "Besides, in most families, dessert follows the main dish."

"See, that's what's wrong with the world," Molly said. "Adults always want to put off the good stuff."

Peter, never known for "putting off the good stuff," nodded agreement, and I could see we were headed for meals of cake and ice cream. Actually, before Molly moved in Peter and I had been known to make a meal of microwave popcorn or chocolate showers ice cream, but now that we were surrogate parents, we were trying to act like grownups. At least, one of us was.

"How was your day?" I asked Peter, to get back on safer ground.

"Not so hot," he said with a grimace. "I found the Morton girl, but she's with a real scumbag boyfriend."

Peter's what you might call a full-service private investigator. He'll take just about any case that walks through his door, but his specialty is runaway kids. Not having much affection for the establishment, he gets along well with the disaffected and disenfranchised. Kids who don't trust anyone old enough to drink without a fake ID will talk to Peter.

He'd been looking for Traci Morton for three days. She'd run away from her domineering father and passive mother in Pacific Palisades. Pressed by police, her friends had revealed that she planned to start a new life in San Francisco.

"The boyfriend's not a pimp, at least," Peter said, distaste sharpening his tone. "But that's probably only because he hasn't thought of it yet, and she's so damn dependent on him that it's going to be hard to get her to cut him loose."

I could see the tension in his face and knew that the case was getting to him. One reason he's so good at his work is that he really cares about kids. But it's sad, hard work and he spends too much time in the painful world of disposable children.

"Have you told the parents?"

"I told them I found her. The old man's as much of a bastard as the boyfriend. 'Just bring her home, and if she resists, you do what you have to. I won't complain,' " he said, mimicking the father's gruff voice. "No wonder the kid puts up with the boyfriend. She probably thinks that's the way a guy shows he cares about you."

"So what're you going to do?" Molly asked. Having run away from home herself, she had her own take on Peter's cases.

Peter grimaced. "There's probably not a good solution for this one. But she'd be safer with her parents than with the boyfriend. If I can get her to consider dumping the scumbag, then maybe she can figure out someplace to go, maybe a relative or a friend of the family who'd take her in."

Molly nodded thoughtfully. "I'm really lucky you took me in," she said, looking at her plate instead of me.

"Hey, kid, you're not so bad," I said. "Especially now that you work for your keep."

Molly had convinced me early in the year to let her work in my office. I'd only agreed to the idea because she'd promised to pull up her grades, and I still had misgivings, but I had to admit that she had not only kept her part of the bargain but was a real asset to the office. She'd taken over many of the dull, repetitive jobs, and under Jesse's tutelage, she could already do things on the computer that I couldn't.

"Can you get the Morton girl to see you again?" I asked, returning to the earlier topic.

"Oh sure, the poor kid's hungry, so I take her out to eat. Long as I feed her, she'll show up."

"Hey, I forgot to tell you," Molly said. "The cops called today."

"Did they call for me or Peter?"

"For me," Molly answered. "A girl I used to know in Palo Alto disappeared. They called to see if I knew anything about where she's gone."

"And do you?" I asked.

"No. I hardly know her, but she's on the *Rack*," Molly replied.

"Ah, the Klingon sex forum," Peter said. He didn't have much interest in computers, but we both kept an eye on Molly's online associates. The *Rack* was a chat room run by a boy in Palo Alto, and its members were mostly kids from that city's two high schools. A recent discussion of Klingon sex had brought together two of its members' favorite topics.

"Very funny," Molly said. "It so happens that the message board had a notice about Chloe being missing last night."

"Chloe Dorn? That's the girl who was in the paper this morning," Peter said.

He got up and went into the living room, returning with a section of the morning paper open to the second page of the local news section. He handed Molly the paper and she nodded as she studied the picture of a girl about her age. She held it between us so that we could both read the article.

The girl in the picture had long, light-colored hair pulled back from a high forehead. Her face was a perfect oval. She looked straight into the camera with large, almost almond-shaped eyes. The eyes were her strongest feature. Otherwise, she was neither pretty nor plain, a girl you'd pass on the street without noticing her.

The article added little to what Molly had learned from the *Rack*. Chloe Dorn had disappeared Saturday night and her parents feared she'd been abducted. She was a good student and very active in her church youth group. In fact, the majority of the article was devoted to the pastor's testimony to her character and his warnings on the dangers confronting today's youth.

"That's an old picture," Molly said, tapping the photo. "She looks a *little* different now." The irony in her voice made me ask what she meant.

"Well, when I saw her about six months ago, her hair was black, for one thing. And she was wearing dark plum lipstick and lots of green eye shadow."

"Do I sense a bit of disparity between the pastor's description and your opinion of her?" I asked.

"She probably doesn't wear the lipstick and eye shadow to church," Molly said.

"That double personality is part of the profile of a runaway," Peter said. "Probably why the cops aren't too concerned."

"But what if they're wrong," Molly said. "Just 'cause she dyed her hair doesn't mean she ran away. How come kids who look one way get taken less seriously than kids who look another way? That's so fucked."

I gave her the watch-the-language look, but I didn't disagree with her. When she'd run away from home, her dress and actions had moved her from the "good kid" category to "bad kid." But she was really the same kid, and she'd been in terrible danger on the streets. I looked at Chloe Dorn's picture and felt a lump in my throat.

I changed the subject. "My new case is in your backyard,"

I told Molly. "It's a skip trace on a programmer who walked off with the source code for a hot new computer game. You might even know him. He was in the vampire LARP."

She didn't know Matt Demming, but she was happy to tell me what she knew about the game he'd played the night he disappeared. "The Palo Alto game's pretty tame, or it was when I was there," she said. "It was mostly computer geeks and some theater people. They're really into playing the roles, you know, running around pretending to be vampires. The Mountain View game is supposed to be wilder; they have some heavy Goth-types."

"Goths?" I said, reminded of my encounter with the real item that afternoon.

"They're the kids who're heavy into night and death," Molly said. "They're all pale and wasted-looking, dye their hair black or bleach it white, have lots of pierces. Very dramatic."

I was relieved to hear disgust in her tone.

"They're the modern-day Romantics," Peter said. "They dress in black or dark red, go for a sort of modified nineteenth-century look—blousy poet shirts for the guys, velvet and lace for the girls. They'd fit right into a vampire game."

"I don't see anything romantic about them," Molly objected.

"Not that kind of romantic," Peter explained. "I mean Romantic as a school of thought. Like the Romantic poets: Byron, Shelley . . ." He stopped when her blank look told him he was way over her head. "Well, they're not really Romantics anyway, they just like to dress that way; they're actually nihilists."

If I'd been throwing around the big words, Molly would just have rolled her eyes, but she worships Peter, and I could see that part of her wanted to understand what he was saying.

"Nihilists are the folks who believe everything's so awful that we ought to just blow it all away even if we don't have anything better to replace it with," Peter said. "Sound familiar?"

"That's the Goths, all right," Molly said. "I used to think they were pretty cool because at least they understood what a shitty world it is. Now, I think they should get a life. So we got left a crummy world, what's the point in whining about it."

The bitterness and cynicism in her tone saddened me. But it was also familiar. I wondered if every generation believed it had been dealt a bum hand.

LOU MARTIN PULLS in behind the crime scene van parked at the edge of a road on the Stanford campus. He cuts his lights and the van fades to a dim, bulky form. The moon is two days past its darkest phase, and the streetlights have been shut off for the next few hours. With luck, tonight Martin and his colleagues will read the story of a murder in traces of blood invisible to the human eye.

In the distance through the trees, bright floodlights illuminate the Cactus Garden. This tangle of ancient succulents and cacti is less a garden than a ruin. Stone-lined paths suggest that it has known finer days, but they were long ago.

It is here that the police believe John Doe was attacked before he was killed. Tiny spots of blood found on wild grasses and two different cacti match the victim's blood type and confirm the importance of a call made to 911 early Sunday morning.

The call came in at 12:52 A.M.—a female reporting a man bleeding badly from a head wound at the Stanford Cactus Garden. When asked for her name, she hung up.

The log reveals that an officer sent to the scene found no evidence of a body. While checking the area, he was interrupted by a group of students who had been drinking, and their response to questions about the 911 call led him to dismiss the call as a prank.

Investigating the area earlier that day with the crime scene team, Martin hadn't been able to fault the 911 officer. There was no large telltale concentration of blood, and the reddish-brown soil was so close to the color of dried blood that smaller spatters were invisible.

It was the cacti themselves that provided the first break. A technician spotted a small, dark red spot on one, and the hema-test strip indicated the presence of blood. Martin and the team had spent much of the afternoon searching for more spots. Tonight they will use Luminol to find what their eyes missed.

Luminol can detect one part per hundred-thousandth of blood, a trace completely invisible even in strong light. A few years ago Martin used it on a garage floor that looked a bit too clean. Sprayed with Luminol and lit by fluorescent light, the floor told a gruesome tale. Spreading circles and bloody footprints glowed blue-green in the darkness.

Martin pulls a flashlight from the glove compartment and climbs out of the car. As he approaches the yellow crime scene tape that surrounds the area, he finds a half dozen people watching curiously. He ignores them, nods at the officer assigned to keep everyone out, and ducks under the tape.

Inside the circle of lights, the scene is lit with a harsh

glare. The blue-gray cacti are bleached almost colorless. Their leathery surfaces, studded with sharp thorns, seem too hostile for living things.

Martin spots Dexter Miller checking the focus of a camera aimed at a spot on the path. Miller is the senior man on the crime scene team. His close-cropped black hair has flecks of gray but there are few lines in his face. He joined the force the year before Martin did and was the only African-American officer for several years.

"We ready to go?" Martin asks.

Miller calls to his partner, "Cut the lights, Mo, and let's see what we've got."

The white floods are extinguished and the area is plunged into darkness. Martin stares into the blackness and waits for his eyes to adjust. Beside him, Miller says, "Looks good. Let's get going. Lights, Mo."

The lights come on again. Miller snaps a picture of the ground, then sets the camera for a time exposure.

"From the spots on the two cacti, I'm guessing this is where he landed," he says, pointing at the ground in front of the camera. "The splatter on that one," he points at a large agave with smooth, spikelike leaves radiating from its center, "is about two feet up, and if I've got the angle right, he was standing there when he was hit. That's where I sprayed the Luminol."

"Let's take a look," Martin says.

Mo cuts the lights and they are back in darkness, then Miller turns on the fluorescent light, and the ground glows blue-green. In the middle of the path, the color is particularly intense, indicating a great density of blood deposits. Around that center, smaller spots glow less brightly.

"Bingo," Miller says, as he snaps the first time exposure.

Martin studies the ground as Miller takes a series of pictures with different exposures. There's a concentration of blood, but it's been disturbed. He's guessing the killer tried to scoop up the top layers of bloodstained earth but missed deeper deposits.

He's computed the time as best he can. The 911 call came from the Beacon gas station at El Camino and Partridge, no more than ten minutes from the Cactus Garden by car. The officer responded almost immediately, so the killer couldn't have had more than fifteen minutes to get the bloody soil up and the body out of there. One person, working very fast, could do it, but not if he had to wrap the head in cloth and the body in plastic. If the wrapping was done here, it points to more than one killer. Martin hopes the Luminol will give him enough information to figure it out.

Miller snaps his last exposure and calls to Mo to turn the lights back on. He picks the camera up and moves it farther down the path. Martin yawns. It's going to be a long night.

UESDAY MORNING I scanned the *Chronicle* for news of Chloe Dorn, the missing girl from Palo Alto. There was no word on her, but a three-paragraph article in the "Bay Area Roundup" section caught my attention. The headline read BODY OF UNIDENTIFIED MAN FOUND IN PALO ALTO. There weren't many details. Just that the victim was a Caucasian in his midtwenties, five feet ten, one hundred and sixty pounds, blue eyes, and dark brown hair.

The description matched Matt Demming. And probably thousands of other young men in the Bay Area.

I called Ari Kazacos and told him about the article.

"It can't be him," he said.

"Why not?"

"It just can't. He ran off. He's out there messing with my head. He can't be dead."

I don't want him to be dead so he can't be dead. Too bad things don't work that way. "Does the description fit Demming?" I asked.

"Well, yeah. But it could fit a million guys."

"I think I'd better check with the police," I said. "I'll show them the picture you gave me, and see what they know."

"No cops," Kazacos said loudly enough to make me jump. "I *don't* want the cops involved."

"If that's Demming's body, they're already involved."

"It can't be, it just can't be." I could hear desperation in his voice.

"It may not be him," I said. "But I have to check."

"I don't want anyone to know about the source code," he said. "We can't let that get out."

"I don't need to tell them anything about your situation unless the body is Demming's. If it is, we'll have to tell them everything."

"Oh God," he said, "and I didn't think things could get any worse."

Things can *always* get worse, but I didn't tell him that.

Before I left for Palo Alto I made copies of Demming's address list and of the papers I'd taken from his apartment, and all my contacts, starting with Ari Kazacos. If the body found in Palo Alto really was Matt Demming's, the police would want that information. I might score points for supplying it to them before they asked. And if I had to deal with the Palo Alto police, I'd need as many brownie points as I could get.

Palo Alto is the town Leland Stanford built for his university when the city fathers of neighboring Menlo Park refused to outlaw the selling of liquor. Today, with a brew pub on every other corner, you'd never guess its origins.

Its main street has one of every chi-chi chain, all skillfully designed not to look like chains. It has street trees and benches, whimsical wall murals, flower boxes. Even the street people look comparatively well groomed.

I knew the Palo Alto police station better than I liked, having damn near been booked for murder there. It was downtown, in a low white building behind the high-rise city hall.

I parked in the underground lot and as I rode up in the elevator and walked around back to the police department, I wondered what kind of reception I could expect. Peter and I had been the star witnesses in a high-profile murder trial, which should have made us beloved by all. But Peter'd also been the star suspect in the case, and cops, like the rest of us, hate to be wrong. So, beloved we were not.

The lobby had been repainted since my last visit. It looked a whole lot better than most of the public facilities in San Francisco, but then the folks in the suburbs have more money and fewer problems to spend it on. They can afford to redecorate.

At the front desk, I asked if Lou Martin, the man who'd handled Peter's case, was still in homicide. He was. I asked to see him.

Martin came out to meet me. He was smiling. I took it as a good sign. I hadn't seen him for a couple of years, but he didn't look much different. His stocky frame might be carrying a few extra pounds but he hadn't fallen victim to middle-aged spread.

Martin had a permanently rumpled look. His dark brown hair was always ruffled as if he'd just run his hands over it, and his shirts looked like they'd been left in the dryer too long. Columbo without the trench coat.

"Catherine, nice to see you again," he said. I'd forgotten

how soft his voice was. Today, I heard a warmth in it I hadn't heard before.

I shook his outstretched hand, and we made small talk as we headed back to his office.

"I hope you're not here on business," he said, as we both sat down.

"I hope not, too," I said. "I understand you have an unidentified body on your hands. I've been hired to find a missing employee who fits the description in the paper."

Martin's smile disappeared and he regarded me solemnly across the desk. "You have a picture?"

I took Demming's photo from my purse and handed it to him.

His face was a mask as he studied the photo. No expression. A sure sign he recognized the face.

"Who is he?"

"His name's Matt Demming. It's him, isn't it?"

He nodded, his expression still tightly controlled. There was something beneath the control. Something I couldn't identify that made my pulse speed up. "Can't say for sure, but it looks like our guy. You know someone who can identify the body?"

"A couple of people he works with. Some friends. No family."

"I'd like the names."

"I'll get them for you," I said. "What can you tell me about how he died?"

"Jesus, after last time I'd think you'd have enough sense to stay away from a homicide. You have a death wish or something?" The soft voice had a touch of steel in it.

I smiled. Martin definitely hadn't changed. "Demming stole something from my client," I said. "His death could be connected to the theft."

Martin regarded me sourly. Clearly our last adventure had not changed his views on appropriate roles for women.

"So you've been interviewing people who knew him?"

I nodded, took the printouts from my purse, and handed them to him.

He didn't offer me a merit badge for good citizenship, but his voice had lost its sharp edge when he asked, "What do you know about the guy?"

I told Martin about *Cult of Blood*, Demming's theft of the source code, and what I knew about the night he disappeared. When I got to the part about the vampire LARP, he leaned forward. If he'd been a bloodhound, his nose would have twitched. "So he was a member of a cult," he said.

"Not a cult, more like a game."

"You're sure of that? Have you met the people in this alleged game?"

"A couple of them," I said. "They're mostly kids and it sounds like a Dungeons & Dragons–type thing."

"A kid got killed a few years ago when his buddies forgot D & D was only a game," Martin said.

"What makes you think it's a cult?" I asked. I had a good idea of the reason for his guarded reaction, and I didn't like it. "Was there something weird about the murder?"

Martin grimaced and studied me silently for a minute. Finally he said, "Can I trust you to keep this absolutely confidential?"

"Yes," I said.

"Because if you leak even one detail of what I'm about to tell you, I'll freeze you out of this case so completely that no one in the department will even speak to you."

"You have my word," I said. Martin wasn't the type to indulge in theatrics. His manner made me nervous.

"Cause of death was exsanguination," he said. "You know what that means?"

"He bled to death?"

"You could say that. He was drained of blood."

I shivered involuntarily.

Martin continued. "As far as we can tell, he was knocked unconscious; he's got a gash on the right side of his head, toward the back. Bled quite a bit but that wasn't the cause of death. Cause of death was two puncture wounds in his neck, one straight into the carotid artery."

"And those puncture wounds, were they close together, like a vampire bite?"

Martin nodded. "You got it. Looks like we got a weirdo on our hands. We're trying to keep it quiet so it doesn't turn into a media circus."

I could imagine the headlines—VAMPIRE MURDERS, KILLER CULT. Major hype. Major pain in the ass for the cops and the bureaucrats.

"He wasn't killed where we found him," Martin continued. "No blood. Coroner figures the killer bled him out somewhere else, then dropped him in the Baylands."

"Do you have an estimate on time of death?" I asked.

"Early Sunday morning."

"So he died after the game. That means the murderer probably has the source code."

"What makes you think that?" Martin asked.

"Demming took it Saturday afternoon. I've searched his apartment, and it isn't there."

Martin looked disgusted. Before he could say anything, I added, "His friend had a key and let me in. We had no reason to think this was a police case."

He wasn't mollified, but he had more serious problems to worry about. "You find anything I should know about?" he asked.

I thought for a moment. "His laptop was missing. His friend assumed that meant he'd gone someplace to work on the game program. The place was pretty messy, hard to tell if anyone searched it before I got there. Oh, and his car's gone."

"How big is this source code?" Martin asked. "Is it on diskettes?"

"It's on a single CD. The easiest thing in the world to carry with you. Or to steal. But he also took the backups, that's a set of CDs with past versions of the program, and they'd be harder to hide."

"This source code. Is it worth a lot of money?"

"Only to his employer, as far as I can tell. The game is almost complete. No one could claim they'd developed it, since a number of people have seen the beta test version."

Martin got a call at that point and had to leave. "I need the names of all your contacts," he said, as he got up and reached behind him for his jacket.

"They're on the top sheet of the papers I gave you."

"I don't suppose it'd do any good to tell you to stay out of this."

I just smiled at him, and he shook his head in disgust. "No, I didn't think so."

I didn't think Martin would get to Ari Kazacos for at least an hour. That gave me time to drive to Redwood City and give him the bad news in person.

"Jesus H. Christ," he yelled, when I told him. "Dead. He's dead." He collapsed in his chair. "He can't be dead. The kid was a genius, the finest designer in the field. A pain in the butt, but a real artist. He can't be dead."

Grif's reaction was much quieter. He just stared at me with his mouth slightly open, a look of total incomprehension on his face, then sank down on his haunches and put his head in his hands.

There was a long silence while the men absorbed the news. Grif sniffed a couple of times, a soft sound loud in the silence.

Finally, Kazacos said, "I feel like a shit even thinking about this, but did they find the source code?"

"No. No sign of it."

"He was killed? Murdered?" Kazacos asked.

"Yes."

"Why? Why would anyone. . . ?" Grif asked.

"The police think it happened early Sunday morning, after the vampire LARP," I said.

"That game he played?" Kazacos asked. "They think one of those guys killed him? Jeez, you suppose one of them actually believed he was a vampire?"

That thought seemed to cheer Kazacos somewhat. "Hey, maybe we don't have to tell them about the source code."

"I've already told them," I said. "And you had better tell them everything you know. Don't try to hold out on anything."

"I don't see why they need to know all our business. It doesn't concern them."

I sighed. Kazacos was truly clueless. "Ari, don't try to play games. If the cops think you're holding out, they'll move you right up to number one on their suspect list."

"Me? But I didn't have anything to do with it."

"They don't know that," I said. "I've personally heard you say at least once that you'd like to kill the bastard."

"But you know . . ."

I didn't know. And not knowing can be deadly.

11

ARI KAZACOS WAS the kind of guy who wouldn't believe he was in trouble until he heard the cell door clang shut behind him. I didn't think his references to "killing the bastard" were anything more than angry hyperbole, but he had motive, and unless he was completely forthcoming with the police, he'd convince them that he had something to hide.

"You talk to him," I said to Grif on the way out. "He can't bullshit the cops. Make him see that."

"I'll try," Grif said, "but when people are giving advice, he doesn't always hear so good."

There was only one thing more I could do. I wrote down the names of a couple of criminal defense lawyers I know and took them back to Kazacos in his office.

"I hope you won't need these," I said, "but if the cops lean on you, call one of these guys immediately. Do not call your corporate counsel."

He rolled his eyes, but he took the paper and put it in his wallet.

As I was on my way out, my pager went off. The number on the display was my office. Grif pointed me to the phone in the reception area.

"Your sister called," Amy announced, when I reached her. "She's really anxious to talk to you. Wants you to call her back as soon as you can."

"Did she tell you what it was about?" I asked warily. Calls from my sister, Marion, are rarely good news. Just about the only things we have in common are our parents and our love for Molly. Now that Molly lived with me, Marion's calls too often related to either Molly's shortcomings or mine.

"No, just that it was *very* important."

Everything is *very* important with Marion. Everything, except my time.

Since Marion lives in Palo Alto, only about fifteen minutes from where I was, it made sense to call her before I drove back to San Francisco, just in case it really was important. I dialed her number, hoping to get the answering machine. No such luck.

"Catherine, oh, thanks for calling back so quickly," she said in a tone so friendly it made me instantly suspicious.

"Amy said it was urgent."

"Yes, yes it is," she said. "A friend of Molly's has disappeared."

"I know. The police called last night," I said. "Molly says she doesn't know anything about it."

"Well, she really wasn't that close to the girl, but her mother is a friend of mine. I was hoping you'd agree to meet with her."

Was Marion, who had nothing but disdain for my career choice, asking me to help her out? "Professionally?" I asked.

"Yes. I was hoping you could help her find her daughter."

"Marion, I'd love to help, but I don't do that kind of work. Peter's the one to call. He specializes in lost kids."

"I don't think Julia would feel comfortable with Peter," she said coolly. Translation: People like my friends do not associate with people like your radical hippie lover.

"Most of Peter's cases come from places like Piedmont and Blackhawk," I said. Translation: The rich and privileged aren't picky about their associates when their kids disappear.

"Would you just see her, please?" Marion asked. "You know how awful it is to lose a child."

I did. Molly had given us all thirty-six hours to learn that painful lesson when she ran away from home. The memory of it was enough to get me to agree to see the missing girl's mother.

Chloe Dorn's parents—Julia and Jeff—lived in a modest neighborhood that was significantly less affluent than the rest of the town. Not poor, not even close, but the houses were smaller and less outrageously priced than their neighbors closer to downtown.

The Dorn house was a single-story cottage in the middle of the block. I didn't need to check for a house number. The gate and tree in front bore posters with Chloe's picture and the word MISSING in large block letters.

Someone in the Dorn family was obviously a gardener. The front walk was lined with brightly colored petunias, and generous beds in front of the house held a variety of plants of differing heights and hues, from deep blue lobelia in front to spires of stately foxglove in the back.

Marion had already arrived. She answered the door when I rang the bell. "I really appreciate this," she whispered, as she greeted me.

The small entrance hall opened into a living room on the right and a dining room on the left. The furniture in both rooms was early American, not antiques but good-quality department store furniture. The wooden surfaces practically gleamed, and I could smell a hint of the lemon furniture polish my mother uses. Like my mother, Julia Dorn probably cleaned house when she was nervous. The bigger the crisis, the cleaner the house. This house was immaculate.

There were two women sitting on the couch in the living room, and in the dining room a large man leaned over a table covered with maps and piles of papers. Marion led the way into the living room and introduced me to Julia Dorn and a woman she identified as a friend from the Dorns' church.

Julia was slender and small-boned with a trim body that probably owed more to genetics than hours in the gym. She wore her shoulder-length brown hair in a casual style that curled softly around her face, framing even features and the same remarkable almond-shaped eyes I'd seen in her daughter's picture. Her skin was pale, and under her eyes there were dark circles she hadn't tried to mask with makeup.

She wasn't what I'd expected. Marion's friends tended to be aggressively upscale—expensively clothed and carefully coiffed. Julia Dorn wore navy slacks and a blue-gray sweater that were attractive but not particularly fashionable. Her house was comfortable but far from upscale.

She rose as I came toward her and extended her hand. Her grip was firm, and she met my eyes with a serious, straightforward gaze.

"Thank you so much for agreeing to help us," she said. There was a softness to her vowels that suggested the South, but not Deep South. Maybe North Carolina.

"I'm not sure how much help I can be," I said, "but I'll do what I can."

"We're so terribly worried," she said, as we sat down. "The police just refuse to take this seriously. They think she ran away, but I know she wouldn't do that." She held her hands in her lap, one grasping the other in a grip so tight that the knuckles whitened. Her friend reached over and put a comforting hand on her arm.

"When did you last see her?" I asked.

"Saturday at dinner. She was going to a party at a friend's house, but she never got there. She just disappeared." Julia Dorn's chin quivered as she fought to hold back tears. I felt my own chest tighten in response, remembering how I'd felt when Marion called to say that Molly had run away.

"Was she walking or driving?"

"She took the bus. I should have given her the car. She asked for it, but her brother wanted to use it, so I let him have it. If only I'd let her take it. . . ." Misery dragged at her voice.

"You said that the police assume she's run away."

"They always assume that when a teenager disappears. Unless someone actually sees the child dragged into a car, they assume it's a runaway situation." Now I heard frustration and anger.

"Do they have any reason to assume that in this case?" I asked.

She bit her lip. "Chloe's been a bit rebellious this year, nothing dramatic, but she's been testing the limits. Six months ago she dyed her hair black, and last month she got her ears pierced when we'd expressly forbidden it."

Only her ears, I thought. That was pretty tame compared to the body parts Molly wanted to decorate with metal.

"She used to be a straight-A student, but she's let her grades slip this year," Julia continued. "I don't mean she's failing," she added quickly, "but she got two Cs."

"None of that sounds terribly dire," I said. "Tell me about her. What's she like?"

"She's a lovely girl. Very bright, a little shy, very sweet. She's not your average teenager. She's really more comfortable with adults than with other kids." She spoke slowly, thoughtfully, and her affection for her daughter was clear in her voice.

"She's a good girl," the friend put in. "She goes to church, teaches in the Sunday school. Not at all the kind to run away."

I thought of Molly and wanted to tell her that there wasn't "a kind to run away." I wondered if Marion had felt the same stab of protectiveness at the unconscious criticism of our runaway.

"We're working with the Polly Klaas Foundation," Julia said. "My husband's up in Petaluma with them now. They've been wonderful in offering advice, and they're making a new poster for us. We're trying to get on the TV news, but so far, we haven't had any luck."

"Too busy covering rapes and murders to spend time on saving a child," the man from the dining room said in a booming voice. He was standing in the doorway now, and his large frame dominated the room. He was well over six feet tall and built like a barrel, not so much heavy as large all over. His thick black hair flecked with gray was brushed back from a face dominated by heavy dark eyebrows over deep-set eyes.

"This is Reverend Seaton," Chloe's mother said, rising to introduce us. "He's our pastor, and he's been very help-ful in trying to get the media to take her disappearance seriously."

Reverend Seaton shook my hand and regarded me with magisterial authority. Here was a man used to taking con-trol. The word "patriarch" came to mind. Not my favorite kind of guy.

"You are the private detective," he said, taking over the conversation. His tone indicated that he had the same dis-taste for private investigators that I had for patriarchs.

I have a poor attitude toward authority. And I don't do subservient except when I'm undercover. "Yes," I said, and turned my attention back to Julia Dorn. "If Chloe was abducted, there's not much I can do for you. The police are far better able to investigate a kidnapping than I am. But if she's run away, I may be able to help.

"I've never handled a case like this, but I have an associ-ate who specializes in locating missing children. I'd like to bring him into the case." I avoided looking at Marion as I said it.

"Whatever you think is best," Julia Dorn said. "We don't have a lot of money, but we'll spend everything we have to get Chloe back."

I didn't want to discuss fees. I'd do the case *pro bono*. For Molly. But I knew that people tend to value less highly those things that are offered free. Jesse once worked for a full week without pay to help the son of a friend, only to have the kid tell him that he must not be a very good detec-tive if he had to give his services away.

"What exactly do you charge?" Reverend Seaton asked, in a tone that announced he was taking control again.

I ignored him and spoke to Mrs. Dorn. "Don't worry about the money at this point. I don't want to take your life savings, and neither does my colleague. What more can you tell me about Chloe?"

She thought for a moment. "She's not a very social child. Doesn't bring friends home much. Her brother's always surrounded by buddies, but Chloe's more apt to be alone.

"It's been hard for her to adjust to life in California. She grew up in Houston. Kids here are more sophisticated, more materialistic than where we used to live. We're a very devout family. Most of the young people she knows here don't understand her faith. They can be very intolerant."

She looked up at the reverend as she said it, and he nodded gravely. I was afraid we were in for a sermon, but he simply intoned, "Too true. Too true."

"That's probably why she became so interested in the computer," Julia continued. "It was something she could do by herself, and I think she felt accepted by the kids she met through it. There was a group of them at school, and she talked with them on something she called 'The Rack.' "

"The Meat Rack?" I asked.

Julia looked confused and distressed. "Is that what they call it?" she asked. "She said it was a chat room."

"A chat room," Reverend Seaton said. "You let her participate in a chat room? Julia, those are places where perverts ensnare innocent children. I've just been preparing a report on . . ."

"Actually," I said, interrupting before he could terrorize the poor woman further, "this particular chat room is run by a high school kid and I think it's pretty harmless. My niece is on the same one."

Marion gave me a look that said I'd have some explaining to do when this was over.

"They may appear harmless," Seaton continued, "but a child has no way of knowing the identity of the person they're communicating with. Chloe could have been lured to a meeting by an adult pretending to be someone her own age. It's happened before."

He was right of course. But I was furious at his insensitivity. Julia looked devastated; it was all she could do not to dissolve into tears.

"We don't know that that happened," I said. "But I'll check on it first thing. Would you show me her room?"

She led me to a small bedroom in the back of the house. The room was a strange mixture of little kid and teenager. Stuffed animals reclined against the pillow on the pink-and-white print bedspread, but the two posters that looked down on them were a threatening figure in black-and-white and a rock group in garish color.

Prints of two of Dalí's surreal paintings bracketed a computer desk with a PC and inkjet printer. A tiny figure of Paddington Bear sat on top of the monitor. It was as though two different people lived in the room.

But of course, they did. An adolescent's room has to house a cast of characters. Watching Molly, I was amazed by the fluidity of personality in a fifteen-year-old. Sometimes it felt like they tried on different sets of clothes at the mall to see who they'd be that week.

The computer was several years old, but it had been fitted out with a CD-ROM drive, a tape backup, and a touch pad instead of a mouse. Since I doubted that the Dorns had the money to support expensive equipment, that probably meant Chloe had friends who knew where to get used equipment and how to install it.

"Did the police copy the files on her computer?" I asked.

"I don't think so," Julia said. "I did tell them about the chat room, and they didn't seem to think it was so awful. They said they would check on it." I could tell that Seaton's words weighed on her. Her tone was a bit defensive, and I knew she must be feeling terribly guilty. Probably just what the good reverend had intended.

"Would you mind if I copied files from the hard drive?" I asked. "I'll only take the ones that look like they might help me understand her better."

"Of course," Julia said. "Do you need to take the computer?"

"No," I said. "I have equipment in my car; I can copy it here. How about a list of her friends. Do you have one?"

"She kept one by the phone. I gave it to the police, but it was printed from the computer so it must be in there somewhere." She gestured vaguely at the computer.

I got my Iomega Zip drive from the car and prepared to copy Chloe's hard drive. She had a dialer program that listed her phone numbers, so I printed that out. Julia stayed with me for a few minutes, then excused herself and went back to the living room.

While I was copying the files from Chloe's computer, I started sorting through the desk. Chloe was no more organized than most teenagers; jumbles of papers were piled in the drawers. Most were schoolwork. I pulled out a few letters, and what looked like parts of writing projects. Near the bottom of the first pile I came across a sheet of paper folded into a small square.

I unfolded it and when I saw what it was, my breath caught in my chest. The top lines read VAMPIRE: THE MASQUERADE, and below were columns of traits.

I grabbed the phone list from the printer. Scanning down it, I found the name I'd hoped would not be there. "Matt."

The list of numbers from Matt Demming's computer was back at my office, but I'd given one to Lou Martin, and if my suspicion was correct, I'd need to talk to him anyway. I pulled out his card and dialed from the phone by Chloe's bed.

Martin was in. "You have something more for me?" he asked, after I'd identified myself.

"Maybe," I said, thinking, God, I hope not. "On the phone list I gave you, there's someone identified only as C.D. Can you give me the number for that one?"

It took a minute to find the number but when he did, it matched the one on the phone I was holding in my hand.

12

LOU MARTIN POPS another antacid tablet into his mouth, but without much hope that it'll damp down the fire in his gut. He hates this case. It has just moved from bad to worse to worse still.

It was bad enough to find an unidentified body drained of blood. Worse when the M.E. got it back to the morgue and found the pentagram carved on the forearm. And worse still to learn that the victim was connected to the teenage girl who'd disappeared the same night.

"Please don't let her be dead, too," he thinks. Dead kids are the worst. You can build defenses against the others, but kids get to him and every other cop he knows. He can't look at the pictures on the MISSING poster without thinking of his own daughter, Melissa. She's eighteen, just out of high school and heading off to college in a week. The Dorn girl is only a couple of years younger. The pain in his gut burns brighter.

The 911 call was made by a female, and the voice

sounded young. It originated from a gas station on El Camino, which suggests that the caller drove there from the Cactus Garden. If it was Chloe Dorn, her parents should be able to identify her voice on the tape. He hopes it was Dorn. That means she could be alive.

He takes another tablet and dials the chief's office. He knows from experience to keep his boss informed. The chief hates surprises.

He delivers the bad news and waits through a long silence at the other end. He knows what the chief is thinking. There are all the messy emotions Martin's been feeling, but for the chief there's also fear—fear of the criticism that they didn't take this kid's disappearance seriously—and dread as he thinks about dealing with the press.

They've succeeded in keeping the details about the body secret, but with the girl involved, holding back information gets much harder, and the chief will have to weigh how long he waits before he drops the bombshell. Martin hopes he'll hang tough and give them time to solve it before he reveals the vampire angle. But he also knows this is a political decision.

"We're going to put a task force together for this case," the chief says.

Martin suspects he'd reached that decision even before hearing about the girl.

The chief names several people, including the juvenile officer assigned to the disappearance and the downtown bike cops, who are likely to know some of the kids in the vampire game. "And George Prizer," he says. "He's studied cult crime. He should be a valuable addition."

Martin winces but keeps his voice neutral. "Discretion is going to be very important here," he says, hoping the chief hears, I don't trust Prizer to keep his mouth shut.

"I'm sure George understands that," the chief says. "I

know you have reservations about the cult angle on this case, but we can't afford to ignore it."

Martin wants to point out that he doesn't ignore anything, but keeps his mouth shut. "Who'll be chairing this task force?" he asks.

"You and George. I know he's a patrolman, but he has expertise you need in this case."

Martin knows all about Prizer's expertise. His bad day just got infinitely worse.

"I don't have to tell you that this is a very high-profile case," the chief says. "Do you know Reverend Thomas Seaton?"

"No."

"Well, you will. He's the pastor of the Dorn girl's church, but he's also on the boards of directors of several national organizations dealing with Satanism and role-playing games. He's well connected politically and very media savvy."

Martin groans and realizes too late that the sound must have been audible over the phone.

"Don't screw around with this guy, Lou," the chief says sternly. "He can act the country hick, but he's very sharp, and a lot of people listen to him. I've got him on our side for the moment by telling him we've got a cult expert on the Dorn case, but if he thinks we aren't taking the cult angle seriously, he'll crucify us in the press."

"What're you telling me?" Martin says sharply. "That I'm supposed to investigate this as a cult killing and ignore the possibility that it might be something else altogether?"

"I'm telling you that you got a victim with a pentagram carved on his arm, who disappeared after a game with a bunch of folks who may or may not believe that they are vampires. I think the cult angle is a damn sensible place to start. You got a problem with that, maybe you want to withdraw from the case."

Lou Martin has thought more than once since he found Matt Demming's body that he wished to hell someone else had been on call. He hates cases like this. Not the case itself, but all the crap surrounding it. Reporters swarming around. Every loon in town calling with crackpot information. Guys like Prizer who want to be part of a big investigation. And the politics. The chief is already freaking out. He'll only get worse if they don't catch the killer fast. Next thing you know, the city council will have their noses in it.

But he's not withdrawing. He's never withdrawn from a case. "No, sir," he says. "If there's a cult killer out there, I'll find him."

13

I'D BEEN MARRIED to a homicide cop; I knew that delivering bad news was part of the job, but one look at Lou Martin's face that afternoon told me just how hard the job could get. Jeff Dorn wasn't home yet, and Reverend Seaton took advantage of that to insist on being present "as Julia's spiritual adviser." She surprised us all by asking me to stay with her.

I'd have given a lot to be somewhere else just then, but Marion and Julia's other friend had gone home, so I stayed. I didn't learn anything new from Martin, but I did learn something about Julia's relationship with the reverend. She was seated between us on the couch, and as Martin told her of Chloe's connection to Matt Demming, she grasped my hand and held on as if she were drowning. She did not reach for Seaton.

When Martin got to the vampire LARP, Seaton nearly exploded. He'd have launched into a sermon about the evils of role-playing games if Martin hadn't stopped him with "I don't think you're helping Mrs. Dorn, sir. If you want to stay, I'll have to ask you not to interrupt."

Julia clung to my hand. I'd wear the imprint of her clenched fingers for days afterward.

Martin was so gentle that I'd have figured him for a real pussycat if I hadn't already seen his harder side. He sat with Julia until she was calm, then began a search of Chloe's room. I called Marion to come back and stay with Julia until her husband got home.

As I was leaving, Martin drew me aside. "This is a murder investigation. I can't afford any loose cannons here. I want you to clear everything with me *before* you make a move. Understand?"

I decided to ignore his reference to loose cannons. "This was a murder case this morning. Why the new restrictions now?"

"This case is going to be a zoo. You met the reverend. He's not just a local preacher. He's a national crusader against role-playing games. I've seen guys like him at work. Lots of politics, lots of media. Then, there's the possibility that we could be looking at a cult or a serial killer. I got enough to worry about without you throwing me any curves."

My dad's a cop, so are a couple of uncles, plus an ex-husband. I never intentionally make things tough for cops. "Okay," I said. "I've got an appointment to see Tony Torres, the guy who runs the vampire game, this evening. Any objections?"

"No, I talked to him this morning. Strange guy, but

probably harmless. I'll be interested to hear what you get out of him."

It was after seven when I got home. I'd forgotten that Peter and I were planning to go to an early movie. A note on the refrigerator informed me that he and Molly had gone on without me.

One of the advantages of having a lover in the same profession is that he understands about screwy schedules and missed dates. The disadvantage is that it almost doubles your time apart. I hoped my meeting with Tony Torres wouldn't last too late.

The game master had suggested that we meet at a coffeehouse near San Francisco State University. While skies were clear at my flat, State is near the coast and was shrouded in thick, chilly fog. The moisture in the air dispersed the light from the streetlamps into an eerie orange glow.

I found the coffeehouse in the middle of a block of small shops. It had that artsy, rundown feel that appeals to students. Inside, the walls next to the door were covered with announcements of poetry readings and political events. Once the air would have been blue with smoke, but a city ordinance had exiled Joe Camel to the chilly street outside.

The waitress pointed toward a corner in the back. It was the darkest spot in a dimly lit room, and I could barely make out the man who sat at a table there. Dressed in dark clothes, he almost disappeared. As I approached the table, he rose, a tall shadow within a deeper shadow.

His black hair was shoulder-length, his deep-set eyes so dark they appeared to be black, too, and his skin olive-toned. A longish face with pronounced features, pleasing but not friendly. Assuming that his neatly trimmed beard made him look older than he probably was, I guessed his age at middle twenties.

"Ms. Sayler?" he said, extending his hand. The fingers were long and fine. Delicate without appearing feminine. His voice was deep, older than his face.

As my eyes adjusted, I realized he wasn't dressed entirely in black. His shirt was a deep wine red. It was silk, cut full in the sleeves and collar, a pirate shirt. But where Damion's Goth outfit had been threatening, Torres's felt theatrical.

"I understand you were one of the last people to see Matt Demming alive," I said.

"One of the last, but not *the* last."

I waited to see where he'd take it.

"Well, the murderer would have been the last, don't you think?" He smiled expectantly, as if to say, "your move."

I sighed. "I'd appreciate it if you'd tell me what happened that night."

He looked disappointed. "Well, it was a big night. Michael, that was Matt's character, had bested Gabriel, Nate's character, and won the right to make a *childe*, a new vampire, and he got to choose from among the mortals. You see, a vampire's victim doesn't automatically become a vampire. Most of the mortals are blood dolls or ghouls. Vampires drink from the blood dolls, but they don't drain them; they're just blood on the hoof or meals on wheels, so to speak.

"To make a vampire, you have to drain the mortal, then just as he's about to die, his sire gives him a drop of the sire's blood."

Torres's dark eyes held mine, waiting for a reaction. I've played "Gross Out the Adult" with Molly enough times to spot the game. Time to switch scripts.

I leaned forward and gave him a hard look. I made my voice low and raspy as I said, "Look, kid, let's cut the crap. This isn't a casting call for 'X-Files.'" It would have been more effective with a cigarette hanging out the side of my mouth, but you can't have everything.

His face broke into a broad grin. "Sam Spade, right? Or maybe Mike Hammer."

I smiled back. "Take your pick, just as long as you answer my questions."

"Sure. I was just doing my Bela Lugosi routine to see where you were coming from."

"I want to know what happened the night Matt Demming died," I said. "That's where I'm coming from and where I'm headed."

"You investigating the murder?"

"No, that's the cops' job. I'm looking for some computer files that have disappeared. And for Chloe Dorn."

"Chloe? Chloe's missing?"

"Since Saturday night."

"Oh, shit." He looked genuinely shocked, but it seemed odd he hadn't heard about Chloe's disappearance.

"You didn't know?"

"No. No. I've been working on this play, so I unplugged the phone, stayed off the Net. I didn't know about Matt until the cops came to see me. Shit, she was with him Saturday."

"Tell me about that night," I said.

He looked up at me. His voice was softer when he spoke, the dramatic inflection gone. "He came to the game a little late, and he was really wired, buzzed. In the game we'd call it 'blood drunk.' He'd just erased the source code from all the computers at his company. He'd figured out how to hack into the system to get at the backup files so he got them, too, and he'd taken the archives.

"He'd been hassling back and forth with this guy he worked with for a week, and it all went nuclear the day before. Something to do with ownership of the company, and the other guy trying to screw Matt.

"So Matt decided he'd teach the guy whose game it really

was. I don't know that much about the business, but he said they couldn't go on without the source code, and he wasn't going to give it up until he had his half of the company."

"You said he was buzzed?"

"He was walking two feet off the ground. Blew our start time because it took us twenty minutes to get him to calm down enough to play. He was totally manic, going on and on about how he was going to be rich, and the game was going to be legendary. Pissed everyone off with it."

"So everyone knew he had the code, and they knew it was worth a lot of money."

"Well," he said, drawing it out, "we knew Matt thought it was worth a lot. I don't know that anyone took him that seriously. Only a few of the players are into computers enough to know what he was talking about."

"Then you started the game?"

"Yeah. First off, you have to understand that it's a game, not a cult or some weird religion. We pretend that we're vampires. No one believes in vampires or worships them. It's a game."

"I understand that."

"I hope the cops do. They tend to get uptight about anything that's a little out of the ordinary. They gave me a pretty tough time."

"They're investigating a murder," I reminded him. "They give everyone a tough time."

Torres seemed mollified. He sat up straighter; he was on stage again. "Each game is like a series of episodes." His hands came together and flew apart. As he talked, they carried on a silent accompaniment. "I'm the storyteller. I give motivation, goals, but it's really just a starting point. The story changes, depending on the players' actions. For example, we started this game several months ago. It involved a conflict between Michael and Gabriel, that's Matt and Nate, and the week before the last game, really the last episode, I'd given

Matt and Nate a challenge. One of them could make a *childe*, and to determine who would have that privilege, they had to perform this series of tasks. So they went off and tried to round up allies, other vampires who'd help them and try to screw things up for their opponent and his allies.

"That was my part of the script. No winner. Not even who would join which side. That all grew out of the game. In fact, up till almost the end, it looked like Nate was going to win, but then it turned out that some of his allies were really double agents working for Matt.

"So this episode started with the winner making his *childe*. And Matt chose Chloe, no big surprise since she is definitely the best-looking woman in the game." He stopped abruptly, then asked in a soft voice, "What do they think happened to her?"

"No one knows," I said.

The waitress came by to refill his coffee and take my order. She obviously knew Torres and was so busy flirting with him that I wondered if she'd remember that I wanted a latte.

"Tell me about Chloe," I said when she left.

"I don't know a lot about her outside the game," he said. "She started playing maybe ten months ago. Came with a girlfriend, Andi, I think. She seems kind of shy outside the game, but once she's in character, wow." His hands emphasized his words.

"She was a minor vampire, first game, but she really developed the role and made that character work. So this game I made her a mortal who was secretly a vampire killer. She was perfect for that role. These guys would think they were stalking her, and she'd lure them away, and wham. They were staked." His voice was full of drama and his hands had speeded up as he talked. Then suddenly he remembered why we were discussing Chloe. His hands dropped to the table and he fell silent.

"You said she was with Demming Saturday night," I prompted.

"Yeah, they left together after the game. She'd really been coming on to him all night." He paused. "A lot of it was in the roles. I mean, Chloe's character, Liza, is one very sexy woman. Bold, brazen. Everything Chloe herself isn't. That happens a lot in the game. People choose roles that are really different from their personalities. It's part of the fun of it.

"And besides, there can be this sexy thing between the sire and his *childe*. I mean, like drinking blood is sexy for vampires. Not that we really drink blood," he said quickly. "I wouldn't permit it. There are some groups where they do. There's a bunch of Goths here in the city who do, but they're a bit crazy, really."

"How about Damion? He's a Goth."

"Damion. Weird kid. He and a couple of his Goth buddies came over from the Mountain View game. They're too weird for us, but I don't want the hassle of confronting them, so I just give them minor roles and hope they'll get bored. The buddies don't come around much now, but Damion's still there."

"Is he dangerous?"

"Oh yeah. That's one reason I haven't blown him off. He can have a very short fuse." Torres's voice had taken on a theatrical quality. I suspected he might be moving back into shock mode. "Several years ago Damion threw another kid through a window. The kid was hassling him, and Damion just blew up and wham. Right out the window. Since then people watch their step around Damion.

"He does the whole slice-and-dice scene, too." Now Torres's tone was conspiratorial, almost gossipy. It was fascinating to watch him move from one role to another. "He's got a bunch of scars on his arms where he slashed himself."

"Like the pentagram."

"Yeah, I think that was supposed to be a homemade tattoo, but he's also got places he just slashed himself with a razor."

"Did you tell the police about him?" I asked.

"Oh, shit, I was supposed to give them a list of the players who were there Saturday and I forgot to take it in." He shrugged. "It didn't occur to me to mention Damion when we talked. Wow! Are you thinking he could be the killer?" He didn't wait for an answer. "Sure, it makes sense. If he thought Matt was hassling him."

But I was on a different track. "You said Damion was weird. How weird? Is it possible he thinks he really is a vampire?"

Torres considered my question. The fact that he had to think about it told me a lot. Though he finally answered in the negative, I knew he was far from sure of his answer.

The waitress was back with my latte and to check whether Torres wanted more coffee. It's hard to make eye contact when you're pouring coffee, especially in such a dark room, but she was working on it.

"Tell me about Matt," I said, when she left. "How did people in the game feel about him?"

Torres paused. He took a drink of coffee, then replaced the cup on the table and turned it between his hands. "Depends on who you talk to," he said. "If you'd asked me yesterday, before I knew he was dead, it would've been easier. It's not a don't-speak-ill-of-the-dead thing, but somehow now his faults don't seem very important."

I nodded. "But if I'd asked you last week?"

"Last week I'd have told you that the newer people in the game thought he was the coolest guy alive. . . ." He winced when he realized the irony of his choice of words. "Folks who knew him longer were less dazzled. Oh hell, the truth is, lots of people didn't like him much.

"See, he had this incredible imagination, and he could

zap you into his fantasy world and blow your mind. He was truly charismatic. Not in how he looked or acted. He was just an ordinary geek that way, but once he opened the door and took you into his world, well, it was like you couldn't get enough of it. You just wanted to be there with him and watch it unfold.

"And before long, you were so into his world that you were adding pieces to it. It was like you became a coauthor of this fabulous story. But Matt was so caught up in his world that he just took everything around him and didn't notice if it came from other people. You could be standing right beside him and he'd be telling someone this cool new thing he was adding to his game, the computer one, and you'd realize it was *your* idea he was describing, but he'd completely forgotten it came from you.

"The first time it happened, people were flattered. The second or third, they began to feel ripped off."

"I take it you had that experience," I said.

"Did I ever." He shook his head and his hands continued to turn the coffee cup, though he seemed unaware of it. "A fair amount of the shareware game comes directly from the street game. I used to have Matt help me develop the scenarios. He was terrific and it was a mind-bending trip to work with him. In fact, when I saw that first game, I jokingly said, 'So where's my share of the royalties?'

"He laughed it off, never recognized that a lot of the stuff was mine. And, of course, there were no royalties, so it didn't matter."

"But there will be with *Cult of Blood*."

"Yeah, and it still has stuff from the street game, but I just decided to let it go. I could have told him not to come to the game, but he is, was, a real asset. It was always more interesting when he was playing. So I decided to hell with it, it's no big deal to me if he uses stuff from the game."

I didn't believe that for a minute, but I didn't challenge

him on it. Instead, I asked, "And the others, what did he take from them?"

"Well, he ripped off Nate fairly majorly by not including him on the *Cult* team, though he said he didn't have a choice since his partner demanded a new artist. I've seen demos of both games, and Grif is definitely better than Nate, so I can see why he made the change. And Matt did get Nate a job on *Cult*, so he wasn't a complete bastard about it.

"And he ripped off a lot of characters from the street game. People develop their own characters, see. They put a lot of time into them and they play the same character over weeks and even months, sometimes years, so they get real attached to them. Sometimes people's characters ended up in Matt's computer games. And they didn't always like what he did with them. Like Damion was so pissed about what Matt did with one of his characters that he stopped playing that character."

We were back to Damion again, the kid who'd thrown someone through a window.

I started to ask more about Damion's relationship with Matt, but Torres was headed in a different direction. "You'd get a completely different story from someone like Ash Klein," he said. "Ash is just a high school kid, a super-geek, but Matt took him under his wing and taught him all about game development. He even helped Ash do his own shareware game, something to do with space pirates, I think. And he got him a job as a tester at Astra. So you see, he could be generous, too."

I asked who had been at the game that night and which of the players were also hackers. He gave me a list. One name jumped out at me.

"Bill Griffen? The animator on *Cult*?"

"Grif, yeah. He's been in the game for about six months. Matt brought him in."

"And he was there Saturday night?"

"Yeah."

Sometimes you learn as much from what people don't tell you as what they do. I'd be having another talk with Bill Griffen.

"I'm cooperating here," Torres said a bit too earnestly. "I gave the cops everything they asked for."

"And what didn't they ask for? What didn't you tell them because they weren't smart enough to ask?"

He looked at me quizzically, then gave me a broad smile. "You're good," he said, "very good. I've already told you a bunch of stuff they didn't think to ask."

I suspected there was more, but I sensed he'd told me all he was going to reveal tonight. "Maybe you'll remember more after a few days. Maybe we should talk again."

"Yeah," he said. "Maybe I will remember more. Give me a call."

Out on the street, the fog had thickened and blew by in tattered wisps. It was movie fog, dense and dramatic, perfect for a darkened street scene in a *noir* flick. It made me realize what had bothered me about Tony Torres.

The scene was just what he would have ordered for his interview with a private investigator, just as the darkest corner of the coffeehouse was the perfect set for his drama. He was as much stage manager as he was actor, and he'd spent a good part of the evening manipulating me as if I were an actor in his private movie. I wondered if he was entirely clear on the line between fantasy and reality. Or if he cared.

14

CHLOE DORN JERKS awake. A thin film of sweat covers her body and her heart is beating too hard. Her eyes search the blackness of the room and find the dim outline of the window in the wrong place. It should be at the end of her bed, but it is off to her side, and it is too large. This can't be her bedroom. It's no place she knows, or should be awakening in the chill hours of early morning.

As she awakens further, she remembers where she is. And she shivers beneath the warm blankets that cover her.

She sits up and wraps the blankets around her. Breathes deeply, hoping to ease the tightness in her chest. It's been three days. Three days since she stumbled over Matt's body in the Cactus Garden at Stanford. She can still see his face, too white in the glare of the flashlight, and the blood startlingly red. Three days since the rustling bushes warned her that his killer was coming back for her.

Maybe she should have gone to the police. She stopped to call 911 from a gas station, told them where to find him, but when they asked her name, she froze. She doesn't even know why.

She screwed up, she knows that. She should have called her parents. But she couldn't do that either. Every day, she's prayed for the strength to call. When she saw the article with her picture in the paper Monday, she almost picked up the phone. She didn't want them to think she'd been kid-napped. But what would she tell them? They'd want her to come home. Mom's voice would get all shaky the way it did when she was trying not to cry, then Chloe'd cave in and tell where she was.

It's all so damn hard. She feels like she's been huddling beneath this blanket forever. During the day, it takes every ounce of energy to maintain the fiction she's spinning about running away from home. Guilt washes through her as she hints at abuse so awful that she can't really discuss it and sees the pity and outrage in others' eyes.

She's staying in Berkeley with a girl she met when Tony invited the Berkeley LARPers to Palo Alto for a special game. Serena is her age but looks older. Her hair is blue and she has several body pierces, "one I can't even show you." Her family lives in a large brown-shingle house in the hills, and Chloe hasn't seen much of them. Serena tells her that they work all the time and pretty much let her do her own thing. They don't seem particularly curious about their new houseguest.

She can't keep on like this. It's tearing her apart. She has to do something, but she's so scared that she can't think clearly. She hates the fear, hates feeling this way.

She walks to the window and lifts the shade. Through a screen of trees, the lights of San Francisco wink at her from the distance. The sky is lightening. In a few hours it will be day. Day Four. She has to do something.

The sky is a gentle blue. A pink blush tints the office spires of San Francisco. Chloe sits in a wooden chair facing the window, but she hasn't really seen the view for at least an hour. She doesn't notice that the blanket she wrapped around herself has fallen off one shoulder.

She has a plan. At last, her sluggish brain has stirred and now it's racing. This can work. She knows it can. It has to.

She remembers someone somewhere, probably in a movie, saying that when reality is too hard, you just have to go with fantasy.

Being Chloe Dorn is too hard. Too scary. But Liza, the vampire killer, wouldn't be scared. Liza would be bold and cunning. She wouldn't quake in fear; she'd go for revenge: quick and sharp and in the carotid. She'd track down the devil's spawn who killed her sire, and she'd see him avenged.

That's the choice really. To be Chloe, the victim. Or to be Liza, the avenger.

She's in character now. Liza can call up the images from Saturday night without feeling the terror, or any of the other emotions of the evening. She can see Chloe and Matt at his place, buzzed by the game and still feeling the pleasant sexy current between them.

She sees Matt's blue eyes and the slight flush of his cheeks. And she feels a kind of heat between them. She remembers the softness of his lips when they kissed in the game. There'd been two games really. The one the game master set up, and the one they were playing with each other. She was his *childe* now, his creation, and she was always at his side, pressing her body against his, playing with his hair.

And his hands were on her, possessive, knowing. Matt was shy, but Michael was a stud. His hand cupped her butt as they walked hip to hip. In the shadows, he'd pulled her close and kissed her. Not a tight kiss like the ones of boys at school, but a long, slow kiss with his tongue playing against her lips until they opened to him.

The same warmth she felt then spreads through Chloe's belly, and the same wild longing. She forces her mind back to his apartment.

They were still more Michael and Liza than Matt and Chloe, she realizes. He'd pulled a couple of beers from the fridge and offered her one. And she, who did not drink and never expected to, took it boldly. She didn't like the sour taste, but the coldness made up for that.

They'd toasted each other and kidded around, and then he'd pulled her to him for another kiss. And this time with his body pressed against hers, she could feel the unmistakable pressure of his desire. She hadn't resisted when he unbuttoned her blouse.

As she remembers the growing heat and urgency, the disrobing and what followed, the messy emotions surface again. She's having trouble staying with Liza. Chloe keeps butting in with her stupid guilt and shame. And even Liza isn't sure it was so great. Even Liza was a bit disappointed.

She pulls her mind from the scene on the bed and concentrates on afterward. Matt was so sweet, so concerned. He hadn't known she was a virgin. Most guys would have been all macho about it, but he was worried about her.

She won't think how her parents would react if they knew what happened. They'd freak if they knew she'd even hung out with a guy in his twenties. But they hadn't known Matt. He was way cooler than the guys at school, though most of the time he didn't seem a lot older than they did.

Sadness washes over her when she thinks of Matt, sadness mixed with fear, but she pulls back into Liza where those emotions can't reach her. Liza would look at that night differently. She'd search for clues to the killer's identity so she could nail him.

First, he has to be someone who's computer-savvy, probably a hacker, because he was sending e-mail messages to Matt that he couldn't trace. And if Matt couldn't find out his identity, then he must be good, very good.

Matt had been expecting a message Saturday night. They'd been playing some kind of game, sort of a catch-me-if-you-can thing. Matt hadn't really explained it very clearly. He'd been expecting the next challenge that night around eleven. But he was late in picking it up and there was a second challenge by the time he logged on at midnight.

The first message was simple: *"Next clue is a thing. I'm putting it in the Cactus Garden, behind the biggest, meanest thorn beast. But you have to get it in the next half hour."* It was signed, *"Raptor."*

"What a dumb name," Matt had said. "But the guy's good, I'll give him that."

The second message had been sent at 11:45. *"Where the hell are you? Don't tell me you're wimping out on the game. The clue will be there between 12:30 and 1. Don't be late. And no fair bringing anyone to help you look. This isn't a party game."*

"Screw that," Matt had said. "You ever been to the Cactus Garden at night?"

She shook her head.

"It's way cool. Come on along. You're my *childe* after all. The *childe* always goes with the sire." He gave her that sexy smile again, the Michael smile.

Chloe had worried about the time. She really needed to be home by one. She'd told her parents she was going to a party at a girlfriend's house. If she was too late, they'd call and learn she wasn't there.

"We'll go at twelve-thirty and I can drop you home by one," Matt had said.

She hadn't really wanted to go. If she could turn back the clock, she'd make him take her home. No, if she could turn back the clock she'd make him stay with her. She'd hang on to him and keep him from that fatal meeting.

No point in thinking about that. Clocks don't turn back. And she can't either.

She remembers the laptop computer then. It's sitting in its black canvas case next to the couch where she put it when she arrived here. If there are clues to the killer, they'll be in the files stored in the laptop. That machine was like an extension of Matt himself. He used a bigger PC at Astra, but he took the laptop everywhere. And anything of importance was kept on its hard drive.

She also remembers the CD. The one that Matt gave her in a flat, square box with a red satin ribbon around it. In the game, he was supposed to give his *childe* something of great value, and he'd chosen the box. She'd returned it to him at home that night, and he'd stuffed it into the laptop case.

He'd taken the computer because he was planning to stop by a hacker buddy's. Did he tell her who or what they were planning to do? She doesn't think so. She just remembers him stuffing the laptop in its case and tossing it into the trunk of his Honda.

She goes back over the ride to the Cactus Garden searching for a clue. Something he might have said that would be important. But she isn't even sure what they talked about. She was worried about the time. That's what she remembers.

She'd been on the Stanford campus hundreds of times, even to the Cactus Garden. It's not really a garden anymore, just a bunch of cactus plants and other spiky things that jab at passersby or sprawl, animal-like across the ground. You can see the remains of stone-lined paths, and the whole place has a neat desert gothic feel about it.

They couldn't see the cactuses from the road. Couldn't really see much more than the outline of bushes nearby. She'd sort of wanted to see the Cactus Garden at night, but Matt had asked her to wait in the car since his secret opponent might be hiding nearby. He'd given her the keys in case the cops came along and told her to move. Then he'd headed off down a path through some bushes.

She didn't have a watch so she doesn't know how long she waited. She remembers getting more and more uptight about the time and being afraid her parents would miss her and call her friend to check on her. Finally, she'd gotten out and followed the direction Matt had taken.

It was darker away from the road. There was some moonlight, not a lot but enough so she could see general shapes. Ahead, a massive dark form seemed to grow spikes as she got closer. Its twisted silhouette resembled a writhing sea monster.

The monster had to be the giant cactus, but there was no sign of Matt anywhere. She called out softly, then moved forward slowly, anxious not to accidentally bang into the sharp spines of a cactus.

She remembers finding the silver cylinder on the path, realizing as she stooped to look at it that it was the flashlight Matt had taken from the glove compartment of the car. In her mind's eye the cone of yellow-white light leaps from her hand to spread itself into a perfect circle on the rocky ground.

Her mind jumps forward, skipping to the moment that the cone of light hit Matt's face. Now she shivers; feels the cold travel through her body and fights against tears. She struggles to hold on to Liza. Liza can look at the blood and stay strong.

She doesn't think she saw the wound. She tries to recall exactly how he looked. He was on his stomach with his head turned, so she could only see one side of his face, and there was a lot of blood.

It seems like she stared at him forever, but it can only have been a few seconds. She'd just leaned down to see if he was breathing when she heard the bushes rustle ahead of her. She tries to remember exactly what she heard. Were there footsteps? Could it have been more than one person?

Liza would know that, but Chloe knows only that she was sure someone was coming. Liza would have turned the light toward the sound and trained it on the killer. Chloe shut it off and took careful steps backward before she turned and ran as fast as she could toward the lights of the road.

Chloe reaches for the blanket and wraps it tight around her shoulders. Even as Liza, it's too hard to send her mind back to that scene.

As she stares out at the San Francisco skyline, she realizes she doesn't have to go back. She made it out of the Cactus Garden. She has Matt's laptop with his files, and somewhere in them is the clue to the killer's identity.

It's time to stop hiding. Time to become the stalker instead of the stalked. She feels alive for the first time in three days.

15

LOU MARTIN HAS scheduled the first meeting of the task force in the conference room at nine o'clock Wednesday morning. When he arrives at 8:45, George Prizer is already there. He's wearing a suit and he's seated himself at one end of the table. Open in front of him is the dark blue binder from the cult crime seminar. It appears well used.

Prizer looks up from the yellow legal pad on which he's making notes and greets Martin. The detective nods in return and unwraps his third stomach mint of the morning. He took the first two when he saw the *San Francisco Chronicle* with its headline, MISSING GIRL LINKED TO SATANIC CULT KILLING.

Martin prides himself on his even temper or at least his

ability to appear even-tempered. But today he is so angry that he doesn't trust himself to speak to Prizer. The story he gave out at the press conference late yesterday afternoon had no mention of cults, satanic or otherwise. He hadn't even referred to the vampire street game, stating simply that the victim and the missing girl were seen together shortly before both disappeared.

So where did they get this crap about a satanic cult? It had to have come from Prizer. Reverend Seaton could have told them about the vampire game, but the unnamed police source spouting psychobabble about the dangers of role-playing games—that had to be Prizer, probably quoting from his blue binder.

Nell Scott, the juvenile officer, arrives just then. Some of the guys call her "Little Nell" because she's barely five feet, but they don't call her that to her face because she's got a wicked wit and a sharp tongue.

Stan Louvis is right behind her. He looks like a jock but is actually a geek, the department specialist in computer crime. Carol Atkins and Mark Chun from the bike patrol, and Ken Shoenfeldt and Al Chavez arrive just before nine, Joyce Lim, right on the hour.

Lim is not a member of the task force. Normally, she wouldn't be here, but this is not a normal case; and since Lou Martin was called away just as she began the autopsy, he wants her here to report the results.

Martin has already provided each officer with a copy of the autopsy report and all other relevant reports and documents. Each manila folder is marked HIGHLY CONFIDENTIAL—FOR YOUR EYES ONLY. From the grave looks on their faces, he knows they've read the folders.

Martin takes his place at the end of the table, opposite Prizer. "Okay, we've got an ugly one here," he says, "and with the Dorn girl missing, it may get uglier. There's a lot of media interest, so the first priority is putting a cork in the leaks." He glares down the table at Prizer.

"What leaks?" Lim says sharply. She runs a tight ship. She has been heard to say, "The only leaks in my department come from the clients."

Martin holds up the *Chronicle*. "I didn't say a word about the vampire game or possible cult involvement, but somebody did."

"I expect it was Reverend Seaton," Prizer says smoothly. "I know that the reporter who contacted me already knew about the vampire game."

"You're the unnamed police source," Martin says. He tries to keep the irritation out of his voice.

"Yes, of course. I asked them to withhold my name because I wanted to check with the task force before making any official statement."

Martin loses it. "You could have bloody well checked with me before you shot off your mouth to the press."

"I don't consider providing background information to be 'shooting off my mouth,' Lou," Prizer says, sounding oh-so-reasonable. "I was very careful not to divulge anything from the autopsy results."

The first response that comes to mind is obscene, so Martin takes a deep breath and struggles to regain his composure. "From here on out," he says, "we have to work together. That means all statements to the press go through one person. I volunteer to be that person. Any objections?"

He pauses. "Okay. You all got copies of the autopsy report. Any questions?"

Atkins, the bike cop, asks about the two neck wounds. "So one puncture was made to drain the blood, but the other was made after he was dead?"

"That's right," Lim says. "What you've got is a simulation, and there's no sign anyone sucked on the wound."

There are more questions, then after a moment of silence,

George Prizer says, "Given the nature of the crime, I'd like to suggest that we bring in an outside consultant on cults. I have the names of several people I could suggest."

"I think we need to do some more investigating before we take a step like that," Martin counters.

"But an expert could help us with that," Prizer says. "They monitor cult crime nationally. This isn't the first vampire killing, you know. And the game these kids were playing, it's played all across the country, and it's been implicated in other crimes. The more we know about it, the better."

Martin has his own ace to play. "Expert help can be very valuable," he says. "And I've already arranged for it. I've asked Mike Silva from the Department of Justice to take a look at this."

Lim nods approval; the others don't seem to know Silva. "He's a profiler for the state, was trained at Quantico by the Feds," he explains. "He's used to dealing with bizarre cases. He should be able to tell us something about our suspect. He'll be here at ten."

Prizer doesn't look satisfied. He'd clearly prefer one of his cult people, but he's been outflanked.

Martin moves on to the next point. "It looks like we have the attack site and time, maybe even a witness." He reviews the information on the 911 call and the blood spatters in the Cactus Garden.

"Blood type matches the victim's," Lim confirms. "Except for one specimen, taken from the barrel cactus labeled *A-9*. It could be the killer's. Of course, it could be from the witness or anyone else who got too close to the spines."

"The blood evidence was pretty badly disturbed," Martin continues. "People've walked through there and kicked up the dirt, plus our killer must have taken away the heaviest concentration. But we've got enough to give us a good idea what happened.

"I've had a couple of sets of photos made." He pulls a thick manila folder from his briefcase and drops it on the table. "George has a set; there's another one in my office. You've got maps of the scene in your folders. The series marked *A* correlates with the photos; *B* gives you the overall scene."

Everyone but Patrolman Shoenfeldt already has the maps out; he rapidly finds his copies and pulls them from the folder.

"You can see on *B-1* there's a service road that runs close to the spot where we think Demming fell," Martin says. "It's too dry for tire tracks, but it's likely the killer pulled in there to load the body into a car. He'd have had to drag or carry it about ten feet. There's no blood anyplace near the road, which is consistent with at least the head being wrapped."

He takes them through his estimate of the time sequence. "It's a lot for one person to do in fifteen minutes," he concludes. "It could point to multiple killers."

Prizer is about to speak, but Scott asks, "You think the 911 caller was Chloe Dorn?"

"The parents can't give us a solid confirmation on that, but it's likely," Martin says. "The call came from a gas station, not the closest place for someone on foot, so it's likely the caller had a car. I'm assuming it's Demming's. We've had a 'Be on the Lookout' for it since we ID'd the body."

"So the Dorn girl may be a witness," Nell Scott says.

"Or she may have been involved and changed her mind," Prizer suggests.

"Either way, if it is her, she's in serious danger," Martin says. "Finding her fast is our first priority."

Everyone is in agreement on that point. They discuss the search, then for the next hour, they go over every piece of evidence and information. Martin's pleased to see that when Prizer can get off his cult shtick, he's a decent investigator—asks good questions, is quick to see things. The others are an asset, too. Nell Scott is as sharp as usual, and the bike officers know everything that goes down on the street. They've encountered the vampire gamers several times, know many of the kids. The two uniforms, who were wild cards as far as he was concerned, turn out to be quick studies.

They spend a good part of the hour discussing the kids in the game. "Most of them are okay," says Atkins, "everything from high school kids looking for something to do on a Saturday night to older guys in their twenties, maybe even thirties. Mostly males.

"There're a few that are pretty alienated, the kind who wear dog collars and black clothes, 'nail heads' with metal hanging off their faces. But there are lots of normal kids, too."

"Any history of trouble?" Chavez asks.

"They can get pretty carried away sometimes," Atkins replies. "Freaked everyone out the night they staged the beating of a homeless woman. We got a slew of calls on that. Got there to find that the supposed victim was one of the players."

They're interrupted just before ten by a knock on the door announcing Silva's arrival. Martin brings him in and introduces him to the team. He's in his early forties, average height, with the spare build of a cyclist. His dark curly hair hits his collar, and he has a broad smile and warm dark eyes.

Martin already knows what Silva has to tell them, the important points anyway. He gave Silva the basic facts over the phone last night, but that was before the profiler had a chance to go over the crime scene report and autopsy information.

"I faxed Mike the information you have in the folders,"

Martin tells the group. Turning to Silva, he asks, "So what can you tell us about this guy?"

"First, the killing was staged."

"Staged?" Prizer asks.

"Set up to look like something it isn't. In this case, the killer wants you to think he's a vampire or that he believes he's a vampire."

"But he's not," Martin says.

"No. If this guy were actually an anthropophage, someone into consuming human flesh or blood, your crime scene would be totally different. It'd be messy as hell. These guys don't leave the body laid out all neat and tidy. They rip into it.

"Think of it this way, if the killer really believed he had to consume blood to survive, then he wouldn't have bothered with a little hole that drained it out slowly. He'd have torn the neck open with his teeth and there'd be blood everywhere."

"But the scene is consistent with a satanic cult," Prizer objects. "They drain the blood to use in future rituals."

"Possibly," Silva replies. "But we don't have any examples of that. I know that some people believe it happens, but we haven't found any actual corpses."

"That's because Satanists are so effective at destroying or hiding the body," Prizer says.

"Maybe." Silva's tone is skeptical. "But I only deal with hard evidence—bodies we've found, cases we've investigated, confessions we've taken. And I have to tell you that your body looks the way someone thinks a vampire's victim 'should' look. That suggests your killer is someone who knew the victim and is trying to direct your attention away from himself."

Martin is nodding, trying not to look smug. Prizer is shaking his head.

Silva tries again. "Look, it happens all the time. A guy

wants to kill his wife but he knows he'd be the prime suspect, so he sets it up to look like she surprised a burglar, and the guy killed her. Only the husband isn't a burglar, he doesn't know how a professional burglar operates. So he makes mistakes, he does stuff a burglar wouldn't do, or he doesn't do stuff a burglar would do.

"Or a kid wants to have sex with a girl and she resists. He gets rough and she ends up dead. He paints bloody symbols on the wall and swears that she was a sacrifice to Satan. But you wipe the bloody symbols away and what you have is a garden-variety sex killing dressed up for an insanity plea."

"I don't understand you people," Prizer explodes. "You'll do anything to deny the possibility of satanic involvement. Is there nothing you could see that would make you think that maybe, just maybe, a cult was involved?"

Silva looks irritated. "I'm not trying to deny anything. You asked me how I interpreted your crime scene. I told you. I think it was staged. Your killer went to a lot of trouble to make this look like a vampire killing. He could believe in Satan; he could believe he *was* Satan, but I'm telling you that he did not believe he was a vampire."

16

ONE LOOK AT my morning *Chronicle* and I wanted to go back to bed. The Dorns' private tragedy was now the public's latest spectacle. The vampire game had been transformed into a bizarre and murderous cult with Chloe as a member and possible victim.

Molly, who rarely speaks before ten, was livid. "I don't believe this. I don't even believe it. What is it with these people? Are they totally out to lunch? Do they have sawdust for brains?" She managed to rant for almost a minute before she slipped in her first obscenity, an improvement I did not comment on.

If she felt that strongly, I could guess what the kids who actually played the game must be thinking. The article would be proof positive to them that no one over thirty had a clue. Worst of all, it would make them even more disdainful of the police and less willing to cooperate.

"Hoo, boy," Peter said, when Molly thrust the paper in his face. He's also not a big talker in the morning. He read the article through while Molly worked on ever more creative metaphors for police stupidity.

"Salem, the sequel," he said, as he put the paper down.

Molly stopped midmetaphor. "What?"

"This thing has the makings of a witch-hunt," Peter said. "You get people thinking that there are a bunch of murderous teens running around doing satanic rituals, and every parent who thinks his kid is acting strange will start seeing witchcraft. Curing adolescence with exorcism should have great sales appeal."

"Yeah, and every kid who wants to freak out his parents will be spray-painting pentagrams on the garden wall," Molly said.

"What's missing here is any concern for what happened to Chloe," I said. "When she was a fine churchgoing young lady, everyone was worried about her. Now that they know she was in the vampire game, it's a different story."

"It always is," Peter said bitterly.

"They assume she's a victim or a suspect, but she

may just be a bystander," I said. I knew I was telling myself what I wanted to hear from the relief I felt when I said it.

Peter nodded. "If she was with him just before, she could have witnessed something, and been too scared to go home. You said she's from a very religious family; that'd make it harder to admit she'd been sneaking out."

"It's as possible as the other scenarios, and a whole lot more hopeful. If she did run away, then maybe there's something we can do. Peter?"

"I'm in. I'd start with kids she might know out of town. If she's running scared, she's probably put some distance between herself and home."

"Demming's car is missing," I said. "That's one thing that's been bothering me. If she has it, she could be almost anywhere."

"Do kids in one vampire game know kids in others?" Peter asked Molly. "Do they ever get together?"

"I don't know," Molly said. "But I can find out."

"Whoa, just a minute," I said. "I don't want you involved in this. You go around asking questions, you could find a killer on your trail."

Molly didn't argue. "I understand," she said. "I've learned a lot since I came to live with you. I'll do whatever you want. But there must be some way I can help Chloe."

A more trusting person would have taken this sweet reasonableness at face value. I simply assumed she was one step ahead of me. Peter wasn't taken in either.

"That's very good," he said. "Did you rehearse that?"

"What?" Molly said, indignation ringing in her voice. "I try to be reasonable and mature and you think I'm shucking you. You never take me seriously."

"Oh, I take you very seriously," I said. "That's why I'm worried."

"You obviously have some ideas of your own about this case," Peter said. "What are they?"

"I know some of the kids," Molly said, calming down. "I don't think it's so dangerous for me to talk to them. I could spend a couple days with my mom. Drop by where people hang out, not ask any questions, just listen. I'll hear stuff they'll never tell you."

When she said "spend a couple days with my mom," I knew how very much she wanted to be involved in this case.

"And?" Peter said.

"Well, Chloe was on *The Meat Rack*; so are a bunch of her friends and the kids in the vampire game. I could monitor it. If you wanted me to post anything, I could do it. That's all I'd do, I promise."

"And when something appeared and none of us were around to respond, or someone asked you to meet them alone with no adults so they could tell you something really important. What then?" I asked.

"I wouldn't go off alone, I promise. I've seen how easy things can go wrong." She paused. "Look, I nearly got both of us killed once. I'll never do that again."

I knew how much it cost her even to mention that night shortly after she ran away when things did go horribly wrong. Some kids might have romantic illusions about danger. Molly was not one of them.

"This isn't like your other cases," she continued. "I know Chloe. I can't just sit around while she's in trouble."

Peter and I looked at each other. "We need milk from the store," Peter said, handing Molly a five-dollar bill. "And Catherine and I need to talk."

She took the money and left without a word.

"Damn," I said, as soon as I heard the front door close. "I don't want Molly mixed up in this case. It's tough enough already without having to worry about what she might do."

"But she already is involved," Peter said.

"I don't have to let her get more involved."

"I don't know how much 'let' comes into it. Short of locking her up somewhere, we have limited control of her actions."

"I'll send her to stay with my parents."

"You could do that, and maybe she'd stay. But maybe she'd feel so betrayed by our lack of trust that she'd run away again. She could end up back in Palo Alto involved with exactly the people you're trying to keep her away from."

He was right, of course, and it made me furious. We did have little real control over Molly. I got up and poured another cup of coffee to give me time to cool down.

"You're saying we'll have more control over her if she's a member of the team than if she's on her own."

"Uh-huh," he said. "There's a guy-saying that if you've got a problem, it's better to have him in the tent pissing out than outside pissing in."

"Charming," I said. "But it seems to me, that depends on which way the wind is blowing."

Molly stayed away long enough to give us plenty of time to discuss managing her role in the investigation. Things would get easier next week when she had school to occupy her days. The public schools were already back in session; unfortunately, Headlands wouldn't start until next Monday.

When she got back, she was obviously dying to know what we'd decided, but she accepted my statement that it was a subject we should discuss at the office with the rest of the staff.

She dressed quickly and emerged from her room wearing her black skirt, salmon blouse, and black wool jacket, an outfit Chris had helped her pick out for times when she wanted to look older and be taken seriously.

At the office we found Jesse back from Seattle. "You

joining the firm?" Jesse asked Peter, as we headed for the conference room.

"I doubt your partner would have me," Peter said.

"Damn right," I said. "We have to have some standards. He's just here as a consultant. A temp."

"A rent-a-dick," Peter added.

Jesse chuckled. "Probably best. We get in enough trouble without having an old hippie like you around."

We started the meeting with Jesse reporting on his trip to Seattle, which had been 90 percent successful but still left some problematic loose ends. Then I brought him up to date on the Astra–Chloe Dorn case.

"Jeez, you do know how to pick 'em," Jesse said, as he scanned the article in the *Chronicle* that I'd brought.

"It was you Astra wanted," I pointed out.

"And to think I was anxious to wind up the Seattle case. Are we officially working for the Dorn family?"

"No contract," I said. "But Julia Dorn asked for my help. Before I knew about the connection between Demming and Chloe, I was going to refer the case to Peter."

"It's dicey working two interlocking cases," Jesse said. "I think we need to parcel them out so one of us is responsible for each. You want me to take Astra?"

"Yes," I said, sliding my case file across the table to him. "Of course, there's a good chance that the answer to one is the answer to the other. If Demming didn't hide the source code and backups, then either Chloe has them or the killer does."

"Why would someone kill Demming for the source code?" Jesse mused. "It's no good to anyone else except Kazacos, and if he had it he wouldn't have hired us to find it."

"You're sure no one else could use it to steal the game?" I asked.

"No way, especially with Demming dead. Anyone trying to market the game would be inviting a murder charge."

"That's what I thought," I said. "But they almost have to be connected. Why else would he be killed the night he stole it?"

"Could Chloe have stolen the code from Demming?" Jesse asked.

I started to tell him that I thought it very unlikely, but instead turned to Molly. "What do you think? You're our expert on teenage psychology."

She looked surprised, then pleased. "I don't think so. You said she and Demming were pretty tight at the game. Didn't you say that he was supposed to give her something of value when he made her his *childe*? I'd bet it was the source code."

We all nodded. "Very nice," Peter said, giving Molly a thumbs-up sign. I made a note to check with Tony Torres on exactly what Demming's gift looked like. But I had a sinking feeling as I did it. If the killer was after the game and Demming had given Chloe the source code, he'd marked her as a potential victim.

It was time to deal with Molly's role in the case. "Molly's asked to be involved in helping to find Chloe," I told Jesse, and outlined what she'd proposed earlier that morning. "I can go along with the idea of letting her monitor *The Meat Rack*; actually going to Palo Alto and meeting the kids seems riskier."

"Especially if they get a hint that she's connected to you," Jesse said.

"Maybe not," Molly said. "I think they'd be cool with it. It's not like you're a cop. I mean, some kids already know you're a private eye, and they think it's way cool. Besides, if I don't ask any questions, they're not going to suspect that I'm trying to find stuff out. I'd just listen, but I'd be able to clue Peter who to talk to and how to approach them."

"You can go for one night," I said, "and I want Peter to shadow you. You'll never see him, but he'll be close by if you need help."

"That's cool," Molly said. She tried to keep her tone casual, but I could tell she was pleased.

"What if Mother Marion gets wind of this?" Jesse asked.

"She'd better not," I said, and Molly nodded vigorously.

"She'll be glad to have me visit," Molly said. "And everyone's going to be talking about that," she waved at the *Chronicle* article, "so she won't be surprised I'm interested."

"Peter'll have the cell phone. You call him anytime you're planning to leave the house."

"Try not to let the sleuthing go too late," Peter said. "I like my sleep."

We worked out the details, then Molly called Marion, who was absolutely delighted that her daughter wanted to visit.

"You be careful," I said to the jubilant Molly. "This isn't a role-playing game. This killer plays for keeps."

17

CHLOE DORN CAN see it was a mistake to tell her story to Serena. She can see the fear in the other girl's eyes. She knows how crazy it all sounds. That's why she was planning to just slip away this morning. But one look at the newspaper stopped that.

MISSING GIRL LINKED TO SATANIC CULT KILLING, the headline screamed. And beneath the headline, there was her school picture next to one of Matt.

They'd gotten it all wrong, of course. It read like something you'd buy in the supermarket checkout line. They'd made the LARP into a bloodthirsty satanic cult and hinted that Matt had been killed in some psycho ritual. They didn't quite know what to do about her. In one paragraph, they had her friends worrying that she might also be a victim. In another, they suggested maybe she'd been part of the cult.

Serena is about to freak out. Chloe can feel her tension. She's trying to be cool, but she keeps tugging on the ring in her ear and running her hand over her short blue hair. There's only one way to prove that what Chloe's been telling her is true. She pulls the paper out and hands it to Serena. Watches as the other girl's eyes grow large and the I've-seen-it-all expression drops from her face.

"Shit," Serena says. "Shit." The yellow Lab at her side whines and pushes its muzzle against her thigh. He can smell the fear, Chloe thinks, it must be coming off her in waves.

Finally Serena looks up at Chloe. "You were really there? When he was killed?"

Chloe nods, then amends it. "Not right when it happened, just after." She takes the paper back and rereads a paragraph in the middle. "But here's something weird. The body was found in the Baylands. He was killed in the Cactus Garden."

"They moved him," Serena says, the quavery quality almost gone from her voice. "What's this shit about a satanic cult?"

"That's the LARP. They think we actually believe in vampires, that we want to be vampires."

"Dumb fucks!"

Chloe reads from a paragraph near the end of the story, " 'Satanists use many devious ways to subvert young people. Seemingly innocent games confuse their moral sensibilities and introduce them to occult symbolism.' "

Serena explodes in harsh laughter. "Oooh, killer cults, vampire madness, drugged-out teens." She holds up her fingers and wiggles them as she makes a witchy sound.

"I was going to go to them," Chloe says. "Tell them what I know, but what's the point? They're so totally out to lunch that they probably wouldn't believe me. Hell, they might put *me* in jail."

Serena is rereading the story. She nods. "Believe it. I mean, you're either a victim or you're one of the cult killers. You were in the LARP after all. You go back now, you're toast."

"I'm not letting whoever did this get away with it." Chloe's voice is harsh with feeling.

"What're you going to do?"

"First, I have to let my parents know I'm okay, but I don't want to call them." Serena nods like she understands, no doubt assuming that Chloe wants nothing to do with them. The truth is that it would break her heart to hear her mother's voice.

"Then, I guess I should tell the police what I know."

"But they'll lock you up," Serena protests.

"They'll have to catch me first. I'll be doing my talking by e-mail."

"Cool. Wait, do the cops have e-mail? And how do you get their address?"

"Off the Web," Chloe says, with more assurance than she feels. Palo Alto's in the heart of Silicon Valley; it must have a home page on the World Wide Web. But she'll deal with that later. "I don't trust them to find the killer," she continues, "not when they're running around looking for cults and crazies."

"Pigs're so dumb they wouldn't know their ass was on fire till they smelled bacon."

"I've got to move the car," Chloe says suddenly.

Serena looks blank. She isn't tracking.

"It's Matt's car; they'll have every cop in the state looking for it."

"Shit. You can't move it now. Wait till it's dark, and maybe we can smear mud on the license plate. No, wait, my friend John has a garage and he and his family are gone for the month."

Chloe feels a surge of gratitude, not for the garage but for Serena's offer of help. She's been figuring she'd have to do this alone, that no one would risk helping her, and here's this girl she hardly knows who's offering to hide the car.

"My old Rabbit's a junk buggy, but it'll get you around."

Now Chloe really doesn't know what to say. "I, I can't get you involved like that," she stammers. "I was just telling you so you wouldn't think you'd had a killer sleeping on your couch."

Serena's face clouds and her features draw in on themselves. "Look, I'm not as fucked-up as my parents and everyone else thinks I am," she says. "I could help you. You don't have to worry that I'll screw up."

"I wasn't," Chloe says, realizing slowly that it's wounded pride and disappointment she's seeing on Serena's face. The yellow Lab whines again. He puts his paw on his mistress's leg and pats it to get her attention. She scratches his ears gently, but her eyes remain on Chloe's face.

"It's too dangerous," Chloe says. "It's not just the pigs, the killer could be after me. I can't risk bringing him down on you."

"You gotta stay someplace, and you can't go after this guy alone," Serena argues. "Once we hide the car, he won't have any way of tracing you here."

Chloe considers it. She could use help, that's for sure.

And she sees that Serena may need to help almost as much as she needs helping. Fuck this indecision, she thinks. I'm Liza now, and Liza takes help where she can get it.

Chloe nods. "Okay. You're in. Let's start with what we know."

"I'll get a pad and take notes," Serena says, jumping to her feet and startling the Lab. She's a model of efficiency as she hustles out and hurries back with a yellow legal pad and ballpoint pen.

"First, the killer is a hacker," Chloe says. "Because he figured out a way of sending e-mail that Matt couldn't crack, so he must have been good."

Serena writes, *"Killer = hacker."*

"And he's someone who knew Matt, at least Matt was pretty sure it was someone he knew."

"What about motive?" Serena asks.

"There's his partner on *Cult of Blood.* With Matt dead, he has the whole company." She gives Serena the background on Ari Kazacos's deceit and Matt's theft of the source code.

"Works for me," Serena says. "A day later and he'd have had to sign partnership papers."

"But there're also all the people who knew Matt had the source code," Chloe says. "He went off about it to all of us at the game that night, and he was in everyone's face with how he'd be hella loaded when *Cult* was out."

"So, like, everyone knew he had the code and it was worth boocoo bucks."

"That's got to be it," Chloe says. "The killer must be planning to put it out himself or sell it to someone else. But he'd still have to be a hacker to pull that off."

It occurs to Chloe at this point that there's a lot she doesn't know about Matt. In fact, there's really very little she *does* know. Maybe she's missing something here. But Liza's voice asserts itself. Don't wuss around here, it tells her. Nail the bastard.

18

JULIA DORN CALLED, midmorning. "Chloe is all right," she said. "One of her friends has heard from her, and she's fine. But she sent the message by computer, e-mail. How can we be sure it really came from Chloe?"

"E-mail always has a return address," I said. "It tells where the message came from. For someone else to use Chloe's address, they'd have to know her password."

"Her friend said something about that," Julia said. "That Chloe was very careful with the password so the message must be from her."

"Have you told the police?" I asked.

"Oh, yes. They're sending someone right over. But I still want to hire your friend who finds runaways. Do you think he'll take the case?"

"I know he will," I said. "I'll put him on the phone in just a minute, but first, what exactly did Chloe say?"

"She said she loves us," Julia's voice caught as she said it, "but she can't come back because it would put us all in danger. She isn't in a cult, and she's sending e-mail to the police telling them what she knows." She paused and took a deep breath. "Why didn't she call us directly?" she asked in a small voice.

"She sounds frightened and confused," I said. "She may not feel like talking to anyone right now."

"I'm so worried about her."

"I know," I said, trying to keep my own emotions from my voice. "We'll do everything we can to help you."

I put Peter on and he made arrangements to see her early in the afternoon. "*After* the police have left," he told me later. With his sixties' distrust of authority and general bad attitude, Peter avoids contact with the police as much as possible.

"Find out who her e-mail provider is," I said. "She's probably using it because she figures it can't be traced, but I'd bet the police can get her provider to pull the records and tell them where those calls originated."

Peter narrowed his eyes and grimaced the way he does when I get too technical for him.

"Honestly, for a guy who's into cultural revolution, you are grazing with the dinosaurs," I said. "If Chloe's sending e-mail to her friends, she must have an account with someone who provides e-mail. It could be a big service like AOL or Prodigy, but I'd bet it's an Internet provider like Hooked or Netcom. In either case, all she needs is a computer with a modem and an account. She can hook up to any phone line, use the modem to dial her service and . . ."

"Stop," Peter said, holding up his hand. "Where's she getting this computer? You said you saw hers at her house in Palo Alto."

"Bingo," I said. "I think you've just solved one mystery. Demming had a laptop computer that was missing when I searched his apartment."

"You think Chloe has it?"

"It's likely, especially since she was with him just before his death."

"And if she's dialing in over regular phone lines, there should be a record of where the calls originated."

"Right, though those calls are apt to be a whole lot shorter than regular ones since it only takes a few seconds to send a short computer file."

"In which case, the cops will be able to figure out where she's staying."

"If she dialed in from there," I said. "If she's sharp enough and scared enough, she may not risk it. I wouldn't. I'd go to someplace public, like the airport."

Peter was about to say something when Molly burst into the room. "Wait'll you see this," she said. "I went on to *The Meat Rack* message board just to tell everyone I was coming home, and as I was scanning back through this morning's messages to see what people had to say about the *Chronicle* story, I found this."

She held out a piece of paper with a printout from a computer screen. The message read,

Hi, I'm baaaack. Reports of my death are, as they say, hella exaggerated. For those of you who saw the bogus article in this morning's Chron, *I did not kill Matt Demming and I did not participate in some weird ritual with people who did. The person who killed Matt was someone he knew. Someone who'd been sending him e-mail messages challenging him to guess his or her identity and making references to the game. I was with him when he got a message that told him to go to the Stanford Cactus Garden, and I went along. I waited in the car and when he didn't come back, I went looking for him and found him lying on the ground with blood all over his face. When I heard noises in the bushes, I figured it was the killer and I hauled ass out of there. That's it, the straight scoop, folks. If the cops can forget the Rosemary's Baby angle, maybe they can catch this guy. But till they do, I'm outta there, on the road, gonesville. I'm telling you all this because maybe someone else knows something that'll help nail the killer. It's got to be someone who Matt knew, and that someone is a good enough*

hacker that Matt couldn't trace his e-mail. Any ideas?
Send me e-mail at bonemeal@silval.net.

It was signed, *"Bonemeal Babe/Liza."*

"Bonemeal Babe is Chloe. It's her handle, the name she uses on the *Rack*," Molly said. "She's okay. It's like you thought, she found him and she's scared. She's okay."

"For now," I said. "Maybe not for long if she's asking for information on the killer, especially if he or she is online."

Molly's excited smile faded. "Yeah. She's really getting in his face. You suppose she's doing that to make him, you know, like, come after *her*?"

"Lord, I hope not," I said. But it was what I feared, and from the look on her face and Peter's as well, I wasn't alone in my concern.

"Liza is her name from the vampire game," I said, looking at Chloe's signature.

"How do you get on the *Rack*?" Peter asked.

"You just log on the Net and go to the *Rack*'s Web site," Molly said. "Then you type in your ID and password."

"So she's going through her Internet provider again. Back to the phone records," Peter said. "You better tell the cops. They're the only ones who can get those records."

I nodded and dialed Lou Martin's number. He was out, but when I mentioned the Chloe Dorn case, I was transferred to someone named Officer Prizer.

He had a pleasant phone voice, and I could hear excitement in it when I told him that Chloe had contacted her friends on *The Meat Rack*. "Is this a chat room?" he asked.

I told him that it was both a chat room and message board run by a local high school student and made up mostly of kids from schools in the area. He peppered me with questions I couldn't answer and he seemed to have completely missed the point that he should be checking the phone records. When he asked for the third time who ran *The*

Meat Rack, I said, "I told you I don't know. He has some weird handle." I thought for a second and it came back to me. "*The Three-Horned Goat*, I think. That's all I know."

"*The Three-Horned Goat*," Prizer almost shouted. "You're sure that's it? *The Three-Horned Goat?*"

Oh shit, I thought, as it slowly dawned on me why this guy was so excited about the chat room and its sysop's handle. I was pretty sure why the kid had chosen a goat; it had to do with the third horn, which was not on the head. But someone concerned about cults could easily turn a carnal reference into a satanic one.

I tried to explain my theory of the third horn, but Prizer cut me off. "How do you know so much about this chat room?" he demanded.

"My niece is on it."

"Ahh," he said. The "ahh" dripped disapproval. "Well, Ms. Sayler, I'd advise you to be very careful about your niece's use of this chat room. You don't know who the other people on it may be. Sexual predators are known to use these . . ."

"Officer Prizer," I interrupted, "I'm aware of the dangers of chat rooms. I was calling to suggest that the phone records for this particular one might help you locate Chloe Dorn."

"You seem to be taking a considerable interest in this case," he said.

"I'm a private investigator. The Dorn family has asked me to help locate Chloe."

"Oh," he said. This guy could get more disapproval into a simple vowel than anyone I'd met.

I made one final attempt to get him back on track. "Chloe Dorn is very savvy computerwise," I said. "Since she's using electronic communication, you might want to consult with Officer Stan Louvis. He has a good deal of experience in this area."

It was a gamble. Prizer might be majorly offended by a civilian making such a suggestion, but if he did consult Louvis, it would not only provide the scientific expertise the investigation obviously lacked, but possibly give me a much-needed character reference. I'd worked with Louvis on a couple of high-tech cases. I hoped he'd convince Prizer that I wasn't a practicing Satanist.

Prizer didn't seem either thrilled or irritated by my suggestion. He did verify my name and phone number twice before he ended the conversation. His tone suggested that he might be adding me to his list of suspects.

"Do I detect that they are not rushing right over with the Good Citizen of the Week Award?" Peter said, as I hung up.

"More like the Witch of the Week Award," I said.

"You sure you got that first consonant right?" he asked.

"They really are hung up on this cult shit, uh, business," Molly said, remembering my restrictions on language at the office.

I reached for the printout of Chloe's e-mail and reread it. "Here's something," I said. "If Chloe's right and the killer had been playing some kind of game with Matt before Saturday night, then he may have been planning the murder for some time. The source code may have nothing to do with it."

Peter leaned over my shoulder. "The game the killer referred to, is that the street game or the computer one?"

"No way to tell. I wonder if Chloe knows?"

"I could ask her," Molly said hopefully. "I mean, I could send her e-mail."

Molly had left the door open when she came in, and Jesse, on his way out, had stopped to see what was happening. I motioned him in and handed him the printout from the *Rack*.

"How would she respond if you offered to put her in touch

with me?" I asked. "You said that some of your friends thought private eyes were cool. Would Chloe trust me?"

Peter answered for her. "Not after the nonsense in the *Chronicle*. But," he paused for effect, "she'd probably trust Molly's boyfriend who's a hacker. And since she was interested in an 'older man' herself, it won't bother her that he's in his twenties." He was looking at Jesse as he said it.

Jesse nodded and got a sneaky grin on his face. "Might not even hurt that he was black," he said. "Make that hacker boyfriend even more an outsider."

"Jesse?" Molly said. "Way cool."

"My, my, what would your mama say about that?" Jesse said in a fake drawl.

"Marion has many failings, but racism isn't one of them," I said. "However, she'll have all of our necks if she finds out what we're doing."

"Molly can send the e-mail from here. She can say she knows how scary it is to be on the streets, and offer the help of her boyfriend, pointing out that maybe he could help figure out who sent those messages," Peter said.

"Maybe she shouldn't go to Palo Alto, then," I said. "I don't want her there once that message goes out."

"Peter can bring me back tomorrow morning, and we'll send the message then," Molly said.

I didn't like it. I didn't want Molly involved at all, but that wasn't a choice.

Molly and Jesse went off to draft the note she'd post on the *Rack*. As they left, I said to Jesse, "It's your job to keep her out of trouble."

"Oh, sure," he said. "Catching the killer's gonna be the easy part of this job."

19

BILL GRIFFEN STUDIES the page of drawings he started last week and frowns. It is the latest installment of his graphic novel. Four panels, two of them inked in color, follow the actions of a young woman dressed in tight black jeans and an even tighter black shirt that molds itself to her full breasts. She follows a man in a flowing cape through streets piled with debris. A pair of feral dogs with ugly fangs charge after her in one frame, only to draw back and slink off with tails between their legs in the next two.

The proportions aren't quite right on the larger dog. Its legs are a bit too long. But that's not the cause of Grif's frown. He's not looking at the dogs but at the girl.

In the fifth frame she turns to face the reader. She's incredibly beautiful, so beautiful that Grif can't bear the thought of changing anything about her. But he has to. He can't leave her as she is, not after all that's happened. Anyone who knew Chloe would recognize the similarity immediately. Those gorgeous almond-shaped eyes, the high forehead, the full lower lip that's just on the edge of a pout. He's captured it all too well.

It's not the work of redrawing her that bothers him. It's giving up those images. And he's not sure that the story will work if he has to imagine another girl in the main role. It's bound to lose some of its power. Can he change the face he sees in his fantasies? No, he won't do that. In his head, she'll always be Chloe. He'll just have to learn to give her a different face when he draws her.

He pulls out a clean sheet of paper and sketches the face of a girl. He makes her face heart-shaped, her eyes narrow. The mouth is still a lot like Chloe's, but he doubts that anyone will notice that. Gazing at the face, he feels disappointed. The soft current of desire that Chloe's image always awakens in him is still. The drawing seems dead.

Works of art can die, just like people, he thinks. Chloe was such an important part of this novel, and after all that's happened, he's not sure how he feels about her anymore. If he had it to do over, and how he wishes he did, he wouldn't have followed her that night.

He looks up from the sketch pad, and his eye is drawn to the hair clip on his desk. It's just an oval of tortoiseshell, probably plastic. He should get rid of it. It's dangerous to have it around. But it's hers, and he can't give it up.

Just looking at it brings back the mixture of anger and pain he felt when he found it at Matt's. He shouldn't have been surprised. He knew Matt liked her. And Matt always got what he wanted.

Grif thinks bitterly of the months of development when they'd sat up all night playing with ideas for the game. "From my mind to your hand, from your hand to my mind," Matt had said. "Soul buddies." Until Grif asked for a better deal on the stock options. Then, Matt told Ari that Grif had done little more than redraw Nate's earlier work.

Nate tried to warn me, he thinks. I should have listened.

Matt's treachery makes his seduction of Chloe all the more galling. Grif's been played for a chump twice. First with the game, now with Chloe. "She's just a high school kid," Matt had said. Well, she sure wasn't such a little girl Saturday night. With that thought the anger he felt then surges through his body again, scorching his mind with its white-hot intensity.

20

WITH JESSE PLAYING Molly's hacker boyfriend, I was once again in charge of the Astra side of the case. I felt a certain relief at not having to face Julia Dorn. The news of Chloe's message would bring her only momentary comfort; then she would realize that her child was still in terrible danger.

A thick gray shroud covered my part of San Francisco. Here they call it "high fog," but it doesn't look much different from what we used to call "low clouds" in Colorado. As I passed Mount San Bruno, the canopy thinned and patches of blue shone through, and by San Mateo, the sky was a light blue dome.

Most things look better in bright sunlight, but at the shabby industrial park where Astra had its office, strong light merely emphasized the faded trim and peeling paint.

Grif answered the door when I rang. Before he could say anything, I said, "You have some explaining to do."

He looked dismayed and awkwardly backed away from me. "I know," he said, taking a couple more steps backward so he could close the door into the work area.

"I should have told you about the game, but I didn't want Ari to know I'd been with Matt Saturday night. He'd have realized I knew about the source code being gone, and . . ." He completed the sentence with a grimace and spread hands.

I kept my eyes on his face and waited to see what else would surface from his guilty conscience.

He shifted his feet nervously. "Look, I know I should have told you, but it wasn't like I knew anything important. You don't have to tell Ari, do you? He's gonna be so pissed if he finds out I knew about Matt taking the source code."

"You'll have more serious problems than Ari's wrath if you hold out on the police," I warned.

He nodded soberly. "I won't. I promise. Are you going to tell Ari?"

"Probably not," I said. "Not now anyway."

"Thanks."

A phone rang several times in the back room. "I better get that," Grif said, relief evident in his voice, "Ari's in his office."

I followed Grif into the back. When I reached Ari Kazacos's cubicle, I realized he was not alone. I waited outside, not wanting to interrupt.

"This could be great, Ari," a woman's voice said. "I mean, you can't *buy* this kind of publicity. I mean, it's too bad about Matt, it's a dreadful, awful thing, but it is also great publicity."

"Only if we find the code," Kazacos said gruffly.

At that point I decided I couldn't hang around and eavesdrop any longer so I knocked on the side of the cubicle. "Hi," I said, "I just wanted you to know I was here. I'll wait in the outer office."

"No, no," Kazacos said, motioning me in and introducing me to Anita Salazar, the marketing manager.

Salazar was a little shorter than I, about five feet five, but her high spike heels gave her an inch of advantage. She had full features in a small face surrounded by a cloud of black, curly hair that reached to her shoulders. "Pleased to meet you," she said. Her handshake was firm. If she was embarrassed that I might have overheard her callous comments, she didn't show it.

"Sit down." She offered me her chair and bustled out to get a new one for herself.

"Jesus, did you see that article in the *Chron* this morning? 'Killer Cult,' what the hell is that all about?" Kazacos said.

"They were referring to the vampire street game he played," I said.

"That's no cult," Kazacos objected. "Next thing you know they'll be saying my game is part of a cult thing. It's even got 'cult' in the title. That's all I need."

"It is exactly what you need," Salazar said from the doorway. "The more the papers rail about it being an evil influence, the more the kids will flock to buy it. We're going to have terrific word of mouth. If we can just get it banned someplace, it'll shoot to the top of the charts."

Kazacos groaned, then turned back to me. "I need some good news. Please tell me you have good news."

"Well, I have news," I said, and caught him up on what I'd learned about Demming's last night and Chloe Dorn.

"So this girl was with him from after the game to just before his death?" he said. "You think she has the code?"

"If she has his laptop, it's likely," I said.

"Great. Then all we have to do is offer a reward and get it back from this girl."

His beaming face told me he hadn't grasped the situation. "Chloe Dorn is afraid she has a killer on her trail," I said. "She's not concerned with the code right now. And she's not going to risk claiming a reward."

"Still it's worth a try," Kazacos said. "Maybe we could find a way she'd consider safe to make the exchange."

"No," I said. "No reward. If the killer was after the code, we don't want to give him more incentive to go after Chloe. And we don't want to bring new players into the game and make it even more dangerous."

Kazacos pursed his lips and frowned. "So what am I supposed to do, just sit around and wait?" he complained. "I told you, I've got to have this game ready to ship."

"I'm working on another angle," I said. "And the police are looking for Chloe."

Kazacos made a disgusted sound. "This is gonna kill me," he said.

"Ari, don't worry," Salazar said. "I'm telling you, even if the ship date is delayed, there's going to be so much buzz about this game, it won't matter."

Kazacos shook his head impatiently. "I don't know. I damn near lost a tester over this. That kid, Ash Klein, his parents are going nuts. They made me move him to the day shift."

"Ash Klein?" I asked. The name was familiar.

"Friend of Matt's. Just a kid, he'd be a senior in high school, except he dropped out," Kazacos said. "But he's smart. Very smart. He showed me part of a game he's working on. He might just be my next partner."

"You mind if I talk to him?" I asked. "Maybe he can tell me more about Chloe Dorn."

"Go ahead," Kazacos replied. "But if you're going to take very long, ask Grif to take over the testing."

I walked to the back of the main room to what Kazacos referred to as the "testing area." Testing lair was more like it. There were two computers with color monitors on a table in front of two of the rattiest armchairs I'd ever seen. Dump-ratty, not Goodwill-shabby. The floor was covered with empty soda cans, sugar cereal boxes, and candy wrappers.

The testers slouched in their chairs, joysticks clutched in their hands, their eyes fixed on the screens of the computers. On one screen a vampire stood poised on the top of a Greek temple, on the other a werewolf stalked toward the viewer. Both testers wore headsets, so it was eerily quiet.

The man on the left was in his late twenties with a long, skinny, brown ponytail and skin that hadn't adjusted to the end of adolescence. The other tester, who I figured was Ash Klein, looked about Molly's age though he must have been a few years older. He was a small kid, yet to get his growth, wiry, and so full of energy that his body rocked and bounced as he played the game. He had an oval face with fine features, thick eyebrows, and Einstein hair.

I tapped him on the shoulder and felt him jump with surprise. He took off the headset and I introduced myself and asked to talk to him. He was only too happy to relinquish his joystick and leave his vampire stranded on the temple.

"You want some coffee?" he asked. His voice was surprisingly deep for his boyish body.

I accepted his offer but changed my mind as soon as I saw the cooking area. New species of creatures were probably evolving in the primal gloop on the counter. "I think I'll have a soda instead," I said.

He opened the refrigerator. It was only a slight improvement over the counter. I figured anything in a can was probably safe.

Klein may have felt the same way, since he handed me a Coke and took a second one for himself. We sat on a couch whose springs had done their share of heavy lifting and given up the effort.

"So how can I help you?" he asked, his dark eyes sparkling with curiosity. "Are you really a private eye?"

I admitted I was, and it seemed to make him unaccountably happy. When I brought up Matt and Chloe his smile faded, but the curiosity still shone in his eyes.

"Do you play the vampire street game?" I asked.

"Sure. That's where I met Matt. And Chloe."

"Did you see anything strange Saturday night?" I asked.

"Well, everything's strange in a game. It's supposed to be. But it's not a cult like the newspaper said." I could hear defensiveness in Klein's voice. "I don't know why adults get so freaked out anytime kids do something they don't understand. The game is great. It's, like, this great way to use your imagination. But do anything with your imagination and you're a weirdo."

"Same with computers," a voice behind me said. I turned to see that the other tester had joined us. He was munching on something that might once have been a sweet roll.

"Yeah," Klein said. "Imagination and computers are dangerous. Especially if you put them together." He gave a sharp, nasal laugh.

"Maybe it's 'cause we don't have a ball," he said, turning toward the other tester, but clearly playing to me as well. "That's it. We need a ball. Anything you do with a ball is cool. Especially if you wear a uniform. I mean, a bunch of guys go out with a ball and chase each other around, bash each other up, maybe break a few bones. That's good healthy fun. We sit around a table and *pretend* to have battles. No broken necks, no blown-out knees. And everyone thinks we're weird, geeks who don't have a life. We need a ball, man."

I laughed and Klein looked pleased. The other tester laughed, too, shook his head, and went to search the refrigerator.

"I don't mean strange the way the ball-people would," I said. "I mean, did something happen that was out of the ordinary for the game?"

He considered for a moment. "If you mean, did anyone act weird to Matt, I don't think so. He and Nate had a huge blowup, but Nate was supposed to be all angry and vowing revenge because Matt beat him, last game. I guess Chloe was coming on to Matt more strongly, but that was in the game, too, 'cause he'd just made her his *childe*."

"Tell me about Matt. Outside the game, I mean."

"He was a genius," Klein said. "A real genius. He had an

imagination that just blew my mind, and technically, he could make a computer do stuff that was awesome."

"And as a person," I prompted.

"Really neat. Generous, a really good friend. He was cool."

I'd have liked a few more adjectives, but I sensed I might have reached the limits of the adolescent male's relational vocabulary. "How about Chloe?" I asked.

"She's pretty cool, too. I don't know her real well. She was in my school, but she's younger."

"Did you know she's posted a message on *The Meat Rack*?"

He looked surprised. "No. What'd she say?"

I showed him a printout of Chloe's message. He read it over carefully. When he looked up, all traces of his flip manner were gone. "Wow," he said. "So she was there."

"And now she's in hiding," I said. "Any idea where she might be?"

He shook his head and reread the message. "It sounds like she's trying to catch the killer herself," he said.

"That's why I have to find her. Before he does."

"I wish I could help," he said, "but I don't know anything."

"She added her LARP character's name to her handle," I said, pointing at the signature on the e-mail. "Do players do that usually?"

"No," Klein said. "We usually keep the *Rack* and the game pretty separate. I mean, some of the same people do both, but we don't talk about the game on the *Rack*."

"Tell me about Liza," I said.

"She's a real kick-ass woman. She lasted amazingly long as a mortal 'cause she was tough and clever. Now that she's a vampire, she's a Toreador, because that's Matt's clan and he's her sire. They're the artistic vampires, lovers of beauty." He paused. "That's probably more than you wanted to know.

Mainly, she's hella fierce, not very powerful yet because young vampires don't have much power, but hella fierce."

"Quite different from Chloe," I observed.

"Oh, totally. I mean, that's what's so neat about the game. You can be what you want to be. Gawd, listen to me, I sound like a commercial. I mean, that's somebody's slogan, isn't it?"

"Probably," I said. "So, Chloe, who's shy and geeky and right now very frightened, can pretend to be Liza, who's fierce and not afraid of anything."

"Yeah," he said, the whole upper half of his body bouncing as he nodded his head. "You think that's what she's doing? Playing at being Liza?"

"I don't know. What do you think?"

The bounce turned to a gentle rocking as he considered it, and one hand beat a rhythm on his thigh. "Yeah, I can see that," he said at last. "I don't know her that well, but I can see how she might do that. Especially if she has the code. You think she has it?"

"I don't know. What makes you think she might?"

He shrugged. "I don't know. I guess 'cause she was with Matt. Of course, the killer could have it."

"Why would someone kill to get the source code?" I asked.

Again he shrugged. "I can't see what anyone would do with it. It's no good to anyone but us."

I watched Klein. He was a twitchy kid, and he'd become more so as we talked about the killer and the source code. The rhythm of his hand had speeded up, and both legs bounced now. I couldn't figure out what was going on with him, but on an impulse, I said, "You've developed your own game, haven't you?"

His hand speeded up another notch. "Yeah," he said. "But it's really different from *Cult*. It's about space pirates— more action, some really cool monsters. Really different."

"And Matt helped you with it?"

"A little bit," Klein said. "Mostly he helped with how to get it out—you know, shareware or sell it to a company. And he helped me get this job so I could learn about the business firsthand and have some cash to get started. He was an incredible guy. I don't understand why anyone would want to kill him."

He took a long drink of his Coke, and before I could ask him more he said, "I really gotta get back to the testing." He was off the couch and halfway to the armchair before I could respond. I'd have given a lot to know why he was so jumpy. Being questioned about a murder case is enough to make anyone nervous, especially a kid, but his nervousness had grown as we talked. I wondered why.

ASH KLEIN WATCHES the lady detective leave. She stops to say some thing to Ari, then she's out the door. He'd like to know where she's headed, but he can't come up with an excuse to ask.

She is pretty sharp, he decides. Too sharp. He'll have to be more careful around her. He senses that he screwed up when he asked about Chloe having the source code. He isn't supposed to be interested in that. He could tell she was surprised by his question.

Otherwise, though, he's done okay. He was suitably

fawning in his praise of Matt Demming. No trace of his real feelings slipped out.

On the screen in front of him, he's a fraction of a second slow in responding to the cyclops he'd forgotten was behind the rock. He takes a hit and loses points. He hates level three of *Cult*. It isn't very challenging, especially after you've played it as many times as he has, and some of the scenarios are really lame.

The game really only takes off in the last three levels. The levels where Matt modified the engine to make everything move smoother and faster. The levels he couldn't have done without me, Ash thinks bitterly.

He's glad now that he didn't bitch to everyone when he found out what Matt had done. He felt so stupid for letting himself be ripped off that he couldn't stand to talk about it.

Three years of work down the drain, all because he just had to show off. Still, the chance to work with Matt Demming, to have that kind of creative genius focused on your game, that was worth some risk.

But he'd lost the gamble. The bastard had given him some useful tips and a couple of good ideas, helped him iron out some problems with his engine, and then stolen it.

His game is as good as dead. He'd been willing to let Matt use the modified engine for *Cult*; after all, they'd developed it together. But when he told Matt he was using it for *Space Plunder*, the bastard had acted like Ash was the one who was ripping it off.

And time was on Matt's side. Once *Cult* was out, everyone would figure that Matt had developed the engine. People might like *Plunder*, but they would still think its engine was Matt's.

But that isn't going to happen. Not with Matt dead and the code missing. He'd give a lot to know where that code is. And even more to keep it from finding its way back to Astra. Without the code, *Cult of Blood* is dead, at least for now.

He wonders how long it'll take Ari to find someone who can rewrite the code. And how long it'll take that person to get the game back to the point it's at now. Months at least. Maybe a year.

A year would be great. He figures his own game will be ready within four to six months, maybe less if he really hauls ass. The modification in Matt's engine that makes the last three levels of *Cult* so good will make his game awesome. And he'll be the first.

That's what counts, being first. When *Cult* finally comes out, only the most sophisticated hackers will notice that the last three levels use his engine, and they'll still remember that his game was first.

I'D PUT IN another call to Lou Martin before I left Astra, and this time I'd been in luck. He was in his office and expected to be there for at least an hour. After my conversation with Officer Prizer, I was anxious to make sure I was talking to the right cop.

Martin looked tired. His shoulders slumped more than usual, and the skin under his eyes was darkened and slightly puffy. Anyone unfamiliar with his usual rumpled state might have assumed he'd slept in his clothes.

"Looks like this case is getting to you," I said, as we sat down.

"I hate it when we've got a kid involved," he said with feeling. "But at least we know she's alive."

"I'd feel better if she weren't pulling this crazy stunt of playing detective," I said.

"What?" His head jerked up and he glared at me. "What the hell do you mean?"

"Didn't Officer Prizer tell you about my call this morning?"

At the mention of Prizer's name, Martin's expression shifted. For just a moment, I saw a look of distaste. Then, he covered it with his usual noncommittal facade and said in a neutral voice, "We haven't spoken since this morning. Why don't you catch me up on your conversation."

I told him about Chloe's message on the *Rack*, and gave him the copy I'd printed out. As he scanned it, his features contracted into a frown. "Damn," he said, as he put it down. "She's begging him to come after her."

"I'm afraid that's exactly what she wants," I said.

He shook his head. "No. Not this kid. Everyone describes her as cautious, fairly shy, not at all the type to take that kind of chance."

"Chloe may be cautious, but Liza is bold and fearless," I said, and explained my theory that Chloe was adopting the persona of her vampire character. "See, she's incorporated Liza's name into her handle," I said, pointing to Chloe's posting on the *Rack*.

"You think she could really do that, transform herself into someone completely different?"

"With the pressure she's under, I think it's possible, for a while at least."

"So she's completely lost touch with reality, thinks she's a vampire?"

"No," I said. "She knows she's no vampire. She says so in the posting. But she needs to act as if she can't be frightened, and her best model for that is the character she's created."

"Okay," he said. "That makes everything about twenty times harder and more dangerous."

I nodded grimly. Outside, a siren shrieked as a patrol car sped out of the police garage. I glanced toward the window but saw only an elderly woman in a coat much too warm for September walking by. She was carrying a bag of aluminum cans.

I glanced back at Martin and caught him staring at the MISSING flyer with Chloe's picture on it. "The fact that she's using a computer may offer some way to track her." I told him what I'd suggested to Prizer.

"Just a minute," he said, reaching for the phone and punching in some numbers. "Stan there?" he asked. After a pause, he said, "This is Lou. Ask him to come to my office ASAP. Thanks."

"I don't know that Officer Prizer took my suggestions very seriously," I said, when he turned back to me. "He seemed more interested in the evils of chat rooms than anything else."

"He thinks he's a cult cop," Martin said.

"A what?"

"A cult cop. It was all the rage a couple years ago. There were dozens of instant experts giving seminars on the satanic conspiracy. These guys'll tell you that there are thousands of people who've disappeared, babies bred for slaughter, children tortured and mutilated, but when you ask for a body or even a part of a body, they tell you that the Satanists are so smart and well organized that they never leave anything for you to find. It's a very neat approach really, using the fact that there is no evidence as evidence."

"You don't think much of them."

"I believe in evidence. Give me evidence of a crime, and I'll go after the criminal. But the last thing you want is cops pursuing a conspiracy when there's no evidence one exists. In my book, that's scarier than any satanic plot."

In mine, too. "I take it Prizer is of the satanic-plot school on the Demming murder."

"Oh yeah. His nose was twitching the minute he saw the body."

"Is he responsible for the quote on role-playing games and the 'killer cult' angle in the *Chron* article?"

Martin nodded and took a bottle of pills from his drawer, put one in his mouth, and chewed it slowly. His expression was sour.

"I'm afraid that article may make things harder," I said. "It's really going to alienate the kids in the game. Most of them don't have the best attitude toward the police; that just makes it worse."

"It makes us look like idiots. That's what it does," Martin said with feeling. He reached for the bottle of pills again, then stopped himself and put it back in the drawer. "Plus, it scares the hell out of parents and brings every nut in the county out of the woodwork."

There was a knock at the door and Martin called out, "Come."

I'd last seen Stan Louvis about six months ago when we were working on the theft of a shipment of microchips. Since then, he'd grown a mustache, acquired a killer tan, and cut his hair in the soft brush style popular with teenagers. I wondered if he had a new girlfriend.

We greeted each other and he pulled up a chair. "Prizer tell you anything about this?" Martin asked, passing Louvis the copy of Chloe's post.

"Yeah, I'm already on it. I sent a request to Judge Halstein for court orders to go after the phone records and the records of her Internet service provider. We should have them soon. But I don't know how much they'll help. The phone records are problematic. The service provider has multiple lines and zillions of calls coming in. It's their help we need, and they're going to be a problem. They've got client-privacy issues. They're small and feisty. I'm afraid they'll fight us."

"Even with a court order?" Martin asked.

"Oh yeah. These Internet guys are real free spirits. They could decide to take a stand and fight all the way to the Supreme Court. But I'm betting a little conversation with their lawyer will convince them it's not worth the pain."

Martin scowled. "And if you can get them to cooperate, can we use this computer stuff to trace her?"

"Maybe. They could track Chloe's log-in activity. They'll know the server she dialed, which should tell us at least the general area, maybe even the city, she's dialing from. And if the server has Caller ID, they'll have captured her phone number. If we can get that, we've got her."

"Only if she made those calls from a private residence," I said. "What if she has a laptop and can go someplace like the airport where the phones are modem-compatible?"

"Then we're screwed," Louvis said.

"Great," Martin growled.

"On a happier note, I talked to the kid who runs *The Meat Rack*, Dan Meier's his name. He's only seventeen, a typical geek. He's scared, and that makes him anxious to cooperate; I don't think we'll have any trouble with him," Louvis said. "He'll contact me if anyone new asks to join the *Rack*. In the meantime, I'm now a member, so I can monitor what's happening. *Pork Butt*'s my handle."

"When did we get this e-mail?" Martin asked.

"A couple of hours ago," Louvis replied. "I forwarded it to you. Should be on your e-mail."

Martin frowned. I had a hunch he wasn't all that fond of computers. "I know it's terribly outdated, but after this, use the phone," he growled.

"Whatever you say, Lou," Louvis said with a cocky grin. "If there's nothing more, I'm off to see if the warrant for those records is ready."

After he left, I said, "Prizer's convinced that the *Rack* is a menace; he's likely to want to shut it down."

"Ain't gonna happen," Martin said. "That's our open line to the Dorn girl. I'm not giving it up."

The phone rang just then and Martin answered it, leaving me to appear not to listen. I looked around the room. Some cops bring in lots of personal stuff; you can see their lives on their bulletin boards. But Martin had a minimum of personal things; in fact, a photo on the bookshelf next to his desk was the only clue to his life away from the office.

The picture showed an attractive young woman in her late teens. She wore a black drape and pearls. A yearbook photo, probably from high school.

"I told you he's a squirrel," I heard Martin say. "He's always calling in. Ignore it."

I wondered about the girl. A daughter? A niece? Whoever she was, I'd bet Martin thought of her whenever he talked with Julia Dorn, just as I thought of Molly. No wonder this case was getting to him.

"Look, just put it all in the log. I'll sort through it later." I could hear exasperation in Martin's voice and he set the receiver down hard enough to make me jump.

"Case like this sure does light up the switchboard," he said. "What more have you got?"

I gave him a quick summary of what I'd learned so far. When I got to what Tony Torres had told me about Damion Wolfe throwing another kid through a window, he nodded and said, "Ah, yes, Damion Wolfe, the kid with all the metal hanging off his face. He is well known to our juvenile division. Been in trouble since he was twelve."

"Is he a suspect?"

"Sure. They're all suspects. He was jumpy as hell when we questioned him. Course, he was probably high and scared we'd run him in for drugs."

"His history of violence makes him a good candidate," I said.

"Well, yes and no. Nell Scott, our juvie officer, says he's probably capable of smashing Demming over the head, but she can't see him planning such a complicated killing. His problem is poor impulse control. He blows up. He doesn't brood and plan a crime like this. Prizer would love to run him in, of course. Just the way he dresses is enough to put him at the top of Prizer's list."

"I'll bet the pentagram sent him through the roof," I said.

"What pentagram?" Martin's usually soft voice was noticeably louder than normal.

"He has a homemade tattoo of a pentagram on his arm."

"Where on his arm?"

"Back of the forearm," I said, indicating the spot on my own arm.

Martin's manner left little doubt that pentagrams were involved in the case somewhere. I raised my eyebrow in a silent question and started to ask, but he cut me off with a shake of the head.

"You got anything else?" he asked.

I told him of the plan to have Jesse pretend to be Molly's hacker boyfriend. "Molly'll send Chloe e-mail offering his services with the computer stuff."

"He can pass for a teenager?" he asked.

"Midtwenties," I said. "About Demming's age."

Martin considered it. "Might work. It's worth a try."

"There's only one hitch," I said. "Your Officer Prizer could be a loose cannon, and I don't want to put Jesse at risk."

"Prizer's got his failings, but he's not going to blow an informant's cover," Martin said. "I'll be sure he knows what's going on so he doesn't decide your partner's a satanic hit man."

I accepted his assurances, but they didn't relieve my

uneasiness. It had started when I talked to Prizer and had grown as Martin described the cult cops and their crusade. True believers, no matter how lofty their motivation, could be as dangerous as the nastiest criminal.

I HAD A pile of work to catch up on, but as I drove to San Francisco, I couldn't get Chloe Dorn out of my head. I was fascinated and touched by her efforts to transform herself into the kind of tough, fearless character she played in the game. That took both imagination and guts.

But courage isn't enough to keep you alive in a dangerous world. And my stomach knotted at the thought of Chloe challenging the killer. I wondered where she was staying. Was she crashing in Demming's car, sleeping on the streets, hooking up with other runaways? While she was on the run, the killer wasn't the only danger she faced.

By the time I got to San Francisco, I knew I couldn't sit in my office and go over paperwork while Chloe was out on the streets. The most likely destination for a runaway was Berkeley. With its liberal social policies and its lively street culture, it was a mecca for disaffected kids.

My heart sank as I looked at the great glowing worm of red lights inching its way toward the Bay Bridge. I was spending much too much time in my car. I considered playing the language tape I'd bought when I decided I could put

commute time to better use if I learned Italian. I made the
usual choice and listened to Emmylou Harris instead.

I'd hoped traffic would lighten up after the Bay Bridge.
It didn't. The area beyond the bridge on the eastern end
was torn up with the seemingly endless effort to enlarge
the Eastshore Freeway and to repair the damage from the
'Quake of '89. At the rate Caltrans was going, it would be
lucky to get the freeway up in time for the next earthquake
to knock it down.

I took the University Avenue off-ramp and drove uphill
toward the campus of the University of California. My destination was Telegraph Avenue, or Tele, as it's known to the
natives. This is the street outsiders associate with hippies
and riots. I saw it first on television in the sixties when mobs
of longhaired students fought phalanxes of police officers
in riot gear and gas masks.

Today it is the kind of slightly grubby street that runs
through most college towns—multitudes of cafés and fast
food places, book and poster stores, shops with the kind of
clothing you wear before you have to get a job. I was definitely overdressed for the Avenue, but I figured anyone over
thirty was invisible except to the panhandlers.

I parked in a large brick structure. The elevator didn't
seem to be running so I took the stairs to the street level. The
stairwell with its stench of urine reminded me of the bear
cages at the zoo.

The sun hadn't set, but deep shadows and a brisk wind
chilled the air. Dried leaves and food wrappers tumbled
down the gutters or piled up against the buildings. The
street merchants were packing away their goods and folding their tables, and ragged street people were already staking out their doorways for the night.

I realized I was a little late. The street was still crowded
with young people, but the crowd was thinning. All

fashions met on the Avenue—preppy collegiate, flannel grunge, baggy gangsta, hippie tie-dye, and black-and-metal punk. Or was it Goth? I still wasn't completely clear on the distinctions.

In front of Moe's Books one group of six heavily pierced teenagers sat in a cluster. They were deeply into black, most of it leather, and metal, much of it hanging from their faces. One girl's hair was bleached fright-white, another's was cherry-red with a heavy black stripe down the middle of the back.

I realized that by now Chloe might look quite different, so I concentrated on the one feature she couldn't change. I looked for those almond-shaped eyes.

The pierced brows made it hard to look at the eyes beneath them. It hurt to see metal poking through the delicate skin above the eye. That was why they did it, I supposed, to have that effect on adults. Seemed like an awfully high price for rebellion.

None of the girls in the cluster resembled Chloe. Nor did the two girls I encountered farther down the street, smoking and arguing with a bored-looking older guy who might have been their pimp. I thought of Traci Morton, the girl Peter'd been hired to bring home, and hoped she'd give up the street life while she still could.

I made two circuits of the street, walking up one side for four blocks, then back down the other, detouring when I got to People's Park to walk around its periphery. Once you looked for them, there were a number of teenage girls, but none had Chloe's almond-shaped eyes. I considered going to the shelters where a runaway might get free food, but I knew from what Peter had said that I was unlikely to find her there. More than likely, she was crashing with someone.

As I got to the corner of Haste Street on the third circuit, a kid in baggy pants caught my eye. I couldn't tell if it was a boy or girl. The figure was slight and the clothes were two sizes too big. The kid was walking fast in a hunched posture. The furtiveness of the movement made me decide to follow.

The kid walked up toward People's Park. He or she looked to be about the right height and weight. I crossed to the opposite side of the street and sped up. As I drew even, a car with a squalling stereo drove by and the kid turned toward it.

The distance was just great enough that I couldn't be sure. The face was a girl's. It didn't look much like the one on the poster, but the eyes were similar.

Unfortunately, she noticed me watching her. She turned away abruptly and headed into the trees at the end of People's Park.

I crossed the street and followed her, but I'd only gotten a few feet into the park when a large man in a filthy black overcoat stepped in front of me. He smelled like a garbage scow and had the bleary look of an alcoholic, not a serious threat. But just behind him were two smaller guys who looked clear-eyed and predatory. From the side a fourth man came in behind me.

I'd miscalculated on the invisibility issue. My blue linen suit, so effective at impressing businessmen and cops, was like a beacon for muggers.

I could just drop the purse and run, but that'd mean hours at the DMV to get a new driver's license, and more time to replace the items I'd lost. Time for Plan B.

I stepped forward, grabbed the arm of the alcoholic, and said in a firm voice, "Gerald, I'm your social worker."

No one messes with social workers. You can go into the toughest part of town and if you look like a social worker, people don't bother you. The other three guys froze, unsure of what to do.

I led the alkie toward the edge of the park, keeping him between me and his two friends, talking in a stern voice about the need to get his forms corrected and his medication adjusted. It was absolute gobbledygook but before anyone figured that out, I was back on the sidewalk where a couple of college kids had stopped to watch what was happening.

As I reached them, I turned toward my charge, who was beginning to get agitated. "You're not Gerald," I said accusingly.

"Who the hell is Gerald?" he demanded, nearly dropping me with the foulness of his breath.

I just shook my head and hotfooted it back to the crowds on Tele. I still had my purse, but the encounter had cost me a possible shot at finding Chloe. The kid I'd been following was gone.

24

DAMION WOLFE STARES at the black candle and tries to concentrate. He's in trouble. He knows that. He just doesn't know how bad the trouble is.

And unless he can remember what happened Saturday night, it may be very bad indeed.

He's set the candle up in the middle of a pentagram drawn on the floor under his rug. He wonders if there are spells or something he could use to call back the memory of Saturday night.

He should never have used so much shit that night. He's not even sure what all he took. He remembers the game. He took some stuff before it, but he remembers it pretty well. Matt ranting on about how he was going to be a millionaire. He remembers that. And he remembers feeling pissed and ripped off by the pumped-up asshole. And Chloe, he remembers her plastered against Matt's thigh, looking very hot in a black mini.

And he remembers after the game going to Alex's and getting ripped. He thinks they went someplace else, maybe with some other people. And he did some more drugs. But that's all so vague, wisps of memory hidden behind layers of fog. Fog. Did they go to a club in the city? They might have. Alex likes clubs. That's it, he'll call Alex.

He reaches for the phone next to his bed and dials Alex's number.

"Yeah," Alex says. That's how he always answers. A challenge in his voice. Damion can see him sitting on his bed with its black silk comforter in his room where the black curtains are always drawn against the daylight. Damion wonders how he got his parents to let him do that to his room. Probably they just don't give a damn. He never sees them when he goes over.

"It's me," Damion says. Suddenly, he doesn't know what to say. He wants to make small talk, ease into the subject of Saturday night, but his head is blank.

"Demonian." It's Alex's nickname for him. "Hey, I got the new *Hellblazer* yesterday. It's pretty cool."

Grateful for a subject, Damion gets Alex talking about the comic, and that spins off into rapping about other comics. When it seems like there's a pause, Damion says, "So I was thinking about Saturday night . . ."

"Oh, man, Saturday night. That was go-od shit. I haven't been that wasted in a long time."

"Me neither," Damion says, trying to find a way to ask

what they did without revealing that he has no memory of it. Finally, he gives up. "I was so gone, there's stuff I don't remember. Exactly what did we do?"

"Oh, man, you too? Maybe there was something in that shit we took. I musta blacked out."

"You don't remember anything?"

"Well, I remember you coming here and us doing the drugs, not a lot more."

Damion's body goes icy cold. He was counting on Alex to remember. "Did we go anywhere? Like to a club, or something?"

"I didn't. I don't know where you went."

"Uh, look, man, we gotta remember. You know Matt Demming, the guy who did the vampire shareware game? He got snuffed Saturday night and the pigs are, like, questioning everyone who knew him."

"Which is you, not me," Alex says.

"Right, but we were together."

"Oh, no, don't you go asking me to alibi you. Wherever you went and whatever you did, I was not a part of it. No way are you dragging me into this."

"Hey, I'm not asking for an alibi," Damion says. "I already told them I was alone, playing computer games. But I need to know what happened Saturday night." He can't bring himself to say what he's really thinking, that he needs to know if maybe, just maybe, he killed Matt Demming.

25

I DIDN'T SLEEP well that night. A case like this was a prescription for nightmares. I was halfway through breakfast before I realized that I hadn't brought in the paper. I always read as I eat breakfast; the paper is the only company I have in a household of people who don't speak before nine. But lately my faithful companion had been giving me heartburn.

It didn't matter that there wasn't any real news on Matt Demming's murder. It was a sensational case, with enough entertainment value to keep it on the front page. I finished my cereal and poured a second cup of coffee before I went to check on today's story.

It was there, right below the fold on page one—the first in a series on role-playing games and Satanism.

I was finishing the article when I heard the front door opening and Molly and Peter in the hall.

"You are so full of it," Molly said in mock disgust.

"No, it's true. If you get an infection, your nose falls off. Not right away, of course, but if you don't get it treated . . ."

They reached the kitchen as Molly delivered her response in the form of a colorful obscenity.

"No one with a nose pierce works in my office," I announced, having figured out the subject of the discussion.

"You're as bad as Mom," Molly complained.

"I'm worse than Mom," I said. "Did you learn anything last night?"

Peter had poured himself coffee and was absorbed in the front page of the paper. Molly had gone straight to the cupboard in search of a second breakfast. She turned around with a look on her face that told me her evening in Palo Alto had paid off.

"Andi was there," she said. "She's a good friend of Chloe's, and she says that Chloe had a real thing for Matt Demming. A major crush, like big-time. She was hoping he'd take her out after the game."

I thought of the condom on the floor at Matt Demming's cottage and felt a bit sick. "Did Chloe date a lot?" I asked. "Was she sexually active?"

"I don't know," Molly said. "No, wait a minute, Andi made some joke about how she was just the opposite of her character. Liza was this super-hot babe, and Chloe was, like, Miss Innocent."

So Chloe'd gotten the date she longed for and most likely it had ended in sex, then shortly thereafter she'd found her lover with his head bashed in. Even for a worldly teen, that would have been emotionally devastating, but for a kid like Chloe, raised on messages of sin and retribution, it must have a whole other dimension. No wonder she was desperately trying to re-create herself as Liza.

Was she overwhelmed by guilt, I wondered. It was easy to see how she might connect their liaison with his death. Unconscious guilt could make her self-destructive. It would explain why she was taunting the killer.

"Earth to Catherine," Molly said, and I realized that I'd spaced out. "Why'd you ask that? What's going on?"

I wasn't about to tell Molly about the condom. I did explain that a date followed by finding your new boyfriend dead would be pretty tough on anyone.

Molly nodded soberly. "Sucks."

"Did Andi say anything else?" I asked.

"She said that the fight between Matt and Nate wasn't all playacting."

"Really?"

Molly had found some English muffins, and after inspecting them carefully for mold, she popped one into the toaster. "Evidently, Nate was really pissed at Matt, and it seemed to be about more than the game," she said. "In fact, a bunch of people were pissed at Matt. Ash Klein sided with Nate in the game even though it went against his character."

"What do you mean, went against his character?"

"Well, as I understand it, Ash's character should have been an ally of Matt's character since they're both from the same clan, but he sided with Nate's character against Matt. Afterward, when they were critiquing the game, Tony called him on it. See, you lose points if you play against character. So if Ash could explain why his character would go against Matt's, he'd get points, but if he didn't have a good reason, he'd lose them. And he didn't have a reason."

"And you figure that means that Ash was mad at Matt," I said.

"That's what Andi says."

"Who else was mad at him?"

"Just about everyone. Even Andi was pissed at him for holding up the game by going on about stealing the source code. Lots of people thought he was bragging. She said, if he'd done that before the last game, he'd never have gotten anyone to side with him against Nate."

"How about Tony?" I asked.

"The game master? All Andi said about him was that he had to really yell at Matt to shut up so they could get on with the game. I don't think there was any love lost between them. Andi says that there was a not-so-subtle power struggle there.

"Tony's a great game master, and he gives everyone a lot

of freedom, but he likes to think that he runs things, and Matt definitely did things his own way. That's what Andi says, anyway."

She took the muffin from the toaster and covered it with cream cheese, then peanut butter, and finally raspberry jam. It looked disgusting. "Do you know Tony?" I asked.

She shook her head. Her voice was muffled by a mouthful of muffin. "Never met him. Andi says his real name is Bob or Fred or something dull like that, so he changed it to Antonio because he wasn't a Fred; he was an Antonio. Sounds to me like he's got the first letter right but I'd spell the rest of it with *s*'s."

"What'd you think of this article?" Peter asked me, while Molly piled still more jam on her muffin. He was holding the front page with its exposé of role-playing games.

"I think it's going to make it harder to get Chloe to trust us," I said. "I also think that the good Reverend Seaton may be exploiting the Dorns' tragedy to build his support on the Peninsula."

Peter nodded. "That's my take on it. He probably believes in the stuff he's putting out, but he's playing on people's fears to get them all stirred up."

"Do you believe what he says about kids becoming identified with the characters they play?"

"That's bullshit," Molly said around her muffin.

"I don't know," Peter said. "I think maybe it's like working undercover. If you do it for too long, it can affect you. To be good at it, you have to pretend that you are the person you're playing, and at some point, you start actually thinking like that person."

"Yeah, but that's not the same thing as believing you're a vampire or a ghoul," Molly objected.

The phone rang and I went to get it, while Molly debated Peter on the effects of role-playing. It was Jesse.

"Joey Marks came through for me," he announced. Joey was a game programmer Jesse'd met on his last job. Since Jesse had cleared him of charges that he was stealing secrets for the competition, Joey owed him one. "He's given me the names of several friends around Palo Alto and he's e-mailed them that his buddy Jesse is coming through, so I've got my intro to the nerds."

"Stay in touch," I said. "If Chloe answers Molly's e-mail, we'll need you fast."

"It's so nice to be wanted," Jesse said ironically.

Molly had captured the paper from Peter and was poring over the Seaton article. Peter stared at his coffee like he was waiting for it to kick in.

"I went to Berkeley last night after I left Palo Alto," I told him.

"Looking for Chloe?"

"It seemed the most likely place."

"Absolutely. Find anything?"

I told him about the kid I'd seen. "No way to know if it was her or not," I said.

"I was planning on going over there today," Peter said. "If she's there, chances are she's linked up with some other kid or group of kids. Berkeley's a haven for runaways. They can get free food, free clothes, free medical treatment, and no one asks any questions. You've got these doctor-lawyer couples who're so liberal that they don't blink an eye when their kid brings home a stray kid. I'm never sure whether I'm looking at utopia or its nightmare opposite."

"What do you mean?"

"Well, on the one hand, it's great that people will take in a runaway. Could be a lifesaver for a kid who's being abused, so those folks are doing a righteous thing. But on the other hand, it makes it so damn easy for a kid to run away. And maybe a kid is on the run not because she's being abused but because her parents won't let her do drugs. That's nothing you want to encourage."

"I don't see how anyone could miss the fact that Chloe's wanted," I said. "Her picture's been in all the papers and on the news, and there are posters up on every telephone pole in the Bay Area."

"You'd be amazed how out of touch people can be," Peter said.

"You want me to come with you?" I asked.

"Nah." He shook his head. "It's hard enough to get kids to talk to one adult. Two makes it impossible, and if that was her you spotted yesterday, she'll bolt the minute she sees you again."

"Molly and I will get that e-mail off to Chloe and hope for an answer," I said. Hoping is not one of the techniques they cover in the investigator's manual, but sometimes it's all you've got.

NINE O'CLOCK, THURSDAY morning. The group that has come to be known in the department as the Vampire Task Force is assembled in Conference Room E, Lou Martin at one end of the table, George Prizer at the other. In what will become a pattern over the coming days, Stan Louvis and Nell Scott sit next to Martin, the two patrolmen, Shoenfeldt and Chavez, next to Prizer, and the bike officers, Atkins and Chun, in the middle across from a young woman with very short dark hair who has been assigned to take notes.

Martin begins with Chloe Dorn's e-mail message and her posting on *The Meat Rack*. "I assume you've all seen this," he says, referring to the printouts. "At least we know she's still alive."

"But not actually a witness," Scott says.

"Not that she admits," Prizer interjects.

"With luck, it may give us a way to trace her," Martin continues. "Stan, what've you got?"

Louvis explains about tracing e-mail. "The court orders for both phone and service provider records have come through. The service provider has agreed to cooperate, and we should have both records soon. I'm monitoring the board now. The kid who runs it didn't save the chat room conversations, but he has backup files for the message board for a couple of weeks, so I've been going over them. Nothing there yet."

"Any discussion of Satan or witchcraft?" Prizer asks.

Louvis shakes his head. "Mostly 'Star Trek,' 'X-Files,' and lots of sex."

"Porn?" Shoenfeldt asks.

"Not really. Just the kind of stuff you'd expect from horny teenagers."

"Have you checked out the members?" Prizer asks.

"I've got a list. As far as I can tell, we have seven who are also involved in the street game—Chloe Dorn, of course, Andi Schecter, Gretchen Borden, Ben Minor, Nathan Sessler, Damion Wolfe, and Asher Klein. Sessler's the only adult, and he's twenty-four."

"The Wolfe kid is a strange one," Prizer observes.

That's Nell Scott's cue to report on Damion Wolfe's record, including the incident in which he tossed a kid through a window. She concludes with her assessment that he couldn't plan and carry through a crime as complex as Demming's murder.

"Maybe not alone," Prizer says, "but he's just the sort of kid to be mixed up with a cult. A loner, socially unsophisticated, in trouble at school, a heavy drug-user. He'd be an easy mark for someone who offered him acceptance."

Sensing Martin's skepticism, Prizer plunges ahead. He can't understand why Martin is so closed-minded, but he figures he can reach the others. "You can see how attractive a cult is to a kid like this. Society says he's a screw-up and tells him he has to give up drugs and straighten himself out. The cult says he's great just as he is. They promise him sex and drugs. He feels weak and out of control. They offer Satan, who's all-powerful."

"And who scares your parents to death," Nell Scott adds. "That's what would appeal to Damion, I think. It's such a perfect way to get back at his parents."

"That's frequently part of the profile," Prizer says. "For a kid from a good Christian home, worshiping the devil is the ultimate repudiation of the parents' beliefs."

"But he can be into Satan without being a member of a cult," Martin comments. Everyone's attention shifts to his end of the table.

"Why are you so set on rejecting the possibility of cult involvement?" Prizer asks, impatience making his voice sharp.

"I haven't rejected it," Martin says. "But we have no evidence of prior cult activity in this area. I've been over the records and checked with D.O.J."

"There was the Night Stalker, the Carter killing, the St. Joseph case in San Francisco." Prizer ticks them off on his fingers.

"Carter was killed fifteen years ago. Ramirez and St. Joseph are both in jail now," Martin responds. "But it wouldn't hurt to check further. Why don't you talk with your sources? Make it seem like a general query. No mention of the Demming case."

Prizer nods. He even smiles.

Martin brings the discussion back to Damion Wolfe. "I've got something more on the Wolfe kid. I understand he has a pentagram tattooed on the back of his right forearm, just about where the killer carved one on Demming."

Suddenly everyone sits up a bit straighter; their excitement is tangible.

"A pentagram? You're sure?" Prizer asks.

"That's what my source tells me," Martin says. "I haven't seen it myself. You ever see it, Nell?"

Scott shakes her head. "No, but he usually wears a leather jacket. I'm not sure I've seen him without it."

"Well, let's bring him in," Prizer says.

"On what charge?" Martin asks.

"Suspicion of murder."

"You can't bust the kid just 'cause he has a tattoo," Martin says.

Prizer doesn't like it, but he knows Martin is right. "We can still put him under the microscope, check his associates, his alibi . . ."

"Absolutely," Martin replies. He senses this could be a good place to use Prizer. "You want that piece of it?"

"Sure."

Chavez clears his throat. "Speaking of evidence," he says, "I think we have something on the murder weapon." He takes a stack of paper from a folder and passes it around the table.

"This is the report on a robbery at Portola Valley Veterinary Hospital, dated August twenty-third, just a week before the murder. Most of the stolen items are what you'd expect, drugs or stuff that could be fenced, but look at item twenty-nine. Three large equine syringes.

"I checked on those. They use them to give antibiotics to horses. They're just the size of the holes in the victim's artery."

"Nice work," Prizer says enthusiastically, as the others nod. "Stolen a week before. The killer clearly planned this well in advance. Were there any animals stolen?"

"Three rabbits," Chavez replies. "We figured they ended up in a roasting pan."

"Not likely," Prizer says. "It's common for cults to mutilate and kill animals."

There's silence around the table. Finally, Atkins says, "They could have used the rabbits to practice finding the jugular vein. Dr. Lim said that would require some experience."

"Check the animal control people," Martin says. "See if they found any dead rabbits." Then he switches gears and asks, "They print the vet's office?"

Chavez doesn't know about fingerprints.

"Well, check on it. If they've got prints, we want copies. Especially if we run in this Wolfe kid," Martin says.

"And we should check them against the Dorn girl's," Prizer adds. In response to Martin's quizzical look, he continues, "She's the last one to see Demming alive and she has his car and computer. She's still a major suspect in my book."

Martin doesn't like it. She may be a suspect, but to him, she looks more like a potential victim.

27

CHLOE AND SERENA sit cross-legged on the rec room floor with the *Chronicle* spread out before them and the yellow Lab begging soulfully for the remains of their bagels. Morning light slants through a side window, running bright bars across the printed pages.

"I don't believe this shit," Serena says, thumping her knuckle on a feature article just below the fold of the front page. Its headline reads, ROLE-PLAYING GAMES: INNOCENT PASTIME OR DANGEROUS OBSESSION?

"'Teenagers get caught up in these games,'" she reads aloud, "'and lose the ability to distinguish fantasy from reality.' Give me a break!"

"That's the pastor of my church," Chloe says. Her voice is thoughtful.

"He's got a few screws loose."

Chloe isn't sure what she thinks of Reverend Seaton. She knows she doesn't like him nearly as much as she liked her pastor in Texas. But he's never seemed crazy.

The article has made Serena so angry that she hasn't bothered to read beyond the first three paragraphs, but Chloe has read the entire article twice. And she's seriously considering the question of whether someone could get so caught up in a game that they could lose touch with reality.

She spent much of yesterday searching through the files on Matt's laptop and found the ones with the killer's messages. She doesn't really know what to make of them. One thing is clear, though. Whoever sent the messages was deeply into Matt's vampire game.

She looks up. Serena is staring at her.

"We need to do something about your hair," Serena says.

"What do you mean?"

"Well, your picture's been in the paper, and there are 'Missing' flyers all over the place. It's only a matter of time till someone recognizes you."

"Oh shit, you're right." Chloe can't believe she didn't think of that one. "What should I do? Dye it? Cut it?"

"Shave it," Serena says. "You'll look totally different shaved. And it'll make it easier if you want to use a wig."

Chloe swallows hard. Dyeing her hair was one thing, but shaving it? Then Liza asserts herself. In for a penny, in for a pound, she thinks. "Okay," she tells Serena.

"You could get a pierce or two."

"No," Chloe says. "No pierces."

"And you'll need clothes, a bunch of different outfits and looks—Goth stuff, gangsta pants—stuff that makes you look completely different."

"And maybe a wig and some real straight clothes, too," Chloe says, getting into it.

"Yeah, and with your head shaved, you could probably pass for a boy. Your tits aren't that big. You could wear baggy stuff and a cap."

Chloe nods. The woman of a thousand faces, she thinks. "Let's do it."

She feels a momentary twinge when she hears the first snip of the scissors and there's a lump in her throat as she watches the clumps of hair hit the floor, but she swallows hard, and fifteen minutes later she's staring at a different person in the mirror.

Her eyes look so much bigger, and her mouth, too. It's like she's looking at a stranger, a rather exotic stranger. This is what Liza looks like, she thinks.

Serena is on home ground now. She has trouble following the computer stuff but cosmetics and clothes are her turf. She pulls out a box full of tubes and pencils and goes to work on Chloe's eyes. She outlines them in black, smears a charcoal shadow on the lids, and stands back and smiles at her work.

She runs to her room and returns with silver hoop earrings and an ear cuff that sends a snake curling up Chloe's right ear.

"You really need more pierces," she complains.

Chloe shakes her head. "I don't even recognize me. No one else will, either."

They spend the rest of the morning in secondhand clothing stores. Chloe is out of money. She's decided to use her auto-teller card to get more, but she knows they can trace it so she'll have to wait till they get to San Francisco. Serena is happy to lend her what she needs.

By lunchtime, she has five outfits and as many looks, a brown wig that's okay if you don't get too close, and two outfits that she can use to pass as a guy. Liza is ready for action.

"So what now?" Serena asks, as they munch on falafel from a food cart. Sitting on the steps of the Cal Student Union, they look down Telegraph with its rainbow array of crafts vendors, street people, and tourists.

"Time to check my e-mail," Chloe says. This is not the easy prospect it seems. She can't just dial in from Serena's. Someone might trace the call back. So she has to find a place with public phones that have modem jacks. Yesterday, she went all the way to San Francisco to use one at the public library. She can do that again but before long, she'll have to find other places.

"Okay," Serena says, "I can drive you to the city, but I still don't see why you don't just use my computer here."

Chloe explains again about the phone lines. Serena can be a rather slow study, and she says things like, "Don't sweat the details." To which Chloe replies, "The details can kill you."

Serena drops Chloe at the Grove Street entrance to the library, and Chloe feels the same mixture of fear and sadness she felt yesterday. She remembers coming here with her parents right after the new building opened—her mom getting all excited by the great open atrium and her dad and brother scouting out all the technology. She wishes now that she hadn't done her bored teenager act.

Her heart speeds up as she steps into the lobby and sees the uniformed guard by the entry. He's only there to stop book thieves, she reminds herself, but she's holding her breath as she walks past him. Standing in the atrium with the floors opening above her, she feels exposed, vulnerable. Anyone could be watching from above. If Raptor is so smart, maybe he could figure out where her message to *The Meat Rack* came from. He could be waiting.

She scans the tiers above her and gasps when she spots a figure on the third floor gazing downward. He doesn't look familiar, but he's too far away to see clearly. She hurries across the open space toward the elevator, head down, shoulders hunched.

She's the last one into the nearly full elevator. The button for the fourth floor has already been pushed. She is startled by the tough-looking, bareheaded girl reflected in the polished metal surface in front of her. Then she feels reassured; even her friends wouldn't know her.

At the fourth floor, she heads for the Business and Technology Center where she knows she'll find phone jacks for the laptop. There are several places at the long blond wood table, and she slides into one, takes the laptop from its case, and plugs into the jack.

Chloe types her log-in sequence and hears the digitized ring and scratchy static that precedes hook-up. She watches the familiar script scroll down her screen, and she's online.

Her throat is dry and her stomach has a weird floating feeling. She hurries to download her mail and log off as quickly as possible. Even this solely electronic connection makes her feel terribly vulnerable, like a bird on the ground.

She doesn't know how easily this call can be traced. Whether the police might be monitoring it even now. And more seriously, whether the master hacker who killed Matt has found some way to track her electronically.

She has ten messages, but they are short and download quickly. She's off-line in less than a minute. She resists the temptation to see who sent the messages and walks through the stacks to find a chair where she doesn't have to worry about someone looking over her shoulder.

As soon as she brings up the list of messages, she gasps. One is from *"Raptor,"* the name the killer used with Matt. The subject line reads: *Advice from a Friend.*

Chloe stares at the screen. It's him. It really is him. The killer. And he's speaking straight to her. Her body is cold; she hugs herself, every muscle tense. Her mind feels frozen, but slowly it begins to function.

"Read the message," she tells herself. She brings it to the screen.

> *Yo, Chloe—*
> *So you want to know who killed Matt? I did, and if you don't want to join him, you'd better back off. No more posts to the* Rack. *No more playing girl detective. Stay away from the cops and keep your mouth shut. I don't*

want to hurt you. You cooperate and everything'll be fine.
Wait for instructions.

Raptor

Pressure in her chest reminds her that she's been holding her breath, and she exhales. She feels an almost irresistible urge to jump up and run out of the library. But where would she go? And how would it be any safer? She has to move into Liza. That's her only chance. Otherwise, she'll sit here paralyzed until the police find her.

As she thinks of Liza, the vampire *childe* steps in to take over. "We wanted to shake the bastard up," Liza says. "Mission accomplished." He must have seen the post on the *Rack.* Does that mean he's a member? Not necessarily, she decides. The gamers are terrible gossips; word of her post is bound to be all over by now.

I'm okay, she tells herself. He can't know where I am. No way he could. She takes slow breaths and tries to think. She should read the other messages. She forces herself to do that.

All but two are from friends. Words of comfort and support. The ninth message is the longest. It's from the police, someone named Lou Martin. He sounds nice, worried and concerned, and he promises to protect her. Sure thing, she thinks. What'll you do, put me in jail?

He warns her not to trust anyone who contacts her by e-mail, not even someone she thinks is a friend. That's a no-brainer. They must think she's hella dumb.

The final message is a surprise. It's from Molly Slater, a girl in the class behind her in school.

"You may not remember me, but we went to junior high together," it says. Chloe tries to remember and gets an image of a girl with short, curly black hair and braces. *"I was one of the kids in black who smoked up the bathroom.*

We had PE together, but I cut most of the time." That's her,
Chloe thinks.

> *I took off for San Francisco last year, ended up on the*
> *streets for a while, so I know the scene. What you're do-*
> *ing is awesome, I'd like to help. You said the killer was a*
> *hacker. Well, my boyfriend is a serious hacker and some-*
> *thing of a phone phreak. He says there are ways to find*
> *out who sent those messages, and he'll help if you want.*
> *You can send him e-mail at jpr66@wenet.com.*

Chloe's pounding heart slows down a bit. She feels weak
and a bit sick to her stomach. Between Raptor and the cops,
she's in a hell of a spot. She wonders about Molly Slater.
Can she trust her? Chloe takes a deep breath and begins
to type.

W E'VE GOT A hit," Molly announced from my office doorway, her face flushed with excitement.
She was waving a piece of paper.

"A hit?"

"Isn't that what you call it when the fish takes the bait?
Chloe's answered our e-mail."

"Terrific," I said. Molly bounded across the room and
dropped the printout of the e-mail on my desk. It was short
and to the point.

Thanks for your help. Can you ask your boyfriend where I can find phones with data jacks or computers with public access. I've been using the computers at the Main Lib, but I'm afraid the cops can figure out where I'm logging on, so I need some other places they can't trace. Thanks.

Bonemeal Babe/Liza

"She's a sharp kid," I said. "And cautious. She's not going to be easy to catch."

Molly nodded soberly. "But that's a good thing, right? Means the killer won't be able to find her."

I wanted to reassure her, to tell her Chloe'd be fine, but a sixteen-year-old kid, no matter how sharp, was still just a kid. The longer she was on her own, the greater the chance that she'd slip up. Molly was watching me anxiously. "I hope so," I said. "I really hope so."

Molly studied the message. "What's a data jack?"

"It's a phone jack," I said. "Like the one where you plug in the telephone or modem." I pointed to the phone jack behind my desk. "Pay phones are connected to phone lines directly; there's no jack, but now a few pay phones have a separate jack where you can plug in a computer."

"And that's what Chloe wants."

"Right. I know there are pay phones with data jacks at major hotels, but those would be almost impossible to monitor. What we need is someplace where we'd be able to spot her when she came in."

"A stakeout," Molly said. I could hear the excitement in her voice.

"But not for you," I said. "Remember, our deal was that you wouldn't be directly involved."

"But you'll have to suggest several places, and that means you'll need extra people to watch them."

I wasn't going to argue. Arguing gives the other guy a

chance to win. "The other possibility is to find public access computers." I picked up the phone and dialed Jesse's pager. If anyone would know about phone jacks and public computers, it was Jesse.

He must have been near a phone since it only took him a few minutes to call in. I explained what I needed.

"Cyber cafés," he said at once. "There aren't too many of them and they're small enough that it'd be easy to spot her. Plus, no one will get suspicious if you hang out for hours surfing the Net."

I'd heard of cyber cafés but hadn't seen one. "How many?" I asked.

"Three in San Francisco, as far as I know. Also, there used to be a combo café and Laundromat with a computer hooked to a phone line. I don't know if it's still around. Pretty neat concept, don't you think, put yourself online and your clothes in the dryer."

Jesse only had the name of one cyber café, Cyberworld. He figured someone there could tell me about the others.

"We'll need someone to stake out these places," I said. "You think you can find some hacker buddies who could handle it?"

"Being paid to spend eight hours drinking coffee and playing with computers? No problem. How many do you need?"

"Depends on what I find when I check the places and how long they're open. At least three or four, maybe double that."

"I'll make some calls," he said.

"How's it going at your end?"

There was a pause while I suspected he was checking around him. "Well, I've talked to several game programmers down here. None of them trust Ari Kazacos and one suggested that he wouldn't be surprised if Ari killed Demming."

"Any reason for that, other than general distrust?"

"I don't think so. But here's something of interest. Ari, unlike many of the producers, is a damn good programmer."

"Interesting. And Demming was killed before Ari discovered that the source code was gone."

"I'd sure like to see Demming's computer to find out how good the killer really is," Jesse said. "Chloe assumes he's a master hacker, but there are ways that aren't too sophisticated to make your messages untraceable."

"Oh, great," I said. The one thing we had that narrowed the field of suspects was our assumption that the killer was a hacker. But if the messages could have been sent by someone with less extensive computer expertise, we were back to start."

"All the killer needed was someone else's password so he could send the messages from their account, and it's not that hard to steal passwords," Jesse said. "You can write a program that captures them and forwards them to you by e-mail. You go to a computer lab, say at a college or university, find a computer where someone didn't log off, and load your program on to that machine. You can even write one that erases itself after it captures twenty passwords, so there's no record that it was ever there."

"But you'd still have to be good enough to write the program."

"It's not that hard, but if you needed a really low-tech approach, you can shoulder surf."

"Shoulder surf?"

"You go into a lab where there are several people working. You log on and look busy but you keep your eye out for someone new to come in. Then when the newcomer sits down to log on, you manage to walk behind him or her so you're in a position to see his fingers as he types his password. People don't worry that someone'll see them type in their password. Sometimes, if it's a series of numbers, they even have it written on a piece of paper and you can just read it over their shoulder."

"And anyone could do that," I said. "They wouldn't have to be a hacker."

"You got it."

"Any way you can tell if that's what's going on?"

"I might be able to tell something from Demming's files. If I can get Chloe to trust me with them. I'll suggest she copy them and send me the copies if she's too skittish to agree to a meeting."

Which brought us back to the issue of finding phones with data jacks or computers with public access. As soon as Jesse and I got off the phone, I called Molly in and asked her to call Cyberworld and get their address and the names of the other cyber cafés.

"I'll go online for them," Molly said. "They probably have a Web site."

"They probably have a phone number," I said. "Check the phone book."

She looked mildly pained to be forced to rely on such a low-tech solution.

Twenty minutes later we were on our way to check out the cyber cafés. Cyberworld was on Folsom Street below Second. The parking gods were with us, and I found an open meter just past the corner. This end of Folsom was industrial buildings and parking lots, a pity since it had a sensational view of the Bay Bridge.

Just at the point where the warehouses gave way to the parking lots, there was a narrow building made of corrugated steel. It was set back from the sidewalk with a slanted front to announce that its aggressive functionality was urban chic, not auto-repair low-budget. Out front there were a couple of tables, and just inside the door a sign made with electrical cables spelled out the letters of Cyberworld.

I'm not wild about industrial chic; I've never gotten into

furnace pipes as a design element, but the place had a nice feel to it. One side of the room had workstations at tables along the wall; the other had café tables in front of floor-to-ceiling windows with a view of the Bay Bridge. Midway, there was a food counter with the requisite espresso machine.

Molly was torn between checking out the computers and the dessert display. Her stomach won out. So did mine when I saw the menu. It was a definite improvement on the geek diet of Skittles and Coke. Here a ham and cheese sandwich was *prosciutto* and Fontina on *focaccia*.

I ordered the sandwich; Molly had a triple chocolate something with cherries on the top. We both had lattes. If I had to do some of the stakeouts, this was definitely my choice.

Cyberworld offered exactly what Chloe would be looking for—computers connected to the Internet where she could access her e-mail account and phone jacks for portable computers. Its long, skinny room meant that anyone working on a computer in the front could see everyone who entered.

The second café, Coffee Net, was in the area behind the Moscone Convention Center, and the third, Internet Alfredo, was on Brannan Street just below the Exposition Center. Both were small enough that one person could easily spot anyone coming in. Unfortunately, Alfredo was open twenty-four hours. That meant we'd need three people to watch it. "You get much traffic in the middle of the night?" I asked.

"Oh, yeah, we get a lot of night crawlers who're really pleased to find a place they can get on the Net," the girl replied.

The final place was the Laundromat café. It was called Brain Wash, and the decor was a funky fifties version of how the future was supposed to look. The counter stools were six-legged rocket-shaped jobs with silvery seats. Here the fare was beer and burgers, and "Don't Be Cruel" was playing on the jukebox. I didn't see any computers.

We walked to the back and found ourselves in a large room full of coin-operated washing machines and an entire wall of dryers. The hum of the machines drowned out Elvis. The clientele included geeky kids who looked like they didn't own a mirror, certainly not a full-length one, brand-labeled yuppies, and tattooed and pierced biker types.

I finally found the computer tucked back in a corner of the café. It was a far cry from the Pentium-chipped, large-screened machines at Cyberworld. This was an old black-and-white workhorse. It was hooked to a phone line, and you got two calls for a quarter. The menu included Telenet, but not the Internet. I tried to access my own e-mail and couldn't.

I crossed Brain Wash off my list, though I'd certainly have brought my laundry there if I lived in the neighbor-hood. The place was a monument to the speed of change in cyberspace. Only a few years ago, its quarter-operated computer was state of the art; now it was museum material.

"Man, that music is the mack," Molly said, as we were leaving. "So retro. Were you, like, an Elvis fan when you were a kid?"

Suddenly, I felt rather like the Brain Wash computer.

29

JESSE HAD PUT out the word that we were paying people to sit in cyber cafés and surf the Net. The response was immediate. By the time I got back to the office, I had three messages. Four more came in within the hour.

I spent most of the evening interviewing for the stakeout team. Molly sat in and provided choice commentary between interviews. McGee, the office cat, also sat in and tortured the cat lovers by ignoring them and the cat haters by jumping in their laps. It was a good chance to watch how they handled distraction, so I didn't dump him outside.

First, there was Gerome, with a *G*, and bright orange hair cut about an inch long all over his head with patchy green sideburns and a sapphire nose stud. Then Leo, who looked exactly like Gunther in "Luann," except that he was a real person instead of a comic-strip character. Then Kirsten of the shaved head and multiple ear pierces who was wearing a granny skirt with a leather bustier and combat boots.

They all seemed plenty sharp and promised that they could split their attention between the computer and the customers, so I signed them up, along with Tollie, who looked like a normal person until he opened his mouth and I saw the tongue stud. He was eighteen and told me he'd be the next Bill Gates.

I did not hire the girl with two-toned hair who was so spacey, a marching band could have walked through the room without her noticing. Nor the two girls in black who looked like they should be auditioning for the witches in *Macbeth*. They got nixed when they described how they sent their consciousness out on to the Web. I needed their consciousness in their bodies watching for Chloe Dorn.

There were a couple of graduate-student types and several twentysomethings wearing brand names on their chests. I'd had no idea how many independent contractors there were in the computer world. None of these kids had regular jobs; all were working, some on major projects. In two hours, I had my team.

I asked them to come to my office at nine the next morning for their assignments.

Peter was in the living room reading when Molly and I got home. I gave him a hug and went to get a beer. Molly beat me to the kitchen and began scouring the cupboards for something of high fat and/or sugar content.

"What's the word from Berkeley?" I asked, as I sank down on the couch next to Peter.

"Nothing on Chloe Dorn yet," he said, "but I put the Morton girl on a plane for Arizona. She's going to try staying with her aunt."

"Congratulations," I said. "How'd you pull that off?"

"The boyfriend finally tipped his hand. He tried to convince her to 'go on a date' with two of his friends who just happened to be dope dealers. She refused, and he beat her up. Fortunately, she got away from him and hid with some other street kids until I got there."

"She was very lucky," I said.

"She'd have been luckier if she'd left a day earlier," Peter said. I could hear the anger in his voice and see it in the set of his jaw.

It was an emotion I'd seen too often over the last six months. I understood it. I knew there was a good reason for it, but the fury that simmered inside him worried me. This wasn't only about Traci Morton.

I put my hand on his. The knuckles were bruised. "Hurt your hand?"

"Okay, I hit the little bastard," Peter said, even though that wasn't what I'd asked. "He spotted us on the street and tried to get her to come with him. He had the nerve to threaten her, right while I was standing there."

"An unwise move on his part."

"Believe it." I could hear a certain satisfaction in his tone. Then he sighed and leaned back against the couch. "All right, I lost my cool. I could have gotten her out of there without roughing him up."

"This is happening a lot lately."

"Not a lot."

"More than it should. How many times have you had to fight your way out of a situation in the past six months?"

"Don't," Peter said, putting up his hand. "I know I have a short fuse right now. I'll work it out."

We'd had this discussion before. Sometimes when the roles were reversed. We were both better at offering help than accepting it. But this time felt different. Several weeks in a Guatemalan jail had wounded Peter and changed him. Before, he'd been slow to anger and only fought when there was no other choice; now he carried a deep rage that erupted whenever he was challenged. And anytime I tried to discuss it, he cut me off.

But there was still one place we came together easily. I snuggled against him and kissed the back of his hand, careful to avoid the scrapes. He put his arm around me and we cuddled together.

"Oh, oh," Molly said, when she came into the room. "None of that, now. You'll warp my delicate psyche."

Another week and I'd be able to send her off to do her homework. I understood why parents looked forward to fall.

"Hey, don't mind me," she said, "I'll just go to my lonely room and see what's up on *The Meat Rack.*"

We went to bed early, not to sleep, but to bed.

Later, as I lay against Peter's body with my head on his shoulder, I thought of his brush with the Morton girl's boyfriend. He kept saying that he'd deal with his problems himself, but now that he was involved in the Chloe Dorn case, those problems affected me directly. In decking the boyfriend, Peter had blown his low-profile status. The kids would be talking about the fight, and that greatly increased the chance that someone would mention his questions to Chloe.

I opened the next morning's *Chronicle* with some trepidation. This should be the last day of the series on the dangers of role-playing games and other cult influences on young people. I was curious to see what Reverend Seaton would come up with for his finale.

He didn't disappoint me. This article focused on efforts of organizations like BADD, Bothered About Dungeons and Dragons, to combat the destructive influences directed at children, but its lead paragraph announced that the Reverend Thomas Seaton and other concerned churchmen would sponsor a "Take Back Our Youth" rally in Palo Alto on Saturday night.

Parents were urged to search their children's rooms for role-playing games, images of vampires or other demonic creatures, and all other games, books, comics, or paraphernalia that glorified evil. They were to bring the offending items to the rally where they would be collected and destroyed.

I was astonished by Seaton's audacity. Palo Alto is a liberal community. Most of its citizens would take a dim view of censoring books of any kind. But the protests would draw the media and grab a top spot on the evening news, and I suspected that was really what the reverend was after.

"Whoa," Molly said, as she read the article. "Search your kid's room. Trash their stuff. It's Gestapo time."

"I take it that means you don't want to donate your comics and posters to the rally," I said.

"I would be so pissed if anyone went through my stuff," Molly said, stopping to retrieve a bagel from the toaster. "It's like kids are supposed to respect adults, but adults can do anything they want. Well, hello, it doesn't work like that. I don't respect anybody who doesn't respect me." Her voice rang with adolescent righteousness. "Where's the jam? And why don't you ever buy strawberry?" she asked in the next breath.

"What if I was really worried about you?" I asked.

"You could talk to me," she said. "Isn't that what people are supposed to do, talk about their problems?"

I thought of how little success I was having getting Peter to talk about his problems and of Molly's long, dark silences. "It isn't always that easy," I said.

The kids on my cyber café stakeout team proved to be impressively punctual. They were all at my office by nine, and a couple showed up at eight-thirty.

I gave them their hours and locations, along with Chloe's photo and a pile of computer-generated pictures of how she'd look with a shaved head and various wigs and haircuts.

The tricky question was what to do when she came in. She'd probably only stay a short time. There was no guarantee that even if they called at once I'd get there fast enough. The plan was that they should e-mail me immediately and follow with a call, then they should try to strike up a conversation with Chloe. She was probably feeling pretty isolated now. I hoped that she'd pause for a few moments of human contact.

Each of the team members practiced his or her approach, with Molly playing the part of Chloe. The girls were good; each one worked out a plausible reason to approach their quarry. The shaved-head, leather-bustiered one was the best. She came over to caution the new girl about "the guy with the spiky hair and bad teeth."

The guys were a different story. They all had pickup lines, or what they thought were pickup lines. I suddenly understood why e-mail and chat lines were so popular with this set. Face-to-face communication was not a strong point. Molly and I tried to coach them. The girls on the team tried to coach them. Several of them got it. With the rest, we'd have to hope that Chloe had a soft spot for the truly clueless.

CHLOE HASN'T BEEN sleeping well. And even when she is asleep, her mind seems to be running on its own. She wakes several times a night, sometimes with nightmares, often with a rough start into awareness that leaves her heart pounding. Raptor's words play like a tape in the background.

She can no longer pray. How can she ask for God's help after she's made the choices she has? It's too dishonest to be

Liza by day and then to pray at night. But the loneliness of it is almost unbearable.

She's up at five but stays quiet until Serena's parents have left the house, terrified every time a board creaks that they've found out who she is and are coming for her. The yellow Lab has become her companion. She steals dog biscuits from the tin in the kitchen so she can feed him during the morning hours while he lies beside the couch where she sleeps. She's tried to get him to climb up on the couch, but he's well trained and just whines when she pats the cushion. This morning, she's wrapped herself in blankets and is cuddled next to him on the floor.

In the cold, dark hours around dawn she feels terribly alone and longs for home and her parents. It's better during the day when she's doing things, but this early morning time is hard. Very hard.

Serena comes down at eight-thirty to announce that the coast is clear. Chloe follows her to the kitchen. Chloe has Raisin Bran; Serena eats Pop-Tarts.

Chloe hasn't told Serena about Raptor's message. She can't bring herself to speak of it; besides, it might make the other girl freak out. "How come your parents don't mind that you're missing school?" she asks.

"I told them it starts next week," Serena says. "Dad has a big project due, and Mom's under some kind of deadline. They can never keep the school schedule straight. If they notice I'm not there, I just say it's International Woman's Day or Malcolm X's birthday." She laughs and looks pleased.

Chloe thinks of how her mother makes a big deal out of school starting and holidays. Her eyes feel prickly with tears. She shakes her head and moves into Liza.

"Where's the paper?" she asks. "Let's see what weird shit they've come up with today."

She and Serena read about the rally. Midway through,

Serena explodes angrily, "That is such bullshit. Man, I'd be so pissed if my parents even touched my stuff."

Chloe's attention is focused on one paragraph in the story. It quotes Reverend Seaton as saying, "The vampire game is a prime example of the dangers of this kind of 'play.' A young man died playing this game. A girl, a member of my congregation, disappeared after playing it. When you encourage young people to imagine that they are evil creatures, you call forth evil."

Chloe wonders if she's calling forth evil when she plays Liza. The reverend would certainly say she is. But being able to become Liza is all that's keeping her going now. And she doesn't think of Liza as evil, but rather as strong. It's true that if she'd never played the game, she wouldn't be here now. But the game isn't evil; it's just a game.

"This is so fucked up," Serena says. Contempt and anger make her voice harsh. "Seems like we're the only ones concerned with who killed your boyfriend. Everyone else is too busy putting down teenagers and the game. I can really see why you had to run away."

As Serena rails against the reverend's crusade, Chloe realizes that she can't go back now. Even if they caught the killer, she's not sure she can face her parents and their friends. They'd expect her to denounce the game and her friends who play it, and that would be a complete betrayal of Matt. She can't do that.

"If you can't go back, you'd better go forward," Liza's voice says. "Time to see what Raptor's come up with today."

She dresses as a boy again—large, loose jeans worn low on her hips, an oversized T-shirt with a denim shirt on top, worn open, a 49ers cap backward on her head.

She doesn't like the idea of going back to the library, but she doesn't know where else to go, and she's scoped it out, has her escape route planned in case she spots a cop. Or Raptor.

In the library, she logs on and downloads her e-mail, and hurries to a safe spot to read it. Her heart speeds up when she sees *"Raptor"* on the list of messages.

The subject line reads: *More Advice from a Friend.* This message is longer than the first.

> *You can get out of this alive. I've got nothing against you, but you have something I want—Matt's laptop, the source code, and the archives. Give me those; I'll give you safe passage.*
>
> *Tomorrow night, put the laptop, source code, and archives in a large cardboard box.*
>
> *Bring the box to Arastradero Lake. Park your car in the parking lot and take the box to the first trail marker past the lake. Leave it there and go home.*
>
> *This is your chance to save yourself. Take it.*
>
> *Raptor*

She feels the same chill and paralyzing fear she felt at the first message. But slowly, she's able to move back into Liza. She's still breathing hard, but her mind calms enough to study the killer's message, starting with the header. The sender's address is Raptor@finet.net. It tells her nothing except that he's slick enough to hide his tracks. But she knew that already.

She turns her attention to his message, the directions for delivering the laptop and game code. Oh right, she thinks. What kind of a fool does he think I am? It's the same setup he used to snare Matt. Park your car in a fairly deserted place and walk to a totally deserted place where he can bash you over the head. Not bloody likely.

She's a bit disappointed in Raptor. She's assumed he is a genius, but this is a lame plan. This note is the first break she's had. She ought to be able to use it some way. But she doesn't know how.

She checks the other messages. There's a letter from her friend Andi telling her that her mother calls every day asking if Andi's heard from her, and could Chloe please send a short message so she'll have something to tell her. Finally, there's a message from Molly's boyfriend with suggestions of places she can go to send e-mail. He also suggests that she meet him so he can take a look at the messages from the killer to Matt. She's not meeting anyone right now. But she's interested in his idea that she could make copies of the files and send them to him. She could include Raptor's latest letter, too. But she needs time to think before she does anything.

The note about her mother bothers her. She can't leave her worrying. So she risks going back to the computer and logging on again. *Tell my mom and dad I'm fine and I love them. I'll come home as soon as it's safe. Tell them not to worry.*

As she clicks on SEND, she knows that her parents will worry, and that she's not fine, and that they know that. But Liza tells her to cut the crap and get moving.

Between waiting for a BART train and missing the bus in Berkeley, it takes over an hour to get back to campus where she's supposed to meet Serena. The afternoon is warm and though the Cal students aren't back yet, the street is full of people. A festive crowd, munching on ice cream or cookies, sipping coffee or soda from paper cups. No Styrofoam in Berkeley.

She walks up Tele, stepping around the tourists who stop to study the tables of crystals, jewelry, tie-dye, and other crafts that line the street. The aroma of cinnamon from Mrs. Fields cookies almost seduces her into parting with a dollar from her dwindling supply of bills. But even the mingling sensations of cinnamon and sunshine, laughter, and the cheerful dulcimer music of a street musician aren't enough to calm the rising panic she's felt since she picked up Raptor's message.

Cool it, she thinks, just cool it. Liza would. Liza would be thinking how to use Raptor's plan against him. She consciously adjusts her walk to Liza, holds herself straighter, takes longer strides, scans the crowd with watchful eyes.

Several blocks up, between Cody's and Moe's bookstores she spots a black-clad group sitting against the building. The skinny girl at the end might be Serena. As Chloe approaches, she recognizes more of the group. Serena calls them wannabe-Goths, but with all the face metal, they look like the real thing to Chloe.

Chloe would find this group of sullen teens intimidating, but Liza approaches boldly and slides in next to a girl with purple hair and a spiky dog collar. "'S up?" she asks.

From her end, Serena greets her and makes introductions. Heads nod, a couple of the guys look her over. No one smiles. She tries to look bored.

"You're the poster girl," the purple-haired girl says.

"Yeah."

"There's a guy looking for you."

Panic surges through her. She almost loses her grip on Liza. It takes her a moment to get control of her voice, then she says in as bored a tone as possible, "Yeah? When?"

"Today," purple-hair says. "Big guy, old, maybe in his forties."

"Name's Harman," a boy with two nose pierces and an earful of studs says. "He's a private eye, specializes in finding lost kids. I've seen him around before."

"That the guy who beat up Orrin?" a girl asks.

"Yeah, beat the crap outta that little weasel," purple-hair says. She seems to approve.

"Orrin's not so bad," the boy says.

"Orrin is pond scum," purple-hair replies. "He beat up that girl. I saw her face. He was trying to pimp her to his druggie buddies."

"Well, the big guy took care of him," the other girl says. "He's okay." She stops to light a cigarette. "Traci, she's the one who got beat up, she says he won't force anyone to go home. Her old man wanted him to drag her back, but he got an aunt in Tucson to take her instead."

"Maybe he could help you," Serena says.

Chloe shrugs. She needs time to think. A private eye. That must mean her parents have hired someone to find her. They haven't given up on her, even when they learned she was involved in Matt's death.

But it doesn't change anything. This guy may not be from her parents. And even if he is, if he could find her here, so could the killer. She has to move on. Fast.

"You ready to go?" she says to Serena. "I got stuff to do."

"Yeah, sure." Serena unfolds herself and stands up. "See ya," she says to the group, as she hurries to catch up with Chloe, who's already walking up the street.

"You don't have to worry," Serena says. "No one's going to say anything."

"Maybe not anyone you know, but lots of people have seen me. Someone'll talk." She quickens her step; her eyes scan the crowd for tall men.

It's harder than ever to stay in Liza. Her illusion of safety, already shaken by the killer's message, is shattered by the news that someone has tracked her to Berkeley. Right now, possibly right on this block, a man is showing her picture, asking about her. It's only a matter of time until he gets an answer.

At Durant, one block from the bus stop, Serena grabs Chloe's arm and pulls her into Noah's Bagels.

"Hey," Chloe objects. "Take it easy."

"That's him," Serena says in a half whisper, jerking her

head in the direction of the street. "Up the block, the tall guy. That's the one who's been asking about you."

"Ohmygod," Chloe says. Her heart pounds and her legs feel weak. She forces herself to move toward the back of the shop, behind the crowd of students waiting for their orders.

"He's coming this way," Serena says urgently. "We gotta get out of here."

Chloe's urge is to hide, but there's no back way out, and if he comes into Noah's she'll be trapped. She takes a deep breath. What would Liza do?

"Come on," she says to Serena. She slips her arm around the other girl's waist. "He's looking for a girl, not a couple. Act like you're my girlfriend."

Serena looks terrified. This'll never work if she can't act natural. Chloe tickles her. Serena jumps and giggles despite herself.

"Keep your head down and toward me, like we're whispering," Chloe orders, as she moves forward, pulling Serena along. She stops where she can see out the window to check on the tall guy. He's stopped to talk with a blond chick who does palm readings, so he's still up the block. They'll only be visible to him for a few seconds if they head toward Bancroft. She pulls Serena out onto the sidewalk.

But once outside, Serena freaks. She looks up the street and freezes when she realizes that the guy is looking straight at them. Chloe tugs at her; she's stronger, but Serena is dead weight. "Come on," she whispers desperately. "Come on."

He's spotted them. How could he miss them with Serena frozen like a deer in the headlights? Chloe drops her arm from Serena's waist and takes off up the street.

There are too many people on the sidewalk. She can't really run without slamming into someone, so she dodges and slips between people as fast as she can. She doesn't look back.

At Bancroft, the light is green and she sprints toward Sproul Plaza. The crowd is less dense here and she can make some speed. Down the stairs by the Student Union and across the lower plaza, she runs, her heart pounding. Then she's on a path that winds beneath tall trees. She keeps running, and she doesn't look back until her lungs are burning and she can't run anymore.

She walks now, struggling to catch her breath. There's no sign of the tall man, but she hurries into a classroom building and looks for a bathroom where she can hide and rest, just in case he's managed to follow.

The building she's chosen is an old one, and the ladies' lounge actually has a small anteroom with a couch and chair. She sinks into the chair, still breathing hard, her heart still pumping, a bit nauseous from too much adrenaline and exertion. She has to move on. That much is clear. Berkeley is no longer safe.

Chloe walks to Serena's, watching all the time for someone following her, checking escape routes. It takes a long time, and the sky is darkening by the time she gets there.

"I'm sorry," Serena says, when she answers the door. "I know I screwed up."

"It's not your fault," Chloe says. "But I can't stay anymore. It's not just me. You're not safe while I'm here."

"Hey, you can lie low. You can stay here, and I can go out and do the stuff you need. I can do it, honest," Serena argues.

Chloe shakes her head. "I have to find a new place. Somewhere outside of Berkeley."

Serena looks sad. She doesn't want Chloe to go, but she can tell there's no point in arguing. "Okay, let me think of who I know who'd take you in."

Serena thinks best with food. She pulls a couple of Cokes

from the refrigerator and a bag of pretzels from the pantry. The pretzels are slightly stale, but neither girl notices.

Serena has three possibilities. She calls the first two. One doesn't answer, the other turns her down. The third is a girl named Tamara, Tam for short. Serena put her up a couple of years ago when she ran away from home. Now she lives in the city with her older sister. "She owes me," she tells Chloe.

The line is busy. Serena calls again. With each call, Chloe becomes more anxious. The yellow Lab senses her distress and stays next to her, even as she paces. Serena suggests watching TV; Chloe tries to pretend that she's interested.

Every ten minutes Serena tries again to reach Tam. Chloe stays in the television room, stroking the yellow Lab. It'll be hard to leave him.

Forty minutes later the line is free. Serena makes her pitch. Tam agrees to take Chloe in.

"Does she know about the murder?" Chloe asks.

"She knows the cops are after you," Serena says. "Said that was character reference enough for her." She laughs, then sobers up. "What about the car? You want to keep it where it is?"

"Yeah. It's like a big arrow pointing at me," Chloe says. "I can always come back to get it if I need it."

"How about the disks?" Serena asks. "I could keep them here for you. No one knows you've been here."

Chloe is torn. Keeping the disks someplace safe makes a lot of sense, but they could put Serena at risk. "I don't know. I think it's awfully dangerous. People have seen us together. What if the killer comes after you?"

Serena dismisses her fears with a swipe of her hand. "I wouldn't be any safer for not having them."

It seems to mean a lot to Serena to be trusted, so Chloe decides to leave the archives and the source code with her. She also makes backup copies of the files on Matt's laptop.

"If anything happens to me, give these to the Palo Alto police," she says.

And then it's time to go, time to move to the next hiding place. If this were a movie, it would be exciting, but all that Chloe feels as she walks toward the bus stop is exhaustion and dread. And the fear that comes with knowing she is very much alone.

31

I KNEW AS SOON as I saw Peter's face that something had gone wrong. "I lost her," he said, taking off his leather jacket and dropping it over the back of the couch. "I was that close, and I lost her."

"Sit down. I'll get you a beer and you can tell me about it," I said. I got two bottles of Sierra Nevada Pale Ale from the kitchen.

Peter was on the couch, leaning back with his eyes closed. He looked exhausted.

"What happened?"

"I spotted her on Telegraph with another girl, but they saw me first. Chloe took off. I chased her onto the campus but I lost her. She's small enough to slip through a crowd, and she's fast."

"Damn," I said. "That's twice we've lost her."

"We won't get a third chance in Berkeley," he said. "After today, she'll move on. I can try to find the girl she was with, but unless I can convince her to trust me, we're back to start."

We didn't discuss Peter's confrontation with Traci's "boyfriend" or what effect it might have had on the reactions of the kids on the Avenue, but we were both thinking of it. Peter lapsed into silence at dinner and hunkered down in front of the TV afterward.

I came in and sat down next to him. "You can't keep it all inside."

"There's nothing more to tell."

I waited. Finally, he turned to me. "The military swooped down on the village, carted us all off, even the women. Believe me, you don't want to know what happened in that jail and it won't help me to tell you. But a lot of people died in not-so-nice ways."

He'd told me that much before, and the marks on his body when he came home had told me more. I slid my arm around his waist and held him. He never fully relaxed.

Peter spent Saturday in Berkeley, and he was in a grim mood when he got home late that afternoon. After hours of talking to kids, he'd found the girl Chloe was with the day before, but she'd refused to speak to him.

"I'm fairly sure Chloe was staying with her, but if she won't talk to me, there's nothing I can do," he said.

"You think she'd talk to the police?"

"Hell, no. And we'd lose any chance that she'll change her mind and call me."

"How about an anti-satanic rally to lift your spirits?" I said.

"That's right. Reverend Seaton's rally is tonight. Sure, I'll go."

"Not unless you lighten up and stop beating up on yourself," I said. "Self-flagellation is a solo activity."

He gave me a weary grin. "Point taken," he said. "Maybe after the rally you can help cheer me up."

I gave him a long kiss. "It's a dirty job, but someone has to do it."

The rally was set for eight o'clock at a plaza about a half-mile from downtown. Peter and I arrived early, to look for a comfortable, and not too obvious, spot where we could check out Seaton's preparations. The sun had just set, leaving the sky turquoise at the horizon and a deepening blue above us. The air was warm, at least ten degrees warmer than it had been in San Francisco, and the night breeze had a sensuous, caressing quality. It was a night for strolling with a lover.

"We need to develop a better social life," I said to Peter.

"Right after the rally," he said, slipping his arm around my waist and pulling me to him.

The plaza was still relatively empty. A few early arrivals sat on benches around the edges or stood talking in small groups. At the far end, men moved equipment near a raised platform with large speakers on either side. In front of the platform was a sizable pile of something that didn't look like trash.

"Think they're planning to burn a witch?" I asked Peter.

"If they are, I'd better get you out of here."

"Oh, thanks. That was witch. With a *W.* "

"Like I said." He grinned. "Better check it out."

We walked over to the pile. "Bears a certain resemblance to Molly's closet," I said, looking down at the assortment of books, games, and mostly black T-shirts. The majority of the books came from Dungeons & Dragons and other role-playing games. The T-shirts sported a variety of skulls, skeletons, and several grisly drawings of vampires sinking their long teeth into victims' necks.

Peter accidentally kicked a stack of comics and it spilled

over, displaying disturbing, threatening images, a gallery of nightmares. Behind us a teenage male voice whined, "Mom, you can't. You just can't."

A grim-faced woman stepped up next to me and dumped a box of comics on the pile. "I bought those with my own money," a tall, tow-headed kid objected. The whine had been replaced by indignation.

"Maybe this will teach you to make better use of your money," the woman said, and walked away. The kid stayed where he was, staring forlornly at his comics. Finally, he gave the pile a vicious kick, swore to himself, and stalked away.

I looked around to see if I recognized anyone. Seaton's bulk made him easy to spot. He stood with several men in front of one of the speakers. Other men hurried up to confer with him, then returned to arrange lights or sound equipment.

Peter and I walked back toward the edge of the plaza where we'd be less obvious, but we took a detour when I spotted Lou Martin standing next to a planter that held a pink oleander bush.

The detective didn't seem to have any official role. He was just smoking a cigarette and apparently staring off into space. He didn't fool me. I'd bet he'd observed more of what was going on than the skinny uniformed cop up in front acting like he was on guard duty.

"Evening, Ms. Sayler, Harman," Martin said as we approached. "Come to watch the festivities?"

I'd never seen Martin smoke before, nor had I smelled cigarettes on his breath or clothes. I wondered if he was a former smoker and the tension of the case had caused a relapse. I knew it had made me long for a cigarette more than once.

I sat on the edge of the planter, resisted the urge to bum a cigarette, and waited to see if he'd say more. Outwaiting the other guy is no game to play with a cop. They're experts at it, but my dad was a cop so I'd practiced with a master.

Martin just kept smoking. Damn. A cigarette is a great prop in the waiting game.

Finally, I gave in. "Reverend Seaton's playing this satanic cult thing for all it's worth," I said. "I must admit I'm surprised the city is allowing him to use the plaza."

"The city is not endorsing the rally, just providing crowd control," Martin said. "For a purely secular event."

"Still . . ."

"The reverend is a very persuasive man, and very skilled at dealing with political institutions," Martin said. A uniformed officer waved to him from across the plaza. Martin excused himself and went to meet him. Peter and I stayed by the oleander and watched as people arrived.

By seven-thirty, there were almost as many protestors as participants. A group of free speech advocates with signs condemning censorship positioned itself near the stage. It included several high school kids and a few college students but was mostly made up of community members. They watched grimly as hordes of men carrying cameras and microphones swarmed over the plaza. It looked for a while like the TV crews might outnumber both protestors and participants. The citizens of Palo Alto were not going to be pleased by the eleven o'clock news.

Across the street, another crowd was gathering. Louder, less well groomed, they were in their teens and early twenties. Rainbow heads, leather punks, curious college kids. Their costumes ranged from grunge to Goth, and while they were in the minority numerically, they had the edge on volume.

The crowd on the plaza continued to grow. It was mostly people in their thirties and forties. A few groups of teenagers. A number of parents with scowling kids. Not a happy crowd. Hushed voices. No laughter.

A couple of school buses parked on the side street and discharged squads of serious-faced, neatly attired teens, church groups by the look of them. No green hair, no metal, no leather. Very earnest.

Just after eight o'clock, the sound system crackled to life, drawing everyone's attention to the stage where Reverend Seaton stood before the microphone. We joined the crowd, staying toward the back. TV cameramen jostled each other in front of the stage, looking for the best angles.

"My fellow citizens," he said, "welcome, and thank you for joining us tonight in this holy crusade."

"Reminds me of a guy named Savonarola," Peter whispered to me.

"He came to a bad end as I recall," I said.

"Yeah, but not until he'd done a lot of damage."

A woman in front of us turned around to glare, and we shut up.

The reverend called for a moment of silent prayer, a nod to the city's restrictions, and the group of earnest high school students sang about "following the light." Then it was Seaton's turn to address the multitudes.

I'd expected hellfire and brimstone, but I'd underestimated the man. He was an excellent orator, and his speech was closer to a lecture than a revival sermon. As he spoke of the danger of role-playing games, I found myself thinking of Damion Wolfe. The kid didn't look exactly stable; it couldn't help his mental health to spend his days pretending he was a vampire.

"I'm asking you to take a long look at what your children are reading, what they're doing with their time," he said. "Is this what you want them studying?" Next to him a man held up several comics with lurid covers and another unfurled posters with evil-looking figures in erotic poses. "Is it healthy for our young people to wear T-shirts that glorify demons or vampires or other evil creatures?" he continued, as his assistants displayed several examples.

"Harmless fun, some would say. A joke. Innocent youthful rebellion. But these are not innocent images. Their intent is not harmless. These are images that glorify evil. These are the images of Satan."

The Goth-and-punk set shouted cat calls and unimaginative obscenities.

Reverend Seaton ignored them. "Your children are not choosing these images. They are being sold them. There are men who make their living marketing them to children.

"There's no limit to their cupidity. Their lust to profit from the debauchery of our youth. Even here, even tonight, they seek to peddle their evil wares." His voice shook with fury and his outstretched arm pointed straight at us.

I turned to see where he was pointing. Behind the audience, four figures dressed in black with their faces painted ghostly white held up two banners. The first read, WHEN GAMES ARE OUTLAWED, ONLY OUTLAWS WILL HAVE GAMES, and the second read, JOIN THE CLAN. *CULT OF BLOOD.* COMING IN DECEMBER.

"Oh, no," I moaned.

"Shame," Seaton thundered. "Shame."

"Shame," the crowd echoed. "Shame. Shame." The chant grew in volume.

The camera crews scurried from the stage to capture the action around the banners. The black-clad faux-vampires were grinning with delight. I wondered if they realized that they might be in real danger.

The police, who had been standing off to the side, moved in and placed themselves between the crowd and the men with the banners. In the meantime, some of the punks came on to the plaza behind the banners. As the crowd shouted, "Shame," they responded with obscenities.

The reverend could have cooled things down. He could

have asked the crowd to turn their backs on the disrupters and ignore them. But a peaceful resolution wasn't on his agenda. Instead, he thundered denunciation at the motley crew of protestors, and of course, they responded as if on cue with louder obscenities.

Sensing a riot in the making, the cops moved toward the protestors, trying to force them back. The group linked arms and shouted defiance. Those who'd stayed across the street rushed to join them.

At that point several kids from the church group charged the banners and tried to wrest them from their holders. Some of the protestors rushed to the defense of the beleaguered vampires, and the battle was on. Members of the opposing groups hurled themselves into the melee. Fistfights broke out, and the cops waded into the mob with their batons out.

Too late, the reverend realized the seriousness of the situation and began urging the crowd to leave the plaza, but less than half the audience followed his advice. The rest withdrew to a safe distance but remained, crammed together, watching the riot unfold.

Suddenly there was a bright flash behind me. I turned to see the pile of comics and games burst into flame. From the intensity of the first blast of flame, it was clear that some part of the pile had been doused with gasoline. Shouts went up as the fire blazed. Excitement spread through the crowd.

Between the shouts of the people and the wail of sirens, the noise was deafening. It was full dark, and in front of us the white high-intensity lights of the television crews lit up pockets of fighting, while behind us silhouetted black figures ran back and forth in front of the orange glow of the fire.

Peter and I tried to move away from the fighting but the crowd made it difficult. Slowly, we worked our way backward and to the side. From the noise level, the cops' efforts to contain the fighting were not meeting with much success.

The crowd thinned as we got farther from the police line and we finally reached a place where there was space to breathe. The crowd obscured what was happening with the cops and protestors; behind us the fire was dying down.

"Let's go," I said, and we headed for the edge of the plaza. We'd only taken a few steps when I was knocked backward and a sharp pain stabbed through my head. The force of the blow didn't knock me over, but it disoriented me, and I stumbled. I felt Peter's arms pull me close to him.

"Shit," he said. "Who the hell . . . ?" He was scanning the crowd for the person who'd thrown whatever hit me.

I automatically put my hand to the spot on my head where the pain seemed to come from. "I think I need to sit down," I said.

Peter was so focused on finding the culprit that I had to repeat what I had said. Finally, he led me to a bench at the edge of the plaza.

I took my hand from the wound. It was sticky with blood and under the light from the street I could see that Peter's shirt was covered with blood.

"What happened to you?" I asked.

"Nothing," he said. "That's yours, I'm afraid." He was still scanning the crowd, his expression fierce.

"Let it go," I said. I was vaguely nauseous and suddenly tired.

He turned his attention back to me and the lines of his face softened. "Let me see," he said, trying to be gentle and only partly succeeding. "It's a scalp wound, probably not too deep, but we should get you to a doctor."

"What happened?"

"I think someone must have thrown something," he said. "But I didn't see what it was or who threw it. Here, hold this against the wound." He put his handkerchief on my head and raised my hand to hold it in place.

"I'm okay," I said. "Just a bit shaken up. Let me sit here for a while until my head clears."

"Catherine Sayler, what're you doing here?" a familiar voice said.

I turned my head and groaned. It was my least favorite television reporter, Malcolm Mercheck. He had red hair, a large nose, and an unusually long neck; tonight he looked like a vulture who'd just spotted blood. The only good news was that his cameraman was busy shooting the dying fire, so we weren't on camera. Yet.

"Are you working on the Chloe Dorn case?" he asked eagerly.

"Go away, Mercheck," I said. "I'm just down here to see my sister."

"How about a statement? Floyd," he called to the cameraman.

"The lady is hurt," Peter said in a tightly controlled voice. "Back off unless you want firsthand experience with what a broken head feels like."

"I'd watch those threats, fella," an official-sounding voice said. It was George Prizer. Things just kept getting worse.

At that point we had one small bit of good luck. The cameraman spotted something more interesting than us and took off toward the other end of the plaza.

"What's going on here, Ms. Sayler?" Prizer demanded. His tone was accusatory.

"Hey, I'm the victim here," I said.

"The innocent don't have blood all over them," he replied.

I don't remember what I said next, something like "You're an idiot," or "That's the dumbest thing I ever heard." It didn't improve the situation. Mercheck was practically salivating; I could feel Peter tense up next to me, and Prizer looked like he was trying to remember what charge he could use to bust me.

Peter pulled away from me and was halfway to his feet. I was afraid he'd deck Prizer. I jumped up and moved between them. "Look," I said to the cop. "I'm sorry; my head hurts. Someone must have thrown something. Mercheck, Officer Prizer is the man you want to talk to. He's an expert on cults."

It was a stroke of genius, if I do say so myself. Mercheck fell on Prizer like he was prime rib, and Prizer was delighted by the chance to preen for the press. Peter and I slipped away as Mercheck was yelling for Floyd to bring the camera. Prizer's moment had arrived.

GEORGE PRIZER IS pleased with the news coverage of what at least one station is calling "the satanic riot." They only ran a short part of his interview, but it was the right part. He'd invoked the danger of cult involvement and warned viewers that some of the scruffy kids they saw battling with police officers might be involved in dangerous rituals. Together with the clip of Reverend Seaton's speech, the piece ought to shake up those complacent liberal eggheads who worship tolerance.

It's past midnight now, time to go to bed, but he's still coming down from the night's events. He sips a glass of bourbon to help him relax.

He's concerned about the involvement of the Sayler woman. He doesn't trust her. She knows too much about bulletin boards and role-playing games. And why was she there tonight, just when her client set off a riot with his provocative signs? He doesn't believe she was hit by a flying object. He's checked; no one saw anything thrown, no one else was hit by anything. The mob did some rock-throwing after the police forced them off the plaza, but that was later. He makes a mental note to check on her on Monday.

The phone rings. He grabs it quickly, hoping it hasn't awakened his wife upstairs. It's Lyle Collier, one of the patrolmen whose beat includes Damion Wolfe's house.

"Sorry to bother you, George, but I thought you'd like to know; we just got a call from the Wolfes' neighbors. The kid's screaming obscenities and breaking things."

"I'll be right there," Prizer says. "Try to stall. Don't wrap this up till I get there."

At the Wolfes' all the lights in the house are on and there're two black-and-whites out front. Prizer hurries up the walk. Collier meets him at the door.

"Kid's split," Collier says. "The parents saw the riot on the news and thought maybe he'd been involved. He came home acting strangely, stoned is my guess, and freaked out when they confronted him. He threw a clock through a window, did some other minor damage, then took off just before we got here."

Prizer goes to meet the parents. The house is in an expensive part of town; one look at the living room tells him these people have money and taste. It's a bit exotic for his liking, but the carved elephant that serves as the base for one table and the metal casks that bracket the couch in place of end tables weren't cheap. This is the kind of room they put in designer magazines.

The people on the couch are too small and plain for this room. The man wears tan slacks and a forest green cardigan over a knit shirt. He's probably almost six feet, but he looks thin and stooped. His body language is Milquetoast. The woman has on a pink running suit in some soft fabric. She's on the plump side with a rosy complexion, looks a bit more substantial than her husband.

Prizer introduces himself, explains he's had some experience with kids like their son, though it's not technically true. They seem relieved by his gentle manner. He's a good listener, doesn't pepper them with questions.

The woman does most of the talking. Prizer senses that she's still in shock from the confrontation with her son. The timing is perfect. In a few hours, the parents will begin to make excuses, to suspect that they overreacted. By morning the rituals of daily life will comfort them, their fears will recede, making it easier to retreat from their son's problems. But tonight everything's still real to them. Tonight Prizer has a chance to reach them.

"You were concerned that he might be involved with Satanists," Prizer prompts.

"Well, not really Satanists," the woman objects, "but unhealthy influences."

Why, Prizer wonders, is it so difficult for these people to say the word *Satan*?

"I understand your concern," he says. "There are some very dangerous people out there. They can take advantage of an impressionable young person."

She swallows hard and nods. Her chin quivers just a bit and Prizer is afraid she's going to burst into tears, which is not what he wants right now.

"Sometimes it helps to understand what's going on if you look at the young person's room," he says. "I could help you do that. I know what to look for."

The father comes to life at that. He's not too shell-shocked to realize that a police officer is asking to search his kid's room. "Well, I don't know," he says.

"I'm sorry if I overstepped, sir," Prizer says quickly. "It's just that I have kids of my own. I know how awful this can be for parents." He pauses, then continues, "But I know some people aren't comfortable with police officers." He's hoping they're the sort of people who won't want to be thought of as "uncomfortable with police officers."

The wife rises to the bait. "Perhaps it would be helpful," she says to her husband.

Please, God, don't let him be a lawyer, Prizer thinks.

The father is a passive sort, Prizer can see his indecision. Definitely not a lawyer, he thinks. "You know just last week we had a young man killed here in Palo Alto," he says. "Probably cult-related."

The mother's eyes are wide. Time to push, he decides. "Well, I'm sorry I can't be of help to you," he says in a sad, slightly resigned voice. He stands. "I hope things work out with your son, that he isn't involved in any of this . . . business."

It's too much for her. She leaps to her feet. "Please don't go. We really do want your help."

He waits. She has to say the words, give him explicit verbal permission to search her son's room.

"Damion's room is upstairs," she says, without looking at her husband, and walking toward the stairs.

"Are you sure you're comfortable with this?" Prizer says, choosing his words carefully. "I don't want to go up there unless you feel I can help."

"Yes, yes," she says. "Please, we want your help. Please let me show you his room."

Prizer hides his feeling of elation as he follows her up the stairs. The father is right behind them.

* * *

Prizer takes it slow. He doesn't want this to look like a search. He walks to the bookcase and studies it. Pulls a large format book down and flips through it, then hands it to the mother. "This is used in a vampire role-playing game. The boy who was killed played that game."

Mrs. Wolfe stares at the book in horror.

Prizer goes back to the shelf. Takes down several comics, all about vampires. He hands them to her. The contents of the bookshelves read like a list from the cult workshop. Anton LaVey, Regardie, Crowley, they're all there. He points out the LaVey book, *The Satanic Bible*.

Mr. Wolfe is looking over his wife's shoulder. He looks torn between horror and fury.

"It's all out there," Prizer tells him. "Right on the shelves next to the games. Kids are encouraged to think of it as play, and the predators are just waiting to draw them in."

He looks around the room. Tries to remember the items on the seminar handout. Occult games and books were definitely there. Candles, drums, gongs or bells, knives, mirrors, ashes, something that could be used as an altar. Then there were the more obvious ones—robes, animal masks, chalices or goblets, crosses, pentagrams. There was more, he knows; he should have gone back over that list to refresh his memory.

There are several candles on the low table by the bed, sticks of incense next to them. The table could be used as an altar. He studies it more closely.

"These could be ritual objects," he tells the mother. "The only way to tell is to see if there are other objects that might be used in a ritual. If your son wanted to hide something, where do you think he'd put it?"

She looks confused. "I don't really know," she says. "Maybe under his bed?" She looks around the room. Under the window is a chestlike bench, heavily carved, probably from somewhere in Southeast Asia. "Maybe in the bench," she says. "We used to joke that it had secret compartments because the drawers come out at the ends, and it's easy to miss them if you don't know where to look."

She shows him how to open the drawers, and gasps in horror as she sees the contents. A knife with a wicked curved blade, a papier-mâché mask of Satan and another of a goat, a pewter chalice, black candles, a black hood, and a tattered notebook.

Prizer is jubilant. I've got you, you bastard, he thinks, but he hides his excitement beneath a mask of deep concern. He shakes his head mournfully. "This doesn't look good," he says. "You were right to be worried."

"I don't understand," Mrs. Wolfe says.

"None of this is illegal, of course. You don't have to be concerned about that," he reassures them, "but it does suggest that your boy may be involved with some dangerous people. Very dangerous people."

"What, what should we do?" the mother asks.

Prizer pauses, as if considering the question. "I'd start by going over his room very thoroughly," he says. "Look for any photographs, names, phone numbers, addresses, other paraphernalia. You want to know who he's associating with. Chances are, there's a group of adults involved, but they'll be very careful to hide their identities. I'll be happy to help any way that I can."

The stress is beginning to tell on both parents. The father looks physically ill; the mother is flushed and agitated. "Yes, yes," she says, "we should look around. We need to do that."

"You look awfully tired," Prizer says. "Would you like to sit down?" Before she can refuse, he says, "I know how hard this is for you. Would you like me to help?"

The father shakes his head. "I never would have

thought . . ." he says. "Thank you for your help, Officer. We'll do as you suggested."

"I wish you luck, sir," Prizer says. "But do act quickly. Your son could be in real danger. Cults rarely stop with one killing."

That has the effect he was hoping for. It focuses them on an outside threat, and from there it's not long before they're begging him to stay and help them go through their son's room.

The search turns up plenty of evidence of satanic involvement. The kid has even carved a crude pentagram into the wooden floor, hidden under an Oriental rug. Bits of melted wax tell Prizer he's been using it for rituals.

They also find drugs, plenty of them, but Prizer plays that down. Talks of rehab programs instead of arrest. He's after something bigger than a drug bust or this homegrown Satanism. He still has nothing linking Wolfe to the murder or to a group of adult Satanists.

"Is there anyplace else he might be doing 'this'?" Prizer indicates the pentagram and the contents of the secret drawers.

"The garden house," the father says. Now that he's committed to the search, it seems to have given him new energy. "It's not really a garden house, more of a glorified potting shed," he explains. "Damion turned it into a sort of clubhouse. Six months ago I noticed he'd put a padlock on the door."

It's pitch-black in the backyard, and the garden house is far from the lights of the main house. A daylight search would be much better, but Prizer can't risk the Wolfes' changing their minds. He calls to Collier, who has remained in the background, to bring Mr. Wolfe a flashlight.

The bright cone of light illuminates a rough shed about half the size of a small garage, its single door secured with a padlock.

Wolfe has no objection to prying off the lock. It comes easily. Short nails inexpertly hammered are no match for a crowbar. Prizer suggests that Collier look around outside, stopping to check that it's all right with Mr. Wolfe. By now Wolfe has forgotten that he's dealing with the police, or maybe he's so horrified by his son's activities that he no longer cares.

The scene inside the shed appears even more bizarre by flashlight. Fragments of it jump to life as they are illuminated, then disappear as the light moves on. Another pentagram on the floor. Candles and wax drippings everyplace. An old mattress covered with a scarlet cloth. A pile of pornographic magazines.

"George," a voice calls from outside, interrupting their search.

They go out to find Officer Collier kneeling near the corner of the shed. There's a pile of wood stacked roughly against the shed and a stack of broken flowerpots next to it. Collier is shining his light into one of the pots. Stuffed into the bottom is a white rag with reddish brown stains and a very large hypodermic needle.

I LEARNED OF Damion Wolfe's arrest on Monday morning at nine o'clock when Lou Martin called to demand if I was the source of the front-page article in the *Chronicle*. I'd expected his call from the moment I opened the paper and read, VAMPIRE KILLER DRAINED MURDER VICTIM.

The paper had all the details Martin had given me about Demming's death and a few new ones. Coming on the heels of Saturday's rally and riot, the revelations were sure to send shock waves through the community. I understood the anger I heard in Martin's voice.

"No," I said. "I told you I wouldn't reveal what you told me and I haven't. Besides, you didn't tell me about the pentagram on Demming's arm, so there's no way I could be the source."

"Okay," Martin said. "I believe you." Not "I'm sorry I suspected you" or "Please forgive my lack of faith." Just "Okay."

I decided to see if I could go for guilt points. Always a long shot with the cops, but worth a try. "I've always been straight with you," I said, trying to sound oh-so-slightly wounded. "I've never given you reason to doubt my word."

"I said I believed you," he said impatiently. Then, "By the way, we have an arrest in the Demming case."

No apology, but a bit of free information. Guilt wins out.

"Really? Can you tell me who?" I asked.

"Damion Wolfe."

"You get a confession?"

"Not yet, but we have very strong physical evidence."

"Damion Wolfe," I repeated, trying to figure out why it didn't feel quite right. "You looking for an accomplice?"

"Why an accomplice?" Martin asked.

"I don't know, but somehow I can't see him pulling off this killing all by himself. I believe he's capable of murder, but this one required careful planning, and the kid looks like he'd have trouble figuring out what to eat for breakfast."

"Prizer's convinced there's a cult involved."

Prizer would be. "Could just as easily be someone who knew he'd be the perfect fall guy."

"Yeah," Martin said.

"Is he a computer geek?" I asked.

"Oh yeah, he spends hours playing those games."

"No, I mean, does he know how to program? Would he be able to figure out how to send anonymous e-mail to Matt Demming?"

"We're working on that. Don't know yet." Then he switched topics before I could ask more. "I hear you saw some action in our little riot Saturday."

"Yeah, and I have three stitches in my head to show for it."

"Prizer figures you were involved in the melee. I told him you weren't the type to duke it out with the cops."

"Thanks for the character reference," I said. "Someone threw something that hit me in the head." I was glad he'd brought up the riot. I was considering calling to ask if there'd been any injuries similar to mine. "Was there a lot of stuff being thrown around that night?"

"Only a few cans and bottles at the cops."

A chill traveled up my spine at that information. "So I was the only one not involved in the fighting who got hit?"

"As far as I know."

Oh great. We were back in paranoia central. It was probably just a coincidence that I was the one who was hit. But every time I told myself that, a little voice in my head said, Yeah, right.

"By the way," Martin went on, "you can tell your client that we're looking into charging him for the police over-time caused by the riot. It would've been nice if you'd mentioned he was going to pull that stunt."

"It would've been nice if he'd mentioned it to me," I said. "Clients are like teenagers, Detective Martin, they rarely tell you when they're planning something stupid."

"Yeah," Martin said. Then switching topics again,

"Look, we've got a whole bunch of things pointing at the Wolfe kid and nothing pointing anyplace else. Strong circumstantial evidence, no alibi, someone who saw him leave the game with Demming . . ."

"Someone saw him leave with Matt? Who?" I asked. At least two people had said Demming left with Chloe.

"Torres. The game master. He said Chloe, Matt, and Damion went off together."

"Torres," I said. "He told me that Matt and Chloe left together. He never mentioned Damion Wolfe."

"I pulled him in Saturday for another chat. Leaned on him a bit heavier, and out popped the info on Wolfe," Martin said. "He seemed nervous about it, was anxious I not tell Wolfe who'd told me."

"Not surprising, given Wolfe's tendency to toss people through windows," I said. "You believe him?"

"With all the other evidence, yeah, I believe him."

I wasn't sure I did. Torres had lied to one of us. I wondered why.

"Your partner hear anything from the Dorn girl?" Martin asked.

Damn. I hate lying to a cop. "No," I said. "Not yet."

"Well, keep me informed."

I hung up the phone and poured another cup of coffee. I had the kitchen to myself except for my ever-hungry cat, Touchstone, who was desperately trying to convince me that I'd forgotten to feed him. It's a good act. Might have worked if he didn't do it every day.

It had been a hectic morning, even for a Monday. Today was the first day of school for Molly, and ever the enthusiastic scholar, she had whined and procrastinated until the last possible moment when Peter and I shoved her out the door for the run to the bus stop.

Peter wasn't far behind her. He had a court appearance.

And I was racing to get to Ari Kazacos to tell him in person just what I thought of his publicity stunt Saturday night. It would be interesting to see how everyone at Astra reacted to the news about Wolfe.

The atmosphere at Astra was completely different from the one I'd encountered on previous visits. First of all, the door was open, there was a secretary at the front desk, and she looked busy. She motioned me toward the back when I told her who I was.

"What's going on?" I asked Grif, as he met me at the door.

"The orders for *Cult of Blood* are just pouring in. And you won't believe the media coverage. I mean, the local stations carried the rally Saturday night, but now with this 'vampire killer' thing, all the major networks are calling. We're going to be on the national news tonight, all three networks."

"How very nice for you," I said. "Too bad Matt had to die for it." I was feeling a bit cranky. I get that way when greed beats out decency.

Grif looked abashed. More than abashed. Confused and sad, like a seven-year-old who's just lost his teddy bear. "Oh, jeez, so much has happened; I can't quite wrap my mind around it," he said mournfully. "I mean, did he really die that way? Like they said in the paper?"

I nodded.

"That's so . . . so gross. How could anyone do that? I mean, I can see, someone gets mad and shoots someone else, but this . . . draining him of blood . . . poor Matt."

His face was twisted with anguish. He looked on the verge of tears. I could imagine he was confused. The same day had offered him the possibility of success beyond his dreams and the reality of a friend's nightmare death.

"He probably wasn't conscious," I said. "I don't think he knew what was happening."

"That's good," Grif said, but he still looked near tears. "I think Matt would have been happy about what's happening with *Cult*. I mean, it was always the most important thing to him."

Probably not that night when someone knocked him over the head, I thought. Death tends to reorder your priorities—fast.

The testers were still in their lair; the mountain of junk food containers next to the armchairs was growing, probably in more ways than one. Ash Klein and Nate Sessler conferred in the doorway to Matt Demming's cubicle. I was surprised to see Sessler there, then remembered that he was working part-time for Astra.

Sessler turned to greet me. With his bat tattoo, he seemed to have two faces; and while he smiled a friendly welcome, the bat glowered malevolently. I nodded at the two men and headed for Kazacos's office.

As I approached, I could hear Anita Salazar's voice, raised in excitement. "Didn't I tell you? Didn't I? There's no such thing as bad publicity."

"The distributor says they'll give it priority. I figure we can give them the disks by Saturday, maybe sooner." He sounded positively giddy.

"You have the disks?" I asked from the doorway to the cubicle.

"Hello, Catherine," Kazacos said. "Not the source code, but we don't need that now. There's so much demand that we're putting the game out as is. We're calling it 'an uncorrected original by master game designer Matt Demming, real-life victim of the vampire killer.'" His fingers made quotes around the words.

"Ah, murder as a marketing opportunity," I said. I was

sick of Ari Kazacos and Anita Salazar. I didn't give a damn if he fired me.

But he and Salazar were too high on the scent of money to pick up on irony. "The buzz is terrific," Salazar said. "A million dollars' worth of word of mouth."

"You didn't tell me Matt had been drained of blood," Kazacos said accusingly. "You never mentioned the vampire aspect."

"Maybe that was because I think murder is a wee bit more important than the sales figures for a computer game," I snapped back. "Are you people out of your heads? Have you completely forgotten that a real person was killed? What the hell did you think you were doing, staging a stunt like that on Saturday night?"

"Now just a damn minute here," Kazacos said, his eyes narrowing. "You work for me. I hired you to find the source code, which, incidentally you did not do. How I run my business is none of your concern."

"No," I said. "It is not. And since it would appear that you won't need my services further, I'll send you a bill and you won't have to listen to my opinion. You may have less success with the police."

"What? What about the police?" Kazacos asked sharply, his tone still belligerent.

"They're considering charging you for the overtime costs of the riot."

"They can't do that," Kazacos exploded. "This is a free country. I can advertise my product any way I please. It's not my fault those family-values nuts tore down my sign and started a fight."

Our argument had drawn Grif, Ash, and Nate. They hovered just outside the cubicle. Standing next to each other, Grif and Ash looked like Mutt and Jeff. Nate kept rubbing his hand across the tattoo on his arm, as if he were caressing it.

"Don't sweat it, Ari," Salazar chimed in. "It's just more publicity. You can sue them for harassment."

She was right. For Kazacos, any publicity made the game more valuable. There was no restraint on his actions. Just as there was none on Reverend Seaton's. With self-interest shining brightly before them, neither one felt the least responsibility for the effect they had on the murder investigation.

It scared me because I wasn't convinced that Damion Wolfe was the only killer. And because Chloe Dorn was still running for her life. These guys were like the people who weave in and out of traffic. They're rarely caught in the accident their behavior causes.

"By the way," I said, remembering the other reason for my visit. "There's been an arrest in Demming's murder."

"Who?" just about everyone said, almost at once.

I moved so that I could see the three men at the door along with Kazacos and Salazar. "Damion Wolfe," I said.

"That's the Goth weirdo," Ash said. He was never completely still. Now he bounced up and down on the balls of his feet.

"Damion Wolfe," Nate said. "Man, I knew he was weird, but I didn't realize he was totally crazy."

Grif stared at the floor.

"Who is this Wolfe guy?" Ari asked. "Is he one of the kids who plays that street game?"

"Yeah," Nate and Ash said at the same time.

"Has he said why he did it?" Ash asked.

"No, he claims he's innocent," I said. "And there's some question whether he acted alone."

"What do they think?" Ari asked. "That there's a cult of vampire killers?" He sounded eager. I could see the dollar signs in his eyes.

"That's so bogus," Nate said. "That's just those right-wing religious nuts."

"I don't know," Ash said. "Can you really see Damion getting it together to do what they say he did? Like, he's so out to lunch he's lucky if he knows what day it is."

"If they're looking for a cult, this could be one of the hottest stories of the year," Salazar said. She and Kazacos smiled slyly at each other. "Like I said, you can't buy this kind of publicity."

I remembered Saturday night—Seaton's fervor, Prizer's suspicions. Or this kind of trouble, I thought.

34

AT THE PALO Alto police station Damion Wolfe is learning a lot about trouble. The police picked him up shortly before daybreak when he tried to sneak back into his house. He's been Mirandized and told he could have his mother and father with him, but he won't even speak to his parents and, to everyone's surprise, he's waived his Miranda rights.

That doesn't mean he's talking. So far, all they've gotten out of him is obscenities.

Prizer and Martin are playing good-cop-bad-cop, with Martin as the tough guy, steadily escalating the pressure on Wolfe. It's time for Prizer to go play Mr. Nice. As he enters the interrogation room, Martin is berating the kid. He stands over him, dominating him physically, his body language radiating threat.

Prizer is a bit surprised. He hasn't seen Martin in this role before. He's been on the receiving end of Martin's hostility, but now he's seeing a toughness he missed before.

They're pushing hard. The next few hours are key. Once the kid is arraigned, the parents will hire a lawyer, and that'll pretty well kill any chance they have of getting him to talk. If they're to get through to the kid, it has to be soon.

"Don't think 'cause you're underage, you'll get off," Martin warns Wolfe. "We'll be trying you as an adult. You know what that means? San Quentin. Not a nice place for a kid like you. Things happen there. . . ." He gives Prizer a quick glance, the sign that it's his turn.

"Ah, Lou, how about I take over here," Prizer says a bit awkwardly.

"How about you back off," Martin says angrily. Prizer knows it's all for show, set up to paint him as the protector, someone the kid will turn to, but he's taken aback by the force of Martin's challenge.

"Hey, Lou," he says in a conciliatory tone, "you're letting the kid get to you. They just made fresh coffee in the squad room. Why don't you get a cup?"

Martin gives the kid an evil look, then shakes his head in disgust. "Yeah, sure, let's see what you can do with him." He starts for the door, then turns back to the kid. "I'll be back. Meantime, you better be thinking on what life'd be like in Quentin."

When Martin is out, Prizer sits down opposite the kid and gives him a long look. The kid glares back defiantly, his features drawn into a surly expression. Prizer feels an instant distaste for him, with his slightly greasy, long, dark hair and pasty white skin. He's a piece of work, this kid, fits to a T the descriptions Prizer's heard in cult seminars.

He reminds himself that Wolfe is as much a victim as

Matt Demming. He didn't start out this way. Someone recruited him, introduced him to satanic rituals, probably ordered him to kill his former friend. Somewhere there are powerful adults who pull the strings, like puppeteers. Those are the people he wants. And only the kid can give them to him.

"Would you like a Coke or something?" he asks.

The kid just glares.

He shrugs. "We're going to be here for a while. I can get you a sandwich if you get hungry." He pauses, not really expecting a reaction yet. "I have to tell you it looks pretty bad for you. We found what we think is the murder weapon and a rag with Matt Demming's blood on it."

"I don't know anything about that shit," the kid explodes. "I didn't kill him. I didn't fuckin' kill him."

"So how do you think those things got in your back-yard?" Prizer asks, his voice neutral, no accusation, just a question.

The kid is silent.

"You had some interesting stuff in your room," Prizer says. "The black candles, the masks, the knife, and the pentagram on the floor." He watches closely for the kid's reaction to the mention of his satanic paraphernalia. The kid just shrugs.

"Where'd you get that stuff?"

"Store in San Francisco," the kid says grudgingly. "It's not illegal, you know."

"No, I know it's not. I was just curious. People usually use those things in a group, you know, like a club."

No answer.

"You part of a group?"

Still no answer. The kid is staring at the door, ignoring Prizer.

"Because I think maybe you were in a group, and maybe

the people in that group are setting you up to take the fall for them."

The kid turns slowly back toward Prizer, watching him with interest.

"I think these people figure that because you're a kid you're not smart enough to realize what they're doing. That you'll take the fall and keep your mouth shut." He pauses, then continues, "Maybe they told you that we can't try you as an adult, which isn't true, and they know that. Or maybe they threatened you, and you're afraid to tell us the truth."

"I ain't afraid of nothing," the kid says, but he has trouble making his voice match the words.

"We don't *have* to try you as an adult. You're seventeen. If you're tried as a juvenile, you go to a juvenile facility, not San Quentin, and you're out when you turn twenty-five. The record's sealed; no one knows about it. You get to start life over. If you cooperate with us, we can work with the D.A. to make that happen."

The kid leans forward. His expression has changed from surly to crafty.

I'm getting through to him, Prizer thinks, and feels a warm excitement, the feeling he gets when he's playing poker and picks up the card that completes a full house.

"I want to help with this," he says earnestly. "The way I see it, those other people are the ones who should be going to Quentin. You're just a kid. You should get a second chance."

The kid's considering it, he can tell.

"I'm getting thirsty. Think I'll get a Coke. You want anything?" he asks. "Soft drink, coffee?"

"I'll have a Seven-Up," the kid says.

"How about a sandwich? Turkey, ham, roast beef?"

"Ham."

Prizer goes out to get the food. Leaves the kid alone to consider his options.

Martin is waiting in the hall. "So?" he asks.

"I think we're close," Prizer says.

"Don't move too fast," Martin warns. Prizer nods and goes off for the drinks and sandwich.

Martin is left standing in the hall, feeling strangely ill at ease. He should be excited, especially if, as Prizer says, they're close to a confession. But the pain burns in his gut and he feels anything but excitement. It galls him to think that maybe he's letting his personal feelings toward Prizer color his professional instincts. He takes another stomach mint from the roll in his pocket.

Prizer is back with soft drinks and two sandwiches. Martin would have withheld food for much longer, but this is Prizer's show. And if he is close to getting a confession, the food will help cement the bond.

Back in the interrogation room, Prizer puts the drinks and sandwiches on the table, sits down, and takes a gulp of his Coke. He waits to see if the kid will say anything. The kid just unwraps the sandwich and starts eating.

"The way this works," Prizer says, "is, you help me with the investigation and I help you with the judge. We have to show that you cooperated."

The kid is studying his sandwich. He doesn't look at Prizer.

"The people who put you up to this, they're going to walk away from you. They'll leave you to take the fall."

"I ain't got nothin' to say," the kid snarls.

Prizer sighs heavily. It's time to give Martin another shot.

35

school situated belongs to the last person to see Matt
Demming alive. A number appears beneath her picture, and
viewers are asked to call the *Chronicle*, which is hosting the
game. Oh no. Chloe doesn't need this.

CHLOE LEARNS OF Damion Wolfe's arrest on the evening news. The "Vampire Killer" is the lead story.
Her new roommate-protector doesn't take the *Chronicle*, so
this is the first she's heard of how Matt Demming died. It's
not an easy story for anyone to hear; for Chloe it's like a fist
through the chest.

First, there's Matt's picture, not a very good one, then a
reporter at the Cactus Garden describing how he was lured
there and knocked unconscious. She listens in shock as the
dark-haired man with the microphone describes the two
wounds, simulating a vampire bite, through which Matt's
body was drained of blood.

Next, there's footage of the Baylands—a wooden walkway above marshy grass. The same dark-haired man tells
how the body was left here twenty-four hours later.

Then, there's a picture of Damion Wolfe, the weird Goth
kid from the game, and the news that he's been arrested.
The reporter describes how on the night of the murder, Matt
and Damion and other kids played a vampire role-playing
game, "a game that obviously got out of hand." Chloe
spaces out when he starts describing the parents' crusade
with their rally-turned-riot Saturday night, but her attention
is yanked back to the screen when her own picture appears
there. The smooth male voice explains that the police are
anxious to talk to Chloe Dorn, the sixteen-year-old high

school student believed to be the last person to see Matt Demming alive. A number appears beneath her picture, and viewers are asked to call if they have any information on her whereabouts.

Chloe looks anxiously at Tam, the girl who's taken her in. Serena told her the story, but Chloe fears she may change her mind about harboring a fugitive, now that Chloe's face is all over the television and papers. She watches for Tam's reaction. It's not easy to read.

Tam is very different from Serena. Self-contained, like a building without windows. There's no clue to what's inside. Solid like a building, too. Chloe finds that solidity comforting. She could use some of that herself.

Finally, Tam turns to her. "What a shitty way to go," she says. "You going home now that they've got the killer?"

Chloe swallows hard. "I . . . I'd like to think that over. I don't know why, but something still doesn't feel right."

"Take your time," Tam says. "I'm going out for pizza. You wanta come or you want me to bring you something when I come back?"

"I think I'll stay here," Chloe says. She has a lot of thinking to do.

Matt was alive when she left. He was alive. She might have been able to save him if only . . . If only what, she asks herself. If only you'd waited around to die with him? I did call 911, she reminds herself in her own defense. *They* could have saved him. They must not have listened to me.

She can't think about how he died. Or if he knew he was dying. If he suffered. No point in that, Liza says. None of it changes anything. The only thing that matters is to nail the killer.

Damion Wolfe. They've arrested Damion Wolfe. She should be relieved. They've got the killer. She's safe now. But she doesn't feel safe.

* * *

Chloe doesn't sleep well that night, not that she's been sleeping well before. But now her mind races on beyond her control. She fears nightmares, but they don't come. There's just the ceaseless chatter of her mind running on.

By morning, she's clearer on one thing. She knows why she still feels at risk. It's pretty simple, really. She doesn't believe that Damion Wolfe is Raptor.

If the police are right that Matt was killed by someone who thought he was a vampire, then Damion is their man. He's definitely crazy enough for that.

But Raptor isn't crazy.

Matt didn't think he was crazy and she doesn't think he's crazy. Not that way, anyhow.

And Raptor wants the computer and the source code. Why would Damion want that? What good would the source code do him? No, Raptor is not Damion Wolfe. He might be using Damion, but the person who planned Matt Demming's death is still out there.

Now the question is, what to do about that. How to flush him out. She could use his own plan against him, lure him to the spot where he planned to lure her, but she'd need help for that, and there's no one she can trust, not when the stakes are so high.

So she works out a fallback plan. It's not ideal, might not even work, but if it fails, she'll still be alive to try something else.

Each venture out requires her to decide who she'll be that day. Male or female. Grunge or punk. Shaved or wigged. With her picture all over, she goes for shaved, with dark eye shadow to mask the shape of her eyes and an exotic ear cuff to draw attention from her features. She wears baggy olive pants with a tight orange T-shirt. She practices letting her mouth droop open, decides it makes her look like a halfwit. Perfect. She's ready to hit the street.

It takes two transfers to get to Cyberworld, one of the

cafés that Molly's boyfriend suggested. She likes its cool industrial-chic lines. There are only two customers inside this morning. She goes straight to the coffee bar, orders a mocha, and asks about using the computers.

The girl behind the counter is only a little older than she is. If she's surprised by Chloe's appearance, she doesn't let on. She enthusiastically describes the setup, asks if Chloe wants help.

Chloe shakes her head, pays for thirty minutes of connect time. "Those the only computers?" she asks, indicating the ones near the door. They seem too exposed, and there's a geeky guy at one who keeps watching her.

"There's one in the back," the girl says, indicating a loungelike area at the rear of the building.

Chloe heads for the lounge. It's easy to log on. She connects to her server and picks up her mail. Breathes a sigh of relief that there's nothing more from Raptor.

First, she calls up Raptor's messages and forwards a copy of them to Molly's boyfriend, asking if he can figure out anything from them.

Her next e-mail is to Tony Torres. For the subject line, she types: *Game Time.* The message is short. It reads: *"Oh master of Satan's cult, your humble servant, Liza, has a suggestion. How about another game? Just to let the puritan bastards know they can't keep us down. Might be interesting to have a wake for Matt. He'd have liked that, I know."*

She's in the process of forwarding a second copy of Raptor's messages to the Palo Alto police with a note suggesting that they check whether Damion Wolfe was a good enough hacker to send it, when she spots the geeky guy from in front approaching. She quickly types: *"What use would Wolfe have for the source code? I don't think he could have done this alone,"* and hits the SEND button just as the geek closes in.

He's slender and only a few inches taller than she is, and

he looks about fourteen. Angry acne sores dot his face, matching the ruby stud he wears in one ear.

"Hi," he says, in a voice that cracks. "Need any help?"

"No," she replies coldly. Her look says, "Go away."

But he doesn't read looks. "You're new here, aren't you?" he says. He's between her and the door, and suddenly she starts to feel nervous, caged-in. She was planning to send e-mail to her mom via Andi, but that will have to wait. She needs to get out of here. Now.

But she also has to erase the personal information she typed in when she logged on. So she turns away and does that while he makes another awkward stab at conversation. It takes less than a minute, then she's on her feet headed for the door.

But he dodges in front of her. "Hey, where you going?" he asks. His voice is too anxious.

She tries to step around him. He blocks her again. "Can I buy you coffee?"

She moves left, he moves left. Her chest tightens with panic.

"Get away from me," she says loudly. "Just get away."

Now the girl at the counter realizes something's going on, and she hurries toward them. Finally, Chloe gives the geek a push and sprints for the door. The girl makes no attempt to stop her.

She runs down the hill. She doesn't see the dark blue van that narrowly misses hitting her or hear the driver yell. Her only thought is that she must keep running.

36

I MISSED CHLOE by three minutes. That's what the kid with the face like a pepperoni pizza said. "I tried to get her to have some coffee," he said. "But she got really weird on me and just took off. I couldn't stop her."

The girl behind the counter was no help. She'd never seen Chloe before. I wasn't at all sure she believed me when I explained that Chloe was the witness to a murder. It didn't really matter since our runaway wasn't coming back.

Too many near misses. She must be thoroughly spooked by now. Fear could make her turn to the police, but more likely she would just work harder at being Liza, and Liza would never go to the police.

I went back to the office with a tension headache squeezing my skull and a ugly mixture of dread, anxiety, and frustration churning in my gut.

The churning turned into a solid knot when I walked in the door and saw the look on my secretary's face. "A message from Chloe," Amy said, holding up a piece of paper.

I scanned the sheet and felt a chill spread through me. The killer had answered her challenge. He was after her. He promised safety, but he wanted the source code and the computer files, and to guarantee that he'd have the only copies, he'd have to kill Chloe.

I wanted to e-mail her immediately and warn her not to follow his instructions, to stay away from Arastradero

Lake, but she hadn't asked for advice. She'd asked for information, and only Jesse could provide that. Besides, after her experience at Cyberworld, she'd be spooked, and it was likely she'd wait awhile before risking e-mail again.

I checked the header. The sender was "Raptor@ finet.net." It was possible that the killer had stolen a password from someone using *Raptor* for a handle, but it was much more likely that he or she had chosen that name and established an account with that as the user name. I didn't know anything about Finet, the service provider, but the police should be able to get the account information from them. At least, we finally had something we could try to trace.

"You think she'll risk taking the computer to Arastradero Lake?" Amy asked anxiously.

"I hope not," I said. "She's a smart kid, but she could be pretty desperate by now. We should be able to get the cops to stake out that spot, but I'll do it myself if I have to."

"Not alone?" Amy asked, looking even more alarmed.

"No, Mom, not alone," I said. Amy is ten years younger than I am, but she fusses like an old lady.

I paged Jesse and waited for a call back.

He got back to me in less than an hour.

"I've met a guy who plays the vampire game in Palo Alto," he informed me. "A programmer at Sega. I told him I wanted to join a game down here, and he's promised to tell me the next time they're playing."

"Good work," I said. "With all the negative press, I'd think they'd lie low, but you never can tell. Molly's also staying in touch with her friend Andi, who's close to Chloe, so she should get word if there's a game happening."

"How's my new girlfriend doing?" he asked. "She staying out of trouble?"

"For the moment," I said. "What do you make of the messages I forwarded?"

"The killer sent them though Finet, which is a server in Finland that'll strip off your return address and substitute a handle. That's why they read, 'Raptor@finet.net.' Finet will know the name of the account that has the handle *Raptor*. So if he was careless enough to use his own account, the cops can probably trace him.

"We're not talking Swiss bank here. Finet cooperates with cops on important cases, so we could be in luck. That's the good news. The bad news is that if Raptor's sharp, he probably stole someone else's password and sent it from their account, in which case, he's untraceable."

"Will Stan Louvis know all this?"

"Oh yeah. He may even have had some dealings with Finet. Some drug dealers on the Peninsula tried to use it last year."

Jesse didn't have any more information for me. He was spending most of his days drinking Jolt Cola and playing computer games. "I've probably killed half a planet's worth of bad guys in the last week," he said. "We better wrap this case up before I die of malnutrition."

I forwarded Raptor's messages to Lou Martin, then headed for Palo Alto.

I got to the police department offices around two o'clock. Martin was in, but it took them a while to find him. He looked tired and even more rumpled than usual when he arrived at the front desk.

I followed him to his office, walking a bit behind him to confirm what I'd suspected. He wasn't exactly limping, but there was something slightly wrong with his walk.

"You feeling okay?" I asked, as we sat down.

"I feel like hell," he said. "I hate cases like this. They give me chronic indigestion."

"Easy to see why," I said. "The messages from Raptor can't have helped."

"They were sent before we arrested Wolfe, so they could have come from him."

"Could have," I said, "*if* he were a hacker and *if* he had a reason to want the laptop and the source code."

"He's not a hacker," Martin said, "but he could have learned to send anonymous e-mail from a friend. And as to why he wants the laptop, he may feel its files contain something that incriminates him."

"And the source code?"

"Who knows. He's a weird kid."

Martin was not in sharing mode. Even if Wolfe had talked, he wasn't likely to tell me, so I switched subjects. "Are you going to stake out Arastradero Lake?"

"Already have," he said.

"So you don't think Wolfe's a solo killer."

"I don't know. And when I don't know, I don't take chances." His expression was grim.

It matched my mood. I was glad the police were staking out Arastradero Lake. But with Raptor stalking Chloe, I couldn't sit on the sidelines waiting for something to happen.

Nate Sessler seemed to know Damion Wolfe as well as anyone, so I headed down to Mountain View to see him. The software store was empty of customers and to my surprise, the guy behind the counter was not Nate but Tony Torres, the game master. In a black T-shirt and jeans, he looked considerably less dramatic than the last time I'd seen him, but even in full daylight, he was a striking young man.

"Hey, it's the private eye," he said, when I came in. "I hear they arrested Damion."

"That's what I hear," I said. "What're you doing here?"

"Nate's working for Astra now. They're pushing to get

the game out and wanted him full-time. I needed some extra cash, so . . ." He spread his hands, letting the gesture finish his sentence.

"What do you think of Damion's arrest?" I asked. "You know him. You think he did it?"

"I don't really know the dude," he said. "But he's definitely weird, so yeah, I think he probably did it." He leaned his hip against the counter. His dark eyes watched my reactions.

"Any reason other than that he's weird?" I wanted to see if he'd tell me that he'd seen Damion leave with Matt.

Torres shrugged.

"I had the feeling he hardly knew Matt."

"Oh, no, they knew each other. I didn't think of it when I talked to you, but after they arrested Damion, I remembered that there was a time almost a year ago when Matt was really into the Goth scene. He wasn't playing the street game then, too busy working on *Cult*, but I used to see him from time to time, and at one point he told me how he'd hooked up with Damion and was going to Goth clubs in the city.

"He said the Goths manifested the dark side and he wanted that dark energy in the game. Said it really fed his creative juices to hang with them." His voice had grown softer and the tone conspiratorial as he talked. He punctuated his words with gestures.

"Could Damion, and maybe Matt, have been part of some sort of Goth cult?" I asked.

Torres shrugged. "Oh, sure. Matt'd really have gotten off on a secret cult, and I can see Damion joining up. There was a cult like that in the South someplace, killed a girl's mother." He drew his forefinger across his throat, and smiled.

I remembered the story. At the time, the so-called cult members had sounded like a bunch of alienated kids who'd committed the kind of violent crime that was all too common now. But with Matt Demming's murder, I had to reconsider my assumptions.

"Did he ever mention a cult?"

"No, just going to clubs. But there could have been a cult associated with one of the clubs."

"Does anyone else know about this?" I asked.

"Probably. If Matt told me, he'd have told other people, too. Why? Does Damion deny it?"

"I don't know. Have you told the police?"

He shook his head. "I don't have any more to do with the police than I have to. That guy, Prizer, he's out to shut down the game. I'm keeping a low profile. We all are."

When he said the part about the low profile, his voice changed slightly, and suddenly I was suspicious.

"No more street games?" I asked.

"Not right now. Not till things cool down."

I didn't quite believe him. It didn't make sense to continue the street game in the current climate, especially with Prizer out to get it. But Torres didn't act out of the same motives as other people. I had the feeling I'd had at the coffeehouse, that he viewed the world as his private movie set, and himself as the director. He might well stage a game just to see what would happen.

And for just that reason, I said, "So did you lie to the cops or to me?"

He looked surprised.

"Come on. You told me that Matt left with Chloe. You told them that he left with Damion and Chloe."

He smiled as if he were delighted to be caught in a lie. "You're good," he said. "But I'd hardly admit lying to the cops, especially to you."

I stopped at Astra on my way back to the city. If Matt Demming had been involved in the Goth scene, maybe someone at Astra would know. And though I was no longer working for Kazacos, I figured he and his crew would still answer my questions.

If anything the activity level there was even more intense than it had been the day before. Kazacos was in his office yelling into the phone. Grif was working at his computer. In a newly assembled cubicle, Nate was sketching something on a drawing pad. And in Matt Demming's cubicle, I could just make out Ash's wild hair bouncing up and down as he banged on the keyboard of Matt's computer.

I started with Ash. I had to speak to him twice before I could grab his attention from the line of code he was typing, and when he looked up, he seemed confused, almost as if he didn't know where he was.

"You're the private eyeball," he said. I noticed that he'd stuck a couple of phone books on the seat of the chair. He still rocked and twitched like a piece of kinetic sculpture. The wild hair was now orange.

"Are you taking Matt's place?" I asked.

He nodded enthusiastically. "Sure am. I am now Ari's lead programmer." He grinned like a happy fourth-grader. "We've got to re-create that source code for the next version of *Cult*."

"Congratulations."

"Thanks. I'm really busy now. Do you need something?"

"Just one thing," I said. "Do you remember if Matt ever went to Goth clubs, maybe with Damion Wolfe and his friends?"

He rocked a bit more slowly as he considered it. "Not that I know of," he said at last. "Course, I only started hanging with him these last six months, so he could have before that. I never saw Matt with Damion."

I moved on to Nate. When he turned to greet me, I had the eerie feeling of being watched by two pairs of eyes. Nate smiled, but his bat tattoo glowered at me over the tattered, cutout neckline of his gray sweatshirt. The tops of the bat's wings were etched just below his collarbone.

When I asked about Matt going to Goth clubs with Damion, he gave me the same answer as Ash. And the same caveat that he hadn't seen much of Matt until recently. "We lost touch for a while," he said, "so I don't know what he was up to before he started LARPing again. But I can definitely see him doing the clubs. Could definitely happen. Matt liked to try weird stuff. The Goths would have appealed to him."

I got my answer where I least expected it, from Grif. He began nodding even before I finished my question. "Yeah. I remember that," he said. "Must have been back in the early days, maybe around the time we were working on the third level of *Cult*. He was into evil, what he called the dark side. He figured the game would be stronger if that were more of an element. So for a month or two, he hung out with a bunch of Goths, and I think he met them through someone in the street game."

He was holding the pencil he'd been drawing with, and now he doodled idly as we talked. "But that was a long time ago, eight or nine months at least. He was done with them long ago."

Demming might have been done with the Goths, but that didn't mean they were done with him.

37

Lou Martin has his own questions about Chloe Dorn, and they have brought him back to her high school. He knows the school well, both as a parent and a cop. Over the last week, he's gotten to know it even better, spending hours talking to kids and teachers. Today he's on his way to see Carolyn Stark, the computer teacher.

He walks down a hall smelling of chalk dust and sweat with a hint of old sneakers and the faint peppermint of bathroom disinfectant. School is out and the hall is rapidly emptying of teenagers. Most seem to ignore him, but a few watch warily. They can tell he's a cop. Or maybe he's a bit paranoid. Maybe they think he's just someone's dad.

He finds room 216, the computer room. Carolyn Stark is waiting for him. She's a motherly-looking woman in her fifties, with gray hair and glasses and an impish smile. Her deep blue sweater picks up the color of her eyes; they have an impish quality, too.

Martin sits in a chair that reminds him of his own school days. The computers that surround him testify to the changing times, but the chair with its desk arm offers a comforting familiarity.

"You know Chloe Dorn," he says.

"Yes," she says. She doesn't remind him that she's already talked to another police officer about Chloe.

"I need to know if she was a hacker," he says.

"Well, I don't exactly know what you mean by that," Stark answers. "She was very good at programming, very proficient, but I don't think she was breaking into other systems, if that's what you mean."

"That's not what I mean," Martin says. He feels like he's trying to speak a foreign language, and his vocabulary is sorely limited. "I mean, would she know how to send e-mail so that you couldn't trace it?"

She considers the question. "I doubt it," she says at last. "Mind you, I don't know how to do that, so I don't know how much skill it requires. But it's not something a kid at Chloe's level would probably know how to do."

"Do you have kids who would?"

"Maybe one or two, though I can't be sure. Neither of them is in the group your people have been asking about."

"How about Ash Klein? Do you know him?"

"Oh yes, Ash was one of my students a couple of years ago before he dropped out. Now, Ash would probably know how to do that."

There is a tap at the door and a girl in jeans and a black T-shirt sticks her head in before Stark can respond.

"Oops, sorry," the girl says, and disappears.

"Ash was already beyond me when he arrived as a freshman," Stark says. "He liked to hang out in my room because of the equipment but there wasn't much I could teach him, not about computers, anyway. It's a real pity he dropped out. There's a lot he needed to learn that he won't get in independent study."

"He works for Astra now," Martin offers. "It's the company Matt Demming worked for."

"I know," Stark says, "and in a few years he'll probably be earning two or three times what you or I make." She catches herself and adds, "There's nothing wrong with that; he's a first-rate talent. But he's also a child, and no one seems to remember that."

"You mean he's emotionally immature?" Martin asks.

"Of course, he's emotionally immature," she says impatiently. "He's a seventeen-year-old male. I'm not suggesting he has criminal tendencies. I was commenting on the state of society more than the state of Ash Klein's psyche."

"I'm not sure I understand."

"A kid like Ash, bright and technologically sophisticated, is still just a kid. He needs guidance." She leans forward in her chair. "In a traditional society young people are initiated by adults. They recognize that the adults possess the skills they need to survive. In our world some of the most prized skills don't come from adults but from peers, because adults can't keep up with technological change. So you've got fourteen-year-old hackers with the ability to do great harm, and they've acquired that skill without the moral influence of adults." She stops and looks embarrassed. "I'm lecturing again," she says. "My kids hate that. Sorry."

"No, go on," Martin says. "I need to understand these kids. This is useful."

"Well, that's pretty much it. That and the fact that so many of these kids, and I'm not talking about just the computer kids, have very little contact with adults. I don't know Damion Wolfe, but I'd bet money that his parents are like so many that I see. They love their kids but they don't have a lot of time for them."

"What about the kids who're in the vampire game?" Martin asks. "You know a number of them. In fact, you probably know some of the older ones. How about Nate Sessler?"

"I knew both him and Matt when they were here. Matt was a lot like Ash, brilliant and quirky, and not at all interested in studying anything but computers. He and Nate were inseparable. They called themselves the dynamic duo. Nate was a good programmer, but not outstanding, and it was the same with his art—good, but not truly original."

"And Chloe Dorn?"

"Chloe's really a very sweet girl. Shy and a bit timid, but very sweet. I don't believe for a minute that she had anything to do with Matt's murder."

Martin is inclined to agree with Stark's assessment of Chloe's innocence, but as to shy and timid, boy, has she missed the call on that one.

Martin gets away from the high school by three-forty and pulls into the underground garage five minutes before the four o'clock task force meeting. The brass discourages parking here since there are a limited number of stalls, but no way is Martin going to brave the mob of reporters who have turned the whole civic center into a media encampment. The Public Information officer is holding regular press briefings, but there's still a feeding frenzy every time a member of the task force is spotted.

He hurries upstairs and stops by his office to pick up his papers and check his voice mail. The first message is the familiar voice of Catherine Sayler informing him that Matt Demming knew Damion Wolfe better than she'd realized. As she explains the connection she's discovered, Martin swears under his breath. How does that damn woman do it? It took his team days of work to come up with the fact that Demming had frequented Goth clubs with Wolfe.

Martin heads for the conference room. Ahead of him in the hall he sees Reverend Seaton. Next to him, George Prizer looks like a poodle with a St. Bernard. Seaton has been invited to attend the task force meeting. It's not Martin's choice, but the chief's decided that Seaton will be less of a threat if he's involved.

The arrest of Damion Wolfe should have calmed things down, but reporters don't give up easily with a crime this sensational, especially not with people like Seaton suggesting that a cult of killers is still on the loose.

Martin ducks into the rest room to take a drink of Maalox. The pills no longer work. The pain in his gut is constant now, sharper some times than others, but a constant burning.

He's the last one into the conference room. He always starts the meetings. Today he begins by introducing Seaton and asking if he'd like to address the group.

"Thank you very much," the reverend responds, "but I don't want to take time from your valuable work."

"You do understand, sir, that everything we say here is completely confidential. It cannot be repeated or discussed outside this room," Martin says. If this works, he thinks, it just might shut the guy up. If it doesn't, well, he isn't planning on revealing anything too sensitive.

Seaton promises discretion, and thanks the task force for allowing him to attend.

"Nothing new to report on the Wolfe kid," Martin announces. "He's not talking."

"He's afraid," Prizer says. "I think he's scared of what the others will do to him."

"He'd do better to worry about what we'll do to him," Martin says. "We'll keep leaning on him. What have we got on physical evidence?"

"We've been back over the Wolfes' house, the shed, yard, cars," Atkins reports. "I've sent a zillion samples to the lab. No matches to anything on the body yet."

"Any more blood evidence?"

Atkins shakes his head. "Not at the house, and the blood on the barrel cactus isn't the same type as Wolfe's, so we can't tie him in that way. The M.E. didn't get much in the way of fibers off the body, and nothing we did get matches to anything we've collected so far."

"Well, keep on it. There's got to be something there. Any decent defense attorney'll claim that the syringe and bloody rag were planted. We need other evidence to counter that. How about interviews?"

The bike cops have been interviewing everyone who knows Damion Wolfe. Most aren't too surprised by his arrest, but none report incriminating conversations. If the kid bragged about his exploits, he didn't do it with anyone willing to help the police.

Martin switches topics and brings up Chloe Dorn's e-mail message. Everyone in the room has received copies of it, except for Seaton, and Martin passes a copy to him.

"I've contacted Finet, no response yet, but I think they'll cooperate," Louvis reports. "This could be our big break."

"I still don't understand where the source code fits in all this," Atkins of bike patrol says. "If the crime was planned weeks before, Wolfe couldn't have known it'd be stolen. And why would he want it anyhow?"

Reverend Seaton clears his throat. "I think I may have an answer to that. I think it's what they call a red herring, something intended to divert our attention. You seem to assume that Chloe Dorn is telling the truth. I doubt that. It pains me to say it but I think she was also a member of this cult, and that she's invented this message from the supposed killer."

Louvis attempts to explain that Chloe couldn't have just made up the e-mail message. "She would've had to establish an account with Finet, then used it to send the Raptor message to herself. It's possible, but it'd take time and a credit source."

"She's not working alone," Seaton says. "She'll have plenty of money."

"If she's in a cult," Martin says. "We don't have any indication of that."

"And we won't have if we don't investigate that possibility," Prizer says. His voice betrays more emotion than he'd intended.

"And what would you propose we do?" Martin asks, keeping his own voice even.

"I think we need to take a close look at whether other people connected to this case might be involved in Satanism. We know Wolfe took Demming to Goth clubs in the city. We ought to be checking on those."

Martin has talked with the SFPD about the clubs. They seem weird but harmless enough. Still, maybe Prizer'll turn up something he missed. "Sure, go for it," he says. He knows he doesn't sound sufficiently enthusiastic, but he's been down that route and hit nothing but dead ends.

Martin waits while the others leave the room. A wave of exhaustion sweeps over him.

He looks up from his papers to see Thomas Seaton standing over him. He automatically rises, unwilling to give the other man the advantage. "What can I do for you, Reverend Seaton?" he asks.

"I thought perhaps you and I might talk a bit."

Martin offers him a chair.

"I'm curious why you refuse to consider the possibility that you're dealing with a satanic cult."

"I don't," Martin objects. "It's just that I don't assume that this is cult-related. I try not to assume anything in a murder investigation."

"Do you believe in Satan, Detective Martin?"

"What I believe has nothing to do with this," Martin says coldly. Seaton's manner irritates him. His gaze is too direct, his speech too commanding.

"It has everything to do with this," Seaton says. "Do you believe that Satanism exists?"

"I believe that there are people who believe in Satanism, and those people are capable of committing crimes just like everybody else."

"But you don't believe in Satan."

"I don't discuss my personal beliefs in my professional capacity," Martin says, barely able to control his anger.

"I just wanted to point out that we *both* have our beliefs," Seaton says smoothly, "and that just as you fear I may be blinded by mine, I worry lest you are influenced by yours."

Martin does not reply and they stare at each other a moment, like two cats on a fence, each unwilling to break eye contact first.

Then Seaton looks down at his hands and back up at Martin. "You think I'm just a kook, don't you? A loony cracker preacher who sees Satan in an innocent child's game. Well, let me tell you that that 'innocent game' killed my nephew.

"I didn't pay much attention when my sister worried over how much time he spent in the basement with his D & D buddies. Just thought it was a phase, something he'd grow out of. Then one night he wrote a long letter to those same buddies, signed it with the name of the character he played, took his daddy's hunting rifle, and blew his brains out."

Seaton's voice is harsh; his eyes moist. Martin has seen the same searing anguish in the faces of the parents of other kids who've committed suicide and once in the father of a teenager who killed his girlfriend. A part of them replays the days and hours before the fatal moment, searching for the point where they might have stopped the clock, changed the outcome. The pain is never over.

38

IT'S A BAD sign when you read the morning newspaper to get news on your case. But that's what I was reduced to, since I wasn't getting a lot of information from any-place else.

This morning's installment was an interview with the Reverend Thomas Seaton. Where in the past he'd managed to assume the tone of an academician commenting on the danger of role-playing games, this time he sounded like a down-home preacher. He warned that Satan walks among us, looking for weak souls to do his bidding. He sounded the familiar theme that those who marketed role-playing games and other "paraphernalia of evil" were Satan's recruiters. And he warned that those who turned a blind eye to this evil were accessories to it.

He didn't name Ari Kazacos as a merchant-servant of evil or Lou Martin as an accessory, but his comments left little doubt of his judgment of them. I probably didn't rate too highly in his book, either. None of that was a big sur-prise. But his characterization of Chloe was, and it infuri-ated me. He described her as a "lost sheep," and used her as an example of the terrible price of being led astray by sa-tanic games. While he professed to mourn for her soul, he seemed to care little for what happened to her body. The aw-ful fear that disturbed my sleep, and Martin's as well, I sus-pected, was missing from Seaton's commentary.

"This guy is a lot more concerned with Satan than he is with Chloe Dorn," I said in disgust, handing the article to Peter.

"He sucks," Molly said around a mouthful of toast. "He is so fu ... ed." Lately, she'd been trying to get around my injunction against foul language by dropping middle consonants.

Peter read the article through, then handed it to Molly. I reminded her that she had exactly eight minutes until she needed to catch the bus for school.

We got Molly out the door with about twenty seconds to spare. "I don't know how it can take so much energy just to get one teenager off to school," I said, as I poured a second cup of coffee for Peter and myself. "I feel as if I've already put in a couple of hours of work."

"You have," he said. "I'm hitting nothing but dead ends with Chloe." His voice was softer than usual, and there was a flatness that suggested resignation. "I've found a couple of kids in Berkeley who saw her last week, but none of them know where she is now. No one on the street here has seen her. She's not following any of the usual runaway patterns and she doesn't seem to have hooked up with anyone from the other role-playing games."

"She's still close enough to San Francisco to send e-mail from here. At least she was on Tuesday," I said.

"I wonder what she thinks of this," Peter said, tapping the *Chronicle* article.

"I doubt that Liza will like being called a 'lost sheep,'" I said.

39

"**T**HE LOST SHEEP" logs on to a computer at the library to continue her correspondence with one of the "evil influences" the reverend so deplores. After her experience at Cyberworld, she's edgy and nervous, checks over her shoulder every few minutes.

> *From: Tony Torres < gamemstr@hooked.net >*
> *Subject: Re: Game Time*
> *To: Chloe Dorn < bonemeal@silval.net >*
> *Date: 10 Sept 21:55:14*

Liza—

The blood of your sire runs strong in your veins, little one. I'm already planning our next adventure. A wake, yes, but not for Matt, for Michael. With Matt's death, Michael dies, too. So since Michael is of the game, we'll honor him in it. You could give the eulogy, if you'll come out of hiding.

The players will be told that Michael was killed between the last game and this one and that Damion's character, Death, has been seized by the Sheriff, but it's known that he didn't act alone. Since Michael was a very old and very powerful vampire, his death must be avenged. The purpose of the game is to catch the killer or killers.

I'll divide the players into suspects and innocents (you may have some suggestions there). Each innocent will be

*given one clue incriminating one suspect—Michael's re-
mains were found on X's territory, something of Y's found
near the remains, Z was seen with Michael just before the
killing, etc. And we'll let it go from there and see what
happens.*

   How about Saturday night?

                                                      Tony

From: Chloe Dorn < bonemeal@silval.net >
Subject: Re: Game Time
To: Tony Torres < gamemstr@hooked.net >
Date: 11 Sept 12:24:17

Tony—
   *Fabu. Saturday's good. I have some clues I'd like in-
serted in the game. I'll send them to you. I don't care how
you use them, but you should use the exact wording because they're the words of the real killer, taken from
Matt's computer files. They're the clues the killer used in
his psycho game with Matt.*
   *I'd love to give the eulogy but I'm on the run till I know
they've got the killer in jail, and I'm not sure of that yet.
So how about I possess Andi and she acts in my stead?*

                                                      Liza

From: Tony Torres < gamemstr@hooked.net >
Subject: Eulogy
To: Chloe Dorn < bonemeal@silval.net >
Date: 11 Sept 18:23:06

Liza—
   *Andi's cool. You can send me what you want to go in
the eulogy, and I'll add some stuff that ought to mess with
some minds. Let the games begin!*

                                                      Tony

40

Our OTHER CLIENTS' problems seemed mundane compared to the Chloe Dorn case, but they weren't mundane to the clients, so I spent a good part of Thursday on catch-up. My mind kept sneaking back to Chloe as I tried to figure out some way to find her.

Just before noon, Jesse called. "Something's up," he said. "James, the geek I'm hanging with, says there's a game set for Saturday night."

"A street game?"

"That's right. Very secret. No one outside is supposed to know, but James just couldn't wait to tell me. The game's in honor of Demming, and there'll be some kind of service since his character's been killed. I've been working on James to see if he can sneak me in."

"So Torres lied to me," I said. "Probably wasn't the first time."

"James admires him, but he's also a bit intimidated by him. Don't take any chances with the guy."

"Do I ever take chances?"

Jesse's laughter was a bit too hearty.

I was furious at Torres, but also excited by the possibility that Chloe might show up at the game. She might even have been in contact with the game master.

That possibility made it worth a trip to Mountain View.

Tony Torres was at the software store where I expected

him to be. He was dressed in black, as usual. I wondered if he was ever offstage. Before he could say hello, I lit into him. "You lied to me."

He looked startled for a second, then like an actor shifting into a role, he smiled and said, "I don't know what you mean."

"I know there's a game Saturday night," I said. "I want to know what else is going on. And I don't want any bullshit. You are about two minutes away from a nasty confrontation with the Palo Alto police."

Mention of the police shook his facade. "I'm not doing anything illegal," he protested.

"No one believes Damion Wolfe acted alone," I said. "They're still looking for accomplices, and there are plenty of people who're convinced that they have a satanic cult in their own backyard. You are likely to be their first choice for grand Satanist."

"Hey." He held up his hands in protest. "It's just a game. Anyone with any sense understands that."

"I wouldn't count on it," I said grimly. "I'm not convinced of your innocence, and I'm more sympathetic than the cops'll be."

"This is crazy. I haven't done anything wrong. There's not a shred of evidence against me. You're just trying to scare me."

I was, and from the expression on his face and the pitch of his voice, I was succeeding. "Things are getting a little crazy out there," I said in a more conciliatory tone. "You're going to need all the friends you can get. I can't see you risking a game right now without a very good reason. I want to know what's going on."

He studied me for a moment, then he said, "Supposing something was going on, would you tell the police?"

"Depends on what the something is," I said. "If it had to do with Chloe, I might prefer to deal with it myself."

"What do you mean?"

"I need to talk to Chloe. I'm not going to force her to go home, but I need to talk to her. I wouldn't turn her over to the police."

He didn't say anything for a while, and his silence told me what I wanted to know. Now, I waited to see if he'd lie or tell some version of the truth.

"Chloe wanted the game," he said at last. "She's not playing. Liza is going to possess a character played by another girl. The theme of the game is the search for the vampire who killed Matt's character."

" 'To catch the conscience of the king,' " I said.

"*Hamlet*. Right?"

"Right. He used a play to catch a killer, and everyone ended up dead."

He nodded and his expression was serious. "We just thought we'd watch how people reacted, see who came and who didn't, if anyone acted weird. I'm not on some superhero trip, I'll tell the police if we learn anything."

"Is Chloe going to be there?"

"She didn't say. She won't be in the game."

"Aren't you worried about the police busting the game?"

"We're not doing anything illegal," he said again. "We have as much right to be on the street as anyone else."

"They could still put enough uniforms around where you're playing to scare everyone off."

"Yeah, but the streets are really crowded on Saturdays when it's warm. There are hundreds of people, lots of them our age; we won't be so easy to pick out."

"Tony," I said, letting my exasperation show, "you're missing the point here. This is a murder case, a very high-profile murder case. The cops know you guys; the minute they see two or three of you together, they'll be all over you."

He sighed, then nodded. "I guess."

"Believe it," I said. "The only way you're going to play this game is if we can convince the cops to let you do it. I might be able to help with that, but I have to know everything that's going down."

Everything turned out to be more than I'd expected. The game scenario, the eulogy Chloe'd written for Matt's character, and some quotes from Raptor's messages to Demming. I skimmed the messages and eulogy and had Torres take me through the game scenario step by step. Then he made copies of everything, and I took the originals.

"I'll call you after I talk with the police," I said, as I left.

He nodded, but he looked like he was already regretting his decision to cooperate.

I made my own copies of the papers Torres had given me before I went to see Lou Martin. I'd convinced the game master that I could intervene with the police, but that had been a bit of role-playing on my part. Getting Lou Martin to go along with my plan was a long shot.

By the time I reached the police department I'd decided that it was too much of a long shot. The game was our best chance to catch Chloe; I couldn't risk having Martin thwart it. I needed to see him to find out if the task force had traced the Finet e-mail account and to learn what I could about the Goth club scene, but I wouldn't risk telling him about the game.

Martin was in a meeting when I arrived and I had to wait almost forty-five minutes before he could see me. That gave me plenty of time to go over Raptor's messages. They began with a challenge, one warrior to another, to a battle of wits. The first offered Demming a puzzle based on events in *Cult of Blood* and promised that if he solved it, he could pose a puzzle for Raptor. A series of challenges followed as each player solved one puzzle and posed a new one for his opponent.

What struck me was the shift in tone that occurred after the first three exchanges. Both players wrote in a kind of faux-medieval parlance that included boasts and insults, threats and challenges. Testosterone dialect. But the level of aggression grew, and the playful quality in Raptor's messages disappeared after the fourth message.

Demming, used to the hyperbole of role-playing, probably missed it. Too bad. Had he paid attention to the escalating anger, even hatred, in those messages, he'd never have gone to the Cactus Garden that night.

41

ONE LOOK AT Lou Martin told me that there hadn't been any breakthrough in the case. Every line in his face seemed to have deepened, and he looked like he'd aged ten years in just a few days.

"I take it that the e-mail message was a dead end," I said, as I took the chair across from his desk.

"Finet gave us the account information. It belongs to a sophomore at Stanford, no connection to Demming. She's a French major who's barely computer-literate, and she was at home in Oregon the weekend Demming was killed."

"So you figure the password was stolen."

He nodded.

"Damn," I said, "I don't imagine Reverend Seaton's crusade is making things any easier."

"No, it's not," Martin said, his voice tight. "The man is

now suggesting that maybe the reason we're not making progress is that there are Satanists in high places sabotaging the investigation."

"You?"

"He hasn't come right out and said it, but that would be the inference."

"Surely no one's taking that seriously."

"Probably not, but it's not making matters easier."

I wondered why Martin was being so candid with me. It wasn't like him to volunteer that kind of information. As if he'd read my mind, he said, "I'm telling you this because if they're looking for Satanists, you could be on the list. Prizer has been asking about you; someone's sure to have told him about the Wyte case."

"But I was the good guy there," I objected. The Wyte case was a high-profile murder I'd helped Martin solve.

"Well, it looks that way. But if you assume that Satanists are incredibly clever people who can arrange killings without being caught, a private investigator who's been involved in several homicides might be a prime suspect."

I started to protest that the whole idea was crazy, but crazy depends on who's calling the shots, and I could see how Martin's logic made a twisted kind of sense. "Thanks for the warning."

"You've been straight with me, and better at keeping your mouth shut than some people who are supposed to be on my team."

"We're both working for the same goal," I said. "I'd like to think we can trust each other, but I don't trust Prizer."

"He means well," Martin said, not sounding very convincing.

I reconsidered my decision not to tell Martin about the game. He would be a valuable ally if I could get him to cooperate. Without his help, there was a good chance that the police would stumble across the game while it was in session and bust it before I found Chloe.

"I think I have a chance to make contact with Chloe Dorn," I told Martin, "but it depends on there not being any police around."

"I can't make any promises," he said.

"Suppose there were another vampire game," I said. "one that was of particular interest to Chloe. Would you be willing to keep your people away from it, if I promised to try to convince Chloe to come in or to meet you someplace?"

Martin considered. Normally, he'd have wanted to run the show, but with the task force involved, that would mean dealing with Prizer and the danger that Seaton would get word of the game.

"There'd be hell to pay if Seaton found out we'd let the game continue."

"Might be worth it to get Chloe to cooperate. She's the key to the case."

He nodded slowly and kept his eyes on me while he thought it through. "Okay," he said at last. "Tell me about it."

"There's a game set for Saturday night. Chloe suggested it, and she's supplying some clues." I handed him the papers I'd gotten from Torres and told him what I knew about the game.

"I figure Chloe'll be there," I continued, "probably in disguise and probably in hiding. We'll try to get Jesse in as one of the gamers. Since Chloe may have seen Peter and me when we were looking for her in Berkeley, we'll need disguises. I think we'll join your local homeless for the night."

Martin nodded, but not necessarily in agreement. Finally, he said, "We'd have to let the bike cops in on it. They know the gamers and they'd call it in as soon as they saw three or four of them together. Then, there are a couple of beat cops I'd have to tell."

"The more people who know, the greater the chance of a leak," I reminded him.

"Hey, it's my neck that's on the line here," he said. "If I wait until the beginning of the shift to tell them, they won't have a chance to talk to anyone else. Especially if Prizer is in San Francisco checking out Goth clubs."

"So you'll do it?"

He nodded, his expression as grim as I'd seen it.

42

GEORGE PRIZER PICKS up a pile of photographs and lays them out on his desk as if he were playing some sort of card game. There are thirty-six photos, each showing a different individual. The pictures have a casual snapshot quality; their subjects are caught walking down the street or emerging from doorways. The faces are not as clear as he'd like. It's hard to get crystal-clear pictures with a telephoto when you can't use a tripod. But they are clear enough.

Twenty-six of the photos are of the people directly involved in the Demming case; the other ten are shots of random individuals, included to test the honesty of an identification. He'd planned to show them to Lou Martin and explain his plan, but after yesterday's task force meeting and this morning's conversation with Tom Seaton, he's changed his mind.

Until now, he's given Martin the benefit of the doubt, accepting his skepticism about satanic cults as the product of naïveté. But slowly he's come to suspect a more sinister cause. At the cult crime seminar the presenters warned that many cult members were community leaders, some even in law enforcement.

It isn't too surprising that a Satanist would be attracted to police work. It's an ideal cover. And the homicide detail offers the perfect position for gathering information and covering up the cult's crimes.

Prizer has wrestled with this question for days, fearing that his suspicions are a form of paranoia. But watching Martin deflect attention from the satanic clubs of San Francisco and focus instead on arcane computer issues has made those suspicions more credible. And now that Seaton has voiced the same doubts, he knows he can't dismiss the possibility.

He suspects that one reason they haven't made progress with Damion Wolfe is that Martin is sabotaging the interrogation. They are seldom in the room at the same time, and there have been several times when he knew he was close to breaking through to the kid, only to find Wolfe's resistance renewed after Martin's time with him.

He's still not convinced of Martin's complicity, but he does know that whether the man is a Satanist or just a tool of Satan, he is hindering the investigation, and it will be necessary to work around him. He's fairly sure that the cult must include at least a few of the people connected to the case. The trick is to find out who they are.

He studies the picture of an attractive blond-haired woman who is locking the door of a blue Volvo. Catherine Sayler. The private investigator. A pushy woman, the type who'd bite your balls off and eat them for dinner. She's always a step ahead of them, knows too much, is involved in the case from too many angles. And now that he knows of her past, that she's been involved in other murder cases, he's moved her up on his suspect list.

Prizer gathers up the photos and returns them to their

envelope. Time to drive to juvenile hall and have a little chat with Damion Wolfe.

The kid shuffles into the interview room with the same sullen expression he's worn since he was arrested. His stringy dark hair hasn't been combed, and his skin is the color and consistency of white paste.

Prizer asks the kid if he wants his lawyer present.

"Fuck 'im," the kid replies. He doesn't like the lawyer any better than he likes the cops.

"So you're willing to talk to me without him?" Prizer prompts, just to get it clear. He is still the good cop. He brings the kid a candy bar and a magazine, asks how he's doing, if he needs anything. The kid is as unresponsive as ever.

"They're going to try you as an adult," Prizer says, sounding sorrowful. "I've tried to stop them, but the D.A. says that if you won't help us, he can't help you."

The kid just stares at the table.

"Are you afraid to talk?" Prizer asks. "Afraid of what the others will do to you?"

"I'm not afraid of nothin'," the kid says, still staring at the table.

"We can protect you," Prizer says. "I know that you think the cult is very powerful. They've probably told you that they can get you anyplace, but that's not true. You give me names, and I'll put them away where they can't hurt you."

The kid is silent.

"I worry about a kid like you in a maximum security prison. You think you're tough, but it's full of tough guys. Bad things happen to kids like you." He doesn't need to define "bad things"; Martin's been explicit about that. "That's why I want you tried as a juvenile."

The kid looks up at him and he can see he's getting through to him. "What would I have to tell you?" he asks.

"You'd have to tell us about the others. The cult members. I promise we can protect you from them."

"I don't know any names," the kid says. "I never heard their names."

Excitement surges through Prizer's body, almost propelling him out of his chair. He realizes too late that it must show on his face, so he doesn't try to hide it. "That's okay. I'll work with you to figure out the names. Your willingness to help is what we need."

"They always held the meetings in really dark places, so it was hard to see, and nobody said their name."

"Tell me about it," Prizer says. "Tell me about the gatherings."

Once the kid starts talking, the story pours out. Groups of people in black robes meeting at the dark of the moon, ritual sex, drugs, black masses. A few details shock even Prizer.

"Did they sacrifice any animals?"

"Oh yeah, kittens and puppies, sheep. But no humans," the kid adds quickly. "I never saw a human sacrifice."

"What happened to Matt Demming?"

"I . . ." The kid stutters, hesitates, then swallows and plunges on. "I don't remember, honest I don't. They gave me something to drink, and, like, I don't remember what happened after that."

"Who was there? Who took you?"

The kid looks wary again. Prizer's intensity scares him, so the cop calms his voice. "I may be able to help you," he says in a softer tone. "I have some photos. Maybe you'll recognize some of the people."

He lays the photos out in front of Wolfe, watching the kid's reactions as he puts each picture down. The kid is restless, anxious. He doesn't seem to know what to do with the pictures.

When they're all on the table, Prizer urges him to study them, to tell him if anyone looks familiar. The kid takes a long time, and he becomes more agitated as he looks at the pictures.

"What happens if I point someone out?" he asks. "Do I get out of jail? Do you put them in jail?"

"I'll start investigating them, gathering evidence. When I've got proof of their guilt, I can arrest them. They'll never know that you identified them. But the D.A. will know, and he'll go easy on you."

Wolfe nods. In his agitation, his head continues to bob, becoming a mannerism rather than a gesture. Finally, he points to two photos. "I might have seen these two at gatherings," he says. "Can't be sure. It was always dark, and the night Matt died everyone was in robes and hoods."

Prizer sweeps the other photos aside, leaving only the two that Wolfe indicated. The photos are of Catherine Sayler and Ari Kazacos.

43

ON A WARM fall Saturday night Palo Alto is full of people. Street musicians fill the air with music—Peruvian pipes on one corner, steel drums on another, students singing harmony down the block. Young couples stroll or settle into tables at sidewalk cafés; families queue up at the ice cream store, college students head for the brew pubs.

At a back table in the pizza parlor, almost a dozen young people dressed in dark colors crowd around a table where

Tony Torres makes final preparations for the game that most have been forbidden to play.

He hands each player a copy of *The Kindred Times*, a newsletter he produces for the game. This edition carries the headline, CLAN LEADER MURDERED; DIABLERIE SUSPECTED. An article announces the death of Michael, head of the Toreador clan, who was found drained of blood and spirit. The Sheriff has proclaimed it a case of *diablerie*, the killing of one vampire by another who seeks to steal his victim's power by drinking his blood. A second article tells of the arrest of Death, who is being held by the Sheriff, pending trial before the Council. It reports that the Sheriff suspects that Death had an accomplice and that at least one other *diabolist*, or murderer, is still at large. The Council has ordered a full investigation.

At another table three male tech-heads, two of them regulars of the game and a third, an African-American who appears to be in his early twenties, leaf through well-worn books and carry on their discussion in lowered tones.

"I played a great Malkavian last game," one reg says, referring to his character's clan. "Completely insane. I had this inferiority complex; I never believed I was wacky enough."

The other tech-head interrupts. "If your character's gonna be an assistant to the Prince of Chicago, you'll want some offensive mental powers, too. Dread gaze or something, just to keep the peace."

The African-American checks his character sheet. "No, I want him to be a sneaky bastard, the kind who sends you taunting e-mail from your own address, you know?"

They all laugh softly.

From the game master's table a slender blond youth, whose efforts at growing a beard have only succeeded in making his chin look malformed, watches the tech-heads.

"Tony," he complains, "who the fuck's the new guy? I thought you said no outsiders tonight."

"He's okay," Torres says. "He's a friend of James's. He played in the Seattle game and I told him he could join us."

"But," the kid whines, "not tonight. Tonight's special 'cause of Matt. It's not right."

"Sasha, don't be annoying," Torres says. His attention is on several of the younger players, who are horsing around. Everyone feels weird playing under these circumstances; the immature kids are dealing with their tension by bouncing off the walls and talking too loud.

"Keep your voices down," Torres orders. "Ash, over here."

Ash Klein hurries over and slides in next to Torres. The game master hands him a folded sheet of paper. "Read this where no one else can see it, then eat it," he orders.

Klein salutes and stuffs the paper in his pocket, then leaves the pizza parlor.

Several blocks away, in the park behind the Senior Center, a couple gets up and moves away rather than share their bench with a homeless woman who looks and smells like she dressed from a garbage Dumpster. The woman seems unaware of them. She leans back on the bench and continues her conversation with someone named "Mickey."

She is largely invisible on her bench. Passersby avert their eyes, and though hers is the only bench with room to sit, no one joins her.

Across the street a tall, unshaven man in tattered clothes and a watch cap much too warm for the temperate evening drinks from a bottle in a paper bag. He sits on the steps of a building owned by a prosperous legal firm. People walking on the sidewalk give him a wide berth.

And in the bushes behind the homeless woman, unseen by anyone in the park, a young girl dressed as a boy finds a good spot from which to watch the open grassy area in front of the benches. She marks the spot with white stones so she can find it again, then creeps backward until she can crawl out of the bushes and make her way back to the main street. There, she takes her place in a doorway and waits for the evening to unfold.

The game begins as the young people leave the pizza parlor. They depart in small groups, anxious not to attract attention. Most have left their costumes at home tonight. They've dressed to blend with the crowd.

The game is called "The Masquerade," since one of the premises is that the vampires must keep their identity secret from mortals. That's part of the fun. To walk down a street full of people, knowing that they are completely unaware of the game. To convert the city into a giant game board where the players know each other and everyone else is an extra in their movie.

Tonight the players feel the masquerade even more keenly. A week and a half of media coverage of Matt Demming's murder and Reverend Seaton's tirades against role-playing games have made the public aware of the game. One false step can lead to discovery and bring the police down on them.

Some of the younger players are giddy with excitement; others are uncomfortable playing at death when the real thing is at hand. The older players are experiencing a range of emotions for a variety of reasons, but they are better at keeping their feelings to themselves.

In this early part of the game, the players operate alone or in small groups. They chat with others, drop clues, probe for information. Some, like Ash Klein, have received special directions or privileged information from the game master. Everyone is busy trying to figure out what is going down.

Downtown is a perfect place for the game, not only

because of the crowds but because the business district is laid out with alleys and walkways, and many buildings have courtyards and outside staircases. Torres has limited the players to several square blocks, but there are plenty of good spaces for the game.

Nate Sessler, whose game name is Gabriel, and Bill Griffen, who calls himself Gibson, both have special directions from the game master. They sit on the lower steps of a staircase in a walkway just off the main street. Nate is wearing a ruby stud in his nose and a silver dagger in his ear. He rubs his hand back and forth over the tattoo on his arm, an unconscious nervous habit. Grif, dressed in black, stretches his long legs, refolds them. He's edgy and keeps stepping out of character.

"We shouldn't be doing this," he says. "It's not right. Death isn't some game."

"Chill out," Nate says. "This is exactly the sort of thing Matt would have loved. You think he'd have liked some minister saying words over him in some church, talking up his immortal soul? Hell, no. He'd have wanted this. All of us on the street, playing the game. For him."

"I don't know."

"Well, I do. We been buddies since we were kids. We spent just about every spare moment together during high school. People thought we were brothers, only we were better than brothers. He was my best friend."

"Yeah, right," Grif says with derision in his voice. "That's not the tune you were singing a few weeks ago. Then, he was a total bastard who stole your game. A leech who lived off the blood of his friends."

Before Nate can reply, they're interrupted by a short redheaded kid whose game name is Striker. The kid is probably about fifteen, but he looks nine, and has a frenetic manner coupled with an obsession for role-playing that has earned him the epithet "gamer goober."

"I hear there's a meeting tonight at eight-thirty in the park," the goober says.

"So I hear," Nate replies.

"You have any ideas about Death's accomplice?" Striker asks.

"Some. None I'd share with a mangy Brujah," Nate says, insulting Striker and his clan.

"Watch out, or I'll read my answers in your insides." The kid tries for menacing.

"Beat it, Striker," Grif says. His voice is impatient.

"You can't just shove me off. I've got an interest in this information, too. What have you two got to hide? I know Gabriel was pissed about losing out on the challenge, but what about you, Gibson?"

"Go be annoying someplace else," Grif orders shortly. Seeing that the goober wants to hold his ground, the animator catches his eye and leans forward. "I'm telling you to leave. I'm *persuasively* telling you to leave."

The kid, recognizing the challenge, replies quickly, "I'm *stubbornly* refusing to move."

Having pitted persuasion against stubbornness, the players must now determine who wins the challenge. After a silence longer than normal, each combatant raises a clenched fist at waist height.

"Ro-sham-bo." The kid sticks with rock, Grif goes for scissors. The goober smiles triumphantly at winning the challenge and changes his posture as if settling in.

But Grif's jaw tightens and his eyes narrow in anger. "If you don't get out of here right now, I'm going to frenzy," he says. The menace in his voice sounds real. The goober takes a step back. Going into frenzy is a serious matter in the game. A character in frenzy is out of control and can do all manner of evil. The kid backs off, wondering what he said that set Grif on such a short fuse.

* * *

By eight-thirty, players drift toward the park. Some have traded information or intimidated others into telling what they know. Several have gone home, unable to handle the emotions aroused by playing a scenario associated with their friend's death.

The sky is blue-black, and the streetlights have come on. Most of the families with children who were here earlier have left, and the remaining adults will move on as the teenagers take over the park. Only the homeless woman remains, a dirty lump of rags snoring quietly on her bench.

Tony Torres stands in an open area not far from the homeless woman. He confers with a pretty, dark-haired girl wearing a navy blue T-shirt. The girl is Andi Schecter, Chloe's friend, who will deliver the eulogy. She is about seventeen, barely five-two, with glasses. She holds a sheet of paper in her right hand.

"I hope I can remember this," she says.

Torres hands her a small flashlight. "Read it if you have to. It's important not to leave anything out."

She nods and moves away as three boys approach the game master.

It's eight forty-five by the time everyone makes it to the park. They stand in small groups, quiet because at the first sign of horsing around Torres is on them. When he senses that everyone is there, the game master signals Andi.

She steps forward and moans dramatically. "I feel . . . I feel . . ." She says, "Liza, is that you?"

Everyone looks around, but she draws their attention back with her voice. "Liza, I can feel you. What do you want?" She jerks her upper body a couple of times and when she speaks again, it is with a strong voice quite different from her earlier one.

"Hear me, kindred, I am your newest neonate, and I call out for vengeance. I demand vengeance against the *diabolist* who killed my sire."

"She's possessed," Torres announces. "Liza has possessed her."

"Will you hear me?" she demands.

The others make assenting noises and gestures.

"Michael was a vampire of great beauty and power, worthy to be named for an archangel. The beast was strong in him, but he fought it bravely and prized what was left of his humanity. The Toreador clan will not see his like again. We have been deprived of a great leader.

"But I come here not to sing his praises, but to demand justice. There are those present who had reason to harm my sire." She turns and dramatically studies the faces before her.

"You, Sarin," she says, pointing at Ash. "You envied Michael's powers. You pretended to admire him, but you envied him. His blood would give you tremendous power. Did you think you could step into his place?"

Ash has been rocking gently on his feet, but with the accusation, he stops, absolutely still. He doesn't speak. He seems frozen.

"And you, Gabriel," the girl says, switching her attention to Nate Sessler, "you envied him, too. He won the challenge and took me away from you. Michael and Gabriel, the battling angels, but Michael was the victor. Did you hate him for his success?"

Nate has nothing to say either. His face betrays no emotion. His hand strokes the tattoo on his arm.

"And you, Gibson," the girl says, moving her finger to point at Bill Griffen, who stands next to Sessler. "Were you jealous? You were supposed to be friends. But Michael was always more powerful. It's hard to be a friend to the powerful."

Grif looks like he wants to protest, but he swallows the impulse and just stares at the girl.

The accusations continue. Most are based on events in

the game, and a few have strange wording that only the
killer would recognize. Tension spreads through the group
as the veil of the game thins and players remember that
Matt Demming really was murdered, and that his killer
could be among them.

I WATCHED THE mock funeral from beneath my pile of rags
and waited for the signal that it was coming to an end. The
dark-haired girl followed her accusations with the com-
mand that the Sheriff question the assembly. "In the name
of my sire, by the blood that was once his and now runs in
my veins, I demand vengeance. Speak. Tell what you know.
Give words to your suspicions."

That was it—my cue to get moving. I didn't know how
long this next act of the drama would take, but I wanted to
be in the parking area behind the bushes by the time it was
over. Those bushes were the natural hiding place for Chloe
if she wanted to watch the show. When she crept out of
them, I intended to be in position to snag her.

Peter should already be across the side street beyond
the parking lot. He would have a better view of the park
from there and could see Chloe if I missed her. Jesse was to
stay with the gamers and watch their reactions to whatever
happened.

I snorted a couple of times and mumbled to myself as I
sat up and looked around. The gamers watched me ner-

vously. I coughed and spat on the ground, then slowly rose to my feet and hobbled off toward the side of the park.

By the time I reached the sidewalk, I couldn't hear what was happening. The gamers were keeping their voices down, anxious not to attract the attention of the cops. I reached my next post, near a Dumpster, and waited for Chloe.

A Dumpster is never a good place to do surveillance, unless the garbage collectors have been there very recently. This Dumpster was ripe, very ripe. Fortunately, my nose was already conditioned to rank odors. Peter, whose favorite disguise is homeless alcoholic, had outdone himself in "conditioning" my clothes. After the first fifteen minutes in them, I craved nothing so much as a long, hot bath.

The group in the park seemed to be breaking up. I waited by the side of the Dumpster, pretending to go through a big sack of stuff I'd stashed next to it. Several kids from the game walked by me, talking quietly among themselves.

The park was emptying, and there was still no sign of movement in the bushes. Maybe we'd guessed wrong. She hadn't come. Or she'd hidden somewhere else. I threw some of the stuff from the bag into the Dumpster.

Where are you? I wondered. And what the devil did you intend with that eulogy? Liza had accused just about everyone in the game, but one of those people could be a murderer and if her charges hit too close to home, she'd just given him added motive to kill her.

I thought I detected some movement in the bushes to my right. A few seconds later, a slight figure crawled out of them and stood up. She was about fifteen feet away. I waited.

She walked toward me, then stopped when she realized I was there.

"How about a quarter for an old lady?" I said huskily.

She shook her head and started to walk by me. When she

was in range, I lunged and grabbed her by both arms. She tried to pull away, but in aikido, you learn to keep a grip, and I wasn't about to let go.

As she struggled, I said, "Chloe, I'm here to help you. Two minutes, give me two minutes."

She didn't have a lot of choice, and when she realized it, she stopped fighting. "Who are you?" she demanded.

"A friend of your mother's," I said. "I'm a private investigator, and I want to help you get out of this mess alive. My name's Catherine Sayler."

"I can't go home," she said.

"I won't make you."

"I won't go the police either."

"You don't have to. But you won't be safe till we catch the killer. And I need your help to do that."

"What do you want?"

I wanted to take her home with me. To keep her under guard until we caught the killer, but for now, I'd settle for getting her to talk to me someplace safer than the edge of a public park. Before I could tell her that, we were blinded by the headlights of a car that had just pulled into the parking lot.

"Stay where you are," a voice from a police bullhorn ordered us.

"You, you tricked me," Chloe said, wrenching her arm free and backing away.

"No," I said, reaching out for her. My hand closed on air as she turned and dashed back toward the park. I was right behind her. Unfortunately, a police officer was in front of me, and instead of grabbing Chloe, he snagged me.

I pulled free, but a second cop grabbed my other arm and ordered me to freeze. I had enough sense not to resist, but not enough to keep my mouth shut. Watching helplessly, while Chloe disappeared into a crowd across the street, sent my temper shooting off the scale, and when I realized that the second cop who'd grabbed me was George Prizer, I let him have it.

"You idiot," I yelled, "I had your witness. She was ready to talk to me, and you blew it. Why the hell couldn't you follow directions and stay back?"

"What the . . . Catherine Sayler," Prizer said, as he recognized me beneath the grime of my disguise. "What're you doing here?"

"If you guys talked to each other, you'd know," I said. "You'd also know that you just blew our chance to get Chloe Dorn to cooperate. Now she's on the run again, back in danger. If anything happens to her . . ." But I couldn't bring myself to finish the sentence because I couldn't bear to think of what might happen to her. Couldn't stand the thought that I had let her step into the open where the killer could draw a bead on her.

"You settle down and answer my questions," Prizer ordered. "I want to know what you're doing here in that get-up."

Well, okay, I did look a little funny, maybe even suspicious, but I was too mad to think about how I looked. "I was doing your job," I said, "trying to make contact with Chloe Dorn. You know, the missing girl, the witness, the potential next victim of Demming's murderer. You guys seem to have forgotten about her. If you weren't so busy doing Satan patrol . . ."

"I think you better come downtown for questioning."

"Are you arresting me?"

"That depends on you."

"So go ahead and bust me." It was a dumb thing to say, but I was too pissed to care. "What's the charge? Calling a cop stupid, dressing like a homeless woman? I don't think that's in the criminal code."

"Obstructing an officer," he said. "For starters."

"Oh, right," I said sarcastically. "Blow the investigation,

bust the witness. This is going to make a great 'wrongful arrest' suit."

"Get in the car before I add resisting arrest to the charge."

"I want to see Lou Martin."

"Martin's in the hospital, a bleeding ulcer," Prizer said, a nasty smile on his face. "I'm in charge of the investigation now."

That explained the screw-up. It also explained Prizer's total cluelessness. Martin had done as I'd asked and not told him of our plan. Unfortunately, at the crucial moment, he went off to the hospital, leaving Prizer to mess things up.

And to arrest me.

At that moment Peter appeared from the direction Chloe had run. He'd sprinkled enough alcohol on his shirt to smell of booze, and did truly look like one of skid row's finest.

"I lost her," he announced, breathing hard from the fruit-less chase. "What a monumental screw-up!" He realized for the first time that I was attached to the policeman. "What's going on?" he asked.

"Keep your hands where I can see them," Prizer ordered. "Who are you? And what's your role in this?"

"Oh, jeez," Peter said.

"Captain Marvel is about to arrest me," I said, then added, "for obstructing an officer."

Peter's a quick study, and he's a lot better at getting con-trol of his emotions. "I think it's time to calm down before you get in a situation you'll both regret," he said in a remarkably neutral voice.

He was speaking to me, but Prizer was too far beyond reason to realize that. "You're under arrest for threatening a police officer," he announced. "Cuff him," he ordered the guy holding me.

I was mad enough not to care anymore, and Peter's rap sheet goes back to antiwar protests, so he's no stranger to a cell. I'd have let Prizer bust us just so I could raise hell in court, but when I looked at Peter, I changed my mind instantly. His face had drained of color and his eyes had the look of a cornered animal. "No," he said in a strained voice, and took a step back.

He wasn't in Palo Alto anymore; he was back in Guatemala. And from the look on his face, they'd have to club him into unconsciousness to get him in a cell again.

I knew I had to move fast if we were to avoid that. "Okay, you win," I said to Prizer. "I was way out of line and I apologize."

"Too late," he said.

I'd used up every bit of self-control I had on the apology. But the expression on Peter's face wrung my heart. I was ready to do anything to keep him out of jail. Prizer wanted groveling, he'd get groveling.

"I'm sorry I was disrespectful," I said, trying to sound contrite. I got about three more apologies out, each more abject than the one before. I was going to choke if this went on much longer.

"You should have thought of that before," he said sternly. He turned his attention to the other cop, "I told you to cuff him," he said. "I'll take care of her."

I was getting desperate. "I admit I was out of line. Go ahead and arrest me, but, please, not my friend. He was a POW. He couldn't take being put in a cell again."

I was gambling that Prizer hadn't read Peter's jacket. I didn't think his name had come up in the investigation, so there was no reason for Prizer to have checked on him, unless Martin had mentioned our previous association.

Prizer looked at Peter. Even he could see that something was very wrong. He hesitated, figured out that he could have a nasty fight on his hands, and probably realized that beating up a former POW might not play well in the press.

After a long pause, self-preservation won out. "You can go," he said to Peter.

But Peter was still lost in the nightmare of the past. He didn't even know we were there. I reached out and shook his arm gently. "Peter, go home. Molly needs you there," I said.

He shook his head and dragged his attention back to the present. He took a deep breath and put his hands out in front of him as if he expected to be cuffed.

"You can go," Prizer said again. "But you," he said to me, "are going to jail."

45

I GOT TO sit in the patrol car while Prizer hassled Tony Torres and several of the other gamers. Most of the players had split the minute they spotted uniforms, and it didn't seem to occur to Prizer that the ones who were still there were less likely suspects.

It's always interesting to watch the movie without the dialogue. You notice stuff you'd miss otherwise. Like the difference in Tony Torres's body language. The usually flamboyant game master stood very still, his eyes cast down, his shoulders slumped so that he looked smaller and less imposing. He nodded a lot, spoke only when asked a question. Was he as thoroughly intimidated as he appeared? I wondered.

Not likely. He'd staged this game with the knowledge

that it might be busted by the cops. When I'd told him that Martin couldn't risk warning anyone beyond the bike patrol officers, he hadn't seemed worried. He was playing his submissive role, just as in the game he'd played the Sheriff. And he was probably enjoying himself tremendously.

The newspaper accounts had suggested that Damion Wolfe had lost touch with reality and come to believe he was a vampire. I wondered about Tony Torres's reality. Were we all just players in his drama? And if so, how much of it had he scripted?

He'd written most of the eulogy. The accusations were his idea, and he'd crafted them to reflect the other players' relationships with Demming. It was a risky proposition. If the killer was in the game, goading him was a dangerous ploy. And not just for Torres, but for Chloe as well.

Chloe. She was out there someplace. Maybe not so far away. Had the killer seen her, realized as I had that she'd shaved her hair? Was he even now following her home to wherever she'd chosen to hide? Or worse yet, catching up to her and offering help?

Her face haunted me. Those gorgeous almond-shaped eyes. The incredible vulnerability masked by bravado. The driving need to feel strong and independent. Like Molly in so many ways. I swallowed around a growing lump in my throat.

Prizer was headed back to the car. He was chatting easily with the cop beside him, and his features had relaxed and were no longer drawn into an angry frown. With a little time to cool off, he'd probably realize how foolish it was to bust me. If I played it right, I'd be sleeping in my own bed tonight.

But that thought brought no relief because I could still see Chloe's face, and the lump in my throat had only grown larger. I might go home, but she wouldn't be any safer for it.

And with tonight's fiasco, I'd lost my one chance to gain her trust.

Prizer stopped to talk to a second officer, and as he did, I realized that he'd offered me a second chance. Getting busted was the best proof I could offer that I hadn't set Chloe up. But she'd have to hear about the arrest, and that meant that a lot of people would have to hear about it. It meant a story in the paper.

I winced as I imagined the headline: PRIVATE INVESTIGATOR ARRESTED AT CULT GATHERING. Talk about bad publicity! I could imagine how that would play in executive suites across San Francisco. I'd be lucky if every single client didn't call and fire me on the spot.

But I thought of Chloe and realized I really had no choice. Even if they did fire me, I couldn't pass up my one chance to reach her.

Prizer gave me the silent treatment on the short drive to the police station. When he took me out of the car in the underground garage, he kept the handcuffs on, and it looked like he really was going to book me. I'd been here once before, under even worse circumstances, so I knew more about the Palo Alto Police Department's procedures than I wanted to. Enough to realize when he took me upstairs instead of putting me in the holding area that he wasn't booking me.

"Am I under arrest?" I asked, as we reached the top of the stairs. Showing too much familiarity with the department's booking procedures didn't seem like a good move.

"That may not be necessary. Let's say we're just having a friendly little chat."

"Ooh, kinky," I said. "Cuffs for a chat. I hate to think what you do for a date."

He frowned and his reddish skin got even redder. "I was hoping you'd cooperate. There's no reason to get hostile."

"I'm standing here in handcuffs after you screwed up my

only chance to help Chloe Dorn. Even someone of your limited intelligence should be able to figure out I'd be pissed."

His face approached tomato and his lips just about disappeared. He took my elbow and led me toward an interrogation room. Getting busted was looking harder than I'd expected.

The interrogation room had two chairs and a table. The walls were Pepto-Bismol pink. Once inside Prizer took the cuffs off. "Sit," he said, pointing at a chair.

"Arf," I said, remaining standing.

"Sit down, *please*."

I leaned against the wall, watching his face reach very ripe tomato. He couldn't sit down without giving me a height advantage; finally, he perched on the edge of the table. "How do you know Damion Wolfe?" he asked.

The question took me by surprise. I'd assumed Prizer wanted to quiz me about Chloe and the game. Martin's warning came back to me. This guy really did suspect me of being a Satanist.

I gave him my best bored, insolent look. The one I learned from Molly.

"Look, there's several ways we can do this," he said. "I can overlook your behavior tonight and let you go with a warning. I can arrest you for obstructing an officer and cite you out here so you can go home. Or I can send you to the county jail for the night. All depends on you."

"You missed one."

"What?"

"You could apologize for being an asshole and escort me to my car," I said.

His face moved from tomato to eggplant. "Okay," he said. "You're under arrest."

I was hoping they'd get the booking procedure over quickly so I could make my phone call. It'd take fast work to make the deadline for the Sunday paper. But Prizer had no deadline, and the whole process took forever.

When they finally got around to letting me make a call, I dialed home and got Peter. "You okay?" he asked.

"I'm fine," I said, "but I need two things. First, I need you to call Jerry Moss at the *Chron* and tell him I was arrested in Palo Alto in connection with the vampire game. Give him just enough to get him salivating. I want the story to get some play. Second, I'd really appreciate it if you'd come bail me out."

"Moss is probably gone by now and tomorrow's deadline is past. I'll bail you out, then we can talk to Moss."

"At least, leave him a message."

"You got it. I'm on my way."

I expected to be transported to the county jail, but Prizer wasn't in any hurry to get me there. He kept making excuses that they didn't have a cop to spare for the twenty-block drive. My bratty self wanted to continue to harass him, but I exercised a bit of self-control and responded to his questions as civilly as I could.

When I finally realized I should be paying attention, I discovered that he wasn't much interested in the role-playing game. He wanted to know where I'd met Damion Wolfe, how I'd known Ari Kazacos before the code disappeared, and numerous details about previous cases. It was a bizarre set of questions. And I didn't like where it was leading. Prizer was fitting me for a satanic hood. And a cell.

46

THE GUY WHO said there was no such thing as too much success was wrong. I'd hoped for a nice little article in the Sunday paper. I missed that, but I made the evening news on all the local stations. And I hit the front page on Monday.

But that wasn't the worst of it. I got calls from my mother in Denver and just about everyone I knew outside the Bay Area. The story of my arrest had gone national.

"Is it possible peace has descended on the Middle East, Bosnia, and the U.S. Congress? Are there no droughts or civil wars anyplace on the planet?" I asked Peter crankily, as the calls poured in.

"Bread-and-circus time," he said. "Bizarre murders are so much more entertaining than foreign affairs."

"You could, like, sell your memoirs and make a bundle," Molly said.

"She'd have to write fast," Peter said. "The public has a short attention span."

"Hey, there's a kid's life at stake here," I said. "This isn't just a scenario for trash TV."

"The worse things get, the more you need to laugh," Peter said.

"Then we'll be rolling on the floor before long," I said. I knew he was right but that only made me more cranky.

"You weren't exactly chuckling when Prizer threatened to bust you."

I regretted my words the minute they were out of my mouth. "No," Peter said slowly, his expression grave. "No, I wasn't." He got up from the table and went into the other room. Molly suddenly focused on eating her cereal.

I followed Peter into the living room where he was putting on his jacket. "I'm sorry," I said. "But we really have to talk. I can't go on like this."

He sat down on the couch. I'd expected anger; instead, I saw total emotional exhaustion. "You're right," he said. "But I can't talk about it. Talking doesn't help. It doesn't bring people back to life. It doesn't stop the torture."

"Nothing can do that," I said. "At least, not anything you can do. You have to stop tormenting yourself." Easy for me to say. Me, who couldn't get Chloe Dorn's face out of my mind. If something happened to her, I'd probably end up in worse shape than Peter. I sat down next to him and put my arm around him. He pulled me to his chest and held me tight.

I spent a good part of Monday on the phone and drafting letters to our clients telling them in language that I hoped was professional and reassuring that I was not really a dangerous felon. By midmorning, my secretary Amy was complaining that we needed to hire a press agent. It wasn't just the reporters. Now we were getting calls from the tabloid news shows. When a producer from a TV talk show called, I considered having the phone disconnected.

It didn't matter that I hadn't talked to the various newspaper and television reporters who called. George Prizer had, and so had Thomas Seaton. With their spin, the vampire game became a gathering of potentially bloodthirsty teens, and my presence there proof of my involvement in the murder. Their references to my previous high-profile cases made it seem like solving murders was proof of complicity.

Marion was obviously impressed by all the coverage. She called to offer support, and within minutes announced that living with me was probably not good for Molly.

"It's not like you didn't know all this stuff," I said. "It's been in the newspapers. I've told you about it. It's just that then I was the good guy and now I'm somehow a moral degenerate."

"I'm not doubting your honesty," Marion said. "It's just that it can't be good for a teenage girl to live with someone who is frequently involved in violent crime."

"It's got to be better than living on the streets," I said. "And besides, you're the one who got me involved in this case in the first place."

It was a low blow and not even quite true, but this was Marion and sisters never fight fair.

I'd called Lou Martin on Sunday, but he'd been too sedated to talk to me. The nurse had said I should call back today.

When he answered the phone, his voice was surprisingly strong.

"I'm glad to hear you sounding so good," I said.

"I don't know about good, but I'm definitely better than before," he said.

"It was an ulcer?"

"Yeah, the doc says it eroded. How's that for a word, eroded? Makes me sound like a pile of dirt. Look, I'm sorry about Saturday night. I passed out before I could take care of things."

"Not your fault," I said. "It did make for an interesting evening."

"Did you get to talk to Chloe Dorn?"

"No. I had her, but before I could convince her to talk to

me, Prizer arrived and she split. You probably know the rest of the sordid tale."

"Prizer's version is that he responded to a call that the vampire gamers were in the park and found a homeless woman struggling with a young boy. According to him, you not only blocked his attempt to capture the Dorn girl, you were uncooperative and abusive when he tried to question you."

"The second part's true, but he's got the roles reversed on who interfered with whom. It took more effort than I'd expected to get him to bust me."

"You wanted to be arrested?"

I explained why I'd pushed Prizer to arrest me. There was a long pause, then Martin said, "I suppose it might work. But I hope you realize it's a high-stakes game. Prizer's convinced you're involved in the cult. He's not after you for obstruction. He wants you for murder."

"I was afraid of that," I said. "And how about you? Are you a member of this cult, too?"

"He didn't come out and say that, but I've been taken off the case. It's a pretty clear violation of department policy to keep your fellow officers in the dark on information relevant to an investigation."

"What'll they do about that?"

"I don't know. I can probably claim that I wasn't thinking clearly because of the pain, or that I was going to notify Prizer but was incapacitated before I could do it. But the important thing is that I'm off the case for now, and everything is in George Prizer's hands. That's not good news for you."

"Or for Chloe, I'm afraid."

"I'd like to help, but there's not much I can do. I'm on medical leave for now, and if Seaton has his way, they'll put me on administrative leave pending a hearing."

"I'm sorry," I said. "I got you in this spot."

"I got myself here. I just hope you can find Chloe Dorn."

He didn't say, "before it's too late," but we were both thinking it.

I wasn't thrilled that the cop in charge of the investigation thought I was a Satanist, but I was even more concerned about the press coverage. Chloe Dorn wasn't likely to contact me if the media convinced her I was a cult member. And there was the small matter of my professional reputation. It was taking a hell of a beating. I had to do something about it.

I called my lawyer. Not Stephen Chin who handles my corporate stuff, but Vince Malone, the meanest, nastiest criminal defense attorney in San Francisco.

"I need you to get these guys off my back," I said. "Can't you threaten them with something?"

"No problem," he said. "I will remind them of the generous settlements juries have awarded individuals unjustly accused in the press. That will do the trick."

"It's so nice to know you're there," I said.

"It's always nice to know that you're out generating business for me," he said. "By the way, I could use some help on one of my cases. And don't tell me you don't do homicides. I read the papers." He laughed heartily at his own joke. At least, I hoped it was a joke.

There was one more thing I could do to reach out to Chloe. I called Julia Dorn. I explained why I'd been at the game and why I'd gotten myself arrested. There was a long pause after I finished.

"Reverend Seaton thinks you're part of the cult."

"Do you believe him?"

"I . . . I don't know what to believe."

"You have to trust your own instincts," I said. "If I'm part of a cult, then Peter is, too, and my sister Marion as well, because she's the one who introduced you to me."

"I don't believe that," Julia said. "You've been much

more concerned with finding Chloe than that man Prizer. He thinks she's a Satanist."

"I need your help if I'm to contact Chloe," I said. "You may be the last chance we have to reach her."

"What do you want me to do?"

"I want to call a press conference where you and I will appear together, asking Chloe to contact one of us. If she sees that you trust me, perhaps she will, too." I knew what I was asking. So did she. It wasn't just exposing herself to the media. It was going against her pastor and probably most of her friends.

"My husband said I wasn't to talk with you again," she said. "He'd be furious if I did what you ask. And Reverend Seaton . . ."

"I know it's asking a lot," I said, "but we have to convince Chloe to trust me. Otherwise, she may turn to someone else for help, and that person could turn out to be the killer."

There was a long pause. I didn't rush her. She was not a woman who asserted herself. She had probably never defied her husband openly, and I was asking her to disregard his orders and risk public censure.

Finally, in a voice close to tears, she said, "I can't. I just can't."

"I understand," I said. And I did. But I felt tears in my own throat and the heavy weight of hopelessness bore down on me. "Please call me if you change your mind," I said. There was no response, but I heard a sob just before the disconnect.

Two hours later I got a call from a client for whom I was scheduled to testify in a kickback case.

"We won't be needing you to testify," the lawyer said. "We've decided to settle out of court."

"Really?" I said. "I thought you had an excellent case."

"Our excellent case depended on your testimony," he said, "and right now I don't know how that would go over with a jury."

I could hear the anger in his voice. There was no point in arguing with him. It didn't matter that I didn't sacrifice children and drink their blood. It only mattered that Prizer and Seaton had created enough smoke to make some people suspect a fire.

Nothing happened in the next few hours to raise my spirits. We got numerous calls from the press, but not a single one from a client or potential client.

Just before five, Amy buzzed me. "Call on line one," she said. "It's not a reporter."

It was Julia Dorn. "Do you really think this press conference can save Chloe?" she asked.

"I can't promise you that," I said. "But it's the only thing I can think of that'll give us a chance."

"Tell me what to do," she said.

TUESDAY AFTERNOON. CHLOE Dorn gazes at her mother's face on the television screen as tears slide down her cheeks. She hugs herself tightly, as if she were cold, but the room is hot from afternoon sun pouring through the bay windows.

She has never felt so empty. The longing for home presses so hard on her chest that she can barely breathe.

"Please, Chloe, wherever you are, we love you. We want you safe," her mother says. "Please let us help you."

She can see her mother's mouth twitch the way it does when she's trying not to cry. She sees the dark circles under her eyes, feels the exhaustion that makes her shoulders slump. It is almost more than she can bear.

This is why I didn't call home, she thinks. I can't do this. I have to be Liza. I have to be strong. Liza would turn off the television, but Chloe can't bring herself to do that.

She switches her attention to the blond-haired woman who stands beside her mother. The face is vaguely familiar. She's seen her somewhere. When the woman speaks, she recognizes the voice. It's the homeless woman from Saturday night.

The reporter has asked about allegations that she's involved in a vampire cult.

"I assume you mean the role-playing game that took place Saturday night in Palo Alto," she says. "That's a game played by young people all over the country. Whether you approve of it or not, it is a game, not a cult. I was observing the game because I hoped that Chloe might show up. I've been working for Mrs. Dorn since Chloe's disappearance; this seemed our best chance of making contact."

"Was she there?" another voice asks.

"Yes. But I only had a few seconds to speak to her before the police arrived and frightened her away."

"What was the reason for your arrest?"

"I don't want to comment on that, except to say that unless I get a public apology from the police, I plan to sue for false arrest."

The camera switches back to the reporter for a wrap-up, then back to the studio for a story on a five-car crash on the freeway. Chloe switches off the television, sits and stares at the blank screen.

Seeing her mother sharpens the longing she's felt since Saturday night. It was hard to be so close to home, tougher still to have to leave. The tears threaten to start again.

Liza wouldn't moon around like this, she reminds herself. But it's getting harder and harder to stay in Liza. It takes so much energy to be strong. And Chloe is very tired.

Why not? she thinks. Why not just give the computer and the files to the investigator and let her deal with it? But the answer comes to her as quickly as the question. Because Raptor is still out there, and until he's caught, she won't be safe.

Besides, she's worked hard to become Liza, to be strong and powerful. She won't just give that up and go back to being a terrified wimp.

She looks over at the single sheet of white paper on the coffee table, the paper on which she's copied an e-mail message. It has an almost magnetic power over her; she's been able to think of little else since she picked it up earlier today.

It is another message from Raptor, promising her safety if she'll just give him the computer and the archives. This time he wants her to leave them at the Pulgas Water Temple, about thirty miles south of San Francisco. The location sounds remote, and at 3 A.M., when he tells her to come, it will be completely deserted.

This message does not arouse the terror that the first two did. Maybe she's losing her ability to feel, like a lab rat shocked one too many times. She can read this without feeling her heart race and her hands turn icy.

She can't go alone. That would be nuts. But maybe she could use the investigator as backup. She'd still be calling the shots, but she wouldn't be completely alone.

Chloe Dorn reaches for the phone.

"She's smarter than they realize," I said. "And that —" Outside, a dog started to bark. I shook my head slightly. We're not wired, couldn't the people at the studio see that — but it was like we were in a room where they'd been paying each house a few dollars a month so that when the house emptied out completely, they'd come in, just cleaning up, and they'd come to clean, and the few that Seaton might not think they'd be willing, could at last be free.

48

JESSE JOINED PETER and Molly and me to watch my appearance on the evening news. I was relieved to see that they'd used the footage I'd hoped they would. It's always tricky dealing with the media. Sometimes when they finish editing the tape, you wonder if you were there when it was shot.

The one thing that you can count on is that they'll take the most sensational quotes and footage, so I'd carefully scripted what Julia and I were to say. We'd given the scripted answers anytime they gave us a chance, and for all other questions, they got the dullest responses we could come up with.

"You think it'll work?" Molly asked, as the segment ended.

"I doubt they'll ask me to anchor 'Good Morning, America,'" I said, "but I think it does what I hoped it would."

"Seeing her mother's bound to have an impact," Peter said.

"It was an incredibly courageous thing to do," I said. "She went against every authority figure in her life, maybe even risked her marriage."

"She'll be under a lot of pressure to recant and denounce you," Peter said. "You know Prizer and Seaton'll do everything they can to convince her that you're Satan's minion."

"She's stronger than they realize," I said. "And, like Chloe, she's discovering that. I don't think she'll cave."

"I hate to bring up petty business concerns," Jesse said, "but your appearance should help soothe some of our jumpier clients."

"I hope so," I said. "Otherwise, that bag lady costume could end up being my work clothes."

"People don't really believe that shit about you being in a cult, do they?" Molly asked.

"Probably not. But we're hired to solve problems. Clients don't have much faith in someone whose problems are bigger than their own," I said.

"Especially when those someones look like a homeless woman and a geeky kid pretending to be a vampire," Jesse said.

"How'd the game go?" Peter asked.

"As an undercover operation, it was a bust," Jesse said. "Every one of the suspects looked nervous and guilty. Even Torres seemed uptight during the scene in the park. But as a game, it was sort of cool."

"Ought to be right up your alley," Peter said. "You spend about half your life undercover pretending to be someone else."

"Don't we all," Jesse said. "We're not so different from the gamers."

"Except that they resolve conflicts with hand-held games or dice. Would that our opponents would settle for that," I said.

Just then the phone rang. As I picked up the receiver, everyone watched anxiously.

"Hello." I tried to keep my voice neutral.

"Is this Catherine Sayler?"

"Yes."

"This is Chloe Dorn."

Thank God, I thought. "I'm glad you called," I said, not wanting to move too fast and spook her.

"You said you'd help me. That I didn't have to go to the police. Did you mean it?"

"Yes," I said. "Tell me what you want." I'd decided that if she called, I'd let her define the situation. Chloe might long for someone to tell her what to do, but the girl on the phone was both Chloe and Liza. And Liza needed to feel that she was in control.

"He's contacted me. The killer. He wants me to leave the computer and archives someplace. I think we can catch him, but I need your help."

"You've got it," I said. "Can we meet, or do you want to do this over the phone?"

Please agree to meet, I thought. "The phone," she said.

Damn. "All right," I agreed. "Tell me what he's asked you to do."

The killer's message was an obvious setup. Chloe was to bring the computer and archives to the Pulgas Water Temple. She was to come early in the morning to avoid the chance that someone would see her and steal the computer.

"And then he can step out of the bushes and whack you over the head," I said.

"That's what I figure. It's why I need you."

"Do you know this place, the Pulgas Water Temple?"

"No," she said. "He said it was out on Cañada Road near San Mateo. What is it?"

"I haven't been there for years, but as I remember it really is a temple, or at least looks like one. It was put up by the water district, and you can hear the water flowing beneath it. At night, it would be an easy place to kill someone."

There was a pause. Maybe I was scaring her. I hoped so.

"I can get someone your size to take your place," I said. "In the dark, the killer will never know the difference."

"I want to do it," she said.

"We'll have a better chance of catching him if you're not there," I said. "I can put together a team that's used to working with each other. It would be safer and better. For all of us."

"I go, or it's off." She said it like she thought she was in a gangster movie.

"Okay," I said, "It's your call, but I'd suggest you let me take a look at the Water Temple tomorrow to check it out. We can't protect you unless we know the layout."

"All right, but he wants me to come tomorrow night."

"Stall him. Don't answer. Send him e-mail tomorrow night telling him you'll come Thursday."

"Okay. But don't call the police."

"You've got my word," I said. "I'd like to talk with you face-to-face. Anyplace you suggest."

"No," she said vehemently. "No meeting."

"How will we stay in contact? How can I reach you if I need to?"

"Send me e-mail," she said.

"Not good enough. How about a pager?"

"No," she said. "You check out the Water Temple. I'll call tomorrow afternoon."

There was a click and she was gone.

49

THE PULGAS WATER temple was built in 1934 at the outfall of the Hetch Hetchy Aqueduct bringing water from the snowy peaks of the Sierras to San Francisco. Water was a big thing in those days, still is here in drought country, and the city fathers celebrated big-time when the project was completed. They constructed a plaster temple for the ceremonies and replaced it a few years later with a permanent one.

You can see it, if you know where to look, from Highway 280 on the way to San Francisco. I've always wondered about it. Now I'd get to know it like a second home.

Peter and I parked in a small lot just off Cañada Road. There was a big metal gate at the opening to the lot. I wondered how anyone would get in at night, then realized that there was no fence attached to the gate.

A dirt path led through some low bushes to a clearing. The temple was to our left. It was a graceful circle of tall columns capped with a frieze and dome. Inside the columns was a low circular structure that looked like it might be an altar. From where we stood, you could hear the rush of water.

In front of a shallow reflecting pool, flanked by plane trees, the temple pointed toward the road.

It was a lovely, peaceful spot, but all I could see that morning were too many places where a killer could hide.

First, there was the path; the brush beside it wasn't heavy, but in the dark it could easily conceal an assailant. Then there were the bushes behind the temple on either side. The only encouraging feature was the chain-link fence that ran across the meadow behind the temple. The thick, low ornamental bushes in front. A giant live oak to the side.

"It'd be hard enough to secure this area during the day," I complained. "It's going to be nearly impossible at night."

"Be easier if we knew for sure there was only one killer," Peter said.

"I don't buy the satanic cult thing," I said. "If I'm their best candidate for cult member, the cops can't have much that points that way."

"Doesn't mean you don't have several people involved," he pointed out.

"So, how many do we need on our side?"

"One for each of the bushy places behind the temple, one near the beginning of the path, one near the end." He held up four fingers.

"And one near the gate, so he can't come up behind her before she gets to the path," I added.

"You want me to find two guys to help?"

"No," I said. "I'll call the Mascotti brothers. They're retired cops who do surveillance for me."

We were interrupted by a couple with a young child who came down the path behind us. The kid was about four and he charged down the path with such abandon that I was sure he'd trip and go flying. But he made it to the meadow and headed straight for the pool, ignoring the temple. I hoped I'd be better at predicting the killer's behavior than I'd been with the kid.

We walked up to the temple, the sound of rushing water growing as we got closer. The structure in the center of the circle of columns was a large, open cylinder with heavy wire across the top.

"That used to be open," Peter said. "When I was going to Stanford, you could look down at the water. I guess one too many freshmen jumped in. The trick was to hold your breath and swim to the ditch at the end of the tunnel." He pointed to a narrow canal about fifty feet beyond a fence behind the temple.

"Well, at least I don't have to worry about drowning," I said.

We tramped around the temple. I'd hoped that the fence surrounded it entirely, cutting off access from anyplace but the road. No such luck. One whole side was open, and there was more than enough cover for our killer to sneak through unseen.

"The biggest danger is that he'll shoot her," Peter said. "He could take her out before we knew where he was."

I'd had the same fear. It's damn hard to protect against gunfire. But Demming hadn't been shot, and that gave me some hope. "It'll be dark," I said. "Unless he's an experienced marksman, I doubt he'll risk it."

"When you're left hoping your enemy's a poor shot, it's not a good sign," Peter said.

"You got a better plan?"

"No, but I'm bringing my gun."

"I don't think that's such a great idea right now."

Peter frowned, then took a deep breath and said, "Okay. No gun. But I'd advise you to bring one."

I shook my head. "Not on your life. And you should be glad. I'd be as likely to hit you as the killer."

"We better check on moonrise," Peter said. "We want this to go down when there's maximum light."

"The moon's just past full. If the sky is clear, it ought to be reasonably bright."

I waited for Peter to tell me that when you have to hope

for clear skies, it's not a good sign. But he just nodded. His expression was grim.

Chloe called at one that afternoon and I made another attempt to get her to meet with us. She refused and wouldn't even agree to pick up a pager. "Just tell me what I should do tomorrow night," she said. "I can borrow a car."

"Plan to arrive around 3 A.M.," I said. "I think that's when we'll get maximum light from the moon. You can park near the gate."

"He said not to do that because it might attract attention," she interrupted. "He wants me to park down the road about a hundred yards."

"Don't," I said. "You'd make an easy target if he's got a gun. Park next to the gate."

"But he said . . ."

"What's he going to do? Refuse to pick up the computer? You can call the shots here. Besides, you don't have to tell him where you'll park."

"Okay," she said. "I'm not really bringing the computer or the archives. I'll bring an empty box."

"That's good, but put some books or something in it so it weighs about what the computer and archives would. It'll affect how you carry it."

"Okay."

"Stay out of the open as much as possible. You don't want to give him a target. There'll be five of us hidden in various places. With luck, we'll spot him before you even arrive, but we can't count on that.

"We'll try to grab him as soon as he shows himself. You'll be safest if you're not in the middle of things. I may yell at you to run or to drop to the ground. Listen for it."

"Okay," she said. "What if he doesn't show?"

"Then just leave the box where he told you and get out of there. My partner will be near the gate. Leave your car unlocked and he'll slip into the backseat if it looks like the killer isn't going to show."

"No," she said sharply. "No one gets in my car."

"The killer could be waiting down the road for you. You don't want to be alone."

"That road runs two ways," she said. "He won't know which way I'm going. I'll be okay."

We argued that point for a couple of minutes. I lost. She was a stubborn kid. I hoped she wouldn't be a dead kid.

THOMAS SEATON FEELS a mixture of anxiety and excitement as he places the phone back on the hook. His efforts are paying off. The private investigator he has hired to keep an eye on the Sayler woman has brought him proof that the Satanists are planning something.

This morning Sayler and Peter Harman spent more than an hour at the Pulgas Water Temple. It is a remote and pagan spot, perfect for a cult's secret rites. The Satanists must be planning their next ceremony, and he has a terrible fear that it might involve the sacrifice of Chloe Dorn.

He's been worried ever since Julia foolishly appeared with Sayler for that press conference. What folly to turn to one of the key suspects in the case! He'd warned her about Sayler. How could she ...? But then, women are the weaker vessel, irrational and easily swayed by emotion.

Times like this made it clear why the Creator had given man dominion over woman.

He's tried to keep an open mind about the Sayler woman. Even when Damion Wolfe identified her, he'd considered that the boy might be lying. But when the woman convinced Julia Dorn to go on television to appeal to Chloe, he recognized a demonic plot to use a distraught woman to trap her own daughter.

Seaton picks up the phone and calls George Prizer. "I think we've got them," he tells Prizer.

Prizer is also excited, but the temple is outside the Palo Alto city limits, so he must get approval from the chief before making arrangements with another jurisdiction.

Two hours later, Prizer calls back. Seaton knows from the tone of his voice that the news is bad.

"The brass won't go for it," he announces in a defeated tone with an edge of anger. "The Sayler woman's got a pit-bull lawyer from San Francisco who's got them scared shitless of a lawsuit."

"But this is their chance to catch her and put her behind bars," Seaton objects.

"Or to have someone up the Peninsula leak it to the press and give her a great chance to charge harassment and who knows what else. Besides, we don't know when this might go down. We can't put a team out there every night for the next month."

"They're going to act soon," Seaton says. "I'm sure of it. And I'm terribly afraid their next sacrifice will be Chloe."

"I can warn the sheriff's department of the danger and ask them to increase patrols, but beyond that, there's nothing I can do." Seaton can hear the frustration in Prizer's voice. He thanks the policeman coldly and breaks off the conversation. Somebody has to do something to save Chloe Dorn. It looks like it'll have to be him.

*   *   *

Reverend Seaton makes a visit of his own to the Pulgas Water Temple that afternoon. He smiles at a couple picnicking on the grass and returns their friendly greeting, thinking how different this place will look in the dark. He is pleased to discover a thick grove of trees across the road from the gate. A good place for a group of men to wait unseen while they watch the gate and the road in front of the temple.

He can get some men from his church to help. That should be easy. No guns. In the dark there's too great a danger of hitting the wrong person. Besides, he's no vigilante. He doesn't want to kill the cultists. He wants them arrested and brought to trial where the community can see the work of Satan exposed.

But they should have some kind of weapons to defend themselves. Maybe bats and heavy sticks. And lights to illuminate the meadow so no one can sneak off in the darkness. A plan begins to form.

He finds a place up the road where they can park a couple of cars without being noticed. Timing is crucial. They have to arrive before the cultists so they can take their positions without being seen, but there's no way of knowing when the cult will gather. It could be as early as tonight, or it might be days from now.

The Sayler woman's involvement makes it easier. As long as his investigator is watching her, they'll know when she goes out at night. It's not a great plan. He could end up mobilizing the troops while she's shopping for groceries, but it's worth a few false alarms to save Chloe.

His nephew's face appears unbidden in his mind's eye and he feels the awful emptiness that has been his companion since the boy's death. This time he will not stand by. Satan will not claim *this* child.

51

THURSDAY MORNING. CHLOE Dorn paces restlessly though the apartment, driven from one room to the next by a wiry energy that hums through her body. She's jazzed, buzzed, wired. Her mind leaps from one thing to the next. It's like she's mainlined twenty double espressos and they've scrambled her brains.

Finally, she feels like she'll climb the walls if she doesn't get out of this apartment. Her haven has become a prison. Outside, she barely sees the buildings she passes, forces herself to pay attention to street signs so she won't become hopelessly lost, and lets the tension drive her forward until it begins to loosen its grip. By the time she gets back to the apartment she is tired but less crazed.

She flops down on the gray-green futon that's become her bed and stares at the dust motes that float in a shaft of sunlight. How many hours till the 3 A.M. meeting? she wonders. She could count them, but it won't make the waiting any easier.

Get a grip, she tells herself, and forces herself to go over her moves at the water temple. She tries to imagine getting out of the car and walking down the dark path, knowing that Matt's killer is waiting. A wave of panic sweeps through her, freezing her thoughts and clamping tight bands on her chest. What if she can't do it? What if she freezes?

Liza won't freeze, she reminds herself. She's not doing

this as Chloe but as Liza. It's just a question of getting back into Liza.

So, I'll do it like the game, she thinks. After all, the whole setup is just like something Tony would dream up. The vampire stalking his prey in the dead of night, luring her to a deserted spot, only to find that prey is really a vampire killer. She feels some of Liza's power return to her. Takes a couple of deep breaths to relieve the tension in her chest.

Raptor's set up a hunt, she thinks, but we'll see who ends up as prey.

That's what's been bothering her, she realizes. The investigator has given her the role of prey. She's supposed to bring the empty box and let someone else take Raptor when he goes after her. Well, that's not the way Liza plays the game.

She needs a plan. And a weapon. Liza wouldn't go into this thing unarmed. Chloe's never shot a handgun, but she's done some target shooting with her brother's rifle. If Raptor gets close enough that she needs to use a gun, aim won't be a problem.

Getting the gun, now that could be a problem. It's not like in the game where you pay the game master a few points for a slip that says "gun." But she's heard other teens talk about buying guns. If you've got the money, there are plenty of people ready to supply the firepower. One of the guys Serena introduced her to in Berkeley was a dope dealer. If he can't sell her a gun, he'll know someone who can.

That afternoon, Chloe Dorn sits on the BART train back to San Francisco, holding her backpack on her lap. She wonders what the gray-haired woman sitting next to her would think if she knew its contents.

The gun is heavier than she'd expected. It's a revolver. Not very big, though Serena's friend assured her that it's just right for her purposes. Small enough to conceal, large enough for accuracy.

Accuracy. Now there's a laugh. There's not even enough time to find a place to practice firing it. She's crazy to take a gun when she can't shoot straight; but she'd be crazier still to go without a weapon.

The guy who sold it to her showed her how to hold it, and she's practiced pulling the trigger when it wasn't loaded. But she knows that shooting will be a whole different experience. There'll be a kick; she knows that from the times she's fired her brother's hunting rifle. And an ear-shattering blast. "Don't freak out and drop it," the dealer advised.

He loaded it for her. Only five bullets, so the chamber is blank and she can't shoot it accidentally. Before she leaves San Francisco tonight, she'll cock the gun, sending a live round into the chamber.

She gets a queasy, floaty feeling in her stomach when she thinks about it, but she reminds herself, it won't be Chloe carrying that gun tonight. It will be Liza. And Liza is capable of anything.

THURSDAY WAS A long day. I'd debated posting someone at the Pulgas Water Temple in case the killer arrived early, but there was too much danger of being spotted in the daylight. So we all waited until after dark to move into position.

Before we left San Francisco I gave Frank Mascotti a cell phone with instructions to call 911 the minute we had the killer. "What do you want me to say?" he asked.

"Tell them you saw a man and woman struggling and he dragged her into the bushes."

"But that's not true," he said.

"Give me the phone," his brother, Joe, said sharply. "I'll do it."

We drove down together and left the car in a pull-out up the road. All of us except Jesse approached from the north, the side of the temple that was unfenced. We moved in through the woods, trying to make as little noise as possible. Jesse drove to the front gate and sat with his car window down and rap music on the stereo to cover the sound of our movement. He hung around for twenty minutes, drinking Coke from a beer bottle, then drove off, only to sneak back on a bicycle an hour later and take his place near the front gate.

The Mascottis hid in the bushes on either side of the temple. Peter took a spot near the point where the path reached the meadow, and I found a place near the end by the parking lot.

We all settled in for a long wait, alert to any sound that might signal the killer's arrival. For the first hour, every movement in the brush set my heart pounding. After that, I was better able to distinguish common sounds from something out of the ordinary.

Moonrise was later than we'd calculated because of the foothills to the east. And it provided less light than I'd hoped for. I was glad I'd talked Peter out of bringing his gun. In the murky darkness where objects and people were no more than dim blurs, even an experienced marksman could easily hit the wrong target.

A bunch of teenage boys arrived just before midnight and finished off a couple of six-packs. They made enough noise that a small army might have taken up positions with-out us knowing.

By two-thirty the moonlight was a little better. The cold was worse, making me long for an extra sweater and a ther-mos of coffee. I was having trouble staying awake. I sucked on hard candies and kept reminding myself why we were there. Once or twice I thought I heard someone in the bushes, but it could have been Peter or one of the others.

Night and exhaustion have their uses. Sometimes the weary mind floats free to glimpse things invisible to day-time sight. As I crouched in the bushes, I realized that I'd been so focused on figuring out how Raptor had sent his messages that I'd missed the significance of the messages themselves. Their thinly disguised rage suggested that the killer had hated Matt Demming long before he'd stolen the source code. It was a hatred that must have grown over time, nurtured by resentment and jealousy. There were only two people who had that much history with Demming, and one had far more reason to resent him than the other.

What you know doesn't count for much in this business; what you guess counts for even less. It's what you can prove that matters. And the only way to prove who had killed Matt Demming was to catch the man who must be even now preparing for a second murder.

It was after three when I finally heard the crunch of gravel as a car pulled off the road at the gate. The engine died, and a door slammed a few seconds later.

It took a little more than a minute for the driver to walk through the parking lot to the beginning of the path. From my vantage point I could see only shapes, no detail, but I could tell that the figure approaching the path was slight and carried a box.

She moved past me, unaware of my presence. She walked confidently, her back straight and her stride pur-poseful. She's doing this as Liza, I thought. I only had a moment to wonder how that might affect her reactions, when a second form stepped out behind her on the path.

"Chloe," I yelled. "Down," as I ran toward the figure.

But instead of dropping to the ground as I'd told her to, Chloe spun around and faced her attacker. "Freeze," she yelled. "I've got a gun."

The attacker and I both skidded to a stop with several feet still separating us. Peter had charged out of the bushes now behind Chloe. He froze, too.

The dark figure in front of me only paused for a moment. Then he turned and dashed back into the bushes, but he'd misjudged, and a large pyracantha stopped his progress just long enough for me to reach him. I stepped directly behind him and grabbed hold of his jacket on either side of his neck.

He tried to pull free of my hold and when that failed, he swung around ready to punch me. I stepped to the far side and turned my hips, swinging him in front of me and taking him down.

He landed flat on his stomach and I pinned him to the ground with my knee on his spine and one hand on his neck. Behind me, Peter called out, "Chloe, it's okay, we've got him. Give me the gun."

My quarry twisted his head and swore at me as he struggled to get up. I pulled out my flashlight and aimed it at him. The first thing I saw in its harsh glare was the ugly vampire on Nate Sessler's arm. I'd been right about the killer. But there was no time to enjoy it.

"Chloe, please," I could hear the tension in Peter's voice and realized that we had a terrified teenager with a gun, quite possibly aimed at my lover.

"Chloe," I called out. "I have the killer. It's Nate—" But before I could say more, I was interrupted by the sound of people crashing through the bushes, and I was blinded by the white glare of flashlight beams. Ohmygod, I thought, he *was* part of a cult.

"Don't anyone move," a voice commanded.

I was trapped between the approaching group and Chloe with her gun, and Sessler was struggling all the harder. I couldn't stay on the ground with him. I grabbed his right hand in a *sankyo* grip and pulled him up as I got to my feet. Sessler screamed as I torqued his wrist.

Two large men rushed at us. I twisted a bit farther, then hurled Sessler toward them. He crashed into the men and all three went down. Another man reached for me, but Peter was beside me now, and he slugged the man before he got to me. There was no time to find Chloe. I prayed she wouldn't fire in panic.

It was chaos, people punching and yelling, and flashlights flickering wildly about, giving the scene a strobe effect.

In the dojo we sometimes practice blindfolded with multiple attacks. Tonight that practice proved a lifesaver. I grabbed one guy who was headed my way and threw him into another. Someone tried to grab me in a choke hold and I dropped forward on my knees, flipping him over me.

I had to get to Chloe. The flashlights should have made that easier, but their beams were jumping around all over the place, and their glare blinded me to darker areas. With all the confusion it was hard to tell how far I'd moved from my original position, and that made it doubly difficult to find the spot where I'd last seen Chloe.

I stayed low and groped my way in what I hoped was the right direction. A light swept over the area in front of me, and for a second I saw her at the edge of the meadow. She was struggling with Nate Sessler. I couldn't see who had the gun.

I dashed toward them, trying to come in behind Sessler. A shot exploded just as I reached them, but their struggle continued. I grabbed Sessler's hair and yanked, pulling him backward, but another man slammed into me, knocking me off-balance and causing me to lose my grip.

Sessler swung around and faced me. We were out in the clearing, and by the light of the moon, I saw he had the gun. Time froze as I waited for him to pull the trigger. But suddenly Chloe was on his back, clawing at his eyes. He fired, but his shot went wide.

With Chloe distracting him, I moved in on his right side, snaked my left arm around his gun arm, grabbed my other wrist and lifted, hyperextending his elbow.

Sessler screamed and struggled. I felt his elbow give as it dislocated. He dropped the gun.

I became aware of the wail of sirens nearby, and a male voice speaking over a bullhorn ordered everyone to raise their hands and stand still. It took a second order and the cops smacking at least one guy before things quieted down.

I was in an awkward position. I couldn't raise my hands without letting Sessler go, and I wasn't about to do that. "You there, let that man go. Raise your hands," the cop ordered.

"This man's the killer from the Palo Alto murder case," I yelled back. "Please have one of your men take charge of him."

"That woman is a member of the vampire cult. She's one of the killers," another voice called out. I recognized it as Reverend Seaton's.

The cops solved the problem by cuffing us both. Sessler complained bitterly about his elbow and demanded to be taken to a hospital, but the cop didn't look impressed. "We'll have a medic check it out," he said.

I was relieved to see that Peter had one arm around Chloe and she was clinging to him for comfort. He had a nasty gash over one eye; she looked frightened but uninjured. She was lucky to be alive.

Next, I checked for Jesse and the Mascotti brothers. Men flailing away with sticks can do a lot of damage. All three were on their feet, but Jesse was holding a cloth to a wound on his head, and there was clearly something wrong with Frank's arm.

The officer in charge called to the cop who'd cuffed Sessler and me, and after ordering us to stay where we were, he left us.

Sessler's hands were cuffed in front of him because of the injured elbow, and he looked like he was in pain. He turned to look at Chloe and I couldn't read the expression on his face.

Suddenly Chloe broke away from Peter and charged at him. "You bastard," she cried. "You killed him. He was your best friend and you killed him."

Peter was right behind her. He put a hand on her shoulder.

"You bastard." She was crying now and her hands were balled in fists.

Sessler took a step back. "You don't understand," he protested. "You thought he cared about you, but he didn't care about anybody. Only himself. He was just using you like he used me."

"He loved you. He got you a job with Astra." She sobbed out the words.

"He got me a job so I could watch him rake in the profits from *our* game. *Our* game. I gave five years of my life to that game, and he stole it. He stole my life." Sessler was crying now. Tears ran down his face. His features were contorted in anger and misery.

"Bastard," Chloe said, and stepped forward as if to strike him. Peter grabbed her arm.

"He killed Matt," she said. "He killed him." Then she dissolved into sobs, and Peter folded her in his arms.

53

THE COPS TOOK those of us who were still on our feet to the county sheriff's offices to sort things out. They stuck me in a room by myself and ignored my request to speak to the officer in charge.

I'm not good at waiting, and the awareness that every minute increased the chance that Nate Sessler might slip through my fingers drove me wild. When the cops called Palo Alto, Prizer would tell them I was the killer, which would make Sessler an intended victim. There'd be no reason to hold Sessler, and once released, he'd have time to destroy any evidence connecting him to the killing, then disappear. Chloe'd never recover as long as the killer was free, and Prizer would destroy my career even if he never got me into court.

I'd done every calming and centering exercise I knew and was still about to climb the walls by the time the door finally opened. A stocky, middle-aged cop, with white hair cut shorter than his mustache, stepped into the room and introduced himself as Sergeant Metcalf. George Prizer was right behind him.

"You haven't released Nate Sessler, have you?" I asked before Metcalf had closed the door.

"We aren't releasing anyone until we have the full story," he said. "Why don't you tell me your side of it."

I did. Metcalf listened attentively, occasionally jotting

down notes in a battered pocket notebook. Prizer frowned much of the time but kept silent.

When I finished, Metcalf asked a number of questions, then turned to Prizer. "All yours."

"Where's Ari Kazacos?" Prizer asked.

"Kazacos?"

"Don't play dumb. Damion Wolfe identified you and Kazacos as members of the cult that killed Matt Demming."

"Really? And did he mention Nate Sessler?"

"Just answer the question," Prizer said.

"I have no idea where Kazacos is," I said. "And I don't know why Damion Wolfe would identify him or me as members of a cult. Sessler's your killer."

Metcalf watched our interchange closely, his expression impassive. I'd have given a lot to know what he was thinking. Early in the interrogation, I'd urged him to call Lou Martin, but he hadn't done it. As Prizer shot questions at me, and Metcalf watched silently, my stomach began to twist with anxiety. If it came down to my word versus Prizer's, I'd lose.

They weren't listening to Chloe or to anyone on my team. That left Sessler. If only the cop hadn't walked away before Chloe confronted him. I remembered his expression as he watched her, his efforts to justify himself to her. It was a long shot, but it was our best chance.

I turned to Metcalf and said, "There might be one way to sort this out. Do you have a room with a two-way mirror or a video camera?"

He nodded.

"Nate Sessler seems to have some feeling for Chloe Dorn. He practically confessed to her while we were waiting to be brought here from the water temple. How about putting them in a room together to see if she can get him to incriminate himself?"

"What the hell . . ." Prizer started to object, but Metcalf looked interested.

"Might be worth a try," he said.

"I'll need to prepare Chloe," I said. "And she shouldn't be in there alone. I'll go in with her."

"This is some kind of trick," Prizer said. "I wouldn't let her near the Dorn girl. Or Sessler."

"You'll be with us when I talk to her," I said, "and you'll be able to hear everything we say when we're with Sessler."

Metcalf finally nodded. "I'll bring the girl." Prizer followed him out of the room, arguing vigorously against the idea.

He lost. A few minutes later Metcalf was back with Chloe. I'd never seen her up close in the light. She was smaller than I'd imagined and looked terribly frail for a kid who'd acted with such bravado. Her face was smudged with dirt and the tracks of tears. I realized that I might be asking more than she could give.

"How do you feel?" I asked.

"I'm okay," she said, her voice not matching her words.

"Can you play Liza for a few minutes more?"

Her face registered surprise, then she nodded. "I think so."

"Nate Sessler isn't talking and if we can't get him to confess, he could walk. I think you might be able to get to him."

"Me? Why?"

"I think he's attracted to you," I said. "Losing you to Matt in the game could have been the final straw that set him off."

Her eyes widened in alarm. "You think he killed Matt because of me?"

"No. He killed Matt because he was jealous. You were just one more reason for his jealousy. He'd been building up to it for a long time."

"I don't see how I—"

"Nate hated and resented Matt. I think he wants you to

accept, maybe share, those feelings. If we can play on his need to justify himself to you, we might get a confession. You won't be in there alone. I'll go with you, and we can play him between us."

Chloe swallowed hard a couple of times. She was clearly near tears.

"I know it's asking a lot," I said. "But Liza could do it."

Her head snapped up. Her eyes looked less confused.

"Can you be Liza again?"

She nodded slowly and I watched as her body transformed itself. Her spine straightened and her shoulders seemed to expand. She spread her feet slightly, widening her stance, and raised her chin so that she looked straight at me, her eyes clear and strong in their gaze.

"Let's nail the bastard," she said.

While Metcalf set up the room and Prizer watched Chloe and me, we planned our strategy. I suggested some approaches and we decided on where to start, but once we were in the room with Sessler, it would be up to Chloe to probe for Sessler's weak spot. I hoped she'd be up to the task.

Fifteen minutes later, Metcalf took us to the room with the video camera and showed us where to stand. As we waited, Chloe bit her lip and her breathing was shallow, but when the door opened and a deputy led Sessler into the room, she straightened and seemed calmer.

"Hey," I protested, "you're not leaving him here, are you?"

"It'll just be a couple of minutes," the deputy said.

"No," I said. "We don't want to be in a room with him. He's a killer."

"Calm down," the deputy said, as he stepped out and closed the door.

Chloe and I backed away toward the side of the room with the video camera. She huddled against me.

"You tried to kill me," she said to Sessler. Her tone was just right, not so much accusative as surprised.

Sessler stared at her.

"I thought you were my friend," she said.

He looked uncomfortable. The bat's head on his throat bobbed as he swallowed hard.

"I just don't understand." She shook her head.

I'd known it was a long shot. Only a fool would talk inside a police station, even if we appeared to be alone. But for most of us, there's a weak point, one accusation that we can't resist answering. A judgment too damning to let stand. I probed for Sessler's.

"He isn't anybody's friend," I said to Chloe, echoing his condemnation of Matt Demming. "He only cares about himself. He just uses other people."

Sessler shifted his gaze to me, and anger flared in his eyes. The muscles of his jaw tightened.

"He used Matt," I said. "Tried to piggyback on his success. Matt was right when he told you that Nate was nothing but a hack animator, a parasite."

Sessler's slightly ruddy skin was now a deep rose; anger narrowed his eyes and pulled his features into a scowl. I could feel his tension. If we could just tighten the screws a bit, we might push him to the breaking point. I squeezed Chloe's arm to cue her.

"I feel so stupid," she said to me. "I trusted him. I even hoped he'd win the challenge in the game, so I could be his *childe*."

"You fell for the wrong guy," I said. "Matt would have taken care of you. Nate would have killed you."

He was shaking his head, but his mouth stayed firmly closed.

"Can't you see what a loser he is?" I said to Chloe. "He did a few drawings for Matt's game and tried to claim credit for the whole thing. He wasn't even good enough for the commercial team. Matt was a genius. Everyone knows—"

"Matt was a bastard," Sessler exploded. "He was a user. He stole ideas from everyone around him. Ask Tony or Grif. He was no genius."

"I suppose *Cult of Blood* was really *your* idea," I said in a mocking tone.

"It was," he said. "And most of the plot was mine, too." He began to enumerate the scenes and episodes he'd developed. I let him go on. It wasn't a confession, but every assertion led him deeper into his resentment and dulled his awareness of where he was.

When he seemed to be running out of steam, I asked, "Was that what your e-mail game was all about? Proving that you were smarter than he was?"

"I was way ahead of him," he boasted. "He never figured out who Raptor was."

"Not even at the end?" I asked. "Surely you let him see your face before you killed him."

"He never knew," Sessler said. "He thought he was so smart, and he never even knew what hit him."

Suddenly, he realized what he'd said. His mouth snapped shut and his eyes darted around the room.

"It's just us," I said. "But don't feel too smug. Damion Wolfe will talk even if you don't."

"Damion doesn't know shit," Sessler said confidently. "I gave him a little present after the game—just the right combo of drugs for a fast high and a blackout. It was sweet dreams and no memories."

"So you covered all the bases," I said. "Planted the murder weapon and gave the police a killer so they wouldn't look for you. But Chloe took the game. Or was it the laptop you wanted?"

"Or was it me?" Chloe asked, when he didn't respond. "Did you really mean to kill me?"

"No," Nate protested. "Never. I just wanted the computer. I wouldn't have hurt you." He took a step toward her, and I moved between them.

At that point Metcalf must have decided he had enough, or that things could be getting dangerous. He opened the door a moment later and seized Sessler by the arm. "I think we've heard enough," he said.

Sessler jerked violently and only succeeded in hurting himself. He was swearing loudly as Metcalf led him out.

Epilogue

NATE SESSLER REFUSED to talk to the police after his performance for the camera, but there really wasn't much left to tell. Close examination of Matt Demming's computer revealed why Nate had been so anxious to get his hands on it. The first two e-mail messages to Demming had been sent through Finet so they were anonymous, but Sessler had sent them before he set up the Raptor account. Finet records tied those first two messages neatly back to him.

The Palo Alto Police Department dropped the charges against me and officially apologized for impugning my honesty. They even gave me a special commendation for my help in the Demming case. The sweet part of that was that George Prizer had to present it. From the expression on his face, I was glad they didn't ask him to pin a medal on me.

Prizer was back on patrol, and Lou Martin was in robbery-homicide again. He was recovering well from surgery and looked better than he had for weeks. As we said good-bye after the official festivities, he put his arm around me and said softly, "You're a fine investigator, Catherine, but I sure hope I don't see you in my office again."

Molly and Marion attended the ceremony, and for once my sister managed to get through a whole afternoon without making any cracks about my profession. She wasn't quite as successful when it came to comments on Molly's attire.

Reverend Seaton and the Dorns were there, too. I hadn't seen Seaton since the night at the Water Temple. Much as I'd have loved to see him spend some time in a cell, I hadn't signed a complaint against him. Chloe's father had been part of the reverend's posse, and I didn't think that sending her old man to jail would contribute to her healing.

Seaton hung around after the ceremony was over. He seemed almost shy. Finally, he came over to where Peter, Jesse, and I were standing. He probably hadn't had much experience with apologies, but his awkwardness made his words seem all the more genuine. When he said, "It's given me a lot to think about," I felt like he really meant it.

Afterward, Peter and I took Chloe out for ice cream.

"How're you doing?" I asked her. "Really?"

"I'm okay," she said. "I feel bad about what I put my parents through. They've been great. I was stupid not to know they would be."

Sitting there, eating fudge ripple ice cream, she looked like a normal sixteen-year-old. But we all knew she wasn't.

Peter and I kept silent, giving her space to talk.

At last, she said, "I'm glad to be home, but it's hard. My parents want me to be their little girl. My friends don't understand why I space out when they start talking clothes and boys. I don't fit anymore."

"You've faced some things most people never have to face," Peter said.

"Yeah," she said. "They want to know all about it, and they get all excited and tell me how cool I was, but they don't have a clue what it was like."

"You have nightmares?" I asked.

"Yeah, and sometimes I see things when I'm not asleep, like parts of it just come back to me."

"That's normal," Peter said. "It gets better. They don't come so often after a while."

She looked from him to me. "Mom says you've worked on other cases where people died."

We both nodded. "We know about the nightmares," I said. "And the other stuff."

"How do you do that?" she asked. "I mean, how do you just go back to doing your work, cooking meals, making small talk. How do you act like nothing's different, when everything's changed?"

"You just do," Peter said. "You know that inside you're all busted up, but you act like you're okay, and it gets better. Not right away." He looked at me over Chloe's head. "But in time."

"You don't pretend it didn't happen," I said. "And you don't pretend that you don't have all those feelings about what happened. But you try not to hang on to them. When someone tells a joke, you let yourself laugh."

There was a pause, then she said, "I don't know. Most of my friends' jokes are pretty lame." She gave us a tentative smile.

We both laughed. "You're going to be okay, kid," Peter said.

A CONVERSATION WITH
LINDA GRANT

Q. *Linda, you seem to choose topics for your mysteries—sexual harassment, computer fraud, bio-tech rivalries—long before they become part of our general vocabulary. How do you go about choosing such cutting-edge subjects?*
A. I write about what interests me. The world is changing rapidly and I'm struggling to understand what those changes mean. I guess that leads me to topics that eventually end up in the headlines. I'm not much concerned with the nuts and bolts of technology, what's under the hood or in the box; but I am intensely interested in how new technologies affect our lives and in the people who work on the cutting edge. They are the new explorers, and they often make engaging characters.

Lethal Genes is a good example of what I look for in the subject of a book. A friend asked if I'd ever considered doing a book on "big science." It was the first time I'd heard the term, and I was immediately curious. When he described how a poorly managed lab could degenerate into a large dysfunctional family, I knew I had a subject that was intriguing on many levels.

I prefer to avoid high-profile subjects. When I'm looking for ideas, I look to the back pages of the paper, and I listen to the stories people tell. When I wrote *A Woman's Place*, I discovered the problem of having a back-page story go big time. I began the book several months before the Clarence Thomas hearings. Within a week of the hearings many people were convinced that harassment in the workplace was over. It wasn't, of course, but I had to make a number of changes in the book because readers' perceptions had changed.

Q. *What was the genesis of* Vampire Bytes?
A. I got the idea for the book the night my then-seventeen-year-old daughter said, "I'm going up to Cal to play the Vampire game. I might be late."

I found the world of role-playing games fascinating (after all, I got to join the game as part of my research), and I even thought, well, at least this subject won't end up on the front page of the paper. But in the year it's taken me to write the book, there have been two murder cases involving teenagers deeply involved in role-playing games, so it's closer to the headlines than I'd expected.

Q. *How do you research these subjects since you're dealing with such nascent ideas?*
A. There are two ways to do research: the library and lunch. I do lunch. I find a source and invite him or her out to eat. I've dined with a criminal profiler, several police officers, scientists, computer game designers, therapists, probation officers. I find them all fascinating, but I've learned to speak softly since other diners do not appreciate hearing about autopsies and crime scenes while munching on a BLT.

Research is one of my favorite parts of writing. I choose subjects I want to learn about and try to give my reader the most interesting things I discover.

Q. *Do you think the fact that you live in Berkeley has an impact on the subjects you choose?*
A. Yes. There are so many companies working with cutting-edge technology here that I'm probably more aware of what's going on in those areas than I would be if I lived

elsewhere. Also, in Berkeley everything is political. We watch politics the way other folks watch baseball; there's always robust discussion of a variety of social issues. That also fuels my writing.

You can see the Berkeley influence in *Lethal Genes*. It's about more than university politics. It also deals with the politics of food, how we decide what research to fund, what problems to solve. In the long run, understanding how to grow food crops in sandy soils without fertilizer may save more lives than the kinds of medical interventions more commonly associated with genetic research.

Q. *Was researching* Lethal Genes, *which takes place at UC Berkeley's plant genetics lab, a particular challenge? Have other books been more difficult to research?*
A. I was fortunate to have a good friend who is the principal investigator of a plant genetics lab. He introduced me to the students, invited me to hang around the lab, and patiently answered my questions. I wanted the book to have a scientific mystery along with the murder plot, and he helped me with that as well. Learning enough genetics to get the scientific background right was the hardest part of the research.

Q. *How true to life are the politics of the genetics lab in* Lethal Genes? *How open were people you interviewed about these politics? Do you think these rivalries could really lead to murder?*
A. Readers who work in different kinds of research labs have told me that the politics are very real. The students I interviewed had worked in a number of labs, and they were only too happy to share horror stories.

People are surprisingly open about describing the problems in their workplace. In fact, I find that I can ask just about anyone why someone in their profession might be killed and they have an answer. Not only that, they have a candidate for the victim. And they have a highly original means of doing in their victim. It's enough to make me glad I work at home. The students I interviewed were no different. In fact, they helped me devise a very sneaky murder weapon.

Could all this lead to murder? The professor whose lab I studied told me he once had to stop one student from pushing another's head into a centrifuge. And while I was writing *Lethal Genes*, a student poisoned the coffee in a lab at a university in New York, so I have to assume that it could.

Q. *Catherine Sayler often faces trouble—even death—when she investigates crimes in the settings you've chosen for her. Have you ever felt threatened while researching a book?*
A. No, thank goodness. Catherine is a good deal braver than I am, though even she is appalled by some of the situations I create for her. One thing I enjoy about the series is exploring how Catherine confronts danger. I grew up being told that because I was a girl, there were places I couldn't go, things I couldn't do. It's great fun to write a character who confronts her fears but doesn't let them limit her, who goes where she wants, and does what she has to do.

The Catherine Sayler Mysteries

by Linda Grant

"She may specialize in corporate crime, but Sayler, a black belt in aikido, is no white-collar wimp."
—*Entertainment Weekly*

Published by Ivy Books.
Available at your local bookstore.

A WOMAN'S PLACE

BLIND TRUST
by Linda Grant

When Catherine Sayler's biggest client goes broke, she can't be choosy about her cases. So she agrees to help First Central Bank find a missing hacker. And as Catherine gets closer, she discovers she's not searching alone.

LOVE NOR MONEY
by Linda Grant

Catherine Sayler thinks that the murder of Mitch Morrison, a loner and a recovering alcoholic, is connected to a respected judge who sexually abused Mitch when he was a child. As she uncovers evidence against the judge, she learns about the perils children face every day—placing both her reputation and her life on the line.

A WOMAN'S PLACE
by Linda Grant

Systech Corporation wants Catherine Sayler to find out who is sending lewd e-mail messages through the company's computer system. But the situation worsens when female employees start receiving photographs of women being tortured. Then Catherine discovers a brutal murder and the perverted killer begins to stalk her.

LETHAL GENES
by Linda Grant

At U.C. Berkeley's plant genetics lab, precious specimens are being trashed, genetic material is disappearing, a favorite staff member dies suddenly, and the lab's brainy researchers start squabbling like children. The big question facing private investigator Catherine Sayler is: Are some of these budding genetic geniuses also experimenting with murder?

Published by Ivy Books.
Available at your local bookstore.

Books that Live

BERTRAND RUSSELL
  Mysticism and Logic $3.00
  Our Knowledge of the External World $3.00
  Sceptical Essays $2.50
  Philosophy $3.00

JOHN COWPER POWYS
  The Meaning of Culture $3.00

G. ELLIOT SMITH
  Human History $5.00

EVERETT DEAN MARTIN
  The Meaning of a Liberal Education $3.00
  Psychology $3.00

JOHN B. WATSON
  Behaviorism $3.00
  Psychological Care of Infant and Child $2.00

H. A. OVERSTREET
  About Ourselves $3.00
  Influencing Human Behavior $3.00

JOHN DEWEY
  Experience and Nature $3.00

FRANZ BOAS
  Anthropology and Modern Life $3.00

W · W · NORTON & COMPANY, INC.
70 Fifth Avenue, New York

us to that final shock of death which brings these two incomprehensible things together; brings them together on the brink of a third thing, more incomprehensible still, the great Perhaps of silence.

THE END

vidual human being are left very much as they were ten thousand years ago. Dubiously, fluctuatingly, they alternate —these ultimate human thoughts—between gratitude to the unknown and indignant stoical defiance. Philosophers have repeated again and again their smooth rational pronouncement that it is foolish to be afraid of the gods. But in spite of philosophy—and doubtless because of our stupid and cruel offences against one another—"conscience doth make cowards of us all." Culture, as some of us have come to understand it, does not take up any dogmatic attitude with regard to the existence, or the non-existence, of God or of the gods. It recognizes irrational hopes and fears. It takes account of many rumours caught on passing winds, of many voices heard in solitary places, of many reef-bells over strange waters. It allows for queer second-thoughts and for startling, mysterious intimations that escape all logical capture. In its patient, slow, dreamy methods of waiting upon the motions of the spirit, culture comes to recognize that there are levels in human feeling that apparently belong to dimensions of existence beyond the chemistry, beyond the electric magnetism, of the whole stellar system.

Remembering these feelings in its calmer and more rational activities culture is loath to commit itself to any final word. In the midst of the turbulence of modern life it offers a calm refuge, a patient, sceptical but not cynical standing-ground, from which we can survey the track of our journey through the years without too much self-abasement and without too many regrets.

For culture has at least this—that it reconciles us to the two destinies, both the inward and the outward, and resigns

solitary hours full of mystical, poetical and metaphysical thought.

The outward destiny of all of us is of course most fatally influenced by public opinion. Except where public opinion is opposed to cruelty—and this, alas, is rare—public opinion is always wrong. Thus in the great struggle between culture and destiny, which resembles those austere contests in classic drama between the hero and fate, culture will be found constantly at war with public opinion. Public opinion is always trying to democratize culture—in other words to prostitute it and change it. Public opinion—led by affected rhetoricians—is always seeking to encourage the latest fashions and obsessions in art, the latest fashions and obsessions in thought, religion and taste. Against all this, culture stands firm; grounding itself upon the eternal elements of Nature and human nature.

The world is very old and the human race is very old. All these problems of human life are difficult and obscure. No ready-made solution can deal with them—not even the best of modern theories about education. What has been suggested in this book is a view of culture, by no means the only possible one, wherein education plays a much smaller part than does a certain secret, mental and imaginative effort of one's own, continued day by day, and year by year, until it becomes a permanent habit belonging to that psyche or inner nucleus of personality, which used to be called the soul. But theories of this kind have been offered to the world for more than ten thousand years. Again and again have they been offered; far more nobly expressed and far more subtly and clearly thought out than in this tentative and hesitant work. But the real deep thoughts of the indi-

more wickedly and effectively than could the most treacherous of lovers!

One learns indeed from the subtle stories of Dorothy Richardson what exactly it is that a mother's influence does to a daughter's life. Every woman is a creator, in the sense of creating a kind of spiritual *ménage* round her, wherever she is. She does this as instinctively as a silk-worm spins its cocoon. But by a terrible and cruel law of Nature there cannot be two *ménages* under one ceiling; so when a girl lives with her mother the deep creative instinct within her, that instinct which is her inward destiny, that instinct which is the very material of her culture, is teased, suppressed, tantalized, unsatisfied.

Even so—for "old maids" under certain conditions can be the most cultured persons of all—an unmarried woman living with her mother can, by sheer intellectual and imaginative power, liberate herself while she is still enslaved. But she must fight tooth and nail for a room entirely her own—never entered by her mother—and for the right to retire to this room as often as she pleases. It is in the direction of cultural solitariness, not in the direction of rowdy parties, that young people's liberty, of both sexes, should be gained.

True culture demands a certain degree of sensuality, of sensual ecstasy even; but this sensuality need not be *gregarious*. Culture, in fact, desires for a young person just the very opposite of what most employers, preachers and moralists desire. These desire for the youth of both sexes, when not hard at work, an exhausting round of lively, gregarious, wholesome, athletic distraction. Culture, on the contrary, desires for the youth of both sexes, long, silent,

dreams. Without long, lovely moments spent in day-dreams
life becomes an iron-ribbed, sterile puffing engine. And that
is what our rulers and moralists of today want to make it
and keep it: a moralized machine. But how cunningly must
we guard our leisure to dream and with what divine un-
scrupulousness must we steal it! Any boy, any girl, who has
spent an hour in happy dreaming has already fulfilled the
purpose of creation. Out of His dreams God created the
world; and shall not His creation imitate Him?

It is against this new-fangled, commercialized motto of
"Service" that culture must lift up her beautiful thousand-
years-old snake's head. Contemplation, not activity of any
sort, is the purpose of the universe—or at any rate of that
universe which all mystics and artists and lovers and sen-
sualists and saints have substituted for the sterile mirage of
objective truth. And every day-dream, begotten of pleasant
leisure, by well-side or fire-side or window-sill, is a sort of
"chewing of the cud" of immortal and god-like contemplation, and is worthy of a high place in the order of a good
life.

Happy are those persons whose outward destiny leaves
them at least one solitary, independent room to retire to at
night. It is a pitiful and a wicked shame when young girls
have to go on for years and years living at home. It is easy
for young men to retain their individuality and live a life
of culture in their parents' dwelling: it is almost impossible
for a girl to do so. There is something about the parental
"aura"—however kind and unselfish her parents may be—
that is deadly to a girl's nature; and as cruel to her culture
as the most insidious drops of poison. Her parents indeed
may be fussing anxiously about her chastity while they
themselves are all the while murdering her noblest culture

inspiration of inventors will cease; when nomadic fellaheen tribesmen and rustic heathen peasantries will bow themselves in passive helplessness under warring Caesars and despotic Tamburlanes. These new rulers of men will have dispossessed of their transitory authority both capitalists and communists, both cosmopolitan financiers and cosmopolitan proletariats; and the high destiny of our race will sink back and sink down into some long epoch of historyless chaos, out of which, once more, in its orbic cycle, in its great new "Platonic year," the creative energy will emerge and enter upon some totally unforeseen, unpredicted avatar.

But confronted as we are by so much vigorous, youthful, violent activity, by so much savage science, it is hard to visualize our present industrialism, whether capitalistic as in America, or communistic as in Russia, as something old, world-weary, "civilized," and in the autumn of its days. Who can tell? Science and machinery may, for all we know, get into quite other hands than those of new predatory conquerors. There may arise some grand, irresistible, devoted free-masonry of men of good will and of wise wits all the world over. If there were enough individual men and women in every country who had acquired in place of an angular nation-spirit a well rounded earth-spirit, who can predict what might not be done?

As things are now, it seems wiser to gather together one's own personal life-forces, one's intelligence, one's instincts, one's imagination, one's will, and make something of the only democracy, the only kingdom one has control of—namely, oneself. It seems wiser to do this than to engage in the already lost cause of re-establishing on wavering and quaking foundations the old local cults.

Any real, beautiful, noble culture is founded upon

ever ignorantly conventionalized, is to insult that noble
hero-worship in the heart of man by which the generations
lift themselves up. But it cannot, all the same, be denied
that the more cultured a person is the more daringly will
he follow some curious bias in his own secret nature in
regard to music and art. The age of sublime, heroic ob-
jectivity in these high matters seems to have been destroyed
forever by the terrible cosmopolitanism of modern in-
ventions.

Behold individualism, rampant, shameless, romantic,
realistic, angelic, devilish, proud, humble, childish, senile,
gay, pessimistic, mad, marches conquering across the whole
terraqueous globe! With cosmopolitan industry, cosmopolitan commerce, cosmopolitan finance dominating the
world, in the wake of cosmopolitan science, what can local,
aesthetic traditions do against such a tide? Still they hold
on, fierce, stubborn, reluctant, earth-rooted, these heroic
racial traditions, each with its own mysterious, sub-con-
scious destiny.

But rapid transportation erases their boundaries day by
day. Day by day the wireless neutralizes them, aeroplanes
drop spiritual poisons upon them; the press, the movies,
cheap translations, vulgarized tourist-facilities, corrode and
corrupt them. Their hidden earth-bound destinies, drawing
sap and pith from their immemorial local legends, are
caught up, are swept away, on one tangential wind after another; and, as they waver, fluctuate, diverge, take alien
colours, alien shapes, their old, revengeful, exclusive, local
divinities forfeit their faithful obedience.

What then is left? Spengler in his great book suggests
that the day will come when grass will grow in the streets
of Berlin, London, Paris, New York, Chicago; when the